Daniel Clarke was born in Bradford, West Yorkshire, the cultural centre of the north of England.

Rather than misspent, his childhood was well spent in the woods that were the backdrop to his childhood home, climbing trees, building dens and most importantly, falling off swings.

This was the birth place for his passions for building and storytelling.

Daniel has had a widely varying career, from labouring to directorship but for the last few years, he has spent most of his time as a stay-at-home dad, giving him a broad knowledge base.

Encouraged by his daughters to follow his passions, Daniel is pleased to introduce his debut novel, *Avenging Angels*.

I would like to dedicate this book to my uncle, Eddie Clarke, who has been a constant inspiration to follow my dreams.

"No matter the difficulties or doubters in your way, believe in yourself as I do."

Daniel Clarke

AVENGING ANGELS

AUSTIN MACAULEY PUBLISHERS™

LONDON * CAMBRIDGE * NEW YORK * SHARJAH

A CIP catalogue record for this title is available from the British Library.

ISBN 9781398441859 (Paperback)
ISBN 9781398441866 (ePub e-book)

www.austinmacauley.com

First Published 2022
Austin Macauley Publishers Ltd®
1 Canada Square
Canary Wharf
London
E14 5AA

Firstly, I would like to acknowledge my daughters, Charlotte and Emily, who turned my own words of encouragement against me, when they bought me a laptop for Christmas and told me to follow my dreams of being a published writer.

I would also like to thank the team at Austin Macauley Publishers for all their hard work in helping my book through its journey from a rough manuscript to a book that I'm proud of. Their foresight to introduce new ways to help writers get published has made my book dream a reality.

Table of Contents

Prologue   11

Chapter 1 The Execution   12

Chapter 2 Maple Tree House   22

Chapter 3 The Fall   36

Chapter 4 The Co-Operative   46

Chapter 5 Mates for Life   56

Chapter 6 The Charmin Problem   74

Chapter 7 Mr Regan   86

Chapter 8 The Mission   106

Chapter 9 Thumb Print Buns   118

Chapter 10 Cover Up   134

Chapter 11 Tracking   148

Chapter 12 Chess   167

Chapter 13 Trust Issues   185

Chapter 14 Friend or Foe   205

Chapter 15 Reunited   227

Chapter 16 Cleaning House   249

Chapter 17 Justice   265

Chapter 18 Reparation   278

Chapter 19 Epilogue   290

Prologue

His phone was ringing. He went to answer it. He knew who was calling and could guess the reason why, but still, it had to be answered.

"Hello," he said.

And barely having time to finish the word, the voice on the other end of the line said with a degree of urgency, "They're going to kill him."

"Calm yourself," he said.

"I am calm."

"We can't intervene, there's too much at stake."

"It's not right."

"I understand but one of the first things we learn is that life is unfair and we can't stop every injustice; we can only do our job and hope for the best."

A moment's silence fell.

"I'm not ok with this; too many people are dying."

"I'll see what I can do but no promises," then he hung up the phone.

Chapter 1

The Execution

Mike's bail had been denied and it was less than a week since he was arrested and charged. All Mike could do on his way to prison was try to figure out how things had turned out so wrong.

When he arrived at prison, he was processed and led to his cell. He saw a face that was familiar to him, a face he hadn't seen for many years. The last time he did, this face was smiling at him with pride and affection, but not today. No, this face was angry and confused.

Mike made the gesture of a slight nod to his friend of old, but received a slight shake of the head as a reply. Then his old friend turned his back to him.

Mike took this as a sign that they were no longer friends and knew well enough not to press the point.

He had seen that demonstration of disrespect before, when other members of their friendship group had been disavowed for acts that the others deemed unacceptable.

You wouldn't expect young thugs to have much of a moral code, but you would be wrong. The fights were usually with rival gangs of their own age, or the occasional run in with the police.

They didn't condone violence or crime towards the old or the young, and although blazing rows with girlfriends was commonplace, god help anyone who let a lass feel the back of their hand.

The two craziest and arguably strongest members of the friendship group, both came from homes where their mothers suffered from domestic abuse, Jimmy's from his father and Dave's, from whichever boyfriend his mother had at the time.

Dave Jackson was the man who had turned his back on Mike. He would have been his best man at his wedding and was godfather to Mike's son and daughter, despite being in prison at the time of the wedding and their christenings.

He was a man Mike had thought he could depend on until the end of days. If he, of all people, believed Mike to be guilty, what hope had he of convincing anyone else.

The next day, Mike kept himself to himself. After all, he had a lot to think about. What happened, how it happened and why it happened, but most important, how could the finger possibly be directed at him.

None of it made sense, and now, to be implicated was more than he could comprehend.

It must be a mistake, surely they've got their facts wrong, is it possible that my children have been assaulted and neither I or my wife noticed.

Had someone really killed them all to cover it up? Did my wife know? Who was it?

After all, they didn't really know anyone in the village well enough who'd have access to the children.

What about the forensic evidence linking him, surely there's been a mistake? These are the questions that kept Mike awake almost three days straight, only occasionally drifting off through exhaustion.

Mike was going for breakfast one morning, despite not really being able to eat, he still had to follow the routine of prison life.

He entered the dining room and queued to get his food when one of the prisoners walking in the other direction whispered "Scum."

Mike, not sure if he had imagined it, carried on in the que but as he passed the table where the prisoner was seated, he heard it again but louder and clearer.

Mike should have kept on walking but being sleep-deprived and suffering malnutrition and stress, Mike snapped at the man, "'av you got something to say to me?"

"Fuck off, paedo," replied the prisoner.

Mike's blood boiled which gave him a wealth of energy. He launched himself at the prisoner with a passion he'd not seen in himself for many years.

Despite the prisoner having almost a foot and 5st on Mike, he was on his back before he knew what had hit him.

Mike's assault was so fast and ferocious, the prisoner didn't have chance to recover himself from the barrage of fists coming from this unassuming wild man.

"I never touched my kids; I never touched my kids," Mike kept repeating.

The attack was so quick that the prison officers didn't get there before Mike had beaten the man unconscious and it still took four of them to prise Mike from his victim.

Mike was restrained and taken to a holding cell to await the prison doctor to be checked over.

It was a couple of hours before anyone came to see him but it wasn't the doctor, it was the governor.

"Mike can you tell me what happened?"

Mike was looking drained. The adrenalin that had fuelled his attack had dissipated and he was in a worse state than when he started the day.

"He called me a fucking paedo," Mike said struggling for energy.

"That's no excuse for what you did to him."

"I didn't hurt my kids."

"That doesn't matter Mike, people here have access to the news and believe what they want to believe, and you can't beat people to a pulp every time someone says something you don't like."

Mike didn't respond and just sat there with barely the energy to keep his eyes open.

"The prisoner you attacked is having to be taken to hospital. We don't have the facilities here to treat him, you will then be seen by the doctor before we decide what to do with you."

The governor then asked the prison officer to close up the cell and went back to his office.

Just over an hour later, two prison officers escorted Mike to the doctor's office.

"Sit here Mike," said the doctor. He seemed a friendly enough chap, thought Mike.

"You got any injuries from the fight? Does anything hurt?"

"Only what he said," replied Mike.

The doctor looked at Mike like he was studying him, trying to weigh him up.

"I'm not here to get involved or judge Mike. I've worked here long enough to know not to ask certain questions or make rash judgements. I'm just here to take care of your wellbeing. Fair enough?"

"Fair enough," replied Mike.

"Now let me take a look at those hands of yours."

The doctor examined Mike's hands and cleaned the blood from them.

"Does this hurt?" the doctor asked as he squeezed and rolled Mike's hands and fingers. Mike shook his head.

"You are very fortunate not to have broken every bone in your hand."

Mike looked at the doctor and thought to himself, fortunate was not a word that would describe his life right now.

The doctor asked Mike many questions about his sleep patterns and eating habits before asking about his state of mind.

Mike would have been annoyed if he had the energy but he cooperated and answered the doctors questions honestly.

"Do you prefer tea or coffee, Mike?"

Mike was a little thrown by the question and had to think for a second, "Tea."

"Could you get us a sweet tea and some biscuits please, officer?" the doctor directed at the prison officers.

"Do we look like tea maids?" replied one of the officers.

Taken aback by what the prison officer had said, the doctor asked him to step outside for a moment. As soon as the door to his office closed, the doctor turned to the prison officer and asked, "Would you like to explain yourself?"

"I'm not here to serve people like him cups of tea."

"People like him?"

"Yeah, child rapists?"

"As I understand it, he hasn't been convicted of it yet."

"Doesn't matter, he's as guilty as they come."

"How do you figure?"

"That's what's wrong with him, it's guilt, now that he's been caught and found out. I've seen it before, you mark my words, he's guilty alright."

"Well, if what you say is true, then I need to keep him in good health so he can be at his trial." Said the doctor.

"You go back in and watch him and I'll get the tea."

The prison officer returned to the room while the doctor went to get the tea, he returned a few minutes later with it, accompanied by a small plate with a selection of biscuits.

"Mike, I need you to eat these and drink the tea."

Mike looked at the plate and before he had a chance to refuse, the doctor said, "You're not leaving here until you've eaten everything."

Mike complied and began nibbling the food and sipping the tea.

"I don't really have anything to help you sleep Mike, but take these pain killers and they may make you rest better as they have a drowsy side effect to them."

Mike took the pills and washed them down with a sip of tea.

When Mike had finished, the doctor said, "The officers will take you back to your cell now and you need to get some rest. You have a lot to think about Mike and you're not going to be any good to yourself if you don't start taking better care of yourself."

"He's not going back to his cell; he's going back to the holding cell until the governor decides what to do with him."

"The holding cell is not sufficient," argued the doctor.

"Governor's orders doc. If you don't like it, speak to him."

The doctor picked up the phone and dialled the extension number for the governor's office.

The receptionist answered.

"I need to speak to the governor," said the doctor.

"He's busy on a call. I'll ask him to call you once he's done."

"If you could please, it's very important."

"We can't wait here all day, so if you're finished, we'll be taking him back and you can speak to the governor when he's free," said the officer raising Mike to his feet and ushering him out of the door.

Despite several more attempts, it was over two hours before the doctor managed to get in touch with the governor.

"I know why you're calling and I've already given the order to return Mike to his cell," said the governor.

"Really. That's great. Why?" asked the doctor.

"I called Mike's solicitor to inform him of the incident and I've had none stop calls all afternoon from the CPS and a couple of high-ranking officials all telling me to play it down and not to create a media storm over it. Even Graham, the prisoner he attacked, has asked for it not to go any further, suggesting that he was at fault."

"You know what prisoners are like. He probably just wants a chance to even up the score," suggested the doctor.

"Maybe but he'll not get his chance."

"What do you mean?"

"Before he gets back, I'll be moving Mike to the vulnerable offenders wing."

"With the sex offenders? Is that wise? He hasn't been convicted yet."

"It doesn't matter. He's in danger. The other prisoners have clearly made up their minds that he is guilty."

"Very well. But I need to see him again as I'm concerned for his health. He's not adjusting well and putting him on that wing may damage his mental health further."

"If this man is guilty of what he's accused, it is where he belongs," said the governor before hanging up the phone.

Mike slept for about three and a half hours that night which was more than the accumulated hours he had slept for the entire previous week.

He felt physically better for it and was sat on his bed waiting for the door to open for breakfast.

He could hear the other doors starting to open and prepared himself to leave his cell.

He stood there with thoughts of what had happened the day before and what would he have to face today.

He stood there for a while before he realised his door was not being opened. Was this part of his punishment or was he being segregated from the other prisoners, like the night before when he had to eat his evening meal alone?

About thirty minutes passed before Mike's door finally opened and he was led by two prison officers to a small room.

The room was bare except for a small table and one chair which were both bolted down. Mike sat in the chair as directed by the officers who positioned themselves behind him.

Within a couple of minutes, the door opened and a prisoner carrying a tray of food came in followed by the governor. He set the tray down on the table and left closing the door behind him.

"Please, eat," said the governor.

Mike slowly started to eat; he was hungry but was still struggling to get anything down.

"I'm arranging for you to be transferred Mike, for your safety and that of the other prisoners."

"Where to?" asked Mike.

"We have a wing here that is designed to keep prisoners safe when there are, special circumstances."

"You mean with the perverts?" Mike said angrily.

"It's not just for sex offenders Mike, it's also for vulnerable prisoners who may be in danger from other prisoners."

"Do I look vulnerable to you? And I'm certainly no pervert."

"Mike, it's like I said to you yesterday. People here are quick to jump to conclusions and I have to think of the safety of everyone."

"If you put me in there, how is that going to look to everyone? It's going to look like I'm guilty and a pervert, I won't go."

"You don't have much of a choice Mike and neither do I. I've had several calls demanding that I transfer you for your safety and you're going."

Mike could see that it was pointless to argue and continued with his food.

After he had finished his breakfast, Mike was returned to his cell and told to get his things together for the move.

Mike realised he had no choice in the matter so did as he was told.

It wasn't until lunch time that Mike was collected from his cell, after all the other prisoners had left the block.

He was led to the far side of the complex to the special protection wing and once he had deposited his things in his cell, he was led to the dining room.

"You don't have long so get your food and get it eaten," said one of the prison officers.

Mike collected his food and looked around for where to sit. There were no empty tables but there was one with only one occupant so he made his way towards it as he wanted as little interaction with the prisoners as possible.

Mike could see everyone staring at him. In fact, the only person who wasn't was the solo diner on the table where he was heading.

Mike sat and quietly began to eat. After a few minutes, a prisoner approached the table and sat down looking at Mike.

"The names Charmin. Well, that's what they call me," said the prisoner with a snake-like grin on his face.

"You must be something special."

Mike looked at him questioningly.

"Two prison officers," he said pointing to Mike's escort, "normal people only get one."

"There's normal people here?" said Mike sarcastically but almost immediately regretting opening his mouth.

"What's that supposed to mean?"

"Nothing. I've had a bad night and I'm not interested in having a conversation."

"I'm just trying to be friendly with you."

"I've got enough friends, thanks."

"Not in here, you haven't," said Charmin, obviously offended by Mike's remarks.

"Listen, just fuck off you fairy princess. I'm not interested," replied Mike.

The solo diner choked on his drink and Charmin jumped to his feet knocking his chair over.

"What you laughing at cunt, I'll snip your throat, you fuck." Charmin said with veins popping out from his neck.

"I see why they call you Charmin," interjected Mike.

"SETTLE DOWN!" shouted a prison officer, "and you, pick that chair up and get back to your own table."

Charmin did as he was told and picked the chair up and as he slowly pushed it under the table, he glared at Mike and said.

"You're a victim, who doesn't yet know it," and with that said, he returned to his table.

"I wouldn't take his threat lightly if I was you," said the diner, "he's here for life that one, so he has nothing to lose except face."

Mike just looked at the diner but was in no mood to strike up another conversation.

He'd barely eaten any of his meal before the prisoners were being ushered back towards their cells and although the prisoners were allowed to socialise once there, Mike went straight to his cell and lay on his bed thinking things over until evening meal time came around.

Evening meal followed a similar pattern, he collected his meal and sat at the same table opposite the lone diner and ate his meal without a word being spoken.

When Mike got back to his cell, he found the doctor waiting for him.

"How's it going Mike? I have regular visits on this wing so it's easier for me to pop down than them transporting half the wing to my office."

Mike entered the cell and sat on his bed.

"You're looking well Mike. How's your appetite and did you manage to get any sleep?"

"I've eaten and I've had a few hours last night."

"Great, I have some more pain killers for you just to help you relax," the doctor handed Mike two tablets and a cup of water.

Mike swallowed the tablets and handed the cup back.

"I'm going to arrange for you to see a psychiatrist and maybe he can prescribe you something stronger to help you sleep. Maybe you'll be able to talk through some of your troubles with him?"

Mike thanked the doctor but was not enthusiastic about seeing a psychiatrist.

He knew if he refused it wouldn't make any difference so he just went along with it.

"I won't keep you doctor; I'm going to try and get some sleep" he said laying on his bed and turning his back to him.

The doctor left with a promise of returning tomorrow.

Within about ten minutes, the pain killers had started to kick in and with a reasonably full stomach from dinner, Mike began to feel drowsy.

Before long, Mike was asleep. He found himself dreaming of his home.

He knew every inch of the house intimately as he'd worked on all of it and was still in the middle of several projects.

At first, he felt at peace but as he went from room to room, he felt like something was missing.

He couldn't quite put his finger on it but his feeling was growing into fear that something was wrong. He started running from room to room, not really knowing what he was looking for.

Mike started to hear something, faintly at first, but it was getting louder and louder until he could make out the voices of his wife and children.

At first, he couldn't make out what they were saying but as it got louder, he realised they weren't talking at all.

They were shouting and screaming, shouting and screaming his name to be precise.

He searched and searched for them but couldn't find them anywhere.

His breath became heavy and he was losing the vision.

Suddenly, Mike woke up to a pulling around his neck. He tried to move but couldn't. He wasn't sure what was happening.

Someone shoved a rag in his mouth and he couldn't raise his hands to stop them.

He was wrapped tightly in a blanket and was being held down by two prisoners, and a third had put a bed sheet fashioned into a noose around his neck, then shoved the rag into his mouth.

Mike wriggled but couldn't break free.

The two prisoners lifted Mike up and carried him to the door.

Mike could now see the third prisoner; it was Charmin. He had tied a knot in the bedsheet and threw it over the door to the cell and trapped the knot in the door jam.

"Let him down," Charmin told the other two prisoners, who dropped Mike and the blanket fell to the floor.

"Right, you two get off and I'll wait to remove the rag"

The two prisoners left and Charmin moved the blanket back to the bed and placed the chair tipped over in front of Mike, who by this time, was struggling less and less.

"Told you," said Charmin with his snake-like grin on his face.

"Victim."

As he could see the life leaving Mike's eyes, he leant in and as he grabbed the rag ready to pull it out, he whispered something into Mike's ear.

Mike's eyes began to water, and a burst of pure anger came over him, which he channelled into one final assault.

He headbutted Charmin, sending him flying across the room with the rag still in his hand.

Mike's throat was too swollen to scream for help but with his last bit of anger-fuelled energy, he kicked at the door trying frantically to raise some attention.

Charmin jumped to his feet but stumbled not realising how hard he'd been hit.

He regrouped himself and fled the cell hearing Mike's thuds getting quieter and quieter as his energy dwindled.

Mike could feel himself losing consciousness but all that was playing in his mind was what Charmin had whispered and as the blackness overtook him, he heard the words once more.

"Your kids didn't die in the fire, they're alive and when I get out of here for killing you, I will get to taste the pleasures of them. Victim."

Chapter 2

Maple Tree House

It was warm for the time of year, and the sun had not yet risen from its slumber as Mike walked to the shop in the centre of the village.

He strolled with an air of wonderment, and the look of a contented man as he passed the picturesque cottages that lined the road of the village he had come to call home.

He had moved there approximately eighteen months ago with his wife Tara and two children, 9-year-old George and his 8-year-old sister, Abigail.

It was a far cry from the council estate where he spent his childhood with its concrete blocks of flats and overcrowded schools.

Despite the differences, there were also the similarities of community spirit that urban areas seem to have lost in recent years, as everyone seems to be becoming more isolated in their own homes.

Not taking time to get to know their neighbours, or even exchange the customary greeting of a good morning, when passing a fellow traveller on the path of life.

Village life could be described to be time-locked, and it often seems to be unaware of the changing face of society and the many challenges it faces.

Mike certainly appreciated the slow pace of life and what he would describe as a more balanced and tolerant attitude towards one's fellow man.

He had worked as a builder from leaving school after landing himself a job as a labourer.

He then attended a training course for joinery which suited him fine coming from a childhood building dens, go karts and sheds.

Mike was now only working part time to be a stay at home father, which kind of made him feel like he was living his childhood all over again, while teaching his children how to do all the things he loved to do when he was younger.

It also made sense for him to stay at home, as he was self-employed, whereas his wife was employed as a teacher and was on a good career path that she loved and was good at.

Unlike Mike, Tara was from a wealthier background and had attended private school and had stayed on for further education in sixth form and then university.

She had a natural passion for science which she taught at a large school in the city.

In some respects, they were like chalk and cheese and except for a unique set of circumstances, may never have met or even spoken to each other.

15 years ago, it was a June night in Nottingham city centre and Tara, with a group of her friends from Uni were out celebrating the handing in of their assignments.

They had been for a meal and then decided to hit the night clubs to blow off some steam.

Tara was a sensible girl, but even sensible girls can have one drink too many, and although the night was not over by most revellers standards, Tara had decided it was time to call it a night.

Tara told her friends and a couple of them agreed to make sure she got safely in a cab.

As they left the nightclub, there were several men arguing with the doorman, who wouldn't let them in as they had clearly had too much to drink.

As Tara and her friends were passing, one of the men got right in the doorman's face and screamed, "why are you being such a dick?"

The doorman pushed the man back with such force, his feet left the ground and desperate to grab on to something, he stretched out his arms and just managed to take a hold of Tara's arm.

In her drunk state and only being of a slight build, she too came crashing down into the road, aside of the drunken man.

In a flash, the drunkard jumped to his feet and launched an assault on the doorman, aided by several of his friends.

The doorman was quickly supported by two of his colleagues, and bodies were either flying or fleeing the vicious onslaught.

Suddenly, one of the drunkards came hurtling through the air towards Tara, who was still on the floor unable to stand due to a sprained ankle.

Despite the assistance from her friends who were equally intoxicated and with all three wearing high heels, it was not the best combination for a rescue party.

A look of fear came over Tara which alerted her friends to the imminent danger, but none of them had time to react.

As they all prepared themselves for what was sure to be a very painful end to their night, the flying body violently changed course.

All three looked up to see a young man who had intercepted the human canon ball, barging him out of the girls' trajectory.

He approached Tara and her friends and in his rough northern accent asked if the girls were alright.

"Yes, but my ankle's sprained," replied Tara.

The young man knelt in front of Tara and said, "Put ya arm around my neck, we need to move ya."

Tara wasn't sure if it was the drink or the speed in which the young man picked her up but her head felt woozy.

He carried her 50 feet to a bench closely followed by her friends and as he sat her on the bench, he asked her, "Which ankle is it?"

"It's ok, it'll be fine if I just rest it," Tara replied.

"Nonsense," said the young man, "let's have a look."

Without hesitation, he lifted Tara's left foot which seemed to be badly swollen.

"That's pretty bad that, ya need to get it seen to," said the young man.

"I'll go to the phone box and call ya an ambulance," he continued when Tara stopped him in his tracks.

"NO!" she insisted, "I just want to go home; I'll walk it off," the young man's face turned from confusion to a smile.

"A lass after my own heart," he said.

"Let me do something about the swelling though."

Before she had the chance to object, he'd already removed his tie and produced a squashed bottle of water from his back pocket and proceeded to soak his tie in the water.

"What are you doing?" asked one of Tara's friends.

"It's ok, it's a cheap tie and we need to support her ankle and get the swelling down," he replied.

He began wrapping it around Tara's ankle and foot as a make shift bandage.

"Where did you learn that?" asked Tara.

"Army cadets," replied the young man.

Tara was impressed with the ingenuity of the young man, and despite being in pain she was appreciative of how firm but gentle his hands felt.

"Right, that should do ya, I'll get one of them taxis to come over here rather than ya having to walk," said the young man, wandering off to the taxi rank.

Tara's two friends who had been stood a few metres away whispering, came closer.

"What an idiot!" one of them said.

"I don't know, it's kind of sweet, helping a stranger," replied Tara.

"Yes, but why, so he can help himself into your taxi and then what will he be helping himself to," interjected the other friend.

"NOTHING, and there will be no taxi ride either. Now be nice, he's on his way back," Tara replied sharply.

"He'll be over in a minute, 'ow's your ankle feeling?" said the young man returning.

"It's throbbing a bit but the pain is not as intense," Tara replied.

"Well, I'll leave ya to it then, I'm sure ya mates can sort it from here," but one of the friends interrupted the young man.

"No, we're not going with her, we're going back to the club," she said.

"Yes, we're going back to the club. Tara seems fine in your capable hands," added the other friend, both still cross over Tara's sharpness.

Tara looked at them but knew better than to say anything as they would only take pleasure if she tried to protest. So, she played along.

"Do you mind sitting with me until the taxi comes," she asked the young man.

"Can do," he replied.

Both Tara and the young man sat on the bench watching her friends make their way back to the nightclub, where the police had now turned up to arrest the brawling drunkards.

"Are you out with your friends tonight?" Tara asked.

"Not so much friends as work colleagues," he replied.

"Where are they? In the nightclub?" she asked as he pointed in the direction that her friends were walking.

"No, that's them getting carted off to the drunk tank to sleep it off."

"Oh, and where do you work?"

He pointed just across the street to an old office block, "Just there, well for the next two weeks anyway. We're refurbing the whole building."

"So, you're a builder then?"

"No, just a labourer but I'm looking at a joinery course, it's much better money if you have a trade."

A taxi pulled up in front of them, and the young man helped Tara to her feet.

As he helped her to the taxi, she tried to hold back the discomfort as she didn't want him to offer his assistance to her home like her friends suggested he would.

Once he had helped her into the back seat, he closed the door and then opened the front passenger door.

Tara was about to tell him that she didn't need him to help her home but he told the taxi driver, "She's hurt er ankle mate, please make sure you help er to er door."

"Nice to meet ya, luv," he said to Tara as he closed the door.

As the taxi set off, Tara asked the driver to slow down and she rolled her window down.

"Excuse me," she shouted, "I feel really rude, I don't even know your name."

"Mike," replied the young man.

"Thanks Mike," shouted Tara as the taxi drove off down the road.

Present day. Mike made it to the village shop which was about a 20-minute steady walk from his house. He liked the walk as it got the blood pumping and Mike liked the quiet stroll to appreciate the beautiful setting, he found himself living in.

"Morning Mike," said the shop keeper, "what can I do for you this morning?"

"Morning, I just need some milk," replied Mike, "We had some cocoa last night and didn't leave enough for a cup of tea, never mind the kids' breakfast."

"Mike, I'm getting mould on the window in the store room and no matter how much I clean it with bleach or anything, it keeps coming back. Could you take a look?"

"I'm a little pressed for time right now but I can pop back after the school run."

"If you wouldn't mind," said the shop keeper as she was handing Mike his change.

Mike left the shop and started his steady stroll back to Maple Tree House, the home he and his wife had bought to raise their family in.

It was an old detached Georgian style house with five double bedrooms set in almost an acre of mature garden, with a further 5 acres of paddocks with stables, which housed three horses belonging to his wife and children.

Mike never really took to horse riding; he had tried it at the request of his wife but after one too many painful falls, he decided it wasn't for him.

Mike was happiest at home doing projects like restoring many of the original features of the house that time had not been forgiving to.

Finding new ways to sympathetically incorporate new technologies into the house to improve the quality of life or make the house more efficient.

Although Tara had lots of input into design, colour and furnishings, Mike was the builder and did all the manual labour.

His latest project was the dining room, someone in their infinite wisdom thought it would be a good idea to gloss over everything that resembled wood.

The doors, the wood panelling and the beautiful decorative fire surround, all of which should have been oak.

The house was definitely a hidden gem, it was so well secluded, it wasn't visible until you actually turned into the drive, after walking down what looked more like a dirt track than a road for about a quarter of a mile.

The entrance to the dirt track was so small that Mike and Tara missed it many times when they first moved in.

The grounds to the property were bordered by ten feet high bushes backed up by forty feet high conifers with no neighbours within a quarter of a mile, it was definitely a private peaceful sanctuary.

Mike turned up the dirt track and was almost immediately hit by the faint smell of fire, which was not completely uncommon as many of the houses still had open fires or fire pits on their patios, so Mike didn't feel too concerned.

After a brief pause to try figure out the direction of the smell, he continued on his way.

As Mike got further down the track, the smell of fire smelt stronger and Mike began to pick up the pace.

A horrifying feeling started to grow in Mike's stomach, and as he came around a small bend in the road just twenty metres before the entrance to Maple Tree House, his growing fear was confirmed.

He could see smoke oozing through the conifers, clearly the fire was coming from his property and it was big.

Mike ran flat out to the gate and stopped only for a second in horror at the sight of his whole house in flames.

It seemed every room had flames burning inside them, flickering out of the open windows.

Mike was no athlete but he covered the distance to the house with a speed Usain Bolt would have been proud of.

As he got to the front of the house, he frantically looked from window to window trying to see signs of his family.

"TARA!" he shouted several times but no reply came.

Still with bottle of milk in hand, he charged towards the front door, and just as his hand reached for the handle there was a loud deafening bang.

The large oak door burst out of its frame towards Mike, knocking him at least twenty feet backwards onto the gravel driveway and then landing on top of him.

Mike lay beneath the door unconscious with a small stream of milk creeping its way out.

A hair line of blood began to run down the milk stream and where it pooled it began to mix and slowly turn the white milk to a darker and darker pink.

Mike woke up surrounded by paramedics and firemen.

"Mike, can you hear me? Mike, can you understand me?" asked a paramedic.

"Yes. Yes," said Mike trying to gather his thoughts, "where's my family?"

The head fireman stepped forward. "We need to know if anyone else was in the house. Mike, was anyone else home?"

"My family," answered Mike, "where's my family?"

"How many people Mike. A wife? Kids?" pressed the fireman.

"My wife Tara and my children George and Abigail. Has anybody seen them?" said Mike in desperation.

"We're looking for them now, just wait here and let the paramedics treat you."

"I'm fine, I can help."

"No, you're not fine, you have injuries that need attending to and you're emotional, so you would only get in the way. Let us do our job and we'll find your family."

Mike had never been described as emotional before, quite the opposite, he'd been described as having no emotions on several occasions.

It wasn't that he didn't feel, he just had a very practical way at looking at things, but he could see what the fireman was saying.

"How old are your kids Mike?" asked the paramedic.

"Eight and nine"

"Boys or girls?"

"One of each," said Mike, then suddenly he jumped to his feet, "The horses!" he cried.

He started running around the house and through the back garden towards the stables.

As he approached, he could see that all three horses were still in their stables, and after a quick search of the other rooms, it was clear his wife had not been out to the horses yet that morning.

Mike started heading back towards the house, he saw the paramedic running toward him accompanied by two police officers.

Maybe they have news on my family he thought and hastened his walk towards them.

"Mike Feather?" asked one of the officers.

"Yes."

"I need you to come with me," said the officer as he pulled out his handcuffs.

"What's going on?" asked a confused Mike.

"We need to ask you some questions and we can't be having you trying to run off again."

"I came to the horses to see if my wife and kids were here."

"They've found your wife and kids," said the paramedic sympathetically.

A small feeling of relief came over Mike.

"Where are they, can I see them?"

"No," said the police officer.

"They were in the house Mike. They didn't make it," the paramedic continued.

Mike's stomach felt like it was in a vice grip getting tighter and tighter.

His legs gave way under him and every emotion he had ever repressed surfaced all at once and try as he may he couldn't control it, not this time.

Out of shear frustration he let out a cry that was no recognisable word, more an unstoppable release of tension.

"Do you mind," said the police officer to the paramedic, "we don't know what his involvement is in all this yet."

"Surely, you don't think he's responsible?" asked the paramedic.

"Look at him. He's heartbroken!"

"You can't judge a book by its cover and I'd thank you to keep your comments to yourself, until we have all the facts."

Mike was oblivious to the conversation, curled up on the cold ground with nothing but pain in his body and mind for company.

The two police officers picked him up by his arms that were handcuffed behind his back, telling him to either start walking or be dragged.

Mike was unresponsive and the officers started to drag him back towards the smouldering house.

The paramedic was not impressed with the way the officers were dealing with Mike, but knew if he said anything, it would fall on deaf ears.

It must have been painful he thought, but Mike was in another level of pain and could care less what was going on around him.

As they passed the house, Mike tried to find his feet several times but the police officers' pace was too quick.

All the emergency services people and a few locals that had gathered, stopped to watch him being carried in handcuffs and put in the back of the police car.

He sat there for about twenty minutes waiting for the police officers who were talking to the firemen and paramedics.

Finally, they got in the car.

"What's happening?" asked Mike.

"We're taking you to the station. We've got some questions that need answering."

"I want to see my family."

"That's not possible, the forensic team need to do their bit. The bodies need to go for an autopsy. Maybe then you can see them."

"You been in trouble with the police before?" asked the other officer phrasing it like small talk.

Mike didn't reply.

He had been in trouble and had to deal with the police several times in his youth but that was a long time ago, still, he remembered the golden rule.

Don't tell the police anything.

Innocent people always make the mistake of thinking that the police are on their side, because they are innocent.

They are often suckered in by the police's tactic of befriending you.

They're only trying to get you to open up, and then they only write down the things that will strengthen their case for you being guilty.

It's all about getting the easy and quick convictions, not what's right or wrong and certainly not about whether you're innocent.

Yes, Mike knew this game all too well to be suckered in.

There was nothing that he had done that could have started that fire.

All his tools had been unplugged and the bottle on the portable gas heater he used had been disconnected, even the paint strippers and other chemicals were kept in correct containers.

There was nothing that Mike could think of but clearly there was some issue that the police wanted to talk to him about.

It was a thirty-five-minute journey into town and despite several attempts from the police to strike up a conversation with Mike, he remained silent for the entire journey.

When they arrived at the police station, they took Mike through to a holding area which was basically a long bare room, with a bench running down one side with partitions every six feet.

It was warm in there but Mike still felt cold.

"It shouldn't be long, just sit down there," said one of the officers.

It was less than five minutes before he was ushered to the desk of the custody sergeant.

"Has he been read his rights?" asked the sergeant.

"Yes Sarge."

Mike couldn't remember being read his rights but he was a little out of it and couldn't remember half of what went on.

"What's he been arrested for?"

"Suspected arson and suspected murder."

"What the fuck!" interrupted Mike "where did that come from?"

"Pipe down son, you'll get your chance to talk," said the sergeant.

"I not saying anything else. I want a solicitor."

Mike was processed without saying another word. Not to even confirm his name, age or home address.

The police officers put him in a cell and left.

Many hours passed and Mike could hear someone walking towards his cell.

Abruptly, the hatch opened, "Dinner time" a voice said.

"I don't want your food. Where's my solicitor?" demanded Mike.

"The officers have gone off duty now so you'll not be seen until the morning, so do you want this food or not?"

"No!"

The hatch closed as abruptly as it opened and footsteps could be heard fading off into the distance.

Mike spent the night pacing up and down his cell thinking of his poor wife and children and how they died.

The agony they must have been in was more than he could bear to think.

He would often find himself on his knees with tears streaming down his face, not quite sure how he ended up there.

Periodically, the hatch on the cell door would open and the voice would say "Are you alright?"

Mike would always answer, "Yes," even though he was far from alright.

Twenty-four hours ago, he was on top of the world and now almost everything that meant anything to him was gone and to add insult to injury, he's in a police cell being accused of causing their deaths.

No, wait a minute. The police officer said murder, not manslaughter and arson. What did they mean?

Are they suggesting I started the fire deliberately, are they saying I killed my family deliberately or that their deaths are a result of some kind of insurance fire scam, that went wrong?

Mike's mind raced around and around with different possibilities and scenarios but not until he was in his interview would Mike know what fanciful scenario the police would throw at him.

What he did know is that he had to be careful because the police officers had, for whatever reason, decided he's guilty, and most times, that's all it takes for an innocent man to go to prison.

The hatch opened again. "Breakfast?" asked the voice.

Mike went over and grabbed the tray and sat on the wooden bed/bench to eat but when he looked at the food, he just couldn't bring himself to eat it.

Despite being hungry and not having anything to eat the day before, he just had no appetite.

He put the food on the floor and laid down.

He wasn't going to sleep; his mind was racing too fast for that and he began thinking of the last time he saw his children.

He'd put them to bed the night before. He'd usually read them a story or sing them a song, not a nursery rhyme but something cool like REM or Oasis.

Despite the fact that he couldn't sing well, his children were his biggest fans and always asked for one more song.

He used to say to his wife, "The kids were so desperate to stay up, they asked me to sing them another song."

Time got away from him as he lay there day dreaming about the fun times he'd spent with his children when suddenly the door opened.

There was a man dressed in smart but casual clothes.

"Morning, I'm Detective Inspector Phillips, I'll be handling your case from now on. Follow me."

They walked down a few corridors and through a big metal door where a man in a very nice suit was waiting.

"This is your solicitor, Mr Regan," said the inspector, "call me when you're ready," and with that he was gone.

"Come with me," said Mr Regan and headed into an interview room.

"Firstly, they haven't charged you yet but you are being detained for questioning. I do believe they're only waiting on the forensic and post mortem reports and you will most certainly be charged with arson and murder."

Mike got angry at hearing this.

"Are you trying to tell me that they think I set the house on fire on purpose."

"Are you telling me it was an accident?" asked Mr Regan.

"No. I didn't start the fire at all. I don't know how it started."

"Well, that's the only piece of information I do have. The fire investigator said there was accelerant used at multiple points around the house and that every room had a window opened to allow the fire to breathe."

Mike had a flash back and remembered the flames flickering out of the windows, "So that's why they're charging me with murder."

"Yes, that and the fact that the bindings around your wife and children were clearly visible."

"WHAT?" said Mike, shocked at this revelation.

"They were tied up?"

"Yes," replied Regan.

Mike slumped into his chair not knowing what to think, with the emotions again trying to surface.

This time he was able to hold them back because as well as being confused, he was angry.

"So, let me get this straight, they're saying that not only did I set my house on fire, I tied up my wife and kids in order to kill them. Why? For an insurance claim or something?"

The solicitor shrugged his shoulders.

"That's the most absurd thing I've ever heard. I loved my family; I would have walked through fire to save them"

"So, I guess we'll be pleading not guilty then."

Mike looked at the solicitor with annoyance, "Did you not hear me? I haven't done anything wrong."

"Right. Well, we better get the officer back in so you can give him your account of your movements that morning."

Mike didn't like the solicitor's flippant attitude and thought, at my first opportunity, I'm changing him out.

Tara's dad was a solicitor and did criminal law at one point, at least I'll be able to trust him, Mike thought.

Inspector Phillips entered the room.

"I understand we're ready to begin," he said.

He set up the recording device which was no longer tapes like the times Mike had been interviewed when he was a youngster, but he still wrote everything down that Mike said.

He read Mike his rights and said, "In your own words, can you tell me what time you woke up and your movements that morning?"

Mike began retelling the story having to pause occasionally for the officer to catch up, but otherwise the officer never interrupted him or asked him to clarify until he ended his narrative.

"Just a couple of things, Mike. Did you see or speak to anyone else except the shop keeper?"

"No one," replied Mike.

"Didn't see any cars or wave to anyone in a window?"

"No, several cars passed me but they weren't anyone I recognised from the village, I guess they were just driving through."

"Were you and your wife having any problems?"

"No; like what?"

"Financial or arguments?"

"No, no arguments and we both earn enough for our needs."

"But that house seems a little out of an unemployed builder and a teacher's pay scale?"

"I'm not out of work, I'm self-employed and part time so I can be at home for the kids."

"Even though, a big expensive property?"

"Tara had a trust fund and I've renovated several properties to work my way up the ladder."

"But who put in the lion's share, you or your wife?"

"It was about even. Is there anything else?" Mike asked clearly getting annoyed at the inuendo style of questions.

"Yes, you said you ran to the house when you saw the flames but you were still carrying the bottle of milk?"

"Yes."

"Well, doesn't that seem odd that if you were in such a rush, you would have dropped it?"

"I didn't think about the milk."

Mike could see the Inspector was looking for holes in his story.

"I think that's everything for now. Do you need five more minutes with your solicitor or are you ready to go back to your cell?"

"My cell? I was expecting to go see my family."

"Not until we clear this up, I'm afraid."

"No offence to Mr Regan, but I want my own solicitor."

"Who's that?" asked the Inspector.

"Tara's dad, Malcolm Briggs."

"That might not be the best idea, Mike," said Regan.

"Sorry Mr Regan. I know him and he knows me and to be honest, you're not filling me with a whole lot of confidence."

"But you're going to be implicated in the death of his daughter and grandchildren, you need someone like me who's impartial and independent."

"He won't believe it, no, Inspector, call him, please."

"Ok Mike, I'll escort you back to your cell first, then I'll call Malcolm Briggs."

Chapter 3
The Fall

It was 10pm on the day of the fire in the Briggs family home, where Malcolm and his wife Beverley were sat reading.

"I think I'm about ready to turn in dear," said Malcolm.

Beverley just raised her eyes for a split second, "Alright dear," she replied clearly still engrossed in her book.

"Have you heard from the kids today?" he asked.

"No, yesterday, they always call on Sunday, unless there is anything in particular they need to discuss," she said with an air of impatience.

"Was work ok?"

She put her book down, "Why do you insist on starting conversations just as you're ready to go to bed. You've had all evening to say something."

Malcolm looked like a naughty child being told off.

"If you're tired, go to bed and leave me to my book."

Malcolm sloped off out of the door and Beverley resumed her reading when her phone began to ring.

Before she had time to answer it Malcolm popped his head around the corner.

"Who's that, calling at this hour" he asked.

The caller ID said Rose, which was the younger of their two daughters.

"It's Rose," Beverley said with a look of confusion.

"Hello, Rose, what's wrong?"

Rose sounded panicked, "Have you seen the news?"

"No, you know we don't watch the news."

"You need to turn it on, Tara's house is on there and they say there's been a fire and three bodies have been found."

"Malcolm, turn the news on quickly."

"What's going on?" he asked while turning on the TV.

"Rose said there's been a fire at Tara's house and bodies have been found."

The TV came on but the sports channel was on. Malcolm quickly changed the channel for the news but the news caster had already move on to another story.

"We missed it Rose, what did they say?" asked Beverly getting increasingly frantic.

"It said three bodies were found and fire investigators were trying to determine the cause of the fire but no further details were available until the families had been notified."

Just then, there was a knock at the door that made both of them jump, and then the doorbell rang.

Malcolm hastened to the door, hoping to see Tara and the kids standing at the other side.

As he approached, he could make out through the stained glass the uniforms of two officers and his heart began to sink.

As the door opened and Malcolm could see the police were alone, he knew what it meant. It could only be bad news.

Bev had come to the hallway and saw the two officers.

"It's the police. They're here," she said down the phone.

"I'm on my way over, I'll be there as soon as I can," said Rose and she hung up the phone.

"Mr and Mrs Briggs," said one of the officers.

"Yes," They both said.

"Please come in," said Malcolm.

He showed them into the sitting room.

"Is this about the fire?" Bev asked.

"Yes, what have you heard?" asked the officer.

"My daughter just told us it was on the news and that three bodies were found. Is that right?"

Both Malcolm and Bev's eyes were fixed upon the officer.

"I'm afraid so."

"Whose bodies?" asked Malcolm.

"A woman and two children."

"God, no," cried Bev and finally let go of the emotions that had been building up inside of her.

Everyone remained silent for a few minutes while Malcolm and Bev comforted each other.

"Would you like me to make you a cup of tea?" asked one of the officers eventually.

But neither of them was in the mood for tea.

"What about Mike?" asked Malcolm, "Have you found his body?"

"He wasn't in the house"

"Where was he?"

"He'd gone to the shop."

"So where is he now?"

"He's at the police station, helping with our inquiries."

"What does that mean?" asked Bev.

"That's all I can say at the moment."

Bev looked at her husband.

"Are you saying you think he's involved in some way?" he asked.

"I'm not saying anything, he's just helping us with our inquiries."

Malcolm had been at the centre of enough cases to know that there was more to it than the officer was letting on.

He reassured his wife that everything would be fine and that he would go and see Mike first thing in the morning.

"Can you tell us how the fire started?"

"Not at the moment."

Malcolm was kicking into solicitor mode.

"We do have some questions for you though," said the other officer.

"Like what?"

"What was your daughter and son in law's relationship like?"

"What do you mean?" asked Bev.

"Were they getting on? Did they have any financial worries?"

Malcolm stopped Bev from answering.

"We've just lost our daughter and grandchildren. We're in no fit state to be answering questions." he said.

"I'm sorry but we need to do our inquiries, surely you can appreciate that."

"I can, but you'll have to come back another time, or we'll come to the police station. Right now we need to process our loss, so unless there's anything else, it's getting late."

The officers could see they weren't going to make any headway and got up to leave.

Malcolm walked them to the door.

One of the officers gave him a piece of paper with his details on and a reference number.

"You can contact me through the station on these details when you're ready to talk."

And with that, the officers left.

Malcolm stood there watching them drive away but really, he was gathering his thoughts, before going back in to comfort his wife.

"You were quite abrupt with them." she said "Why?"

"They were fishing for dirt."

"Dirt? We have nothing to hide."

"Trust me Bev, it's not wise to say too much."

"Do they think Mike is responsible?"

"They always look at family first. I'm sure it's nothing to worry about."

Just then, they heard the front door go.

"It's just me" shouted Rose.

"Don't mention this to Rose, we'll talk when she's gone."

Rose didn't leave all night. She cried herself dry of tears.

It was about 08:30 in the morning and Malcolm had made Bev and Rose a cup of tea.

They were sat on the couch cuddled up going through months of Facebook and Instagram messages and photos to somehow feel closer to Tara and the kids.

"I'm going to get cleaned up and go to the police station." said Malcolm.

"I'll come with you." said Rose.

"No sweetheart, someone needs to stay here with your mother."

"Isn't she going?"

"No, I'm not up to it and it's your father's world, let him do what he needs to do and he'll call us when he knows something."

"Ok but call us as soon as you've spoken to Mike. He must be out of his mind with grief."

Malcolm did his normal morning routine of a shower and a shave, he put on his suit and looked like he was ready for a regular days work.

There was nothing normal or regular about today and although he looked to be gliding along like a swan on the water, beneath the surface, his brain was working overtime.

It was nearly 11 o'clock by the time Malcolm arrived at the police station.

He handed over the piece of paper with the officers details at the front desk and asked to see him.

The desk officer came back a few seconds later and told Malcolm someone would be with him shortly and offered him a seat in the waiting area.

After about twenty minutes, Malcolm was just about to ring the desk bell when a door flung open.

It was Inspector Phillips.

"Malcolm Briggs."

"Yes."

"You've saved me a phone call."

"Why's that?"

"Your son in law asked for you as his representation."

"Has there been any more developments? Do we know what caused the fire?"

"I think it's best if we have a chat first and I can bring you up to speed before you see Mike."

The Inspector took Malcolm into a room and told him the circumstances of how the fire was started and how the bodies were found bound up.

Malcolm was accustomed to hearing gory details but it was never personal and he had trouble composing himself.

"We're still awaiting the autopsy report but it's a good bet that Mike will be charged, regardless of what it says."

Malcolm took a second to compose himself.

"It all seems circumstantial to me. Do you have any hard evidence"?

"Not yet, but he did try to flee the scene and enquiries are still ongoing."

"I think I'm ready to see him now."

"You don't have to do this. We have another solicitor who was with him this morning."

"He's family and I have to hear it from his own lips."

"Ok, wait here and I'll bring him to you."

It seemed like an eternity for Malcolm with his mind a hurricane of information to process and questions to be answered.

He knew the police tactic of building up a case on the thinnest of evidence and how they used irrelevant information to justify their reasoning but there were questions that needed answering.

What possible explanation could Mike have for trying to flee and how in such a short space of time could this all have happened.

It did seem unlikely that a third party had entered the house and committed this crime, all within the space of less than an hour.

Malcolm's phone rang. It was Rose.

"Hello."

"Hi dad. Have you seen Mike yet?"

"Not yet sweetheart, they've gone to get him now."

"Have you learned anything new?"

"The police have told me what they have so far but there's reports from the experts to come in yet."

"What have they told you?"

"It's pointless me giving you snippets of information, I'll give you a full run down when I'm back home."

Rose felt like she was being kept out of the loop.

"I'm not a child dad, tell me what's going on?"

"I know you're not a child but there's too much to go into over the phone and Mike will be here any second. Where's your mother?"

"She's getting a shower."

Malcolm could hear a door open and footsteps walking down the corridor.

"I think Mike is here, I have to go," and Malcolm hung up before Rose had chance to say anything else.

The door to the interview room opened and in walked Mike.

The two men greeted each other with a very firm and awkwardly long hand shake.

Neither of them was the kind of men that hugged other men, and although in these circumstances, it would have been appreciated, the handshake was the next best thing.

The men sat down and Mike ran through his story.

Malcolm listened patiently and carefully with his full attention.

He felt a little relief when Mike explained that he ran to the stables to see if Tara and the kids were there. It clearly made more sense than him fleeing the scene.

Mike also told Malcolm how the police were trying to pick holes in his story and dig for dirt on their relationship.

"It's standard practice," said Malcolm.

"I know but I thought I'd pre-warn you."

"Let me just organise my thoughts, Mike."

The two men sat in silence for a good ten minutes when Malcolm broke the silence.

"There are a few difficulties Mike. The fire was deliberate, the binding of the…" He paused with a lump in his dry throat.

"The binding of the bodies and this all happened in a short space of time while you happened to be out of the house"

"I know and try as I might, I can't explain it." said Mike.

"Mike, I don't know the details but I know you had a troubled youth. Could anything have caught up with you from that?"

"No. Definitely not."

"Are you sure?"

"It was kids' stuff and nobody holds a grudge for twenty years over a black eye and a bust lip."

"Mike, I've defended people who've held grudges for less."

"I'm positive it's not that."

"Ok, let's move forward."

Just then the door swung open and the Inspector walked in followed by a forensic officer.

Sorry for the interruption but we need to do a swab test on Mike.

"Why?" asked Malcolm.

"It's just standard procedure," replied the Inspector.

The forensic officer opened his kit and took two swabs of Mike's DNA. He packed his equipment away and the officers left as abruptly as they entered.

Malcolm gave chase.

"INSPECTOR!"

"Yes."

"What's going on?"

"What do you mean?"

"That wasn't routine, you don't take swabs like that unless there's DNA evidence. What aren't you telling me?"

Mike couldn't quite hear what was going on so he thought he'd get nearer to the doorway of the interview room to eavesdrop.

"Take some advice Malcolm, walk away," said the inspector.

"What is it?" pressed Malcolm.

The inspector could see he wasn't going to keep Malcolm quiet.

"The coroner's been in touch, the kids have been sexually abused and the DNA points to Mike. This is just a formality now but he will be formally charged shortly."

"No, no, this can't be right," said Malcolm shrinking back against the wall.

"The DNA doesn't lie," said the inspector just as Mike got in earshot.

"What do you mean DNA doesn't lie?" said Mike emerging from the doorway.

The inspector directed an officer to escort Mike back into the interview room.

"What's going on? Malcolm?"

Malcolm still steadying himself against the wall looked at Mike. The blood had drained from his face and his eyes were bloodshot.

"What's wrong Malcolm?"

"Mike," said Malcolm with a look of utter shock and disbelief as the officer prised Mike back into the interview room.

"I need to get out of here," said Malcolm.

"Do you need a minute; I can get you a cup of tea?"

"No, I just want out of here, now."

The inspector led Malcolm to the front desk.

"Will you be ok?" he asked but Malcolm just hurried out of the door without a word.

Mike was sat in the interview room concerned for Malcolm but more confused about what had just happened.

About ten minutes later, the inspector came in followed by Mr Regan.

"What's he doing here?" said Mike.

"Your father in law has gone and I don't get the feeling he'll be coming back." said the inspector.

"What did you say to him?"

"Mike Feather, you're under arrest for the murder of Tara Feather and the murder and sexual exploitation of George and Abigail Feather?"

Mike was speechless, he wanted to ask so many questions but was in complete shock.

They carried on talking around him but he'd zoned out and couldn't even process what he'd just been told. It was like he was on auto pilot and the driver had gone for lunch.

"We may as well take him back to his cell, we're not going to get anything out of him like this." said the inspector.

"He needs to snap out of it before we go before the judge tomorrow," said Regan.

Mike was taken back to his cell and spent another sleepless night, and it wasn't until the early hours that his driver decided to make an appearance.

Another untouched breakfast came and went and a little after nine, he was collected from his cell and taken to the interview room.

Mr Regan was waiting for him.

"We don't have long before we're up before the judge."

"What do you mean?" asked Mike "Where's Malcolm?"

"The police want you remanded because you tried to flee."

"I told you, I didn't."

"Yes, the stables, well the police don't believe you and at the moment, it's irrelevant, even without that, they'll get it on the evidence alone."

"What evidence?"

"You were told yesterday; your DNA was found on the children confirming sexual abuse."

"I NEVER TOUCHED MY KIDS."

"Calm down Mike, outbursts are not going to help you."

"Where's Malcolm?" Mike repeated.

"He left. I don't think he was comfortable defending you, so you're stuck with me, it's too late to call anyone else."

Mike felt sick.

"What's next?" he asked.

"It's just a remand hearing so you just need to confirm your details and after the solicitors have spoken, the judge will remand you to prison."

"100% positive on that?"

"I've been doing this job a long time Mike; I can guarantee he's not going to release you with these charges."

When they got to court it went exactly as Regan predicted. The police told the judge of how they had to chase him down.

Fucking liars, Mike thought to himself and had to hold himself back from saying it out loud.

Mike stood there silent while the Judge granted their request.

He was handcuffed and led away to be transferred to prison.

"I'll meet you at the prison," said Regan.

The last person to leave the court room was Inspector Phillips.

He left the court house and headed straight for the police station carpark where his car was parked.

He got in his car and drove to a side street by some industrial units.

He looked around to make sure there was nobody else in sight.

When he was confident the coast was clear, he pulled back the corner of the carpet mat to reveal a small phone cut into the floor lining.

He pressed the number one button on the speed dial and waited for an answer.

"Hello," said the voice and barely having time to finish the word, Phillips said with a degree of urgency, "They're going to kill him."

"Calm yourself," said the voice.

"I am calm."

"We can't intervene, there's too much at stake."

"It's not right."

"I understand, but one of the first things we learn is that life is unfair and we can't stop every injustice, we can only do our job and hope for the best."

A moment's silence fell.

"I'm not ok with this, too many people are dying."

"I'll see what I can do but no promises," said the voice and hung up the phone.

Chapter 4
The Co-Operative

He could faintly hear something. At first, he thought he may be dreaming.

No, there it is again, and there's a beeping noise. What is it?

He couldn't quite make out what they were saying but it was getting louder and clearer.

If I open my eyes, I'll be able to see who it is at least.

He tried to open his eyes but it felt like they were sewn together.

He tried again and again until his eyes finally started to open but they felt like someone was pulling them in the other direction.

The light was blinding and he had to squint, he didn't want to close his eyes for fear they wouldn't open again.

There were several figures around him and they were moving closer.

It seemed like one of them was trying to talk to him but he couldn't quite make out the words.

His eyes began to focus, a man in his thirties was in front of him. "Do you know where you are?"

He tried to answer but couldn't speak.

"Try not to move, you're in hospital. You're safe now, Mike."

Phillips made another call.

"Hello." Said a voice.

"Thanks," said Phillips

"I told you I'd try."

"You did, what's the plan to stop them trying it again?"

"Better if you don't know."

"Fair enough, I've got to go," and with that Phillips hung up the phone.

No sooner had he hung up when he got a call on his regular phone. No caller ID it said.

Phillips answered the phone, "Hello."

"Good Morning," said a voice in a deep Welsh accent even though it was nearly 11pm.

"Good Morning," replied Phillips and the caller hung up.

Phillips started his car and drove out of the city, before long he found himself in the remote country lanes.

As he drove up a narrow lane, he could see a Land Rover in a layby with its hazard warning lights on and it's bonnet open.

He pulled in behind the car and got out, he approached the driver and they both stood silent for a second looking at the engine.

"He's not happy," said the driver in a strong Welsh accent.

"What does he expect? Look at the idiots he uses."

The driver looked at Phillips angrily, "Have you something to get off your chest?"

"He was supposed to die in the fire as a murder suicide like the others but you fucked up."

The driver's face began to turn red but Phillips carried on.

"Then it was supposed to be guilt-riddled suicide in prison but the amateur brigade fucked that up."

"I don't like your tone, if you're such a fucking professional, you kill him."

"It's not just about killing him you idiot; it's about making everyone sure of his guilt. It's about making it such a shameful and disgraced set of circumstances that people will be too shocked to want to look at it too closely."

The Welshman launched a fist at Phillips.

Phillips was expecting it as he'd been trying to provoke him. He blocked the punch and twisted the Welshman's arm up his back.

"Try taking a swing at me again and I'll break your arm clean off," said Phillips secretly getting much satisfaction from the pain he was inflicting.

"GET OFF ME."

Phillips let go and the Welshman took a minute to gather himself.

"Was there a reason for calling me to this meeting or did you just need the exercise."

"He wants you to take care of this."

"So, I've got to clean up your mess now."

"It wasn't my idea."

"I'm not so sure on that, I want to speak to him."

"That's not going to happen."

"It is if you want me to clean this mess up. My only job here is to keep you out of view from the official investigation and guarantee your anonymity."

"Your Job is to do as you're told and in the interest of self-preservation, I suggest you do."

"Are you threatening me?"

Phillips kicked the Welshman in the knee and punched him in the temple.

The Welshman went down and Phillips knelt on his neck and pulled his arm up his back which pushed his face so far into the cold wet mud that he could taste it.

"Don't ever threaten me, you're just an errand boy and you're easily replaced."

"Get off me," the Welshman half gargled through some water that was pooling in his face imprint.

"Not just yet, I want your full attention first, do I have it?"

"Yes."

"If he wants me to clean this mess up, I want to hear it from his own lips and when I've sorted out your fuck up, I'm no longer obligated to you, do you understand."

"Yes, I understand."

With that, Phillips let the Welshman up and said, "Get yourself off and get yourself cleaned up, you've got a busy night ahead."

The Welshman got in his car and drove away into the quiet countryside.

Phillips watched him go and had a smug look on his face. He didn't like the Welshman and revelled at the opportunity to serve him some discomfort.

It took the Welshman some time to get home, weaving through country lanes, dirt tracks and fields to avoid road cameras, stopping at intervals to check he wasn't being followed.

It was a real art moving around the country without being noticed but it was getting harder.

He lived in a little cottage in the middle of the countryside, his house sat in the centre of a plot of about one acre of unkept gardens.

Although there was a main drive to the property, it also seemed to have several dirt tracks leading through the fields to either side and the woods to the rear of the property.

He entered the cottage through the kitchen door and no sooner was it closed when he started unscrewing a hook that was in the wood cladding that covered the wall.

Once the hook was out, he slid the piece of cladding up half a centimetre and it came away from the wall to reveal the white foam insulation which had a hole cut out of it just big enough to fit the iPhone it housed.

He took out the phone, switched it on and once it loaded, he went into his emails and began to write a new email.

It read. Weather is getting colder. Need to act quickly.

Once he'd finished, he saved the email to drafts and switched the phone off.

He put the kettle on and started to disrobe.

He put his clothes it the washing machine and got a cup from the cupboard'

He took a nearly depleted bottle of whiskey and emptied it into the cup, filling it just over halfway, then topped it off with hot water from the kettle.

He took it upstairs and got himself a shower and some clean clothes.

It was nearly 2 am by the time he came down and he when straight to the iPhone and switched it on.

He went into drafts to the email he'd saved earlier but it had changed, it now read, do you think we could have 2 ¼ inch of rain.

He deleted the message and retyped. No, at least 2 ¾. And saved it to drafts again.

He refilled the kettle, opened a new bottle of whiskey and made himself another Hot Toddy.

He checked his drafts every couple of minutes but it took about ten minutes before the message had changed.

It now read. Make it an even 3.

He deleted the message, switched the phone off and returned it behind the panelling.

After quickly finishing his drink, he left the house, got in his Land Rover and drove down one of the tracks through the woods.

Twisting and turning his way on and off road for 45 minutes, he found himself in the woodland of a large country estate.

He parked up, switched his engine off and lit a cigarette.

Barely halfway through his cigarette, he saw a set of bright white headlights heading toward him.

He got out of his car and headed over to the Range Rover that had stopped with its window down.

It was too dark to see the driver but the Welshman knew him well. He'd worked for him for twenty plus years.

"What is the problem now," said the driver. He was well spoken with a commanding presence about him.

"It's Phillips, he said it's not his job to kill Mike Feather and he won't do it unless he hears it from you personally and he wants his freedom afterwards."

"He's beginning to be more trouble than he's worth, I'll have to give this some thought," he said.

"What is wrong with your face?"

"Phillips hit me."

"Why?"

"Because he called me a fuck up, so I took a swing at him."

The driver scoffed at the Welshman, "You are a fuck up. This is all your fault."

"I couldn't help what happened," he said trying to defend himself.

"We need to move forward. Tell Phillips I don't want Mike Feather talking to anyone and arrange a meeting with him through you tomorrow, before breakfast should work best, we need to move quickly."

"You're going to meet face to face?"

"Yes, and after he's cleaned up, I'll cut my ties with him and you can cut his throat."

A smile grew over the Welshman's face.

The window went up and the Range Rover headed off back into the darkness whence it came.

The Welshman stopped halfway home and got out his phone. He looked in his phonebook there were only three entries labelled D, P and R.

He scrolled down to P and pressed call.

"Hello," said Inspector Phillips.

"Good morning."

"Good morning," came the reply and the Welshman hung up.

The code was straight forward, there were four prearranged meeting points that each had a different time of the day as a code word which were Morning, Afternoon, Evening and Night.

When the Welshman asked Good Morning, he was asking if they were good to meet at the first meeting place.

If the response came back Good Morning, it was ok to meet but if the response came back without the Good for example just, Morning, then it was inconvenient to meet and he must choose a different location or call back at a later time.

If the response came back as a simple Hello it was not safe to talk as someone was in earshot.

But if the response was good bye it meant danger was imminent.

Simple to remember and it didn't mean anything to anyone who didn't know the code.

It was nearly 04:30 by the time Phillips got to the rendezvous.

"What's the message?" asked Phillips who was in no mood for small talk due to the lack of sleep and the cold temperature.

"He's agreed to meet you."

"When?"

"I've to take you there now but it will take a few hours."

"Let's get started then."

"First, I need you to leave your phone and any other electronic devices in your car then I'm going to have to search you."

Phillips looked annoyed but did as he was ordered, it was to be expected they would take precautions.

After searching him thoroughly, the Welshman led Phillips to the back of the Land Rover and opened the back door.

He lifted the carpet and opened a trap door that was hiding a cavity that was big enough for three adult bodies at a push.

"You've got to be joking."

"Get in."

"I'm not getting in there."

"Then you're not going to see him."

Phillips thought for a second and begrudgingly climbed in.

"Drive like a twat and I'll break your arms for real," he said as the Welshman closed him in.

It was pitch black but quite comfy due to all the padding. Phillips would have been quite relaxed if it wasn't for the off-road driving.

After about thirty minutes, the Land Rover stopped. That was quick thought Phillips until he heard the Welshman speak.

"We'll be stopped here for about ten minutes, so be quiet."

The Welshman was at his house to use the iPhone to send a message they were on their way.

He made himself another Hot Toddy and went upstairs.

He returned about five minutes later with his empty glass in one hand and a hand gun in the other.

He thought how wonderful it would be to walk outside and put a bullet through Phillips skull, but he knew his time would come when he was of no further use.

He checked the phone for the confirmation email and it was there. He put the phone away and went back to the car.

Without a word to Phillips, he set off and it was nearly 06:00 when they stopped again in the middle of the woods.

"Get out," said the Welshman opening the trap door.

Phillips clambered out; it was still dark but his eyes were already acclimatised from being in the compartment.

He could see well enough to see the gun in the Welshman's hand.

"What's that for?"

"Don't worry, it's a necessary precaution."

"Well, put it away, it's not needed."

"Sorry, orders. He's strict when it comes to security."

"Ok, so what now?"

"Now we wait."

It was about 15 minutes before they could hear a vehicle coming. It was the Range Rover.

Phillips looked at the Welshman who nodded his head.

The Range Rover stopped and the window came down and Phillips approached.

"I need you to clean this mess up and quickly," said the shadowy figure.

"I need to be free of your grip."

"What's your hurry, we look after you, don't we?"

"The cost is too high."

"You could gain advancement through our organisation; we have a large co-operative that takes care of each other."

"I'm not interested."

"We helped you out of a tough spot, you would have definitely seen jail time if not for our assistance."

"One mistake that I'm beginning to believe would have been better for me to admit too and take my punishment."

The driver thought a while.

"Then I guess we have an agreement; you make Mike Feather disappear and I'll make the evidence against you disappear."

"Guarantees?"

"My word."

"Fair enough," said Phillips after a few seconds thought.

"Send the Welshman over."

Phillips went back to the Land Rover where the Welshman returned him to the compartment before going to the Range Rover.

"Something's wrong."

"What do you mean?" asked the Welshman.

"He wasn't surprised to see me, which means he expected to see me, how is that possible?"

"What do you want to do?"

"Keep a close eye on him and either when he's taken care of Feather or at the first sign of trouble. Kill him."

"Consider it done."

It was about 7am by the time the Welshman dropped Phillips back at his car and when he retrieved his phone, he saw that he'd missed twelve calls.

"Fuck sake."

"What's wrong?" asked the Welshman.

"I've had 12 missed calls."

"Is that a problem?"

"No one calls 12 times in the middle of the night unless there's a problem."

Just then, the phone rang again.

"Phillips," he answered, "what?"

The Welshman moved closer to try to hear the other person on the line but couldn't quite make them out.

"What about the guard?" asked Phillips.

He listened for a minute and said, "I'm on my way," before hanging up the phone.

"So, what's the problem?" asked the Welshman gripping his gun in his pocket.

"Mike Feather has jumped the gun and escaped custody."

"What do you mean jumped the gun, you helped him escape?"

"No, I was going to."

The Welshman was just about to draw his weapon and shoot Phillips when his attention was diverted to the sound of a motorcycle getting closer.

The motorcycle passed them and had barely got out of sight before Phillips continued.

"That's how I was going to justify killing him by getting the armed police to shoot him as a dangerous fugitive."

"Ahh I see," said the Welshman taking his hand off the gun.

"And how are you going to do it now?"

"The same, he'll turn up somewhere and we'll be waiting when he does."

"That's not much of a plan, what if he goes into hiding or leaves the country?"

"Guilty men leave the country, and nobody's going to hide him now that it's been made public what he's done."

"You better be right. The boss is not going to be happy with this news."

"He's confused and is looking for answers to clear himself, so he'll most likely return to Maple Tree House or try to talk to the in-laws to protest his innocence."

"What about his family?"

"His parents will be monitored; he doesn't have any siblings."

"Friends?"

"None that he's seen for over ten years. He's got nobody to turn to?"

Phillips got in his car and left for the hospital while the Welshman went to report the latest development.

As soon as Phillips entered the city, he found himself a place to park up.

The streets were already crawling with people on their way to work but Phillips was confident it was safe to make a call.

He took the phone from under the carpet and hit the speed dial.

The call was answered after the first ring, "I've been waiting for your call, what took you so long?"

"I met the Welshman's boss this morning and I can confirm it is our prime target."

"That's great news, how did you manage that?"

"They want me to kill Mike, am I to thank you for his early departure from hospital?"

"Yes, I told you I'd get him out."

"Great, you need to keep him on ice for a few days until we can end this."

"That might be difficult. I don't have him."

"What do you mean you don't have him?"

"He blindsided Peters and took off."

"Shit, we need to find him before the police do."

"There's one more problem."

"What?"

"He knows his kids are alive."

"How?"

"The idiot who tried to kill him told him."

"And you think he'll go looking for them?"

"Wouldn't you, but what worries me is how."

"What do you mean?"

"He has no resources so he'll probably go to the press and if he does, the kids are as good as dead and our investigation will be over."

"Then you need to find him."

"We're not amateurs, we're already on it."

Chapter 5

Mates for Life

Mike was laying in the hospital bed. They'd moved him to a private room with a prison officer as a permanent fixture sat in the corner.

They had given him something to take the swelling down on his throat but didn't want him going to sleep until he was out of danger.

He couldn't stop thinking about what Charmin had said to him.

The more he thought about it and the possibility of some conspiracy behind it, it actually made more sense than the thought of him committing this horrible crime.

He needed to get back to prison, to get to Charmin and make him talk.

Just then, an orderly came in.

"Who are you?" asked the prison officer.

"I've been asked to see if either of you want a drink or something to eat."

"I'll have some water," replied Mike.

"What about you officer, coffee and a sandwich or some biscuits?"

"Yeah that sounds great, anything will do."

The orderly left and returned just after the nurse had done her 4am round.

"Here we are, I'll leave it on the table for you to sort out and I'll pop back for it when you're finished."

Not even ten minutes had gone by when Mike, who'd closed his eyes was disturbed by a gentle hand on his arm.

It was the porter. "We have to leave," he said.

Mike looked at the prison officer who was slouched sideways in his chair fast asleep, with the quarter filled coffee cup still in his hand.

"Have you drugged him?" Mike asked.

"You're smarter than you look," said the porter.

"Why?"

"Because we need to get you out of here."

"But I don't want to go, I need to go back to prison."

"I take it back, you're not smart, don't you see that they're trying to kill you."

"That's why I need to go back. The man who hung me knew something about my kids."

"What did he tell you?"

"That they're still alive."

"He's right they are, but you won't be if you go back to prison and you'll be of no help to them. So get out of bed and let's go, we don't have a lot of time."

Mike got up and started to get dressed in some clothes the porter had given him.

Who is this porter? Why is he helping me? If he's police then why is he breaking me out instead of going through official channels?

There were too many questions but one thing was true, if Mike went back to prison, he wouldn't be able to help his kids from there.

"What's the plan?" asked Mike.

"Just stay close to me and I'll guide you out."

"Listen pal, I don't know you and have no reason to trust you so, what is the plan?"

The porter looked annoyed but thought it would be just quicker to explain.

"I have a car in the parking lot and when we get to it, I'm going to drive you somewhere safe."

"And then what?"

"My colleague will explain everything when we get there."

"Where?"

"We're running out of time Mike; I am trying to save your life."

But Mike wasn't sure, maybe they we trying to get him alone to kill him. Mike decided he had to ditch his guardian angel and fast.

The porter guided Mike down corridors and stairways, until they found themselves coming out of a service door at the bottom of some steps near the carpark.

"Right, the car is a grey Audi about three rows back," said the porter, taking his key out of his pocket.

"What about cameras?"

"They've been down since I got here, just walk normally and no one will even notice us."

It's now or never, thought Mike, and as the porter turned his head to look at him and say let's go, he hit him hard on the temple.

The porter was stunned but hadn't gone down. Mike hit him again and this time the porter fell.

"Sorry pal, but I just don't trust you," said Mike as he took the key and rushed up the stairs.

He quickly made his way to the third row and saw a grey Audi; he pushed the button on the key fob and the lights came on and the doors unlocked.

Mike started the car and left the carpark with the advice from the porter freshly running through his mind, slow and steady, not to attract attention.

He wasn't sure where he was going but he knew he had to put some distance between the hospital and himself.

The car had tinted windows but he pulled down the sun visor to hide his face from street cameras.

He headed for the motorways thinking it would be the fastest way to leave the area, there was so much to think about but he had to think about the immediate problems.

There was plenty of fuel and he figured the car wouldn't be on anybody's radar as the porter seemed to be very professional.

But still, he needed to make one modification.

As he was approaching the motorway, there was a business park with shops, a cinema and gym.

Mike pulled into the carpark and parked between a few cars that were parked outside a shop that was unoccupied.

He searched the car for anything useful but found nothing until he looked in the boot, where there was a dark blue sports bag.

He looked in the bag and found a change of clothes, a wallet and buried beneath them was a hand gun in a holster.

Mike took the wallet and zipped the bag back up.

Before closing the boot, Mike found the tool kit and removed the screwdriver.

He looked around the carpark, it was early but the gym seemed to have an early spin class going, so there were a few cars in the carpark.

Mike was looking for a car that was similar to the one he was driving. There were a few Audi cars but only three in dark grey or black.

He took the screw driver and removed the two number plates from his car and put them under his jacket.

He walked over to the car that was furthest and best secluded from prying eyes and began to change the number plates for his.

It was a risky move but a necessary one as Mike wasn't a hundred percent sure how safe his car was.

If he just took the other cars plates, the owner would most likely report it to the police straight away but by replacing them with his they probably wouldn't even notice.

The added bonus of course is that if anyone did report the car missing, the police will be chasing the wrong car.

All time wasting for the police which would give him more time to figure out his next move.

Mike put the plates on his car and set off for the motorway still not sure where he could go.

He came across a road sign that said M5 North and M5 South. North, he thought to himself.

He knew he couldn't go to his parents' house but he knew more people up north and virtually none down south as they were mainly his wife's friends.

As he entered the slip road for the north bound carriage way, "Jimmy," he said out loud.

He hadn't seen Jimmy since the christening about seven years ago but that shouldn't matter, but then he remembered Dave's reaction in prison.

It wasn't like he had many options so it was settled. Jimmy would have to listen to reason and help. After all, he, like Dave was a godparent to Mike's kids.

Mike's parents had moved to Yeadon, a much nicer part of Leeds for their retirement years but Jimmy still lived in Seacroft which wasn't the worst place to live.

A lot of the high rises had been pulled down and replaced with a shopping centre, with some new housing developments the area had greatly improved.

Mike was positive that the police would concentrate their surveillance in Yeadon, so it would be safe to go to Seacroft.

He arrived in Seacroft a little after midday and parked the car about half a mile away from Jimmy's house next to what used to be industrial land when they were kids, but had now been redeveloped into a housing estate.

He weaved his way through the streets and snickets that were unfamiliar to him, until he found himself in his childhood playground which bordered the old council estate.

Floods of memories came back to him, as he walked the streets, he used to call home.

He eagerly scrutinised every car parked or passing, ready to bolt at the first sign of the police. It gave him a nostalgic feeling.

Jimmy's house was three doors away, but Mike turned up a dirt track that led to the rear of the houses where there was a row of garages, that last count jimmy owned 6 of the 9.

Jimmy was an entrepreneur, is the way he would describe himself, but in truth, he would deal in almost anything.

He had one finger in every pie, and another on the pulse of the estate, even the straight people turned a blind eye to his dealings because he kept the estate relatively crime free.

Mike knew he was a creature of habit and he did most of his business in the evenings, so unless he was taking his crew out quad biking in the woods, or Dave's son to football, he was rarely up before midday.

All the garages were locked up, so Mike went to the back gate to Jimmy's house, which like his fence was 6ft tall and had a sign on it "Beware of the dog" it read.

The dog it referred to was a German Shepard called Rebel that Jimmy found wondering in the woods as a pup, about fourteen years ago.

One of our mates said, look at that pup out on its own, what a rebel, and the name stuck.

Surely, he must be dead by now thought Mike, but as he slowly opened the gate, he saw the old dog raise himself and start walking with a limp toward him.

It had been about eight years since they'd seen each other and Rebel did not take kindly to strangers.

He'd bitten several prowlers in his time and the odd friend who startled him. But he seemed to recognise Mike and put his head under Mike's hand, essentially asking for a stroke.

Mike hugged Rebel, it was the first comfort he'd felt since the morning of the fire and his eyes began to well up.

"As soon as I heard you'd gone on the run, I figured you'd turn up here," said a broad Yorkshire accent.

Mike turned around to see Jimmy stood there bare topped in tracksuit bottoms and trainers holding a cup of tea.

"Even at his age, there's not many that can get that close to him," Jimmy said.

"Can we talk?" asked Mike.

"I think that would be wise Mike because I'm struggling to understand what they're saying about you."

"It's not true Jimmy, none of it."

"Then come inside and tell me, kettle's just boiled."

The two men went inside and Jimmy made some tea, "Have you eaten?" he asked.

"Not really."

"Here's some biscuits, eat some and I'll make us some breakfast while you talk, but first, how did you get here so quickly, did you chore a car?"

"Yes, I took it from the guy who broke me out of the hospital."

"There was no mention of a second person on the news."

Mike pulled out the wallet he took from the sports bag in the boot, "This is the guy," showing Jimmy his licence.

"Mr Jason Peters," he read from the licence, "And where is Mr Peters now?"

"Last time I saw him, he was unconscious at the bottom of a stairwell at the hospital."

"By your hand?"

"Yes."

"Let me understand this right, a man breaks you out of the hospital and you knock him out and steal his car?"

"Pretty much, yeah."

"Ok."

"It's ok, I changed the plates on the car and left it right at the other side of the old rec."

"Did you disable its tracker?"

"No, I didn't even think of that, FUCK."

"Don't worry, have you still got the key?"

"Here," said Mike, passing over the key while Jimmy made a call.

"Boxer, grab whippet and get your arse over here now," then Jimmy hung up the phone without waiting for a reply.

"There's something else, there's a bag in the boot with some clothes in it and a hand gun," said Mike.

"And you left it in the car?"

"I didn't want to be caught carrying it."

"Fair enough, right, let's get to it, what's going on?"

Mike ran through the high lights as he knew his time could be interrupted at any moment, and Jimmy listened patiently.

When he finished, Jimmy stayed silent, digesting the crazy tale he'd just heard.

While taking the bacon off the grill to make the butties he said, "It sounds farfetched Mike."

"What, more farfetched than me doing that to my family, come on Jimmy you know me better than that."

"People change and I haven't seen you for a long time."

"Fuck you Jimmy, I didn't touch my family and if…"

Jimmy stopped him, "Chill yourself Mike, I'm not saying I don't believe you; I'm just saying it's a bit farfetched."

"I need your help; my kids may still be out there in the hands of paedophiles."

"Hang on."

Jimmy went to the door and opened it. Two men in their mid-twenties came in and Jimmy closed the door behind them.

"Fuck me, that's Mike Feather," said one of the men.

"Ok, keep it down Boxer," said Jimmy, "Mike, this is Boxer and the quiet one is Whippet."

"I remember Boxer, you alright lads?"

"We haven't got time for that, we've a car to move."

"What car?" asked Boxer.

"It's a grey Audi A5 parked at the other side of the new housing estate," said Mike.

"Listen lads, two things that are very important. You must take the car to Guiseley and dump it somewhere quiet, but don't disable the tracker."

"And the other thing," asked Boxer.

"Bring me the bag from the boot but don't get caught with it as there's a gun in it."

Jimmy gave the men the key and they were gone as quickly as they came.

Turning back to Mike's problem Jimmy asked, "So what's your next move?"

"I don't know, I was going to go back to prison and make Charmin talk but Peters told me they would kill me if I went back."

Jimmy thought for a second, "Dave."

"No good. Dave turned his back on me when I first arrived."

"Dave has always been a hot head who's quick to jump to the wrong conclusion but if your kids are alive, he'll get it out of this Charmin fellow."

"How will you ask him?"

"His Mrs takes the boy down to see him once a fortnight and she's down there now. I need to call her and see if she's gone in yet."

Jimmy got on the phone but just then, he heard a car pull up outside.

"Shit," said Jimmy.

"What's up?" said Mike springing to action.

"Settle down Mike, it's just the wicked witch of the north," Jimmy's pet name for his long-term girlfriend Cath.

"She may not be happy to see you, but don't worry, I'll speak to her."

Mike had known Cath for a long time but she didn't like Tara.

She said Tara was a snob and when she met the rest of her family and friends at Mike's wedding, let's just say the English dictionary uses the incident to describe the words frosty and reception.

Cath came through the door dressed up like she was ready to go for a night on the town.

As the door swung shut behind her, she saw Mike and stood frozen to the spot.

"Cath," he said.

"What the fuck are you doing here?"

Jimmy stuck his head through the front room door, "Cath come in here."

"What's that dirty bastard doing in my house?"

"CATH," shouted Jimmy, "Come in here, I'm trying to make a call and then I'll explain."

Cath went into the front room without looking at Mike.

Just then, Jimmy's call was answered, "Hello Julie."

"Hi Jimmy," answered the woman on the other end of the phone.

"Have you been to see Dave yet?"

"No, it's not until tomorrow morning."

"I need you to do me a favour, I need you to pass a message on about Mike Feather."

"I don't think that's a good idea, it's hit Dave pretty hard what Mike's done."

"Tell him we think the kids are still alive."

"What do you mean?"

Jimmy told Julie the tale that Mike had told him and made her promise to ask Dave to look into it.

As soon as Jimmy put down the phone, he turned to Cath.

"You fucking mug," she said.

"Excuse me!"

"You really believe that bullshit story, how fucking gullible are you?"

"We'll see soon enough; Julie is going to speak to Dave in the morning and he'll find out what this Charmin knows."

"And what's he going to do until then, he's not staying under my fucking roof."

Jimmy Snapped at Cath, "It's not your fucking roof, it's my fucking roof and if you don't fucking like it, you can go back to your mum's for a couple of nights."

"You're taking your friend's side over me?"

"No, I'm on the side of my god kids and if there's the smallest chance that they're out there being hurt by some fucking sicko, I'm going to do whatever it takes to help them."

"You haven't seen them or him since the Christening."

"What does that matter?"

"I'm not staying here with him so I'm off until he's gone."

"Listen woman, if you grass on him, you're grassing on me."

Cath stormed out of the house slamming all the doors behind her.

"Sorry man," said Mike.

"Don't be. If she's right about you though, you won't have to worry about anyone else trying to kill you. I will."

There wasn't even an attempt to cover it up with sarcasm so Mike knew he was serious.

Jimmy and Mike spent the rest of the day trying to reason out the events, analysing every detail to see what Mike had overlooked.

"You said there were several local people there when the police carried you to the car, did you recognise them?" asked Jimmy.

"Yes, there was a local farmer who is often up at that time of the day, the shop keeper who saw the emergency services and came to have a nosey no doubt, the last two were our closest neighbours, a really nice gay couple."

"Gay?"

"It's not what you think. It's two women who are in their sixties."

"And you didn't see anyone else?"

"No."

"What about this farmer?"

"He's the one who found me, he pulled me out from under the door and called the emergency services."

"He'd have left you to die if he was involved, but he still may have seen something."

"Surely the police have questioned him."

"But the police are already convinced they have the right man."

"True."

This went on for hours and before they knew it, the clock said 21:30.

"It's late and we haven't even had tea."

"I am a bit peckish," said Mike looking in the empty biscuit tin.

"Boxer should have been back hours ago. I'll phone him and he can pick some fish and chips up on his way."

Just then, Rebel started barking.

"Stay here," said Jimmy and he went out of the back door.

"Fuck me Boxer, what you doing, you know better than to come through the back gate."

Boxer was flat backed to the fence with Rebel growling at him.

"Rebel come here. Good boy."

"It's no good calling him a good boy, he'll think it's ok."

"It is ok, he's doing his job, keeping weirdos out."

"Funny," said Boxer creeping past with Rebel still snarling at him.

Both men went inside the house.

"Why you sneaking in the back way like a junky?" asked Jimmy.

"I'm on foot. My car's been wrecked."

"You've had an accident?"

"It was no accident, I had to cut up a car that was following Whippet."

"I dropped him near the park and he made his way to the car on foot."

Jimmy put the kettle on and offered Boxer a cup of tea.

"Yes please, oh hi Mike."

"Carry on," said Jimmy impatiently.

"Before he approached the car, he had a good look about and noticed a similar Audi across the road a little ways up."

Mike sat at the table and gave his full attention.

"He figured that wasn't your Audi as it had someone sat in it.

After a couple of minutes, he felt confident there weren't any cops about so he got in the car and set off.

As he got to the top of the road and was turning left, he noticed the other Audi do a U-turn, he made a few pointless turns through the estate and the other car was matching his course.

I'd already set off to Guiseley when I got the call from him, I was in Alwoodley so I told him to meet me there where the traffic calming bollards are for a pinch."

"Here's your tea."

"Thanks," wrapping his cold fingers around it.

"Well, he came along the road and as soon as he'd passed the bollard, he booted it."

"I saw the other Audi also speed up, so before he could make it through the bollard, I had to put my foot down and I only just got there in time but the arsehole rammed me."

"You crashed into them?" asked Mike.

"No, they crashed into me and popped my radiator."

"Whatever, I told you, you can't handle the power of that Subaru," said Jimmy.

"Fuck you, I was stopped, he hit me and besides I had right of way."

"So, you got his details for insurance?" asked Mike.

"Not exactly."

"What exactly?" asked Jimmy.

"He bullied his way past me and shot off after Whippet."

"You muppet."

"It's ok he didn't catch him. He's not called Whippet for nothing."

"Are you sure?"

"Yes, he called me after he dumped the car and wanted to know what to do with the bag, so I told him to take it home and wait there."

"Good lad, but we'll better go get it before he gets drunk and starts shooting up the estate," said Jimmy with a chuckle.

"Boxer, when you've finished your tea, go get the bag and I'll phone a curry in for when you get back."

Boxer finished his tea and left for Whippet's house that was only three streets away.

Jimmy ordered the takeaway to be delivered and Mike went upstairs to the bathroom.

On the way down, he kept stopping to look at the photos on the wall, photos that spanned over thirty years of family and friends.

Jimmy had not often ventured out of the borders of Leeds and had no interest in traveling abroad.

Yorkshire was all the world he needed and was as beautiful to him as any Caribbean beach.

Mike entered the room to find Jimmy on the phone looking intense and concentrated in thought.

"Don't get seen, we'll be there shortly," and he hung up the phone.

"We may have caught a break."

"What's going on?"

"The Audi boys are back. They're in Whippet's house."

"What's your plan?"

"My plan is to have a chat and find your kids."

"Let's go," said Mike eagerly.

"One stop on the way."

"Where?"

Jimmy gave Mike an awkward look and shot out of the back door with Mike hot on his heels.

"Shouldn't you have locked up?"

"I can't. I've got no keys," replied Jimmy.

"Why?"

"Keep it down Mike, we're here."

"Shit isn't this…"

"Yep, Cath's mum's."

They entered through the kitchen door and were met with a blizzard of abuse.

"What the fucks he doing here?"

"I need the key for the shed."

"Get him out of here."

"I don't have time for this," Jimmy lost his temper, "GET ME THE FUCKING KEY NOW!"

You could hear a pin drop, Cath was clearly stunned, Jimmy had never really snapped like that at her before and despite all their arguments, she never felt in fear of him hitting her until today.

She quickly grabbed a key from the hook and threw it to him not wanting to get too close.

Jimmy rushed outside to the shed.

"He shouldn't speak to her like that," said Cath's mum who was sat at the kitchen table equally stunned.

"Whippet's in trouble," said Mike.

"They're all in danger while you're here," sniped Cath.

Jimmy came back carrying a canvas tool bag, "Let's go," he said as he threw the keys on the worktop.

As they turned the next corner, they passed the Audi. They knew it was the same Audi due to all the damage from front to back on the driver's side.

Whippet's house was fourth on the right just after Mrs Cannon.

Mrs Cannon had lived in the same house with her husband for over forty years until he died two years ago.

She was well known and a well-liked character on the estate.

The council tried to move her to a tiny retirement bungalow after her husband died, which broke her heart until Jimmy intervened and bought the house.

Word is that he only accepts half the going rate of rent from her but she always sends it with a dozen buns every month.

As they approached the house, Boxer stepped out from the privets in Mrs Cannons garden that stood as a barrier between the two houses.

The three men used the privets as a shield to prepare themselves.

Jimmy opened the bag and handed Boxer a sawn-off shotgun and Mike a hand gun, taking a sawn-off shotgun for himself and tucking a hand gun in the back of his jeans, he kicked the bag under the bush.

"How many Boxer?"

"Two, they're in the kitchen with Whippet."

"Right, let's keep it quiet to surprise them. Me first, then Boxer, then Mike. I don't want you exposing yourself until we have them under control."

"Ok."

"And nobody shoots unless they do, I want to talk to these fellas."

They started to creep around the privet to Whippet's house but as they did, the security light came on at the side of the house.

"Fuck, go go go," said Jimmy and the three men rushed for the door.

Peters was stood behind Whippet, holding him in the chair while his colleague delivered blows, every time he failed to answer their questions satisfactorily.

"Where's Mike Feather?" Peters asked again, but before he had chance to deny any knowledge Peters saw the security light come on.

He barely raised his gun before the door flung open; his colleague turned to see three men rush in all carrying weapons.

A few loud seconds went by with everyone shouting at each other to drop their weapons, and then silence fell just as quickly.

"Mike, tell your friends to drop their weapons," said Peters.

"Why would I do that?"

"Because I'm a professional and I won't miss."

"And I'm a mad bastard with a sawn-off shot gun bitch, I won't miss either," said Jimmy.

"We're the good guys here," said Peters.

"Yeah, you look like it. What do you think Whippet, do you think these lads are good guys?"

"Shoot the bastards," replied Whippet.

"Hello. Hello," said a sweet little croaky voice, "who's there?"

"It's Jimmy, Mrs C."

"What's all the noise Jimmy? I can hear it over the telly."

"Sorry Mrs C, we'll keep it down."

"Yes, ok and tell your friends not to slam the gate on the way out."

"Will do, Mrs C," said Jimmy turning back to Peters.

"Right."

"Jimmy?"

"Yes, Mrs C."

"Could you ask Arthur to be on time tomorrow to take me to Asda, I want to beat the rush."

"Will do."

"He was late last week and we didn't get there until after 10, then it takes forever cos all the pensioners are there and they don't stop talking and you can't get on."

"I'm here Mrs C, I won't be late," shouted Boxer.

Jimmy looked at Boxer and mouthed, "Why?"

"Oh Arthur, I want to be there for 08:30."

"Ok Mrs C, I just need to pick another car up cos mine's off the road."

"What's wrong with your car, have you crashed it?"

"I'll tell you all about it tomorrow, I'm a little busy at the minute."

"Oh ok, don't get another one with the silly seats, it's hard to get in and out at my age and I feel like I'm glued in."

"I'll try, Mrs C."

"Mrs C," said Jimmy.

"Yes."

"I'm sorry but we're right in the middle of something and we need to get finished to keep the noise down, I'll pop in at the weekend for a catch up."

"Yes, ok, I'll have some thumb print buns ready, cos I know they're your favourite."

"Ok, get yourself inside where it's warm and lock the door behind you."

"Yes, ok, see you later."

"See you later Mrs C."

"See you later Mrs C," shouted Boxer.

Jimmy looked at him again, "Shut up," he mouthed.

"Yes, ok Arthur, don't be late tomorrow."

"I won't."

Everyone remained silent listening to Mrs Cannon going in the house and locking the door, the silence continued for a few seconds longer just to be sure.

"Daft old bag," said Peters' companion.

Jimmy, Boxer and Mike all turned their guns on him.

"No disrespect meant," he said quickly.

"Listen Mike, you need to come with us, we're trying to keep you safe until this is resolved," said Peters.

"He's safe with us," said Jimmy.

"I have orders."

"I don't care, he's not going anywhere with you."

Peters thought for a minute and said, "Ok, but you must keep out of sight. The police have orders to shoot you on sight and if they don't kill you, you'll not live long in prison."

"Who wants him dead?"

"I can't say any more. I think it's better if we leave now."

"You aren't going anywhere."

"Don't do this, it won't end well for anyone."

"Do I look like I give a fuck, where are his kids?"

"I don't know."

"And why don't I believe you?"

"I don't know where they are, that's the truth."

"Are they alive?"

"We believe so."

"Then who died in the fire?" asked Mike.

"I really have said all I can say."

"Listen mate, his wife is dead and his kids are in the hands of a paedophile gang, so what difference does it make if you tell him who the kids in the fire were?"

"I'm not authorised to tell you anything. If you came with me then maybe my superiors could tell you more."

"I told you, he's not going anywhere. Now I'm going to give you to the count of five and then me and Boxer are going to off load in your knee caps."

"I can't tell you anything."

"Five."

Peters raised his gun.

"Four."

"You'll be the first to die."

"Three."

"I'm trying to save his kids."

"Jimmy," interjected Mike, "Give me a second here."

"Ok, but I'm not starting again, I'm only pausing."

"Do you mean it?" Mike asked Peters.

"Yes."

"Then why don't you pull in the people you know are involved and force it out of them."

"It's not that simple."

"Two," said Jimmy.

"Please Jimmy," said Mike standing in front of the shot gun.

"Why's it not that simple?"

"Because we don't know all the players yet, if we miss just one of them, they will kill the kids and disappear."

"What makes you think my kids are still alive?"

"They keep them alive until they're either too old or used up and then they swap them out."

"I think I'm starting to understand now," said Jimmy.

"They kill the kids and swap them for live ones."

"But why kill the parents?" asked Boxer.

"Parents can identify the kids better than anyone and if there's disgrace attached, then no relative will have the stomach to look into it too deeply," said Peters.

"So why didn't you stop them two weeks ago?"

"Were not deep enough into their organisation to know it was happening until after the event."

"So, his wife is dead and his kids are in the hands of these fucking monsters cos you're playing fucking guess who?"

"It's not that straight forward. Cases take time to build, evidence needs to be gathered and we need to expose all the players."

"Yeah and while you're playing Sherlock fucking Holmes his kids are…are in danger," Jimmy took a breath.

"Get the fuck out, we'll find them ourselves."

"Hang on, pal."

"I'm not your fucking pal and you're of no fucking use, so take a walk while you're still able."

The two men started making their way towards the door.

"Oh," said Peters, "Do you have my wallet, it's not in the bag."

Mike took it out of his pocket and passed it to Jimmy who held his hand out. Jimmy walked over to Peters, handed him the wallet and lent in close to whisper in his ear.

"Don't ever lay a finger on one of my boys again," he said softly, then headbutted Peters as hard as he could from such a short distance.

Peters took the blow surprisingly well and recovered straight away. He didn't say anything, the two men exited the house.

As they walked down the path, Boxer popped his head out of the door.

"One more thing boys."

They turned around and looked at him with stone faces.

"Don't slam the gate."

Chapter 6
The Charmin Problem

None of them could sleep that night. They ate curry, drank beer and revelled at the dangerous situation they found themselves in.

Jimmy thought it better for everyone to stay together in case Peters returned with reinforcements.

As the morning crept upon them and the beer wore off, the conversation became more serious about where they should go to find answers.

"We can't just wait for Dave to get answers. We need to do some looking into it ourselves," said Jimmy.

"Where do we start?" asked Mike.

"There's two people I can think of that need to answer a few questions."

"Who's that?" asked Boxer.

"The Farmer may not be involved but he must have seen something."

"Who else?" Asked Mike.

"The doctor who ran the tests. How did he mistake the kids for Mike's kids?"

"Good point," said Boxer.

"So how we going to get our hands on them?"

"We need some clean transport first, then we'll go see the farmer first as he'll be easiest to get to."

"Shit," said Boxer, "Mrs C is expecting me in an hour."

"Right, let's get organised. Boxer you take my car and sort Mrs C, I'll call Micky and borrow his Range Rover as it has blacked out windows which would be better for moving Mike about."

"Don't leave without me," said Boxer as he left.

Jimmy made a few calls and Mike went for a shower while Whippet kept alert and on guard.

Julie made it through security and sat with her son Ashley in the visiting area waiting for Dave to be brought through.

It wasn't a bad visiting area; they've made them more family friendly in recent years.

It wasn't long before Dave was led into the room.

"Hiya love," he said in his booming voice.

Julie stood up and they gave each other a kiss.

"Hiya son."

Ashley put out his hand to shake hands but his father pulled him close and gave him a strong hug.

He loved his dad and wasn't embarrassed but he was coming to the age when public show of affection were awkward.

They spoke for a while about school and sports, the conversation was all centred around his son as usual.

Dave was very proud of his son and missing his upbringing was probably the only thing that he regretted about his incarceration.

"Give us a minute son. I need to speak to your father."

Ashley went and sat at another table and put his earphones in.

"What's wrong?"

"It's about Mike."

"Has he tried to contact you?"

"No, but he needs your help."

"He'll get nothing from me, except maybe a bullet through his skull."

"You need to listen."

"No, I don't."

"I got a phone call from Jimmy."

"I should have known he'd fall soft."

"The kids are still alive."

"What?"

"They're still alive."

"Explain."

Julie told him everything that Jimmy said yesterday and how he called her this morning to update her on last night's events.

"The guy confirmed it in front of all four of them. The kids are being held by a paedophile gang but he wouldn't give any more details."

"Jimmy should have broken his fucking skull open."

"Calm down Dave, I've only told you because of the kids, but you've only got a couple of years to go and I need you home."

"You're being taken care of, aren't you?"

"Yeah but it's not the same. I need you; Ashley needs you."

"How could I hold my head up if I didn't help them kids?"

"I know you have to help but use your brain not your brawn."

"I'll make the little bastard talk."

"Please Dave, control your temper."

"Don't you worry lass, stay by your phone and don't tie it up talking to your stupid friends."

"I need to get back," he said standing up.

"We've still got some time left."

"Them babies don't have any time."

Julie understood and gave him a hug and a kiss.

Dave gave his son a kiss on the head and rushed to the prison officer to be escorted back.

"Where's dad going?" asked Ashley.

"He's not feeling well, son."

As soon as Dave returned to the block, he went straight to see Paddy, a prisoner who'd been at the prison for fifteen years and knew all the gossip.

Paddy was in his cell reading when Dave walked in without knocking.

"Dave?"

"I need to talk."

Paddy could see that Dave was agitated, so he put his book down.

"Sure, what can I do for you?"

"What do you know about a little fairy called Charmin?"

"The paedophile?"

"Yeah."

"Well, the first thing he's anything but charming."

"What else?"

"Sorry Dave but why are you asking?"

Dave relayed the story as it had been told to him.

"They're crafty bastards these Paedos," said Paddy, "What's your plan?"

"I need to get my hands on him and find out where they're holding the kids."

"It's doubtful he would know and he's in special protection so how are you going to reach him?"

"I was hoping you might have some ideas and he can give me his contact's name and number."

"What happens if he tips them off?"

"You let me worry about that."

"Ok, well the problem is getting you close to him without preying eyes."

"Just get me close and I'll do the rest."

"The only way is to get you transferred to the special protection wing."

"You got any ideas?"

"I have one idea but you're probably not going to like it."

"Whatever it takes but it needs to be quick. Also, do we know anyone over there that can be trusted"

"There's a couple of brothers convicted of raping a drunk girl between them, that hate the paedos, big lads that no one fuck with."

"Did they do it?"

"Who knows, but they swear she was willing at the time and got angry when they mugged her off in the morning."

"Can I get them on side?"

"Yeah, they both have families on the outside that would appreciate £500 each."

"I may need to get a message to my wife after and if I get caught, it could be difficult."

"Don't get caught, but if you do, there's a young Chinese lad that mops the detention area. Give him the message for me and I'll contact your wife."

After leaving his wife's details with Paddy, Dave went back to his cell at Paddy's request to wait for a mystery visitor.

About half an hour went by when a prisoner called Baz came in to Dave's cell, he was of an equal size to Dave and he was carrying a photo of a young boy dressed in a football kit.

He threw the photo on Dave's bed and said, "Let's get to it," coaxing Dave off his bed.

The prisoner looked out of the door at two prison officers that were nearby and said "perfect," he turned to Dave.

"Are you ready?"

"Ready for what?" but barely had he finished the words when bang. Baz hit Dave.

Dave recovered quickly and launched an attack on Baz and the two men wrestled through the door and were brawling in front of everyone.

The whole cell block transformed into a school playground with all the prisoners egging the brawlers on like children.

The prison officers, like teachers, trying to break the kids up, 200lbs kids.

The prison officers assisted by a couple of their colleagues eventually managed to split the two men.

"What the hell is going on"

"He's a fucking nonce," screamed Baz.

"What?" said Dave.

"He stole a picture of my son and I caught him wanking over it."

Dave looked up at all the prisoners whose eyes were fixed on him and noticed Paddy in the centre of them.

"Is this true?" asked the prison officer.

But before he had chance to answer a prisoner ran out of his cell with the photo held high for everyone to see.

Chants of paedophile and pervert arose from the prisoners and a few stray kicks hit Dave as the prison officers aided his retreat from the mob.

After the officers left him in a holding cell, Dave chuckled to himself and said, "Clever boy, Paddy."

It was over an hour before they returned for him.

"You need to go to the doctor's office."

Dave didn't argue and went with them.

"What happened Dave?" asked the doctor.

"I'd rather not talk about it."

"A prisoner caught him wanking over a photo of his son and attacked him."

"Well, let's take a look at you, does anything hurt?"

"No," answered Dave annoyed with the prison officer.

"You've got a few bruises forming."

"It's fine, I'm ok."

"Ok. Well, if you're sure, you can go back to your cell."

"Not a good idea, doc." said the prison officer.

"What do you mean?"

"It took us an hour to get the prisoners back in their cells. We almost had a full riot on our hands."

"So, what do you suggest?"

"I need you to authorise moving him to the special protection wing."

"Why me?"

"The governor's not here, he's off dealing with the escapee."

"Very well, Dave we are going to transfer you to the special protection wing until the governor gets back and things have settled down."

"Fair enough," said Dave and stood up.

"What's your rush don't you want some pain killers?"

"Nah doc, I'm just tired."

As soon as Dave was shown to his new cell, it was time for evening meal.

He followed the rest of the prisoners to the dining room and after collecting his meal, he looked around for a place to sit.

He wanted somewhere he could observe the other prisoners without having to speak to them.

He noticed one table with only one occupant and decided to sit there.

The only other table with few people on it was a table two away from him with two big lads that were about 6ft 5" and built like power lifters accompanied by a younger lad of a slight build who couldn't be more than twenty years old.

He figured these were the brothers he was looking for.

Now all he had to do was identify Charmin, and from what Paddy said, he'll be the mouthy one full of his own self-importance, surrounded by a group of yes-men.

Dave turned to his dining companion, "Who's that with all the stories?"

"Why do you want to know?"

"No reason, just new here and trying to get the lay of the land."

"He's trouble."

"Well, he seems popular with the ladies."

"Yeah that must be why they call him Charmin but I assure you he's anything but."

"Charmin, eh?"

"Yep," said the lone diner examining Dave and trying to weigh him up.

They spent the rest of the meal in silence with Dave just observing.

When they were herded back to the block, Dave followed the brothers back to their cell and followed them in.

"Are you lost?" said one of the brothers when they noticed him.

"Are you the Nelson brothers?"

"Who wants to know?"

"My name is Dave, and I was told you may be able to help me out for the right compensation."

"We don't work for paedos, so fuck off, fairy."

"I'm not a paedo," said Dave, trying to keep his temper in check, "I'm here to talk to someone and I need security."

"Not interested."

"Not even for £2000 each?"

The brothers looked at each other for a few seconds as if they were reading each-other's thoughts.

"You have our attention."

"Can we speak in private?"

"Young Bobby's with us and he'll need paying also."

"What use is he?"

"He's a good lookout and its non-negotiable."

Dave didn't bother to argue, he needed their help so it was on their terms.

"I need some time alone with a prisoner called Charmin."

"That nasty little fuck, why?"

"He's got some information about where my godchildren are being held and he's going to tell me all he knows."

"It won't be easy; he always has two body guards with him and you would have to silence all three before they call for help."

"Now you see why I need your help."

The boys thought for a minute.

"The best time would be after breakfast as most of the prisoners and guards will be at visiting."

"Yes, it's visiting for our wing tomorrow. They try to keep us separate from the rest of the prisoners," added the other brother.

"Do you guys have anyone visiting?"

"No, not for a long time."

"What if Charmin does?"

The brothers laughed, "Nobody visits that freak of nature."

"No visitors at all?"

"No."

"What about phone calls?"

"Not that I've noticed."

"He saw his solicitor last week," said young Bobby.

"His solicitor, are you sure?" asked Dave.

"Yes, it was that Mr Regan, he does most of the sex offenders cases, I only noticed because it was getting late and I was on my way back to my cell for lockup."

"What day?"

"Friday."

"Definitely?"

"Yes, it was the day before that paedo hung himself."

Dave decided not to tell them about Mike and they spent the rest of the evening talking strategy for tomorrow's assault.

Before leaving, Dave asked if they could get the information about Regan to Paddy, then he went straight to his cell.

The next morning, Dave went for breakfast and sat with the lone diner again, as he didn't want to draw attention to his alliance with the brothers.

"You looking for more information," asked the lone diner.

"No, just somewhere to eat my breakfast in peace," replied Dave.

"I thought you'd made friends with the Nelson brothers."

Dave looked at him quizzingly.

"You were in their cell for a while yesterday evening."

"You don't miss much do you, is there a problem?"

"Not at all, just making small talk."

"Any other observations you've made?"

"About you? You don't seem like you belong here."

"What do you mean?"

"You're clearly not one of them, and you look like you can take care of yourself, so I'm wondering why you're on this wing"

"You should never judge a book," replied Dave.

"True, I mean take our friend Charmin over there, he doesn't look much but he's ruthless and armed at all times."

"Really, I suppose a man like that makes enemies easily."

"Most certainly." and with that the men spent the rest of their meal in silence.

When breakfast was finished, Dave went back to his cell and was thinking about the obvious warning.

The prisoners were starting to leave for the visiting room when Dave got a visit from young Bobby.

"We've dropped lucky, one of Charmin's body guards has gone to visiting."

"Great, but tell the boys not to move until they're all in the cell. We don't want anyone seeing anything."

About 10 minutes after young Bobby left, Dave got into position near Charmin's cell waiting for his opportunity.

Time was passing and there were three prisoners nearby talking to a prison officer and they didn't look like they were going anywhere.

Dave looked across at the brothers in frustration, but then Bobby left his post and walked past the prisoners and officer, then disappeared around the corner.

Dave and the brothers were confused until they heard a cry of pain and the officer and prisoners ran to see what the problem was.

A smile came over Dave's face and the adrenaline kicked in as he hastened to Charmin's cell.

The bodyguard was stood in the doorway talking to Charmin and put his arm across to block access when Dave approached.

"Are you Charmin?" asked Dave looking through the door.

"Who's asking?" said his bodyguard.

"My name's Dave and I'm new on this wing."

"So what?" asked Charmin.

"You look like a man of influence around here."

Charmin lapped up the compliment, "What can I do for you?"

"Can I come in to talk away from eavesdroppers?"

"Sure," said Charmin, giving a royal wave to his protector to clear the way.

As soon as the brothers saw Dave enter Charmin's lair, they started casually moving closer.

Dave extended his hand which Charmin took.

"It's a pleasure to meet you," said Dave, as some sort of count down, then BANG.

Dave thrust a head butt and knocked Charmin to the ground.

Charmin's bodyguard rushed in and grabbed Dave before he had a chance to turn. Dave was trying to wriggle free when he saw Charmin raise up in front of him.

Charmin had a sharp object in his hand and launched himself at Dave.

Dave managed to kick out and Charmin flew back against the wall like a rag doll, banging his head against the wall he fell to the ground dazed and disorientated.

The brothers entered the cell, one of them had some material stretched between his hands and looped it over the bodyguards head and hooked it in his mouth.

The other brother tucked himself to the left-hand side and began to repeatedly punch the bodyguard in his lower ribs and kidney, fast and hard, until he was on the floor, struggling to breathe.

The brothers gagged and hog tied the bodyguard, then threw him in the corner of the room while Dave secured Charmin.

"Cheers lads, better if you leave me to it now. No need you getting caught."

The last thing the brothers saw as they left was Dave lifting Charmin up and pulling his trousers down.

Dave slapped Charmin to bring him around.

Charmin found himself gagged and strapped to a chair with his penis on full show.

"Now I don't have enough time to escalate the pain so we're going to jump straight in at the top."

Dave grabbed hold of Charmin's penis and inserted a match into the end of it.

"Mike Feather, the man you tried to kill last week, who put you up to it?"

Charmin just looked at Dave with defiance.

"Where are Mike's kids?"

Again nothing.

"Have it your way," said Dave as he struck a second match, "Last chance."

But Charmin's eyes remained cold and piercing.

"If you change your mind give me a nod," said Dave, as he lit the match in the penis.

Charmin's eyes flared as the match did, and he began frantically shaking his body to put the flame out.

Suddenly and uncontrolled, he began to urinate out of fear which dislodged the match and extinguished the flame, but not before it slightly burned the tip of his shrinking penis.

"Wow, didn't see that coming," said Dave, "Are you ready to talk?"

Charmin shook his head violently.

"Ok, no chance of pissing on these ones."

Dave forced two matchsticks horizontally behind Charmin's eyelids, "Are you going to tell me what I want to know?"

Charmin shook his head, more in a 'please don't do this' way, rather than defiance. He had tears streaming down his face but Dave didn't care.

Dave leaned in close and in a soft but menacing voice he asked, "Tell me, when the kids that you raped and then sliced open with your knife, cried…did you care, or stop?"

Dave struck a match and grabbed Charmin's hair to steady his head, as he brought the flame closer and closer, Charmin began to desperately mumble something.

Dave blew the match out and released his grip.

"I'm going to take off your gag, but if you try to call for help, it's going straight back on and I'll burn your fucking eyes right out of your fucking head."

Charmin nodded that he understood and Dave released the gag.

"It was Mr Regan; he ordered the hit on Mike."

"And the kids?"

Charmin dropped his head and started to cry.

"Where are the kids?" Dave persisted.

"The Welshman has them."

"Who's the Welshman?"

"He works for the big boss, a powerful man who kept him out of jail a long time ago and now he works for him."

"Who's this boss and where do I find the Welshman?"

"I don't know anymore, I promise."

Dave looked at him and could see a man that was broken and telling the truth.

"So, you're of no more use?"

He pulled Charmin's head back and replaced the gag, he gripped his hair and struck another match.

"The next time you approach a child, they'll see you for the monster you are," and he lit the matches in his eyes.

Even with the gag Charmin's screams were making a lot of noise so Dave left the cell and closed the door behind him.

The brothers were stood by the corner that Bobby had disappeared around watching that drama that had just about come to an end.

Dave headed straight for the security office.

"What can I do for you?" asked a prison officer.

"I need to call my wife to let her know that I've been transferred to this wing, she doesn't know yet."

"Can't it wait?"

"I don't want her hearing it from anyone else, I owe her that much."

"Ok take a seat and I'll get authorisation."

Dave sat there for less than five minutes but it felt like hours.

"Ok Dave, here's the phone, make it quick."

Julie had barely left the hotel when the call came through.

"Hello," she said.

"Hi love, it's me."

"Dave, what's up?"

"I need you to listen very carefully, I've had a disagreement with another prisoner and I've been transferred."

"Not again, where to now?"

"Just listen, not to another prison, just another wing but I need you to get a message to my solicitor, Jim. Tell him there's a solicitor down here that knows all about it called Mr Regan"

"Mr Regan, right."

"But Mr Regan is not in charge so he will have to speak to his boss."

"Boss?"

"Yeah, and one more thing, last time I spoke to him and asked about the kids, tell him they're with the Welshman this season."

"The Welshman has got the kids this season"

"Phone him straight away and tell him to do whatever it takes."

"I will. What's that"

An alarm bell started ringing in the background.

"I love you babe."

"I love you too," but Dave had already hung up.

Chapter 7
Mr Regan

It was about 2pm when Jimmy, Mike, Boxer and Whippet were driving into the village that Mike and Tara had called home.

"Keep your head down Mike. This place is crawling with cops," said Jimmy.

"Go straight through the village and about half a mile past the shop, there's a turning on your right, that will take us on the hills behind my house and that's where you'll probably find the farmer," said Mike.

Boxer followed Mike's directions and sure enough as they rose up into the hillside, they could see the farmer in one of the fields fixing a fence.

"Fuck me Mike," said Boxer, "Is that your house?"

Mike looked down at the fire damaged property that had been boarded up. "Yeah…that was our home."

"No wonder you left the estate, that's beautiful."

"Not for me," said Jimmy, "No neighbours, no community."

Mike could have argued that there was a great community spirit but he remained quiet.

Boxer pulled up at the gate to the field were the farmer was working.

"Mike, it's probably better if you stay out of sight for now, I'll speak to him."

Jimmy got out of the car and entered the field.

"This is private property," shouted the farmer.

"I was wondering if I could have a word with you," replied Jimmy.

"I've no time for reporters."

"I'm not a reporter, I'm a private investigator."

"Private. Does that mean you're working for that paedophile?"

"No."

"I should have left him to burn, after what he did to them youngsters, I've nothing to say."

Jimmy could see he had plenty to say on the subject but had to be careful on how to get it out of him.

"I work for the wife's family. They're convinced he had an accomplice."

That peaked the farmer's sympathy.

"You mean like a girlfriend?"

"Or a boyfriend."

"Aye I suppose it could be, there's nowt as queer as folk."

"In the weeks leading up to the fire, did you see anyone who looked out of place?"

"No, we're always getting fly tippers so I keep an eye out for strangers."

"No cars that weren't local, or any locals snooping around the property?"

"No but there is another lad you could ask, if you can find him."

"Who's that?"

"Not sure on his name but he's always running about the country lanes and cutting across fields in his Land Rover."

"Do you know where he lives?"

"No, I don't really know him that well, we've only spoken a couple of times. I thought he was a fly tipper and went to confront him but he keeps looking for new plots of land."

"Did you take down his registration?"

"No, sorry."

"Is there anything else about him you can remember?"

"He's a Welshman, if that helps."

"Thanks for your time," said Jimmy and headed back for his car.

"Excuse me lad," shouted the farmer.

"There's one thing I remember about his registration."

"What's that?"

"The last three letters were my initials, ANS, if that helps."

"It gives me something to chase up, thanks again."

When Jimmy got back in the car, Mike was eager to hear what if anything he had learned.

"I'll tell you one thing Mike, it's a good thing you didn't get out, I think that old timer would have shot you on sight," said Jimmy chuckling.

Jimmy then shared all that the farmer had told him.

"Does it sound familiar Mike, this Welshman in the Land Rover?"

"I can't say that it does."

"We need to get some digs for the night and come up with a plan for finding this Land Rover."

"There's a caravan site in the forest that we can rent a static, day by day"

"Does anyone know you there?"

"No, it was a lad in the pub who said he rents them when he pulls on a night out, so he has some where to take them."

"So, they can accommodate at short notice?"

"Yeah, and they're cheap."

"Right that's sorted. Let's get booked in and we can then get back to business."

After getting the keys for the static caravan, Jimmy picked up a leaflet from the office for car rental.

"We'll get two cars for Boxer and Whippet, I'll stay with Mike in the Range Rover, that way, we can cover more ground."

"Are we looking for this Land Rover?" asked Mike.

"We're not, them two are."

"What we doing?"

"We're going to find this doctor guy who did the autopsy and find out how he fucked it up."

They rented two cars and headed back to the caravan to freshen up and get some sleep for an early start the next day.

As they ate dinner, each man had his own thoughts running through their minds. Boxer eventually broke the silence.

"How did you meet your lass Mike?" he asked.

"A night out in Nottingham, she twisted her ankle and I used my tie to bandage it."

"Knight in shining armour eh, and she give you her number or did she thank you in person?"

"Boxer," said Jimmy shaking his head, "Mike's Mrs is a proper lady; she wouldn't sleep with him until the wedding night."

"Really?" asked Whippet.

Everyone looked at him wondering if he was really that gullible.

"We didn't have mobiles in them days and all I got was her name."

"Not even a kiss, I'd have taken my tie back."

"That's why you'll never get a lass like Tara," said Jimmy as he winked at Mike.

"So, if you only got her name, how did you hook-up?"

"I was working on the building site across the road from the night club, I told her I was working there while we were waiting for her taxi."

Mike started getting emotional.

"You don't have to do this Mike, Boxers just a nosey git."

Mike composed himself, "It's alright Jimmy."

"Two days before the job ended, I was cleaning up and the lads who were taking down the scaffolding started wolf-whistling and making rude comments to some lasses.

"I went to the window to see what the monkeys were causing a fuss over and could see Tara and her friend crossing the road away from the site so I ran down the stairs and into the street, but couldn't see her.

"About an hour later, we stopped for lunch and I went to the café to get my dinner, I'd barely had a fork full when I saw her walk past the window, so I left my food and ran out to catch her.

"She was surprised to see me but she said that she'd been to the building site to find me but the howling monkeys had scared her off.

"She handed me a bag and when I looked inside there was a brand-new tie, she said mine had been damaged so buying me a new one was the least she could do.

"I asked her if she fancied meeting later for a drink and she couldn't because she was on her way to the train station to go home for a week to rest her foot, but she would give me a rain check."

"What's a rain check?" asked Whippet.

"I didn't know either but it meant she'd meet me another day that was more convenient, I didn't let on that I didn't know what it meant but I said I had to get back to my food as we only had two days to finish the job.

"She asked me for my home phone number but we didn't have one as my dad just thought it was a device for debt collectors to pester you on, I told her I couldn't remember the number.

"She took my address and said she'd write and that was it, she was gone again, I went back to the café and they'd thrown my food away, so when they tell you that when you meet your true love, you get an empty pit feeling in your stomach, well, I did. I was starving all day."

The men all laughed at Mike's misfortune.

"Did she write to you then?" asked Boxer.

"Yeah."

"And he wrote back twice a week but she wasn't getting the letters," said Jimmy.

"Why?" asked Whippet.

"Because she was at Uni and her little sister was opening them and throwing them, she didn't approve of me, she thought her sister should have married a professional."

"Little bitch," said Whippet.

"Not really, I thought the same, I sometimes still do."

"Mike, that's enough, that girl loved you with all her heart and I'm not just saying this because you're my mate but she couldn't have picked any one better."

Mike looked at Jimmy with affection.

"Right, enough of this crap," said Jimmy, "Off to bed, we've got a long day ahead tomorrow."

Inspector Phillips was in a layby needing a little privacy to make a call. He pulled out the phone from under his carpet and pushed the number 1 speed dial.

"Hello," said the voice on the other end of the line.

"I've tried you a few times today, where have you been?"

"I had to give a report in person."

"In person?"

"Yep, I was summoned."

"Summoned?"

"Yeah by that pompous little bureaucrat, Luke could have taken a message."

"It's not a problem, have you recovered Mike yet?"

"Not exactly."

"What do you mean exactly?"

"We tracked him back to Leeds, he's got some friends up there that are protecting him."

"Then send the boys in to extract him, by force if necessary."

"They tried."

"And they were beaten by a bunch of council estate gangster wannabes?"

"Peters and Mac were both there, and they said Mike and his friends came in armed to the teeth with shotguns and pistols."

"Really, he didn't seem the type."

"Never judge a book, Peters said it would have been a blood bath if they'd tried to take him."

"So where is he now?"

"We're not sure, he was staying at the house of one Jimmy Dutton, but they disappeared this morning."

"Well, I've also been summoned by the Welshman so I'll get back to you if the police get a sniff of them."

Phillips hung up and hid the phone back under the carpet before setting off to rendezvous with the Welshman.

The Welshman had been waiting a while for Phillips to turn up, which he didn't like as it made him feel exposed.

Phillips pulled up and exited his vehicle to a frosty reception.

"What time do you call this?" asked the Welshman.

"I can get back in my car and leave," said Phillips sarcastically, "I don't need to be wasting my time here."

"We need an update."

"Nothing's changed. I'm still looking for Mike, which is where I should be now instead of running back and forth to you."

"Every minute he's out there we're at risk."

"Did you just bring me here to state the obvious?"

"We want to know what's being done to resolve the problem, because it doesn't seem like your heart is in it."

"First of all, this is your mess I'm cleaning up, and secondly it seems to me you've completely underestimated Mike Feather."

"You will also lose out if this man isn't stopped."

"Are you threatening me?" said Phillips advancing on the Welshman but stopped dead when the Welshman produced a gun.

"Don't think I'm going to let you put your fucking hands on me again. Now go find Feather and kill him."

Phillips backed up and got back in his car without saying a word and drove away.

He got back into the city about three in the afternoon and found a secluded place to make a call from the phone under the carpet.

"Hello."

"Quick update," said Phillips, "The Welshman is constantly armed now."

"Did he threaten you?"

"More setting some boundaries."

"I see, well just watch your back."

"No news on Feather?"

"Not on our side."

"Ok, I need to get back to the station, bye."

It was about nine in the morning and everyone was showered and dressed when Jimmy returned with four breakfast flat cakes and four cups of tea.

They sat there quietly eating while Jimmy produced two maps and two marker pens.

"Right boys, using Mike's house as the centre point, I've divided the maps into two halves, I think it makes sense that this lad doesn't live across the river, so I think we'll be looking towards Wales."

"Just cos he's Welsh, don't mean he lives there," interrupted Whippet.

"If he lived on the other side of the river, he'd have to drive for miles and cross roads that all have cameras, we are assuming that he's trying to avoid them."

"Sorry."

"Don't apologise, it's better to say something stupid than not to say something clever."

Whippet laughed.

"Both take a map and a marker and run the Marker along the roads you've checked, check every house but pay particular attention to remote properties and farm out buildings."

"What if we get challenged?" asked Boxer.

"Tell them you're selling solar panels and you're checking to see if the building roofs can support them, no one wants that crap on their roofs so they'll just tell you to do one."

"Actually," interjected Mike, "down here there's a lot of people who would be interested in that, so better to tell them you're looking for scrap metal and if they have some, tell them you'll come back later with a van."

"They'll definitely tell us to piss off."

"It's ok Boxer, at least you'll see if they have a Welsh accent," said Jimmy.

"Should we check in hourly," asked Whippet.

"No just check in with each other, a simple text message every half hour with your location should be fine, unless you find something there's no point jamming up the phone lines."

"Ok Jimmy."

"Me and Mike will see what we can find at the hospital and if we don't hear from each other, return here when it's too dark to search and we'll pick it back up tomorrow."

After finishing their breakfasts, they all set about their tasks with energy and purpose.

As Mike and Jimmy headed into town, both men were deep in thought and over forty-five minutes had passed in silence before it was broken by Mike.

"Thanks Jimmy."

"Don't be daft lad, there's no need."

"There is, you and your boys are putting yourselves in harm's way for me."

"We look after our own."

"But you haven't seen me for years and them boys don't know me and none of you owe me anything."

"Would you turn your back on me if I needed you?"

"You know I wouldn't."

"Well, there you go and by the way, what makes you think I'm doing it for you, you arrogant little shit."

Mike looked at Jimmy confused.

"I'm doing it for my god kids."

Mike's eye watered over, "I love you man."

"Go all soppy on me and I'll slap you. Now get your game face on, we're nearly there"

Just then Jimmy's phone started to ring.

"Put it on speaker, Mike."

"Hello," said Jimmy.

"Hi Jimmy. It's Julie."

"Hiya love, what can I do for you?"

"I've got a message from Dave."

Jimmy and Mike listened carefully to the message.

"I'm not sure if it makes sense to you Jimmy, but that's what he said word for word."

"Hi Julie, it's Mike."

"Hi Mike."

"It makes a lot of sense; we're trying to trace a Welshman now."

"Good, I think Dave might be in trouble."

"What do you mean?" asked Jimmy.

"An alarm started sounding, he told me he loved me, then hung up."

"That doesn't mean he's in trouble, Dave isn't shy about how much you mean to him. I'm sure he tells you all the time that he loves you."

"He does, but it's the way he said it, and then he hung up without waiting for me to say it."

"You said you heard an alarm, so maybe the prison officer ended the call."

"You didn't hear him Jimmy, he just didn't sound right, oh and I almost forgot, he said do whatever it takes."

Jimmy and Mike looked at each other, both with the same thought, that was what Dave used to say when they were outnumbered and it was expected of you to do as much damage to the opposition as possible.

Not out of malice but as a pure self-preservation survival thing.

"Dave can take care of himself Julie and he wouldn't do anything to jeopardise getting out to you and Ashley."

"I know my Dave and when I told him about Mike's bairns, he had that look in his eye and I knew something was going to happen."

"I'm sorry for getting you all involved Julie," said Mike.

"It's not your fault Mike, Dave is the man he is and wouldn't be able to live with himself if he didn't do all he could for them little ones, it's why I love him."

"Thanks Julie and when this is all over, I'll do whatever I can for Dave and if there's anything you need, don't hesitate to ask."

"Just find them bairns and whatever trouble Dave is in, it's a small price to pay." And with that, Julie ended the call.

"Fucking Regan," said Mike.

"Who is he?" asked Jimmy.

"He was the solicitor who was assigned to me."

"Clearly, that's not a coincidence."

"He must have been there to guarantee I went to prison, so they could have me killed."

"And this Welshman also can't be a coincidence."

"No, but who connects them and what made them choose my family, and more importantly where is this bastard holding my kids."

"I'm sure if Charmin knew, Dave would have got it out of him but now it's our turn."

"What do you mean?"

"We need to get our hands on this Regan character and make him talk."

"Shouldn't we help the boys look for the Welshman if he's got the kids?"

"We don't know where the Welshman is but Regan can't be hard to find. He advertises his address."

"Fair point, and he can probably lead us to the Welshman."

"And if he can't, this boss of his definitely can."

Jimmy took the phone and searched for the address of Regan's firm.

"Got it, I better update the boys."

He called Boxer, "Boxer."

"Yes Jimmy."

"We've got some news."

"That was quick."

"It's come from Dave; it seems the solicitor that was looking after Mike is involved so we're going to see him now."

"Do you need back up?"

"No, we can handle one solicitor, but the other piece of information is that someone known as the Welshman has the kids."

"Fucking hell. It's all falling into place now."

"Yeah, you two keep looking and be careful, don't take any risks and let me know as soon as you have anything."

"Will do."

"You inform Whippet and I'll get back to you if I find out anything else."

Jimmy hung up and set the sat nav for Regan's office.

"Right Mike, lets pay this bastard a visit."

It took them about an hour to reach Regan's office and at the same time Regan was just receiving a call from the prison.

"Hello, this is Mr Regan."

"Please hold for the Governor," said the receptionist.

"Mr Regan."

"Yes, what can I do for you Governor?"

"We've had another incident with another one of your clients."

"Which one?"

"Nicolas Butler, goes by the nickname Charmin."

"What's he done now?"

"He's dead."

"Dead, how?"

"Murdered in his cell."

"How and by who?"

"We're questioning a prisoner now that we suspect is involved and I can't go into too much details but it looks like he was tortured and his heart gave out."

"Tortured how?"

"I'm sorry but I can't give details yet, we're waiting on the police sending someone to interview the prisoner."

"Does he have representation?"

"No, and he doesn't want any, he was pretty clear on that point."

"When did this happen?"

"About 2 to 3 hours ago, the main reason I'm calling is, we don't have a next of kin for Nicolas and wondered if you did."

"He does have family but they disowned him when his crimes came to light."

"Understandable but he's dead now and they may want to bury him."

"To be honest, I think they're more likely to rejoice at the news of his death. One of his victims was his own nephew."

"Ok but I have to ask, so if you could forward me their details, I'll make the call."

"I will dig them out for you, can you tell me who the police are sending for the interview?"

"I've no idea I'm afraid, they just told me someone would be here as soon as possible."

"Ok, thanks for the call Governor and I'll get you them details asap."

Regan put the phone down and thought for a few seconds before picking it back up to make a call.

"Hello, Judge Spruits office."

"Hi Joan It's Regan here, is the judge available for a quick chat?"

"I'm sorry. He's out to lunch, I can pass on a message."

"No, it's ok. It's a personal matter, when is he back in court?"

"At 14:00, do you want me to get him to call you back?"

"No. Could you tell him I'm on my way to see him."

"Ok, will do."

"Thanks Joan. See you soon."

Regan grabbed his coat and bag; told his secretary he'd be out for the rest of the day and left for the court house.

Meanwhile Jimmy and Mike had been scoping out Regan's office.

"I'll call his office and see if he's in," said Jimmy.

"What about your number showing up on his phone records?"

"It's ok, open up the glove box there should be a couple of phones and several throw away sim cards."

Mike got out a phone and inserted a sim card. Then Jimmy called Regan's office.

"Hello, can I speak to Mr Regan. Oh, ok, no message, I'll call back," said Jimmy ending the call.

"Is he out?" asked Mike.

"No, he's on another call."

"We can't take him from this place or interrogate him here, it's too public."

"You're right, there must be loads of businesses in that block, we'll have to follow him home from work."

"What if he uses public transport?"

"I'll follow him on the public transport and keep in touch with you so you can follow in the car."

"Cool, let me put your number in this phone."

"I'm just going to go to the office block, to ask that security guard if there's an underground carpark, if you see a traffic warden just drive around the block."

Jimmy walked across the street and into the office block.

"Hiya pal," he said to the security officer.

"How can I help?" he replied looking happy that someone needed his assistance.

"I've got an appointment here tomorrow and wondered if there was an underground carpark?"

"Who's your appointment with?"

"Greens Solicitors" said Jimmy, picking a name from the board at random.

"Ok. Well, if you come to reception, I will announce you before you go up."

"And the carpark?"

"No, you'll have to use the multi-storey."

"So, there's no carpark at all?"

"No public carpark no."

"What about staff?"

The security guard looked at Jimmy questioningly.

"My interview is for a job."

"Oh, I see, are you a solicitor."

Jimmy's patience was wearing thin from the ridiculous amount of question this lonely security guard was asking.

"No, I'm a bailiff."

"I was going to say you didn't look like a solicitor."

Just then Jimmy's phone rang.

"Hello."

"Jimmy, it's Mike."

"What's up?"

"Regan just walked right passed you."

"Where?"

"He's just walked out of the door."

Jimmy rushed out of the building.

"What does he look like?"

"He's to your left, he's wearing a suit carrying a brown satchel with a coat over his other arm."

"Right, got him, put your phone on hands free and I'll keep in touch with you."

Jimmy followed Regan on foot across town to the court house.

"He's gone into court Mike, I'll wait here until he comes out and you find somewhere to park up, there's always a few quid in the centre consul, use it to pay for parking and grab yourself a sandwich if you want."

"A few quid? There's a grand in here."

"You never know when you need a bit of cash. I tell all my boys to keep a bit of emergency money in their cars."

"Ok, do you want a sandwich bringing down?"

"No, we don't want to risk anyone seeing you so just grab me something and I'll have it later."

Regan got to the Judges office and was sent straight through by his receptionist Joan.

"Mr Regan. What can I do for you?" said the judge.

Regan closed the door behind him and the judges welcoming tone changed to a quieter and more sinister tone.

"What the hell do you think you're doing?" asked the Judge.

"Charmin has been tortured and murdered in prison."

"And…"

"What if it was something to do with this Mike Feather business."

"Do you have any evidence it's connected?"

"No, but it is a little coincidental."

"No, it's not, the timing might be odd but I'm sure that little animal had lots of enemies."

"What about the torture?"

"That place is full of animals it doesn't necessarily mean he was tortured for information. Who's investigating it?"

"I don't know, the Governor was still waiting for the police to turn up."

"Ok, I'll get Phillips on it. Who could possibly be compromised by Charmin?"

"Just me and the Welshman."

"The Welshman met with Phillips yesterday and he's no closer to catching Feather."

"Does Phillips know about me?"

"No, he just knows about me and the Welshman."

"He's met you?"

"It was necessary to get him on board."

"It's not like you to expose yourself though."

"It doesn't matter, once he's taken care of Feather the Welshman will take care of him."

"And in the meantime, what if they did get my name from Charmin?"

"It's highly unlikely, Mike wasn't there long enough to make friends and god knows where he is now."

"Ok but I'm not sure I'm up to this anymore, and I'm certainly not up for being tortured."

The Judge thought for a second.

"If it is Feather and they come looking for you, we need to be ready."

"What do you mean ready?"

"Just go about your normal business, and if anyone turns up and starts questioning you, to the point where you need to answer."

"You mean if they torture me?"

"Well, I wouldn't expect you to volunteer the information but yes if you are pressured into giving some information, give them Phillips name."

"Why Phillips?"

"Because it will give Phillips the chance he needs to get Feather and if they do get the better of him, they can do our dirty work for us."

"But then, they'll come back for me."

"I'll get the Welshman to send Devon to watch your back."

"I'm not comfortable with this plan."

"We're not even sure there's a problem yet, just go back to your office and wait for Devon to make contact."

"I'm not going to the office, it's too easy to find me there. I'm going to get my car and stay at a hotel in the countryside, until we know what's going on."

"Fine, just let me know where you are and I'll send Devon to you."

Regan got up to leave.

"Oh Regan!"

"Yes."

"Don't ever bring personal business to my office again, go through the proper channels."

Outside, Jimmy had perched himself on a bench some distance away from the entrance to the court house, but not too far to see clearly who was leaving the building.

Like a hawk, he saw his rat emerge and as he passed, Jimmy called Mike.

"He's on the move Mike, where are you?"

"I'm two streets away from his office, just up from the NCP."

"On the route he took to get to the court house."

"Cool, it figures he'll take the same route so if it's clear enough, I'll knock him out and throw him in the motor."

"A bit risky, Jimmy."

"We need to take some risks, Mike."

"Ok, it's pretty quiet up here, the lunch time rush has died off."

"Great, we'll be there in a couple of minutes."

Mike kept one eye on the wing mirror for Regan and Jimmy and the other eye on the surrounding area to see if the coast was clear.

"We're coming around the corner now Mike, is it clear?"

"Yeah, it's looking good."

"Right, he's crossing over to your side, so I'm going to hang up now, if there's a problem just switch the car lights on."

Jimmy hung up and quickened his pace on the other side of the road to overtake Regan, but as he was about to cross the road, Regan diverted into the NCP carpark.

Jimmy ran across to Mike.

"Take the motor inside the carpark and I'll find him," he said, before running into the NCP after Regan.

Jimmy could see the lift had just passed the second floor on its way to three so Jimmy set off running up the stairs.

When he reached the third floor, he went back to the lift and saw that it had stopped on the fifth floor, so he set of running up the stairs again to the fifth floor.

As he entered the parking level, he could see Regan about 25 metres in front of him, fumbling in his bag for his keys as he walked towards his car.

For a big man, Jimmy was surprisingly light on his feet, he covered the distance so swiftly and quietly like a hawk swooping down on its unsuspecting prey.

Regan didn't stand a chance, the first he knew of Jimmy's presence was a blow to the back of his head.

Regan flew forward and was dazed by the blow.

Jimmy quickly pounced on him and dragged him between two cars and before Regan had the chance to recover, Jimmy dealt a knockout blow to his right temple.

Jimmy called Mike, "We're on the fifth floor, come get us but drive normally, we don't want to attract attention."

Mike pulled the Range Rover up at the side of Jimmy but by time he had jumped out to help, Jimmy had already thrown Regan like a limp ragdoll into the back seat of the car.

"I'll get in the back to keep him quiet, you drive" said Jimmy.

"Where we taking him?"

"Head for the forest of Dean and we'll find a quiet spot."

Jimmy had put Regan on the floor and rested his feet on top of him so he could feel any movement.

It was over an hour later before Regan showed signs off regaining consciousness and they were just entering the forest.

"What's going on?" a muffled voice spoke from the floor.

"You'll find out soon enough, now keep quiet or I'll knock you the fuck out again."

"I haven't done anything."

Jimmy kicked Regan in the back, "I said shut the fuck up."

Mike could hear Regan blubbering and as a rule he didn't approve of bullying weaker people, but all he could think of were his children and whether they were getting beaten for crying.

"Right, use the four-wheel drive and find us somewhere private," said Jimmy.

Mike turned down a foresters track and drove about a mile into the seclusion of the forest.

"This is good enough Mike."

Once Mike had stopped the vehicle Jimmy pulled Regan up from the floor to his knees.

"Mike, what's going on?" asked Regan.

Jimmy slapped him hard across the head.

"Don't you dare open your mouth again bastard, we'll ask the questions and you'll answer them."

"But I don't understand what I've done wrong."

"I'm not making myself clear, obviously," Jimmy pulled out his gun and pressed it against Regan's head.

"It's going to be very difficult for you to stay alive today Mr Regan, so I suggest you listen very carefully."

"If you kill me, I won't be able to answer any of your questions."

"Don't worry I'll be putting a lot of holes in you before you die, my current record is eighteen."

Regan flopped in despair.

"Right, first question, get this wrong and the first bullet goes through your foot. Are Mike's kids still alive?"

"I don't know what you're talking about."

BANG. Jimmy put a bullet through the sole of Regan's left foot. Regan screamed out in agony and Jimmy gave him a few seconds to get accustomed to the pain.

"That's one, you have at least seventeen wrong answers left."

"Please no more," begged Regan.

"Then answer the question, are Mike's kids still alive?"

"YES," he blurted out, "Just please don't hurt me anymore."

"Does the Welshman have them?" asked Mike,

"Yes."

"And where can we find this Welshman?" asked Jimmy.

"I don't know."

BANG Jimmy shot a hole through the right foot.

"WRONG ANSWER," shouted Jimmy.

"I swear, I swear, I don't know."

"Then who does?" pressed Jimmy.

Regan went quiet trying to think.

Jimmy leant in close and said, "The next one is taking out your left bollock, who is your boss? Does he know where I can find the Welshman?"

Jimmy put the gun under Regan's backside and pressed it against his balls.

"PHILLIPS, Inspector Phillips. He can lead you to the Welshman."

"Is he in charge?" asked Mike.

"Yes, Yes, he's in charge."

"Where do I find him, before you tell me you don't know, my friend here is looking for any excuse to blow your nuts off."

"I have his home address."

"One more question, what's the Welshman's real name?" asked Mike.

Regan started crying.

"What's his name?" said Jimmy.

"Please don't shoot me, please don't."

"Then answer the question."

"I'd tell you if I could, but I don't know," he said, sobbing into a ball on the floor.

"I believe you," said Mike.

"Keep an eye on him Mike, I need to get something from the boot."

Jimmy returned with a bag, he pulled out some tie wraps and bound Regan's hands and feet together. He then took Regan's shoes and socks off and pulled a spray can.

"This may sting a bit, it's spray on plaster," he said with a smirk on his face.

Regan moaned a little when he sprayed it on but I think he was in so much pain that his body was becoming numb.

"Don't be falling asleep dickhead, we need that address."

"It's in my phone, if you untie me, I'll get it for you."

"No, give me the code and I'll get it for myself."

"It'll be quicker if I do it."

"If you don't want to say goodbye to your testicles, you'll give me that code right now."

"12 7 65."

"I'm in, what's it under."

"Greg Phillips."

"Got it, right let's put you somewhere safe. Then we'll pay Inspector Greg Phillips a call."

"I need a hospital."

"You need to pray we get Mike's kids back or you'll need a priest, not a fucking doctor."

Jimmy gagged Regan and got out of the car to speak to Mike.

"This piece of shit is the best lead we have, so I'm going to pull the boys in to watch him and we'll go see this Phillips."

Mike was a little quiet.

"What's wrong Mike?"

"I'm just worried about the kids. If this Welshman knows we're on to him, he might dispose of them."

"That's why we need to move fast."

"I know you're right but still there's something niggling in the back of my mind."

"It's your call Mike, what do you want to do?"

Mike thought for a second.

"Like Dave said, whatever it takes."

It was about half past eleven in the morning when Phillips checked in.

"Had a sleep-in, have you, Greg?"

"I didn't get in until five so I've had a few hours if that's ok with you."

"What's been keeping you up?"

"Trying to track down Feather's friends."

"Were the in-laws any help?"

"Not really, just confirmed what we knew already about Jimmy."

"Well I'm glad you called; I've got an update for you."

"Have you found Mike?"

"No, it's that creature Charmin that we've been watching. He's dead."

"Dead, how?"

"Someone tortured him and his heart gave out."

"Tortured?"

"Yes, they set fire to his cock and his eye balls, it sounds like torture to me."

"Do they have someone for it?"

"Yes, they didn't catch him in the act but they're holding a guy called Dave Jackson. Does the name mean anything to you?"

"No, should it?"

"You're going to love this."

"Spit it out man."

"Dave Jackson comes from the same estate as Mike Feather."

"No?"

"Yes."

"That might be who Rose mentioned, they must know each other."

"Not sure yet but you can take an educated guess."

"What's he in for?"

"Manslaughter."

There were a few seconds silence while Phillips gathered his thoughts.

"Who are these people?" he finally asked, "And how does this unassuming, middle-aged, law-abiding builder know such people?"

"I don't know but I'm considering putting them on the payroll."

"This job has a finesse side to it nowadays. Maybe you could get away with that shit in your day but we can't."

"Well finesse doesn't seem to be having much success right now but you're right, big brother doesn't turn a blind eye anymore."

"Right, I had better get back to the station."

"Don't mention Charmin until it comes through on official channels."

"Do I look like an amateur," and with that, Phillips hung up.

Chapter 8

The Mission

Colonel Rodger Haigh had been in the army a long time and was now head of a small unit attached to MI5.

He'd hand-picked every man on his team and looked after them as if they were blood relatives, which meant even when they fell out which was often, they still rallied around each other when things got hard.

Their specialty was infiltrating far right groups and stopping them carrying out terrorist attacks.

This time their mission was to crack and dismantle a high profile and well isolated paedophile ring.

Not their usual mandate but this organisation had ties throughout the legal system, media, police force, NHS and even government level protection.

All his team were soldiers except one, the youngest of their group Luke May, often referred to as the nipper, he was their tech support and was as proficient at his job as they were at theirs.

The other team members often teased him that he was wet behind the ears or still wearing short pants but in reality, they all respected his skills.

The other six members of the team were Major Greg Peel posing as Inspector Philips, Major Jason Peters and Sargent Conner (Mac) White who all came from the SAS regiment.

Captains Dug Normanton and Mandeep Singh were Royal Marine Commandos and Captain Dawn Smith a pilot from the RAF, so it was fair to say the team was well equipped to handle most situations.

None of the group had partners or children which is another factor why they were chosen.

Haigh had been ordered to infiltrate the organisation, discover the extent and identity of its members and shut it down.

Haigh was to report directly to a minister called Gordon Hayes.

Hayes said he had received a letter from a colleague, who had committed suicide through guilt from his part in the organisation, which had outlined a couple of the members with influence.

It was from that information that Haigh got his team inside the organisation.

It was Tuesday morning after Mike's escape and Haigh had been summoned to the minister's office, which already had got his back up.

He was not happy with leaving his post mid-operation to pander to wet nose ministers.

Over an hour, he was sat there waiting and was considering leaving when he was finally called in.

"Please take a seat Rodger," said the minister.

"No thanks, I took a seat outside over an hour ago."

The minister didn't appreciate the sarcasm.

"I'm sorry but it's been quite busy this morning."

"I'm busy too, so can we get to the reason I'm here so I can leave."

"I can't decide whether you're being direct or arrogant."

"Let's call it both, why am I here?" pressed Haigh.

The minister opened a window on his computer.

"I've been reading over the reports you submitted last night and this morning."

"Yes."

"Well, what's going on?"

"What do you mean?"

"One of your men interferes with an execution of Mike Feather, then another helps him escape custody who is then assaulted by him, and then last night having found him your men left empty handed after being chased off by a group of council estate hooligans."

Haigh could feel his blood boiling but quickly composed himself.

"I thought your men were professionals."

"I beg your pardon?"

"They've risked exposing themselves all for one man."

Haigh couldn't bite his lip any longer.

"My men are professionals, and nobody has been exposed, yes they did do it all for one man, an innocent man whose wife has been murdered and children kidnapped."

"There's a bigger picture here."

"I know but my man in the prison acted like any good man would. He heard a commotion and called for the guards, there's no evidence that anyone helped Feather escape from the hospital."

"And what's your excuse for your men losing to a bunch of untrained low-level thugs."

"Have you ever had to look down the barrel of a gun?"

Hayes didn't answer.

"Didn't think so, when three men are pointing shotguns at you, I don't care how good you've been trained, the only thing you can do is walk away, if they'll let you."

"Well, in future, I want you to run all decisions past me before you implement them."

"Not going to happen."

"Excuse me?"

"I was told to report to you, not answer to you."

"I'm in charge of this operation."

"But we don't work for you."

"We'll see about that," said Hayes, picking up the phone.

Haigh walked to his desk and put his finger on the phone to hang it up.

"You make your call, but keep this in mind, my team is not easily replaced, like let's say, a minister, do you really want to piss off the team that has your back."

And with that Haigh left the minister's office.

When he got back to his base of operations, Luke was there to greet him.

"How's it going boss?"

"Don't ask."

"Ok, Greg's been trying you."

"Did he leave a message?"

"No."

"Can't be that important then, anyone else been in touch?"

"Nope."

"I'll be in my office."

Just then, Greg called again and Luke put it straight through to Haigh.

After Haigh had finished, he came out of his office.

"What's happening with Feather?"

"Not much, we've done background checks on all Mike's friends from last night, and apart from the odd arrest for petty crime and the odd assault when they were kids, there's nothing."

"There must be something, where do they work?"

"They don't."

"So, they're on benefits?"

"Nope."

"So, they're criminals?"

"That would be my guess, but there's no police file on any of them even being known associates or suspects in any crime in the last twenty years."

"Well, that just makes them successful criminals."

"Jimmy Dutton submits a tax return for earnings from property he rents out."

"What property?"

"He practically has a house on every street on that estate."

"You could have started with that; do you have a list of the addresses?"

"Yeah, I passed it on to Peters and Mac, they're checking them out now."

"Well, that's something at least."

"Oh, the registration that Mike put on the car is registered to a woman in Cheltenham, I gave the details to Dawn."

"Any connection?"

"Afraid not, she didn't even realise the plate had been changed, she was at the gym yesterday morning and we're guessing Mike changed it there."

"What's Dawn doing now?"

"I suggested that she had a cup of tea with the old lass that lived next to the house where Peters tracked his bag, as she seemed to know the friends of Mike's."

"Bet she loved you for that one."

"I told her I feared for the boys' safety."

"Did she buy it?"

"No, she called me a sexist little snot."

Haigh laughed, "You'll be getting your arse kicked boy if you're not careful."

"She can pin me down anytime, boss."

"Oi, behave yourself, she's your colleague."

"I'm only joking, boss."

"Getting back on track, how did Dutton afford so many houses?"

"He bought them back in the nineties when they were going for around £5k a piece."

"And how did he pay for them?"

"Cash, but don't ask me where he got the cash, cos I can't find anything to suggest he or his family had that sort of money."

"So, we're assuming it's criminal gains filtered into property."

"Seems that way."

Dawn reached Mrs Cannons house at about half past two, and as she drove down the road, she could see Peters and Mac sat in their car a few doors up.

She didn't stop as she didn't want to attract attention, so she called them instead.

"Don't tell me you two idiots are here to watch my back?"

"Not exactly, we're checking out some of the other properties owned by Jimmy Dutton," answered Peters.

"Good, cos I'd hate to see you get beaten up by an old lady."

"Funny but you're not that old."

"You're cramping my style so jog on."

"We're leaving, but we'll only be a couple of streets away."

"I'm sure I'll be fine."

"You'd be surprised how loyal people around here are to Jimmy and his friends. We've hit a brick wall with everyone we've spoken to and it's not fear, it's respect."

"Well, that's why I'm here to try a little finesse."

"Crack on then and show us how it's done."

Dawn hung up and exited the car, as she went through the gate it slammed behind her.

Peters and Mac winced.

"That's not a good start," said Mac.

As Dawn approached the door it opened to her surprise.

Dawn was confronted by a sweet looking little old lady with a slight build and a white head of hair.

"Was that you?"

"Was what me?"

"Who slammed the gate."

"Yes, I do apologise it got away from me."

"Well you need to keep a hold of it."

"Yes mam."

"Are you being funny?"

Dawn was confused, "No mam."

"I'm not a mam, I'm a Mrs."

"Of course, my mistake, Mrs Cannon, isn't it?"

"It is, now who's asking and what do you want, I don't buy anything you know."

"Well, that's good cos I'm not selling anything."

"What do you want then?"

"A bit of local knowledge"

"I'm busy, what local knowledge? Are you with the council?"

"No, I'm looking to buy property in the area and I was told that you have lived here a long time and no the people and the area better than anyone."

"Why would a nice girl like you want to move here for, who told you I've lived here a long time, too many people gossip if you ask me."

"I'm not moving here; I'm looking to invest in rental properties."

"Oh, sorry sweetie. Jimmy rents all the properties around here, well the council have a few as well."

"Who's Jimmy?"

"Why do you want to know about Jimmy?"

"You just mentioned him."

"Oh yes, well I've nothing to say about Jimmy. He's a good lad, now I'm busy so I've got to go."

"Just one more question."

"What is it with all these questions?"

"Is there a lot of crime around here?"

"Crime, what do you mean crime?"

"Burglaries or car theft?"

"Not around here sweetie."

"So, there's a good police presence?"

"Police, no why?"

"If there's no crime I thought you must have regular police patrols."

"No love, no one would burgle one of Jimmy's houses."

"Are you alright Mrs C?" asked Cath who was passing.

"Hiya Cath, yeah I'm alright."

"Who's the busy-body?"

"She's just asking me questions about Jimmy."

"What, who the fuck are you?"

"Cath, mind your language."

"Sorry Mrs C, why you asking questions about r Jimmy?"

"I'm not, I'm looking to buy property in the area and I was just getting some local knowledge."

"Well go ask an estate agent and leave Mrs C alone."

"We're getting on just fine thanks," said Dawn.

"Mrs C, get yourself inside and lock your door, I'll deal with this silly bitch."

Mrs Cannon went inside her house and Cath got on her phone.

"Hiya luv, there's some bitch down here hassling Mrs C, get down here."

"I don't want no trouble," said Dawn.

"You've already got trouble bitch," said Cath, blocking Dawn's exit from the gate.

"Move."

"Make me. I'd like to see you try."

Dawn tried to open the gate and Cath pulled it shut again.

"Last warning."

"Fuck you, bitch."

Without any more warnings Dawn lunged forward and punched Cath in the solar plexus.

Cath flew back against a parked car and Dawn retreated to her car but as she was getting in, she saw two women running around the corner.

"GET THAT BITCH," shouted Cath who was still trying to recover.

Dawn closed her door and started the car but the women were kicking the car and trying to open the door that she'd locked, as she drove off one of the women grabbed her rear wiper and ripped it clean off.

Dawn sped off down the road thinking, crazy bitches.

As she left the estate her phone began to ring, she answered without even looking at the name, she was so angry.

"Hello."

"Leaving so soon?"

"Mac."

"You seem to be in a hurry, is everything alright?"

"There's some crazy inbred bitches living there."

"What happened to finesse?"

112

"Fuck you Mac," she could hear them both laughing as she hung up the phone.

It was after six by time Dawn got back to base and she was still regretting not getting out of her car and beating the women who'd launched the assault on her.

She thinks it's what the men would have done and that it makes her look weak because she didn't.

"Hi Dawn," said Luke.

But she ignored him and trudged her way passed him and into Haigh's office.

Haigh looked up from his laptop.

"What did you learn Smith?" he asked.

"Nothing," she said, as she flopped on his couch.

"Except that northern council estates are full of crazy bitches."

"I could have told you that and saved you a trip."

Dawn looked at Haigh waiting for an explanation.

"I grew up on a northern council estate."

"What's wrong with them people?"

"Nothing, you just don't understand them."

"Fucking crazy."

"No, they're a close-knit community that looks after its own, and turns a blind eye on Jimmy's activities in return for his protection."

"That's crazy."

"It happens all the time, how do you think the Kray twins rose to power?"

"Because they hurt people?"

"Yes, but nobody in their own community would turn them in, because they looked after their own."

"Went down eventually though."

"True, but that's because they went too far and made waves with the wrong people."

"Well, Jimmy Dutton seems to have that community firmly in his grasp."

"If it's any consolation, Peters and Mac didn't do any better."

"It's not, where are they?"

"They're staying in Leeds as that's the only lead we have on Mike Feather."

"Should we really be wasting so many resources on this guy. He clearly doesn't want to be found."

"It's the damage he could do if he goes to the press or goes after the wrong people."

"What if he goes after the right people?"

"That could be dangerous too, they could kill his kids if he gets too close."

"Has Greg been in touch?"

"He has, I think the Welshman pulled a gun on him."

"First Peters and Mac and now Greg, do you think it's time we were armed."

"Peters and Mac were armed but it didn't do them any good."

"Where's Greg now?"

"He's gone to see Mike's in-laws to see if they can shed some light on his connections."

"Well, let's hope he has better luck."

It was dark by time Inspector Phillips reach the home of Malcolm Briggs. He identified himself to two police officers who were on sentry duty.

"Don't expect a warm reception," said one of the officers.

Phillips proceeded to the house and rang the doorbell. He was considering pressing it again but he could see some movement through the glass.

It still took a while for the door to be answered but eventually Malcolm opened the door, looking like a different man to the one Phillips met several days ago.

Malcolm was unshaven and wearing casual clothes looking very emotionally beat down.

"Hi Mr Briggs, can I come in?"

Malcolm just waved Phillips in without saying a word.

Malcolm closed the door and Phillips followed him into the sitting room where Beverley was sat.

"Have you found him yet?" asked Malcolm as he sat down.

"No, not yet, but we won't stop until we do."

"So why are you here?"

"May I sit?"

"Sure."

"I'm just looking for some insight into your son in law."

"Don't call him that," snapped Bev.

"Sorry, that was insensitive of me."

"It's ok Inspector, it's not your fault. We know you have a job to do but we told the officers yesterday, we don't know anything about Mike's friends and associates," said Malcolm.

"Actually, I was thinking after the officers left, Rose may know more than us as she met some of them on the hen party," said Bev.

"Can I have Rose's details?"

"No need, she'll be here any minute."

"Ok, I'll wait for her, if you don't mind."

"Not at all, would you like a coffee?"

"That would be lovely, thanks."

"I'll get it," said Malcolm.

Malcolm went to the kitchen to get the drinks.

"How are you coping?" Phillips said to break the awkward silence.

"Not great, to be honest with you, but Malcolm is taking it far worse."

"Why?"

"He's spent his life defending bad people and he blames himself for not seeing Mike's true character."

Phillips felt bad that he couldn't tell them that Mike was innocent and that the kids were still alive to at least give them some measure of hope, but he knew the best way to do that was to return the kids.

"The one thing I've learned in my career is that there is no stereotype, and we never can tell a man's true nature just by looking at them"

"I keep telling him that but it makes no difference."

They sat there for about twenty minutes before Malcolm returned with the drinks.

"I didn't know how you had it so I made it standard white with two but I can remake it if it's wrong?"

"That's perfect, thanks Malcolm. I was just thinking do you have any photos from their wedding day."

"We have a few but most of them were at Tara's house," said Bev.

"Could I see them please?"

"I'll get them," said Malcolm.

Phillips watched a broken man trying to be useful and it hit him to his core.

While Malcolm was gone Phillips heard the front door open and close.

"That's probably Rose."

And sure enough, a few seconds later, Rose entered the room.

"Who's this?"

Phillips stood up and introduced himself but got a frosty reception.

"Why are you here, have you caught the bastard?"

"Rose," protested Bev.

"No, that's why I'm here."

"What do you mean?"

Just then, Malcolm walked in with an arm full of photo albums.

"What are you doing with them?"

"They are for the Inspector, he's trying to track down Mike's friends."

"Your mother said you may be able to shed some light on Mike's past," said Phillips.

"I don't see how."

"Didn't you tell me some girls from Leeds were at the hen party."

"Yes mum, but we didn't really get on and I don't think they turned up to the wedding."

"Who's this?" asked Phillips, holding up a wedding photo of Mike, Tara, Rose and another man in a suit.

Rose looked at the photo and her emotions got the better of her.

"That's Mike's best man, Jimmy, I think," said Malcolm.

"Don't you remember his full name?"

"No, sorry."

"I just remember he was a big loud obnoxious arsehole," said Rose.

"The wedding certificate," interrupted Malcolm.

"His name will be on the wedding certificate; you can get a copy."

"Thanks Malcolm. That's an excellent idea."

"It is Jimmy," said Bev, "He was at the christening, I'm sure I saw you talking to him, Rose."

"Yeah, I was just being polite, he was one of the god fathers. I remember he told me the other one couldn't attend because he was in prison," said Rose.

"Do you remember his name?"

"It's not like we were best friends, it was just a short conversation, you're lucky I remember his name."

There was an awkward silence.

"Sorry," said Malcolm.

"Don't be, you've been a massive help, can I keep this photo?"

"Sure."

"I'll make sure you get it back."

"Don't bother," said Bev, "I don't want anything to do with that man in my house."

Phillips didn't argue, people in grief are unpredictable and if he managed to return their grandchildren and set the record straight, they will probably change their minds.

Phillips went back to the station to see if there was any progress in the search, but as he expected there wasn't.

The police had done all the standard procedures, checking cameras, questioning friends and family and putting surveillance on them.

Phillips got himself a sandwich and a coffee and settled himself in his office for a long night of search through public records for anything that could shed some light on where Mike could be.

He thought of his visit to Malcolm Briggs and the unbearable pain that they were all going through.

Greg got a girlfriend pregnant when he was seventeen but the baby was still born, he decided to wait until he was older and more secure before trying to settle down and have a family.

With the twists and turns of life, it hadn't worked out that way for him but he did have hope that there was still time.

He tried to put himself in Mike's position to try understand how he must be feeling and thinking, to try and determine what his possible next move would be.

But to be fair, he couldn't imagine how anyone could not suffer a complete mental break down after being through what Mike had.

It gave him a determination to carry on and a new passion to complete his mission.

Chapter 9
Thumb Print Buns

Phillips got to the station and went straight to the canteen wanting to give the appearance of normality but in reality, he was chomping at the bit to get the job at the prison.

He knew he would get the job as it was connected with the co-operative, and his chief superintendent was involved.

Although he had never directly spoken to Phillips, it was him that passed Phillips details on to the judge, and buried the rape case against him.

After eating, Phillips went to his office to find the chief superintendent sitting at his desk.

"Sir," said Phillips.

"Having a late start, Greg?"

"I was up until late last night chasing leads on Mike Feather, sir."

"I know you were. Any progress on that?"

"A little sir, we're looking into some associates in Leeds."

"I'd like to see the report on that but I've got another job for you first."

"I thought this was top priority?"

"So is this," he snapped, "There's been a murder at the prison and I need you to go investigate and question the suspect."

"Ok."

"And Greg, keep everything you learn to yourself and bring it directly to me when you're done."

"You don't want me to file a report?"

"Not until you've spoken to me and then we'll decide the best way to proceed, it's a sensitive matter Greg."

"Got it."

"Greg, don't fuck it up," he said as he left the office.

Phillips got to the prison a little after three and was shown through to the governor's office.

"Hi, Inspector Greg Phillips."

"Governor Fred Davis, I would have expected a quicker response?"

"Were busy looking for the prisoner you misplaced," Phillips said flippantly.

The Governor didn't look amused.

"I'm sorry I've been up all night looking for Mike Feather and if you don't mind, I just want to get on."

"Ok, well I think forensics are nearly finished, so we'll go to the cell first, if that's ok with you."

"That's great."

The governor escorted Phillips through the prison to the special protection cell block.

"I understand you have a suspect in custody," asked Phillips.

"Yes, Dave Jackson."

"What can you tell me about him?"

"He's in for manslaughter, he caught a man assaulting his mother and beat him to death."

"And the assault on his mother wasn't taken into account?"

"It was but his assault was so brutal, he followed the man who had crawled out to the garden after the first beating and punched his head repeatedly so hard that it left an imprint in the ground. That, with his lack of remorse, got him convicted."

"What's his behaviour been like here?"

"Not a single incident until this, he has all his privileges and his wife and son visit every two weeks without fail."

"Sounds like a model citizen."

"Not quite, he does have a short fuse and temper to match."

"I thought you said he had behaved himself?"

"Here he has, but he was transferred here from Armley in Leeds where he put seven of his fellow prisoners in the infirmary."

"Seven?"

"Yeah, but I've had a good repour with him up until now and I told him if he behaved, I'd give a favourable report to the parole board."

"Has he had any other visitors other than his wife?"

"No."

"When was her last visit?"

"Yesterday, do you think it has anything to do with this?"

"Not sure, did the visit go ok, did they argue?"

"I'm not sure what they talked about but from the CCTV it seemed to be something important, and then Dave cut the visit short."

"Anything else?"

"Yeah, as the alarm was being raised, Dave was making a call to his wife."

"Do you have the recording?"

"Yes, I can give you access to it from the security office after we've been to the cell."

"Were there no witnesses at all?"

"Yes, one but he's been transferred to hospital."

"Why?"

"Several broken ribs and a punctured lung, he was found tied up on the floor next to Charmin."

"Has he said anything, did he see anyone?"

"He's not in any fit state to be questioned yet, so we don't know."

"I'll go see him when I'm finished here."

They arrived at Charmin's cell which was a buzz of activity with forensic officers taking physical evidence and pictures, ambulance staff waiting to remove the body, cleaning staff waiting to move in and all guarded by prison officers.

Phillips told the Governor that he would handle it from here and suggested there was no need for him to hang around, but the Governor stated his intention to stay.

The last thing Phillips needed were people looking over his shoulder, especially as he was supposed to keep his findings secret.

"Ok, but please let me do my work and we'll discuss it later."

Phillips asked the forensic team if it was safe to enter the cell and he was admitted.

"We're nearly done," said the lead investigator.

Phillips looked around the room. It was a standard cell with a single bed, a desk and chair with a tv and games console but no photos of any loved ones or any personal items.

Charmin's body had been transferred to a body bag on the bed, and there was a kind of outline on the floor to mark where the other prisoner lay bound.

"Doesn't it bother you?" asked the investigator.

"What?"

"The smell, got to be the worst, burned flesh."

"I have a blocked nose."

"Lucky you, I've been doing this job nine years and it's the worst smell I've ever come across."

Phillips had lied, he didn't have a blocked nose, he'd spent plenty of time in foreign countries where bodies have been burned for a multitude of reasons.

Open air cremations to ethnic cleansing sites, he'd had to deal with wounds on himself and colleagues that have had hot shrapnel inside.

It was fair to say that he had become nose blind to rancid smells.

"Can I see the body?" asked Phillips.

"Sure, have you got a strong stomach?"

"I'll be ok."

The investigator opened the body bag to reveal a skinny little man with bad burns to his eyes.

"Is that the only injury?"

"No, there's been a couple of blows to the head and a blow to the chest that looks too big for a fist and then there's this."

The investigator grabbed Charmin's penis and pulled back the foreskin to expose a burn mark.

"It looks like a match was inserted in his urinary meatus and set alight."

"Inserted in his what?"

"The hole in the end of his penis."

"That's got to have hurt, why isn't there more damage?"

"It looks like he urinated on the match."

"So, then they moved on to his eyes. It seemed someone wanted to cause Mr Butler a considerable amount of pain."

"He was a paedophile and as I understand it, a particularly nasty character at that, I'm sure he had a que of people wanting to cause him considerable pain."

If the goal was to kill or hurt Charmin, they wouldn't have gone to the trouble of binding him to the chair, they could have stabbed him or poured melted sugar over him to scar him.

Considering the risk of discovery, someone wanted information and was willing to risk everything to get it, this was one of the most ruthless tortures that Greg had ever seen.

"Are you transporting him out now?"

"The Governor wants to wait until the prisoners have gone to dinner."

"Is there anything else I should be aware of?"

"I'd say it took more than one person to do this."

"Right, well I'll leave you to it."

Phillips left the cell and asked the governor to take him to the security office.

"Do we have any CCTV of the cell area?" he asked.

"Apparently not."

"Why?"

"We've been waiting for funding to upgrade the system."

"Are there cameras?"

"Yes, but the hard drive suffered a malfunction and because the prison officers could still monitor the area it wasn't considered a priority."

"But the prison officers didn't see anything?"

"No, they said they were concentrating on the prisoners being transferred for visitation and the officer on the wing, was dealing with a young man who was throwing a tantrum and hurt his leg kicking a wall."

A diversion Phillip's thought.

In the security office, the governor handed Phillips a pair of headphones so he could listen to the phone call between Dave and his wife.

Phillips listened to it several times and wrote every word down with a couple of side notes.

"I think I'm ready to speak to Dave Jackson."

"I have him in a holding cell, I'll have him moved to an interview room."

"No, I'd like to see him in the holding cell."

"That's against protocol."

"There's cameras in an interview room and I want him to be relaxed."

"I don't like it; I can't guarantee your safety in a holding cell."

"You don't need to worry. I've been in tuff rooms before."

"Ok, we'll be close by, and I'll have several officers on standby."

The Governor guided Phillips to the holding cell where they were joined by four large prison officers.

"A little over the top," commented Phillips.

"Don't underestimate this man, he can turn on a pin head."

"I'll be fine, just keep out of sight."

The Governor had the officer open the holding cell and moved his team a couple of metres away.

Phillips entered the cell to find Dave laying on the bed with his eyes closed, his hands were still handcuffed.

"I'm Inspector Phillips, can I talk to you for a second?"

Dave opened his eyes for a second and glanced at Phillips and rolled away from him.

"You need to talk to me Dave."

But Dave ignored him.

"You're going to have to speak to me at some point."

Dave rolled back over and looked at Phillips.

"Why, do I not have a right to remain silent?"

"It may have escaped your attention but we're not in an interview room, there's no cameras or recording equipment."

"That may be, but it doesn't change the fact I can't help you and I've nothing to say."

Dave rolled back over.

"You don't even know why I'm here or what I want."

But Dave didn't move.

"Dave, can you look at this?"

Dave didn't move.

"Please Dave."

Dave turned around and opened his eyes, Phillips was holding the wedding photo he'd got from Malcolm.

Dave tried to play it cool.

"What's this?"

Phillips lowered his voice.

"You're friends, Mike Feather and Jimmy Dutton."

"Not friends of mine."

"I don't have time to play games, Dave."

"Then fuck off, I didn't invite you here and I've got nothing to say to you."

"Ok I'll leave and pull your wife in for questioning."

Dave lunged at Phillips but Phillips was ready for him and struck Dave in the throat with an open hand.

Dave landed on the bed with a thud and within seconds the door to the cell flung open and in rushed the prison officers followed by the Governor.

"Is everything alright?" asked the Governor.

"Calm yourselves, Dave tried to stand up and lost his balance, that's all."

Phillips helped Dave to sit up.

"Did you hurt yourself, mate?"

Dave didn't answer.

"Thanks boys but everything is under control."

The Governor and officers reluctantly retreated back to the hall.

"Now we've got that out of the way, as you can see, there's a good reason to keep the volume down."

"Stay away from my wife," Dave said in a threatening way.

"Dave, I can see you're a resourceful man and I can certainly respect your loyalty but I'm not your enemy."

"Worse, you're a copper."

Phillips could see that getting past Dave's distrust for the police was not going to be easy.

"If you don't want to talk, just listen."

Dave looked stone-faced at Phillips.

"I know you're somehow connected to Mike Feather and that you attacked Charmin. What I don't know is, whether it was just an interrogation or a revenge attack for him trying to kill Mike."

Dave remained quiet.

"I'm guessing from the coded conversation you had with your wife that you got the information that you were after."

"You don't seem to need my help."

"I need your help to find Mike. There are people out there trying to kill him."

"Sorry, I've no idea what you're talking about."

Phillips was getting frustrated.

"I'm guessing you've sent them after Mr Regan. Do you not realise that going after these people could get Mike killed or worse."

"What could be worse?"

"He could get his kids' killed."

Dave examined Phillips; every fibre of his body told him not to trust this policeman but he was not like any copper that Dave had ever met.

"Firstly, you're a copper and every word out of your mouth is a lie, and secondly, like I keep telling you, I don't know what the fuck you're talking about."

Phillips could see he was never going to get anywhere with Dave.

"Ok Dave. I can see you don't trust me."

"And finally, the penny drops."

"If I got you access to a phone, could you at least get a message to Mike and ask him to call me."

Dave laid back down and rolled over.

Phillips shook his head in despair.

"If you see sense and change your mind, ask the Governor to call me."

Phillips headed for the door.

"I'm not your enemy, Dave."

Dave turned over.

"Maybe, but I do know one thing for sure."

"What's that?"

"You're definitely not my friend."

Phillips completely understood what Dave was saying, he had no reason to trust him and from Dave's perspective, he was just a police officer trying to gain trust.

He left the cell and joined the Governor.

"He knows the game too well; he's not saying anything."

"Sorry, we get a lot of that in here. Do you have anything to go on?"

"Not yet, I'm going to go to the hospital to question this other prisoner that was in the cell."

"You'll probably find him just as much help. I'll show you out."

"As they were leaving, the prisoners were returning from dinner. Phillips stopped to watch them go by and got lost in thought for a second."

"Are you ok?" asked the Governor.

"Yes, sorry, I was just gathering my thoughts, making sure I hadn't forgotten anything."

"Shall we proceed?"

"Yes, please do."

Phillips signed out of the prison and sat in his car for a while gathering his thoughts. After about twenty minutes, he started the car and set off for the hospital.

He thought he'd better interview the prisoner with the punctured lung before reporting to either Haigh or the chief superintendent.

On arrival at the hospital, he went directly to A&E. He showed his credentials to the receptionist and asked to be directed to the prisoner.

The receptionist made a call and asked Phillips to take a seat as the doctor would be with him shortly.

It took a good fifteen minutes for the doctor to come and Phillips was getting a little impatient. He didn't need to speak to the prisoner, he was just being thorough but considered it a waste of his time.

"Hi, are you the inspector?" asked a young doctor.

"I am."

"If you follow me, we'll go to my office to talk."

"I'm here to talk to the prisoner, not you," he said, letting his impatience get the better of him.

"That's not going to be possible."

"This is a murder investigation."

"I appreciate that, but he's dead."

"How?"

"He drowned in his own blood in the ambulance."

"And you couldn't have informed the prison."

"I did about twenty minutes ago."

"Did he say anything before he died."

"I don't think he regained consciousness, but the prison officer is in the canteen and he'd be the best person to ask."

Phillips marched away from the doctor towards the canteen without so much as a fare thee well.

The prison officer was tucking into a treacle sponge pudding with custard by the time Phillips arrived.

"Are you the officer supposed to be guarding the prisoner that was brought in."

"He doesn't need guarding, he's dead," said the officer bluntly, "Who are you?"

"Inspector Phillips, why haven't you reported in with the prison?"

"I'm waiting on the doctor's report."

"Tossing it off more like."

"I don't answer to you and I'm allowed to get dinner, I already missed my lunch."

Phillips looked at the man and thought he's never missed a meal in his life.

"Did the prisoner regain consciousness in the ambulance?"

"He was in and out but died twenty minutes into the journey."

"Did he say anything?"

"It's funny, you would think if you were close to death you would call out the names of your loved ones, but this trash just kept repeating the name of his solicitor."

"And who is that?"

"Mr Regan, he represents most of these freaks."

"Are you sure he didn't say anything else?"

"He just kept moaning Regan, get Regan."

Phillips left the officer devouring his pudding and headed back to his car.

Phillips headed back to the station but stopped off in a quiet street to make a call.

"Hello," said Haigh.

"It's definitely something to do with Feather."

"Charmin?"

"Yes."

"Did they get anything from him?"

"Yes, and I think I may have an idea where Mike is going to be?"

"Well, don't keep it to yourself, man."

"I think they're going after Regan."

"Anything else?"

"Yes, it seems Charmin told them the Welshman had Mike's kids."

"Well, they'll go for him first, won't they?"

"Doubtful, the Welshman is very cautious and unlike Regan, doesn't advertise his address."

"Did you get this from Dave Jackson?"

"No, he wouldn't say a word. He called his wife and gave her a cryptic message which wouldn't mean anything to anyone who wasn't familiar with the co-operative."

"Have you got a copy of it?"

"Yes, I wrote it down word for word."

"Email me a copy of everything you have and I'll get Luke to sift through it, do you think this Dave could be convinced to call Mike off?"

"Not likely, he's an immoveable object. He doesn't trust me because he thinks I'm just trying to befriend him, to get him to confess."

"Not sure about that."

"He has a deep distrust of the police."

"That may be, but from what we're learning about these people, they're fiercely loyal to each other. Would you do what Dave did for one of your mates?"

"Dave's a criminal."

"For doing what we get paid to do."

"We have a chain of command."

"They live by a code of conduct."

"And anyone who breaks that code, dies."

"So, sometimes they go a little overboard, you've killed bad men and the only difference is, you were ordered by your government."

Greg took a breath, "I knew you'd take their side."

"I've just been around long enough to know that one man's villain is another man's hero, and if circumstances were different, I could be where Dave is and he could be one of your team mates."

"There has to be a line we don't cross."

"And that's why the world needs people like Dave, to cross the lines we can't."

"You can't mean that, people taking the law into their own hands would be chaos."

"It's people who make laws and people who give us our orders, who's to say if they have it right?"

"We don't have time for a philosophical debate, but if it makes you happy, I have an idea on how we may be able to get Dave to open up."

"I'm all ears."

"You haven't pulled Dug yet, have you?"

"We were just discussing that."

"Don't, I'm going to see if I can get Dave released from isolation so you can get Dug to talk to him."

"I don't think it will work but it's worth a shot."

"I need to report back to the chief superintendent and if I'm right, he's going to want this prison business burying."

"Ok and I'll pull Peters and Mac back from Leeds to watch Regan."

Phillips hung up and wrote an email detailing his findings, then set off for the police station.

Mike and Jimmy dropped Regan at the caravan and waited for the boys to get back.

"He don't look too good, Jimmy."

"Neither would you if you'd been shot through the foot."

"What if he dies?"

"He's not going to die."

"How can you be sure?"

"The bleeding has stopped or at least nearly stopped, and the bullets haven't damaged any vital organs, like I said, he'll live."

Just then, Boxer turned up.

"Where's Whippet?"

"He was further out than me but he won't be long, where is he?"

"In there," said Jimmy pointing to Boxer's bedroom.

"Why'd you put him in my room?"

"Because it was the first room I came to."

Boxer opened the door and saw a middle-aged man laid face down on the floor, his hands and feet tie-wrapped together and another tie wrap connecting his hands to his feet.

"Hog tied, cool," said Boxer.

"Fuck me, Jimmy. He looks in a bad way, he's not going to die on me, is he?"

Mike looked at Jimmy.

"No, he's not. Just change his bandages and keep him quiet."

Boxer picked up his phone and made a call.

"Whippet, Stop at the shop on the way back."

"Sure, what do you want?"

"A shit load of bandages, a bottle of vodka, a bottle of whisky, a six pack of beers and a couple of sarnies."

"Got it, I shouldn't be long I'm about twenty minutes out."

"See you soon."

"Planning a party?" said Jimmy as Boxer put his phone away.

"Vodka for his feet, whisky to keep him quiet and the beers for me, in case he dies."

"He better not die, and you better not get drunk."

"Three beers a piece is hardly going to get us pissed."

"You need to have your wits about you."

"Ok Jimmy."

"Me and Mike are going to get off now, it'll be dark soon and I want to get familiar with the area before we make our move."

As Jimmy and Mike drove to Phillips house, Mike wanted to talk strategy.

"What's your plan Jimmy?"

"What do you mean, we get our hands on Phillips and make him talk."

"How are you planning on getting your hands on him, you can't just knock on his door and shove a shot gun in his face."

Jimmy looked at Mike with confusion.

"What if he has a family Jimmy? What if there's kids in the house?"

"Then it will give him more incentive to talk."

"I'm not ok with hurting kids, Jimmy."

"And you think I am?"

"Not physically but seeing their dad threatened and hurt can hurt them emotionally."

"Fair point Mike, but on the other hand, seeing his kids bound and gagged might give him an ounce of understanding how your feeling?"

"You want to tie his kids up?"

"Mike, sorry but you need a bit of a reality check. Do you think your kids went willingly, no, you can bet your arse they tied them and gagged them."

"I know Jimmy, I think about it all the time."

"I know pal and I'm sorry but we have to show we're a worse alternative to keeping quiet, otherwise, they've no fear of us and have no reason to talk."

"Ok Jimmy, but even whatever it takes has its limits."

"Have a little faith, Mike."

"I do Jimmy, and you have to also consider that we're here to get the address of the Welshman and then we're going to have to secure Phillips and whomever else."

"I'll get the boys to bring Regan here."

"Sounds like a plan, you know we're definitely going to be in harm's way after this one. The police don't take it lightly you going after one of their own, even if he is bent."

"They're all bent," replied Jimmy.

It was about 7:30 in the evening when they arrived at the address that Regan had furnished.

It was a detached property standing in its own grounds on the edge of a village.

"Let's have a drive around first Mike to get a lay of the land."

"Yeah, it doesn't look like anyone's home, anyway."

As they passed the house Jimmy's phone rang, Mike put it on speaker.

"Boxer, what's up, is Regan alright?"

"Yeah, fuck him, Whippet bumped into the Welshman."

"What?"

"Yeah, he was just coming out of the shop and he saw a Land Rover cross the road from one dirt track to another."

"Did he follow him?"

"He tried."

"What do you mean tried?"

"He spun the car around and shot down the track but it was getting dark, he didn't want to attract attention so he left his lights off, but it meant he had to drive carefully."

"And," said Jimmy impatiently.

"He caught up with the Land Rover going through a field up a rocky hill, he said there was no way his car would have made it."

"He lost him."

"He sped around the country roads but by time he got there, yes he lost him."

"There were no tracks or anything?"

"It was too dark to see any, he called me and I told him to mark it on his sat nav on his phone and get back here."

"I suppose that's best, we're here but no one is home, so we're in for a wait."

"Ok Jimmy, I'll get Whippet back out there at first light to find them tracks."

"Good man, tell Whippet good job and he'll get himself a Bruicey Bonus if he finds that son of a bitch."

"Boxer."

"Yes Mike."

"Make sure Whippet knows not to be a hero and not to confront the Welshman on his own."

"No worries Mike, Whippet knows his limits. He's a dam good driver but he couldn't fight his way out of a paper bag."

Boxer hung up so Mike and Jimmy could resume their recce.

The property couldn't be accessed from the rear as a new small housing complex had been built there, with only one way in and out, it was well lit and too open.

Phillips front drive wasn't overlooked from across the road and neither of his neighbours could see into his garden due to the mature bushes.

Only people passing the front of the house would have a view of the property but in this quiet village that wouldn't be too big an issue.

"It looks like your idea of knocking on the front door might be an option." said Mike.

"Yeah, it's still early, so let's grab something to eat and pop back, you never know they may be out to eat themselves."

"On a school night, doubtful."

"These middle class house wives might have big fancy kitchens pal but they don't all use them."

"Tara did."

"Yeah, well she was a one-off pal, you wouldn't catch Cath cooking a meal," laughed Jimmy.

"Is that why you never made an honest woman of her?"

"Nah, these modern-day lasses are constantly going on about not being a down trodden house wife, they don't have a clue what a relationship is."

"They aren't all like that."

"The ones I meet are, they want treating like princesses but ask them to boil an egg and you're a sexist pig."

"Can't you boil your own egg?"

"I can, and I do, but I don't buy a dog to bark myself."

"Wow, and they dare to call you sexist!" said Mike chuckling to himself.

"You know what I mean Mike. Take Mrs C, you wouldn't call her down trodden would you?"

"Fuck no, I think her poor husband got more clips around the ear than all of us put together."

"Yeah, and usually for palming her buns and passing them on to us."

"Can't believe she's still making you them."

"It's because I refuse to increase her rent so she makes it up in thumb print buns."

"I can smell them now."

Both men paused for a minute to saviour the memory.

"Well, back to the point, that house was her domain and she kept it spotless and took pride in it, he went out to work and handed his wage over to her and after she'd taken for the overheads, she'd tell him how much pocket money he could have for his bacci and beer."

"Things are different now; women want to go out to work as well."

"And that's fine, but the problem with it all, is that there's no one left to look after the home and nowadays people can't survive on one wage."

"So, you're saying that we should send all the women back home?"

"Not at all, men can be just as good at looking after the house and kids, what I'm saying is that people should stop disrespecting the role of the housewife."

"Or househusband," interrupted Mike.

"Exactly, and they should get better tax relief to encourage people to be full-time home makers."

"Fuck me Jimmy, you should run for government."

"Stop taking piss dickhead, you know I'm right."

"I actually do agree with you pal but I'm not sure it'll work nowadays, there's too many single parents out there and people who think that's acceptable."

"Dickheads, right you stay in the car and keep out of sight while I go into the chippy, don't want to risk you being seen. After all, your face is probably all over the wrapping paper."

Jimmy closed the door and went to the chip shop laughing all the way.

Although Mike could appreciate Jimmy's views, it didn't stop him thinking what a Neanderthal he came across as, and was it Cath that needed to change or him.

After about fifteen minutes, Jimmy returned with two lots of fish and chips and a bag full of cans of pop.

"Not sure how good they'll be," Jimmy said climbing in the car.

"These bloody southerners can't make fish and chips to save their lives."

Neanderthal, thought Mike and laughed to himself.

Chapter 10
Cover Up

The judge was watching the clock, every second felt like a minute and every minute an hour.

The clock reached 16:25 and the judge who'd stopped listening to the case an hour ago, announced that there would have to be a continuance.

Everyone was surprised by the announcement but the judge said the case was going to need more time, no one was in a position to argue with him so the court session was adjourned.

The judge retired to his chambers and told his receptionist Joan that he wasn't to be disturbed. He got changed out of his robes and gathered his personal items.

"I'm leaving for the day," he said as he rushed past Joan.

It was almost six o'clock by the time he reached his home. He parked out the front and rushed straight to his study.

His home was a large manor house called Churcham Hall, set within 40 acres of woodland and farming, with a good-sized equestrian facility and three cottages.

One cottage was let to a husband and wife who managed the estate; they had been in the judge's service for over ten years.

They lived there with their seven-year-old daughter who the judge and his wife doted on, as their own children had yet to supply any grandchildren.

The home had been in his family for several generations, it had been passed to the judge when he was 43 years of age, after his father died aged 89.

His mother passed away 30 years earlier at the age of 40 while he was at boarding school, and his father didn't even bring him home for the funeral.

It was actually his headmaster who broke the news to him and his wife who comforted him through his grief.

It was the judge's belief that his mother had died at his father's hand as he was an awful drunk and was constantly challenging his wife over having affairs.

He went through so many staff and had to pay a small fortune in compensation to men he had beaten, just to avoid jail.

Towards the end, he was a complete recluse and being an only child, it was the judge's duty to take care of the estate and his affairs.

Once in his office the judge removed a secret panel from the fire surround, which was one of the features and quirks of the house, it had secret compartments hidden all over, dating back centuries.

The children of the house in each generation would make it a game to see who could find new secret compartments.

He removed a smart phone and switched it on, he opened the email and wrote, "Possible storm coming, 2 inches of rain expected" and saved it to drafts.

He put the phone down and went to the kitchen to make a coffee and when he returned, he had a reply which read, "3 inch would be better."

He deleted the message and wrote, "you have 2."

A new draft was saved almost immediately with just one word, "Ok."

He hid the phone back in the fire surround and sat with his coffee thinking when there was a knock at the door.

"Hello," said the judge.

The door opened and a mature woman popped her head through the opening. It was his wife Margrett.

"I'm not disturbing you, am I?" she asked.

"Not at all, dear."

"I saw your car out front and wondered why you hadn't parked it in the garage."

"I thought I'd take a drive around the estate later."

"Ok, I didn't expect you home for a couple of hours, I'm afraid I haven't started dinner yet."

"It's not a problem, we'll eat after my drive."

The Welshman got himself together and secured his property before setting off to meet the judge, it would only take 30 minutes if he took the direct route, but the Welshman had learned a long time ago to live under the radar.

His life style choices have seen him persecuted and beaten within an inch of his life.

His child hood was no better with his weak mother turning a blind eye to his sexual abuse from his own father, just so he would not turn his attention to her.

As he got older, his father's cruelty extended to making him have sex and beat his own mother. He said he was teaching him not to be a victim.

It only ended because his father beat and raped a boy from his school that had called on him to play out. His father held the boy down afterwards and made him rape the boy too.

The police turned up the next day and the whole family was arrested, convicted and sent to prison.

His father was murdered in prison by a relative of the boy, and his mother committed suicide within days of being locked up.

The Welshman was sent to Borstal but the poisoning from his father was in too deep, and his lack of empathy soon got him a reputation as a ruthless rapist.

He was facing a life sentence for kidnapping two young brothers, David and Tommy Jones, 7 and 9, who he raped and tortured for weeks until the older of them died.

He got caught by chance trying to dump his body by two male police officers, they were sat in their car trying to deter people parking up to have sex.

It turns out the police officers were there having gay sex, despite both being married men.

All the evidence got misplaced before the trial and all charges were dropped. It never came to light what the officers were doing there and their careers in the force continued and flourished.

Since then, no one has come close to the Welshman and he's been living completely off grid.

The Welshman drove down one of the tracks at the back of his house, he made his way over the hills and back roads for his rendezvous with the judge.

He knew the roads so well but there were points where he had no option but to cross main roads.

He was entering a village where one such crossing was necessary, he approached the main road and look carefully both ways, he was not only paranoid he was also cautious as not to have an accident.

Most criminals get caught by making the slightest of errors. And the Welshman couldn't afford any errors.

It was clear to cross but he still proceeded slowly as cars that race around tend to get noticed.

He continued along the track until he reached an opening in the wall to his left, this is where his Land Rover came into its own as he turned off road and headed up the hill.

It was a rocky ride that no normal car could traverse but it wasn't a problem for his 4x4.

As he got to the top of the hill, he saw the trees at the bottom of the hill glow up red, he hadn't noticed a car following him, it was getting too dark to drive without lights and he certainly didn't see any lights following him up the track.

He decided to air on caution and park up to observe the car.

After hiding the Land Rover in some trees just off the road, he grabbed his gun from under the passenger seat, he found himself a good vantage point to watch from.

He couldn't see the car anymore but he thought it wise to be patient and wait for a few minutes.

He was glad he had as not long after, a car came racing over the hill and came to a stop at the top of the hill where he had emerged and re-joined the road.

The Welshman kept low and took a firm grip of his gun as the driver emerged from his car.

A skinny young man exited the vehicle and stood at the top of the hill, taking in the view, maybe thought the Welshman.

He definitely didn't look like the police, he looked like a junky joy rider but the Welshman wasn't taking any chances and didn't break cover.

After a couple of minutes, the joyrider got back in his car and seemed to make a phone call as he drove away at speed.

It could have been innocent but the Welshman was too suspicious and wouldn't use that route again for a while.

After all, the car couldn't have possibly followed him from before the village as he'd driven down a river bed, that was challenging enough for a Land Rover and would have been impossible for a car.

He got back in his 4x4 and continued with his journey being extra careful to check he wasn't being followed.

He got to his meeting with the judge about 10 minutes late to find the judge waiting for him.

"What took you?" asked the judge.

"Sorry boss, I thought I was being followed."

"Were you?"

"No, it was just a joyrider looking for short cuts."

"Are you sure?"

"Yeah, I observed him for a while and made sure I wasn't followed."

"We can't be too careful at the moment."

"Why, what's up?"

"Regan came to my chambers earlier today. He informed me that Charmin has been murdered."

"Murdered?"

"Yes, and pretty gruesomely at that."

"What do you mean?"

"Regan thinks he was tortured."

"How so?"

"He had his penis and eyes burned."

"That would make most people talk, do they know who did it?"

"They're holding a guy called Dave Jackson, does the name mean anything to you?"

"No, do we know anything about him?"

"He's a northerner, convicted of manslaughter."

"Wasn't Mike a northerner?"

"Yes, but what are the odds they'd know each other?"

"I don't believe in coincidences."

"Ok, I'll look into it deeper; you need to get Devon to keep an eye on Regan when he gets in touch and lets me know where he is."

"What do you mean?"

"He's gone to check himself into a hotel until this is all sorted, he's worried that Charmin has given his name over."

"It's getting a bit messy boss; do you think we should get rid of the kids and lay low for a bit?"

"Are you crazy, I promised Pierre first place next time we had fresh merchandise and he's due next week, do you realise how much money that is, not to mention the influence he has?"

"Just asking. We can always get more merchandise. There is an infinite supply," the Welshman said with a smirk on his face.

"We wouldn't be even talking about this if you were all capable of doing your jobs properly, I'm not going to lose these kids because people are losing their nerve."

"I'm not losing my nerve," snapped the Welshman.

"I was referring to Regan."

"Right."

"A lot of effort has been invested and I, like you, want my reward."

"I'll get back to you if I find anything out, in the meantime get Regan his protection," said the judge, before getting in his Range Rover and driving off.

It took the Welshman one and a half hours to get home, being extra vigilant, due to what he had learned from the judge and the joy rider he'd seen earlier.

He had stopped halfway there to make a phone call.

He opened his contacts list, scrolled to the entry D and pressed call; it wasn't long before the call was answered by Devon with a Welsh accent.

"Hello."

"Good morning," said the Welshman.

"Good morning to you, sir."

"Come for tea."

"Will do."

That ended the call and the Welshman continued his journey.

It was 22:25 when the Welshman saw headlights coming up his drive, the car pulled around the back of the house.

The Welshman put the kettle on and when the knock on the door came, he shouted, "Come in," and the door opened.

In walked a tall middle-aged man, at first glance he looked smartly dressed but on closer inspection, his clothes looked as old and tired as the man himself, as if they had aged together.

He clearly hadn't shaved that morning nor showered by the smell of him.

Devon was an ex-police officer who had been asked to resign, after several complaints of inappropriate behaviour with several teenage girls.

He was now working as a private investigator/ minder, mainly for the judge, doing background checks on families who were potential targets.

"Hot Toddy?" asked the Welshman.

"Don't mind if I do," answered Devon, "What's up?"

"We need you to shadow Regan."

"Ok, why?"

The Welshman explained about what had happened to Charmin and the involvement of Dave Jackson.

"The name doesn't ring a bell," said Devon.

"It can't be just a coincidence."

"Do you want me to look into this Dave Jackson?"

"No, we've got Phillips on that."

"I don't trust him; he doesn't sit right with me."

"I don't trust him either but no matter, this will be his last job."

"What do you mean?"

"After he finds Mike Feather, he's outlived his usefulness," said the Welshman, passing Devon his drink.

"Has the judge sanctioned this."

"He has."

"Excellent," said Devon, with a smug grin adorning his unkept face.

"So, where's Regan?"

"Don't know yet, he's going to let the boss know when he settles himself in a hotel."

"It's a bit late, shouldn't he have called in by now."

"Depends if he's drunk or not, by what the boss said he was pretty shook up."

"Didn't think he liked Charmin."

"Who does?" laughed the Welshman.

"But I think it's more the thought that, whom ever had Charmin tortured, may have got his name and may be looking to extract information from him in the same manner."

"Shit, can't think I'd keep my mouth shut for long if someone set fire to my love truncheon."

Both men laughed and told stories, drinking their whiskeys into the early hours waiting for the call from Regan.

It was a quarter to eight in the evening when Phillips arrived back at the station, he found a note waiting for him ordering him to go to the chief super intendants office, immediately on his return.

When he got to the office the chief super intendant was on the phone but the inspector was waved in and he made his excuses to end the call.

"It's a fucking mess," he said after hanging up the phone.

"Yes sir," replied Phillips.

"Is it connected to Feather?"

"Not that I can see."

"Maybe you're not looking hard enough, there are better ways to kill a man than burning his penis and eyes out, it must have been an interrogation."

"You're forgetting that Nicolas Butler was a paedophile and a particularly nasty one at that."

"Your saying it's a revenge attack."

"I'm just saying it's a possibility."

"And what does this Dave have to avenge unless he knew Feather?"

"I checked with the prison, even though they were on the same wing, they never spoke so much as a single word to each other."

"They grew up near each other."

"Yes, but beyond that, I can't find any connection."

The chief thought for a second. "What's your next move, to establish a connection?"

"No."

"No?"

"I assume you want this put to bed to stop people looking too closely."

The chief remained silent but looked at Phillips with his full attention.

"I suggest we pin it on his bodyguard who passed away in hospital."

"Explain?"

"He had means, opportunity and motive."

"Motive?"

"Maybe Charmin took advantage of him, hence why, he burned his penis."

"And what about Dave Jackson?"

"Let him go."

"What, are you mad?"

"We can keep looking in to him, and if it becomes clear that he is looking into the co-operative, we can deal with him quietly."

The chief had a smile growing on his face as the inspector's plan became clear.

"What about the governor, will he buy it?"

"He'll have to, but there's a prison officer that could be a problem, unless I can convince him it would be in his best interest to write his report favourably."

"What do you mean?"

"He needs to say that the bodyguard had broken free of his bounds himself to attack Charmin, also, in the ambulance, he asked for Mr Regan, the solicitor, so we can say he was admitting his guilt."

"Seems neat if you can convince this prison officer."

"Everyone has a price, you know that."

"Get on with it."

"Yes sir," said Phillips as he got up to leave.

"One more thing, Regan has gone off grid to a hotel until this is sorted. He's worried someone is coming for him."

"Sensible, where is he?"

"He hasn't checked in yet, you just get this prison business sorted ASAP."

"Yes sir."

Phillips went back to his office and called the prison, it seems the prison officer who found Charmin's bodyguard and escorted him to hospital, was about to finish his shift but had not yet returned from the hospital.

Phillips told them to call the officer and tell him to remain at the hospital until he got there.

On his way to the hospital Phillips stopped off to make a call and update Haigh on his plan.

He reached the hospital a little after 9pm but the prison officer was nowhere to be found.

He called the prison who confirmed that they had conveyed the message but suggested that the guard may have gone home as he didn't seem happy with the request.

Phillips got his address and mobile number then headed for his car.

Once in his car he called the prison officer.

"Hello?"

"This is Inspector Phillips, we spoke earlier."

"What do you want?"

"I'm at the hospital where you were instructed to wait for me."

"My shift ended at 9."

"This is a murder inquiry and you will make yourself available for questioning."

"I don't answer to you."

"Not only do you work for the prison service and should know better, you will make yourself available or I'll send a couple of officers to arrest you and we'll have this conversation at the station."

"On what charge?"

"Obstruction, then my shift may end and you can sit in a cell until I get back on duty after two days off."

The officer thought for a second, he knew the inspector could inconvenience him with any excuse, so he decided to play ball.

"I'm nearly home if you want the address?"

"I have it, just make sure you're there when I get there."

Ten minutes later, Phillips was at the prison officers home, a two-bed town house that had seen better days.

After knocking on the door, the prison officer opened it and flippantly invited the inspector in and started to walk off expecting him to follow him.

"No," said the inspector.

The officer looked at him.

"We'll sit in my car; I need to talk in private."

"I live alone."

"All the same, my car," said Phillips directing the officer out of his home.

Phillips was worried about recording devices and as he was about to coerce the officer, he thought it prudent to have him on his turf.

Once both men were in, Phillips told the officer to switch his phone off so they weren't disturbed.

"Right, your account of what happened from the time you entered Charmin's cell please, and this time be as specific as you can."

"This is all going to be in my report, why can't it wait until I hand it in tomorrow?"

"I need to be clear what is going in your report, so do you."

"What do you mean?"

"What one writes in a report can determine the path of his career. Get it right and one could be moving up the ladder, but get it wrong and one could find yourself unemployed at best."

"Are you threatening me?"

"So, you're as completely dumb as you first appeared, think less of a threat and more of an opportunity."

"What opportunity?"

"This business is bad enough but with the escape of Mike Feather, your prison will end up under review, and you know what that means, heads will roll and jobs will be lost."

"I've done nothing wrong; I have nothing to fear."

"Except that a man was tortured and murdered right under your nose."

"Wait a minute."

"A suspicious person could suggest you turned a blind eye."

"That's a lie."

"Is it, you've made your feelings clear that you don't like paedophiles."

"That doesn't mean I wouldn't do my job."

Phillips thought for a second.

"Let's approach this from a different angle, what do you want, what is your ambition?"

"Ambition?"

"There must be something you want?"

"Not really, although I wouldn't mind getting off the special protection wing."

"Write your report the right way and I guarantee that within 24 hours, you'll be off that wing for good."

"What exactly do you mean by the right way?"

"Nobody but you saw the body guard restrained, did they?"

"No, I released him from his restraints before anyone else arrived to administer first aid."

"All you need to say is that it looked like he had broken from the restraints himself and we can say that he had killed Charmin in revenge."

"Are you suggesting Charmin tied him up and assaulted him?"

"Yes."

"And what about Dave Jackson?"

"We don't need an enquiry or a court case. This way everyone is dead and it's neat and tidy."

"And Dave gets away with it?"

"We'll make sure Dave is punished in another way but what difference does it make. Charmin probably deserved what he got ten times over."

"I'm not sure the governor will buy it."

"Don't worry about the governor, we have people over his head and besides, his neck is on the line too."

"Can I have some time to think about it?"

"We don't have any time, it's now or never."

The officer didn't see that he had any other options, so he agreed.

Phillips produced some paper and a pen, and the two men spent the next few hours writing the officer's statement.

It was almost 2am before Phillips returned to the police station, and it was another two and a half hours before he was finished writing his own report.

He managed to get a couple of hours sleep on his office couch before he was woken up by the chief super intendant.

"Is it dealt with?" he asked, in his usual abrupt manner.

"Good morning to you too, sir."

"Is it done?" he asked impatiently.

"Yes sir, I've emailed my report to you and the governor, and the Prison officer is on board and will be handing his report in first thing this morning."

"Can we rely on this man?"

"He wants off the special protection wing and I promised him it would happen, so you need to make whatever calls and we're set."

"Hope you're not planning on sleeping all day. We still have Mike Feather to find and the back ground on Dave Jackson to check."

"I'll be on with both asap but I'll be going home at some point to get a shower and change of clothes if you can spare me for five minutes."

The chief didn't look impressed by the jibe and left the inspectors office.

After grabbing a coffee and a bacon butty from the canteen, the Inspector buried himself in his work and for the next three hours labour, he found himself no better off for it.

Time to go home and get a shower, he thought and just as he arose from his chair his mobile rang.

He looked at the caller ID and it was the chief.

"Hello."

"Phillips what are you on with?"

"Actually sir, I was just about to go home and get a shower. Why?"

"Regan hasn't checked in, his wife called after he didn't come home or call, just to see if he'd been here with a client."

"If he got drunk, it is possible that he's still asleep."

"I agree but it's still worth looking into."

"As soon as I've showered, I'll make it my first priority."

The chief put down the phone in his usual abrupt manner.

Mike and Jimmy had taken it in turns with the surveillance of Phillip's house through the night.

Mike took first watch while Jimmy slept and they changed around at 3:30 in the morning.

It was nearly 9am when Mike awoke, he had slept well due to pure exhaustion.

"You should have woken me up."

"I was enjoying the peace and quiet."

"Any movement at all?"

"Nothing."

"We are sure we have the right house?"

"That little weasel better not have lied to me, do you think I should go in and have a look around?"

"Not just yet, let's get some breakfast first."

"Good idea," said Jimmy.

"My stomach has been rumbling for over an hour."

"That's because you didn't fill it up with beer last night."

Both men chuckled as they set off in search of breakfast, and it wasn't long before they came across a trailer café in a layby.

It was a portacabin style trailer with a port aloo at the side of it.

"Come on, we can sit in and eat."

"Is that wise?" asked Mike.

"Here, put this hat on and sit with your back to them, you should be fine."

Mike put the baseball cap on and kept his head low.

As they walked into the café, the counter and kitchen were on the left-hand side and the tables were on the right.

Jimmy approached the counter and Mike used his cover to make his way to a table unobserved.

"Two full breakfasts please love, with two teas."

"You want toast or bread?" asked the woman serving.

"Toast please."

"That will be £15.20."

Jimmy could feel the Yorkshire man inside him wanting to protest at the price but he kept his lips firmly shut and paid the bill.

"I'll bring it all over to you," said the woman, as she handed Jimmy the change.

Jimmy joined Mike and the two men sat in silence reading newspapers from over the last week.

It was over ten minutes before their breakfast landed on their table.

Jimmy looked at it with a sinking feeling in his stomach thinking that it wasn't worth a fiver, never mind the £15.20 it cost.

Mike could see what was bothering Jimmy and just silently smirked as he tucked into his meal.

What made it worse is that they were trying to keep a low profile, so Jimmy couldn't even protest as he normally would.

Instead, he just scowled at Mike who seemed to be getting too much pleasure from his discomfort.

As the men were firmly into their meal, they heard a car pull up outside and although they couldn't see it, when its engine switched of and door opened, they heard the familiar sound of a police radio talking and bleeping in the back ground.

Both men's attention heightened as they listened to the footsteps walking towards the café.

"Morning Geoff," said the woman behind the counter, "Usual?"

"Yes please, but to go today," replied the officer.

"You busy?"

"As always."

"You still looking for that escapee?"

"Yes, but I think he's long gone now."

"Really?"

"Word is, he's gone up north, so you're safe for now."

The officer looked around the room, while the woman got on with his order.

When he looked in the direction of the two men, Jimmy sat up straight and gave him a nod and returned to his meal, which they were both eating a little bit slower now.

It didn't take long for the officer's order and he left directly.

Jimmy and Mike had finished their meal and left the café just as the police car was leaving, so they could see what direction he was travelling.

He headed off in the opposite direction to the one they were heading.

"Bet that got the blood pumping," Jimmy said, as they got in the Range Rover.

"At least we know they think I'm in Leeds."

"Yeah, let's get back and see whether Phillips is home yet."

Chapter 11
Tracking

Devon was still asleep on the couch when the Welshman left for an early rendezvous with the Judge.

There was no word from Regan, no news on Mike and the Welshman was feeling uneasy sensing that there was more to it all.

How Mike survived in prison, how he escaped prison, what happened to Charmin and now the disappearance of Regan.

The Judge thinks Regan is sleeping off a hangover and there's no way Mike could have gotten to Charmin.

He puts everything down to circumstance and coincidence, but the Welshman sees conspiracies and cooperation at every turn.

Surely, one man can't be that lucky he thought.

It was after 10am when he returned home to find Devon still fast asleep and after a quick check of his emails to make sure there were no updates, he woke Devon up.

"Come on you lazy fucker, the days half gone."

"What time is it?"

"About half 10."

"Ok, have you heard from Regan?"

"Nope, the Judge thinks he's drunk but I'm not convinced."

"You think something has happened to him, like somebody got to him?"

"Maybe."

"And if they have, then what?"

"They'll be going after Phillips."

"Is that a good or a bad thing?"

"It depends, Phillips is handy enough so if it's just Mike, he should get the better of him, kill him and it's over and done with."

"And if there's more and they get the better of him?"

"Then it's just a matter of how much pain he can stand before he gives the rest of us up."

"I think it may be wise for me to keep an eye on Phillips, and if Regan turns up, then I can switch to him," said Devon, as he prepared himself to leave.

"I agree, my understanding is that he's at the police station but is planning to go home at some point as he was there all night, so head there and I'll update you if I hear anything else."

Devon left for Phillips house, and after he had gone, the Welshman locked the door behind him, he then unlocked and opened an internal door that led to a cellar.

At the bottom of the stairs there was a second door that was not in keeping with the house, it was a thick fire door.

Through the fire door was a corridor with three further fire doors.

"You seem to be learning," said the Welshman.

"It's been 47 hours since I last heard a peep from you, one more hour and you'll have earned some food."

It was nearly 7am by time Whippet had showered and was ready to leave, he was hoping to get to the spot where he saw the Land Rover in time for full sun light.

He wanted to cover as much ground as possible before any signs had disappeared or darkness hampered him.

He thought he'd start his search at the last place he saw the Land Rover at the top of the hill and see how far he could follow that trail before tracking where it had come from.

When he arrived at the top of the hill, he got out of his car and started to descend on foot to the point where he could not follow the Land Rover.

The ground was firm and despite the little moisture that was there, the tracks were barely visible.

But as he got closer to the lane at the bottom where the trees shade kept the ground softer, he could see the tracks more clearly.

He took out his phone and took several pictures and notice that one of the front tyres had a different tread to the rest.

This was massively helpful, as around the country side where every man and his dog has a 4X4, it would be an almost impossible task to track just one.

Armed with this information, Whippet went back to the top road and drove up and down stopping at every access point to fields and dirt tracks looking for signs of the Land Rover.

He found where the Welshman had stopped to observe him, although it didn't dawn on him the purpose for the stop.

After a quick search of the area, he assumed it was a toilet stop or a U-turn and he gave it no more thought.

He managed to track the tyre marks for a few miles but completely lost track of it after a couple of hours.

He marked every twist and turn on his map, then decided to return to the start point to back track where the Land Rover may have come from.

Once back in the village, he turned up the lane he'd seen the Land Rover pull out from, he didn't get very far as the lane ended after 50 feet at a stream.

He got out of his car and approached the stream; he could clearly see tyre tracks coming down the stream from the right, and they matched the ones he'd been tracing.

He looked up the stream and thought there's no way my car is going to make it up there, and then he looked at his new white trainers.

After a second's pause, "Sorry boys," he said to his trainers, as he started walking up the bank of the stream.

About a quarter of a mile up the stream he found where the Land Rover entered from a track in a field.

The track ran for another quarter of a mile up to the roadside which was accessed via a gate, and Whippet could just make out the tyre marks coming from the left.

Whippet opened the map App on his phone and thought it didn't make much sense, that even though the road led straight to the village, the Welshman had chosen to drive up the hill to drive down the stream.

As he ran down the road, he kept his eyes open to see if and where the Land Rover joined the road.

He hadn't even gotten halfway before he found an opening in the hedges big enough for a vehicle to pass through.

Although he couldn't see any distinguishable tracks, it was clear that a vehicle or two had passed through recently.

He continued down the road and found no other access points, but what he did find was a traffic camera, the type they use to track stolen cars which gave Whippet an idea.

Once Whippet got back to his car, he called Boxer.

"Whippet, is everything ok pal?"

"Yes mate, I've followed the trail as far as I could in the direction it was heading, then I lost all sight of it."

"So, what you on with now."

"I came back to the village to track where he came from, and I had to walk up a fucking river and climb a fucking mountain."

"What river and what mountain."

"Ok, a stream and a big fucking hill but Jimmy owes me some new trainers."

"You didn't get them mucky, did you?"

"Mucky, they're fucking ruined."

Boxer laughed.

"Is all you've phoned for to bitch about your trainers."

"No, I've had a thought, this guy is clearly trying to avoid road cameras, yeah."

"That's what we think, yeah."

"Well, if you get a map that shows the location of all cameras, we can check it against the route he's taking and maybe figure out where he's going or been."

"I thought you had that App already."

"I did on my old phone but I didn't really need it as I know where they all are back home."

"Fair enough."

"Besides, as I'm driving and running around and you're sat on your arse, I figured you could look into it."

"Sat on my arse, I'm watching Regan."

"Isn't he dead yet?"

"No, he's still asleep though and there's no more alcohol if he wakes up."

"I'm sure there's a frying pan in the cupboard."

Both men laughed.

"I was hoping the little paedo would bleed out but it seems to have stopped."

"Maybe we can shoot him in the knee caps after this is all over."

"Sounds good to me pal," said Boxer, as his phone bleeped.

"What's this?"

"It's me Boxer, I've sent you pictures of my map and where I tracked the Land Rover to."

"Ok, I'll get on with it now and if you send me updates of where you're going now, I'll try help guide you from here."

"Will do."

"Be careful, and Whippet…"

"Yes Boxer."

"Good job, pal."

Whippet hung up; he started his car and headed for the gap in the hedge.

Once through the gap the was only one direction to take, it wasn't so much a track but he drove around the hill until he came to a gated field.

After passing through the gate, making sure to close it behind him, after all, he didn't need angry farmers chasing him down.

He made his way to the other side of the field where again there was only one possible exit.

There was no indication to say what direction the Land Rover came from and just as he was trying to decide which direction to head, he realised it was dinner time and remembered there was a chippy back in the village.

So left it was, and he could check for possible routes on the way.

He couldn't see any access points down the country road, and when he reached the end where it met the main road, he noticed cameras 25 feet up from the junction.

He can't have come this way, thought Whippet.

After getting his fish and chips, Whippet sat on a bench outside the Chippy and pulled up a satellite map on his phone, and studied it while eating.

Boxer had covered the table with his map, he had begun to mark in red marker all the cameras within a mile of the Welshman's route.

He hadn't finished when he heard a repeated thudding coming from the bedroom.

He opened the door and kicked Regan in the leg.

"Shut the fuck up, I'm trying to concentrate."

But Regan was mumbling something and had tears streaming down his face.

Boxer lent over, "I'm going to take the tape off your mouth and if you start shouting, I'm going to put it back on and beat you senseless."

Regan nodded his head in affirmation that he understood and Boxer ripped the tape off.

"I need the toilet."

"Piss in your pants, I'm sure it won't be the first time."

"I don't just need to pee."

"And?"

"Please, you can't let me lay in my own faeces."

Boxer thought of the smell.

"Ok but don't expect me to wipe your arse" he said, as he replaced the tape across his face.

He left his hands and feet bound but untied the rope that was connecting them and dragged Regan from the bedroom to the bathroom by his feet.

Regan winced in pain and more so when Boxer dragged him to his feet.

Boxer yanked Regan's pants down and shoved him onto the toilet, he then grabbed a bunch of toilet paper and put it Regan's hand.

"Hurry up."

When Regan had finished, Boxer yanked him up and pressed him against the wall while he pulled his pants up.

Regan was mumbling again.

"What now?" said Boxer, ripping the tape off.

"My foot needs looking at."

"It's fine, you'll live."

"Could you at least give me something for the pain?"

Boxer grabbed Regan by the throat and got right in his face, he then whispered very menacingly.

"You'll get nothing until Mike gets his kids, and if them babies have been hurt in any way, I promise you, you'll really know pain."

He dragged him back to the bedroom and threw him to the floor, then replaced the gag and rope.

"Unless you have some clue on how to get Mike's kids back, I better not here so much as a fart."

Boxer shut the door and returned to his map and continued to fill in the camera positions.

After he finished, he followed each road from the last point that Whippet could confirm the Land Rovers position and found that there was no road route the he could have taken.

He then looked at satellite images of the area for possible off-road routes.

There were only two options, one led into what looked like a quarry and the other into a wooded area, which looked like it was part of a large estate.

Whippet had left the Chippy and was heading back to the last spot he had tracked the land rover to.

He left the main road and turned down the country lane, and about 75 feet in, as he twisted his way around a few bends.

He noticed a gap in the hedges that was barely visible from the direction he was travelling, and completely invisible from the other direction.

It wasn't even visible from the satellite images as the hedges had formed an archway over it.

Whippet pulled over and got out to examine the ground.

The Land Rover had definitely passed this way, it had practically had to do a U-turn and its wheels had left good impressions.

He managed to follow the tracks of the Land Rover for about another two miles, across roads occasionally but mainly sticking to dirt tracks and fields.

He was just approaching a wooded area where there was a bit of a cross roads, which led in about five different directions.

The two to his left went through the wooded area and the two to his right went through the fields.

He got out of his car to try to determine which direction the Land Rover had come from, but to his surprise, there were multiple tracks coming and going in all directions.

A smile grew on his face as the significance of the find hit him.

The trail he was tracking must be heading towards the Welshman's home, as he clearly used this junction often.

He marked the intersection on his map and sent all the updates he had collected to Boxer.

No sooner had the message sent when his phone started to ring, it was Boxer.

"Hello."

"That was quick Boxer, I only just finished sending the text."

"What text?" said Boxer, as his phone beeped.

"That text, so why are you calling?"

"I've had a look at what you sent me and I've got a couple of things for you to look into."

"What is it?"

154

"I can only see two possible options for where the Land Rover could have gone, without passing road cameras."

"Where?"

"The first is a quarry."

"No," interrupted Whippet, "I checked it."

"Ok, the second is what looks like an estate."

"The one with the seven-foot wall?"

"It does look like it has a wall but it also had a drive."

"It does, but its tarmacked and I couldn't see any tyre tracks, it also had a tall wooden gate that was locked, so I decided not to get arrested for trespassing and follow the other trail, which has paid off big time."

"What do you mean?"

"The pictures I just sent you is of a cross road in a field which has multiple tyre tracks, I think I'm close to where he lives."

"That's excellent, you've definitely earned a new pair of trainers, pal."

"You had to remind me."

Boxer laughed.

"Be extra careful Whippet, I'm going to call Jimmy and see what he wants us to do."

"Ok pal."

Boxer hung up and called Jimmy.

"Yes Boxer," answered Jimmy.

"I think Whippet is closing in on the Welshman."

"Good, we really need to find that house."

"Is everything ok?"

"Tell Whippet he doesn't have to worry about the Welshman, just find that house ASAP."

"Ok Jimmy, what's wrong?"

"I'll get back to you Boxer."

Jimmy hung up, as Boxer wondered what he meant about the Welshman.

He opened the texts from Whippet and marked them down on his map and looked at the cross road on satellite images.

He could see the wooded area and scrolled around it, there seemed to be only one house nearby at the other side of the woods.

He called Whippet. "Hi pal, what did Jimmy say?"

"He said you don't have to worry about the Welshman anymore, and we need to find that house."

"What does he mean by that?"

"I'm not sure but I've looked on satellite images and there's a house at the other side of the woods."

"Yep I've seen it too."

"I know Jimmy said not to worry but I still think you should approach with caution."

"I've pulled the car behind some trees and I'm planning on walking in."

"Good idea pal. Update me ASAP."

Whippet hung up and set off along a foot path towards the house.

Jimmy and Mike headed back to Phillips house after their breakfast only stopping briefly at a petrol station to top the tank up and grab some supplies.

The brush with the police at the café made them decide not to eat out again.

It was approaching 11am by time they returned and Jimmy parked in the lane opposite the house.

"It doesn't look like anyone has been home yet," said Jimmy.

"I'm guessing that means he probably hasn't got a family," replied Mike.

"They could be away."

"Again pal, not on a school night, I think it's more likely he lives alone."

"Do you think I should take a closer look?"

"No, I think I should."

"And what if you're seen?"

"By whom?"

"A neighbour or what if the post man turns up?"

"Ok Jimmy, you've made your point but don't do anything stupid."

"Like what?"

"Like break a window or kick the door in, we don't want to tip our hand."

"I'm just going to look through the windows, trust me."

Jimmy got out of the Range Rover and walked casually towards Phillips house, remaining vigilant of any movement from neighbours or passing vehicles.

Once he was in the garden he was pretty well shielded from the neighbours and was quick to make his way towards the rear of the property.

The kitchen door was to the side of the property and Jimmy tried the handle gently, to satisfy himself that the door was locked.

He then moved to the rear and the first window looked in on the kitchen where the side door opened into.

He looked through the window looking for signs of life.

Jimmy jumped when he found a sign of life in the form of a cat, that jumped on the counter to welcome him.

"Don't do that, puss," said Jimmy, as he moved on to the second window.

This window looked on to the dining room, which had some double glass doors on the opposite wall which were open and led to the front room.

Jimmy could see straight through the house and out of the front window, it struck him how tidy everything looked.

Jimmy went back to the kitchen window which was made up of two panels, on one side a full-length opening window and on the other a window pane.

As Jimmy studied the window a smile came across his face and he headed back to the Range Rover.

Once there he opened the tailgate and started delving in the bag with the assortment of tools.

He pulled out a thin flat head screwdriver, a wood chisel and a pair of pliers.

"What's going on?" asked Mike as he got in the Range Rover.

"No-one home except a bloody cat that shit the life out of me."

"So, what are the tools for?"

"I'm going in."

"I thought we agreed no breaking in."

"I'm not going to break anything; the windows are externally glazed."

"But they're usually glued in when externally glazed."

"Yeah with a sticky back foam strip."

"Which you can't get to from the outside, it needs to cut from the inside with a knife."

"Ye of little faith."

Jimmy pulled out a lighter from his pocket and started to heat up the end of the small screwdriver.

Mike watched in silence as Jimmy after a short time put the lighter away and grabbed the pliers and started to bend the end of the screwdriver to a 90-degree angle.

"That will do nicely." said Jimmy.

"Do what?"

"After removing the beading, you insert the screwdriver and hook it behind the glass and run it all around, job done."

"What a mis-spent youth you've had, and what about his alarm system, you have seen the box?"

"I've seen it and I've also seen that it only works on contacts on the external doors and windows."

"Are you sure there's no PIRS?"

"All the internal doors are open and the cat has free roam of the house, so no PIRS, I'm no amateur kid."

"Sorry Jimmy, I'm just being cautious, I meant no disrespect."

"None taken pal, I know what's at stake and you're right to question everything."

Jimmy jumped out and headed for the house, with his pace a little swifter but still with caution.

He used the wood chisel to remove the UPVC window beads from the dining room window, which was bigger and lower down than the kitchen window.

He inserted the bent screwdriver and worked his way around the pane, cutting through the foam seal quite easily.

Once he'd gone all the way around, he used the hook to pull the pane out and it came out with ease, he then placed it on the floor and entered the property.

He was almost immediately joined by the cat who clearly wanted attention, even if it came from a man who had just broken in.

Jimmy picked the cat up and looked at him.

"You're no guard dog, but you still managed to shit the life out of me."

Being careful not to be seen from the front windows he walked around the house looking for any photos to confirm that Phillips lived there.

There were no photos anywhere in the dining room or living room, nor could he find any old letters or newspapers.

He went to the kitchen and again there was nothing to suggest who lived there.

The cat jumped out of his arms and went to his bowls on the floor, both were empty.

"Are you hungry kid, when was your last meal eh?"

Jimmy filled the water and searched the cupboards for cat food and found several pouches of which he took one out, opened it and put it in the cats bowl.

After feeding the cat Jimmy went upstairs to continue his search.

On the first floor, there was a family bathroom and three bedrooms, the smaller of which was set out like an office.

Jimmy started with the office, and sure enough in the office there were bills, neatly filed away in the filing cabinet in the name of Mr Gregory Phillips.

Jimmy had the confirmation he wanted but to be thorough he searched the two bedrooms before replacing the window pane and re-joining Mike in the Range Rover.

"It's definitely Phillips house. I found some bills with his name on them and the council tax bill has him as the only resident."

"You replaced everything you disturbed right?"

"Yeah."

"You don't sound 100% sure."

"I fed the cat."

"What?"

"I couldn't let him go without."

"Some hard man, put an animal or child in front of you and you turn to mush," said Mike, with laughter.

"Compassion and caring for those who are defenceless is a corner stone of a real man, cowards and bullies are uncaring and cruel."

"You're right pal, I'm just taking the piss."

"Thing is pal, there's something not right with this picture."

"What do you mean?"

"I can appreciate a well-organised home; I think it speaks volumes of a man who has a well-organised wardrobe."

"What, you're saying you're impressed with his wardrobe?"

"Not just his wardrobe, his whole house is organised and everything is in its place."

"Easier to keep a house tidy and organised when you don't have kids."

"True, but this guy has no trinkets or memorabilia, it doesn't look to me like he spends a lot of time here."

"He has a cat, so he must spend some time here."

"There's a cat flap and he probably only has a cat, to keep the rats at bay."

"Well, we can't wait here too long; what do you think we should do?"

"I still think he'll be here at some point; it is the best place to grab him."

"How long should we give it?"

"We'll give it another 24 hours, if he ain't here by tomorrow morning, we'll look at ways to draw him out."

"Draw him out?"

"He may be aware we have Regan."

"If they do, they may not want to keep the kids, they may think it's too risky."

"Mike, stay focused. My understanding of these people is that they'd rather cut off their bollocks than give up a child."

"Not sure that makes me feel any better, pal."

"What I'm saying is that you need to assume your kids are alive, and once we've got them back, I'll hold these bastards down and you can cut their bollocks off."

"Ok Jimmy, stay positive."

"Good lad."

"I could do with a toilet though."

"Just piss behind the Range Rover."

"It's not just a piss I need."

"I told you to go at the petrol station."

"I was worried about getting spotted after the near miss with the police in the café."

"Here take these," Jimmy handed Mike the chisel and bent screwdriver, "There's a toilet under the stairs, it's the first window after the kitchen."

"What if he turns up while I'm taking a dump?"

"I'll call you and I'll be straight over."

"Ok," said Mike, as he got out of the Range Rover.

"One more thing, Mike."

"Yeah?"

"Don't leave any evidence."

Mike closed the door and set off as Jimmy chuckled to himself.

After approaching the house cautiously, Mike removed the window and climbed in, as with Jimmy he was greeted by the resident cat, but he wasn't here for pleasantries so he quickly made his way to the toilet under the stairs.

No sooner had Mike left Jimmy's view, when a car came driving into the village slowly.

Jimmy crouched down in the Range Rover as people pay more attention to a parked car with someone sat in it.

He waited for the car to pass but it didn't, it stopped and reversed into the side street in front of the Range Rover.

From his concealment, Jimmy listened as the engine stopped and he heard the cars door open and close.

His adrenalin began to pump around his body as he readied himself to pounce on the unsuspecting motorist.

He wasn't sure whether it was a visitor or a neighbour but he was sure it wasn't Phillips, surely, he would have parked in his drive if it was.

The footsteps were faint but seemed to be getting fainter, Jimmy decided to peek and see what direction the motorist was heading.

"Fuck," said Jimmy, as he viewed the motorist entering Phillips garden, his first thought was to call Mike but he was worried the motorist would hear the phone ringing.

He had to warn Mike. A text seemed the best option, it would only be a beep but what to write.

DANGER CLOSE. It was short and to the point.

Jimmy sent the text while observing the motorist who seemed to be acting peculiar, he hadn't gone straight to the door as one would expect.

Instead, he seemed to be examining the property, looking it up and down as he walked around it.

Jimmy watched as he walked around the side of the property and thought of the window pain, and how there was no way he was going to miss it.

Jimmy was light on his feet and quickly left his vehicle in pursuit of the motorist, who had now disappeared behind the building.

On seeing the window pane removed, the motorist removed a gun from a holster beneath his coat and quickly launched himself through the opening.

Mike who hadn't received the text was just finishing up, and as Jimmy was running past the side door, he heard the toilet flush.

As Mike exited the lavatory, he was confronted by the barrel of a hand gun.

"Mike Feather, I presume," said the motorist, in a broad Welsh accent.

"Welshman," said Mike.

To the motorists surprise Mike lunged at him with the speed and ferocity of a tiger, and the two men fell to the ground wrestling over the gun.

Despite Mike's passion and vigour, the motorist was stronger and began to overpower Mike.

Jimmy didn't even break his stride when he got to the opening, he leaped through the opening like it was barely there, and dive bombed the motorist who was just about to pull the trigger.

He hit the motorist in the side of the head with such force he broke two fingers in his hand.

The motorist flew off Mike and landed on the ground like a dead weight, Mike jumped to his feet and rushed to him.

"Please don't be dead," he said as he shook the limp body.

Jimmy picked up the gun and put a hand on Mike's back, "You're alright, pal?" he said.

"It's the Welshman, Jimmy."

"How'd you know?"

"He had a fucking Welsh accent and you've fucking killed him."

Jimmy grabbed the motorist and put his fingers on his neck.

"He's got a pulse."

He then licked his finger and put it below the motorists nose.

"And he's breathing."

"For fuck sake Jimmy, you shit the life out of me."

"Well, he's not dead but he is out cold, let's tie him up before he wakes up, then he'll wish he was dead."

Mike ran to the Range Rover to get the tool bag to restrain the motorist, all stealth was gone as he ran flat out there and back.

They tied him to one of the dining chairs and Mike started slapping him to try and bring him around, but it wasn't working.

"Wait a minute, Mike." said Jimmy, going to the kitchen and returning with a kettle of water.

"Wait," said Mike, as Jimmy was about to pour.

"It's cold," and Jimmy poured it over the motorist head but that didn't do the trick either.

"What do you think he's doing here?" asked Jimmy.

"Calling on that bastard, Phillips."

"I don't think so, the way he was looking around the house, it looked like he was up to no good."

"What do you mean?"

"He didn't knock on the door."

"He could have seen that Phillips car wasn't here."

"Then why not wait in his car until Phillips came home, no he looked like a thief casing the joint."

"He could be checking on the property for Phillips."

"Again, I don't think so as he would have tried the door handles," said Jimmy.

The two men thought for a few minutes.

"Who carries a gun unless they intend on using it?" said Jimmy.

"What do you mean?"

"If they know about Charmin and Regan, maybe he's cutting his ties."

"You mean he's here to kill Phillips?"

"It's a possibility, but whatever his reason for being here, I think we should work on the assumption that Phillips will be home soon, to be on the safe side."

"Wait, if you're right and he is severing ties, what does that mean for George and Abigail."

"It means he'd rather sacrifice his friends than lose the kids."

"I hope you're right Jimmy, I don't know what I'll do if they're—"

"Ehh, stop that, they're fine and we're going to find them, whatever it takes."

"Yes pal, so what now?"

"I think we should both stay in the house and try and wake this arsehole up."

"And what if Phillips turns up?"

"We'll keep a watch and if he does, we can play them off against each other, they're not going to stay quiet for long when they see what we do to the other one."

About an hour and a half past and the motorist still hadn't regained consciousness, Mike shook his head at Jimmy who shrugged his shoulders.

Just then Jimmy got a phone call from Boxer telling him that Whippet was closing in on the Welshman.

"What was that?" asked Mike.

"Whippet thinks he's close to this bastard's house," Jimmy said pointing at their prisoner.

"That's great news."

"Yeah, maybe we should get Boxer to drop Regan here so he can help him out."

"Sounds like a plan to me, Jimmy."

Jimmy tried calling Boxer back but his phone was engaged, just then Mike dropped to the floor.

"What's up Mike?"

"Phillips is here."

"Quick, put the Welshman on the floor so he sees him but not his bonds."

Mike and Jimmy positioned the motorists body on the floor.

"Right Mike, you hide in the toilet and I'll hide behind the door, and when I say, we'll attack him from two fronts."

"Ok, Jimmy."

"Yes."

"Don't hurt him."

Both men took up their positions and waited for their prey to fall into their trap.

Both Jimmy and Mike had that feeling they had so many times as children, when they were preparing to ambush a rival gang or had been cornered by superior numbers.

It's a little bit of fear and excitement rolled in to one but this time there was a genuine need for this fight, with real consequences should they lose.

Mike never had any fear when they were teenagers and was well known for it, but he felt fear today, his children were relying on him winning.

Phillips got out of his car and approached the back door when he was intercepted.

"Hello Sophia, have you missed me?" he said, bending down and picking up the resident cat, who had fled the earlier battle.

He entered the house and put Sophia on the kitchen work surface.

"Let me go to the toilet and I promise I'll feed you."

Mike and Jimmy prepared themselves.

"What the hell!" said Phillips as he saw the unconscious motorist on the floor.

He rushed to the man's assistance and as he knelt down, he saw that the man was bound.

He didn't have time to raise before Jimmy was on his back, "Now," shouted Jimmy, as he landed.

Phillips pushed up and thrust his head backwards and caught Jimmy square on the nose.

Jimmy stunned from the blow lost his grip and Phillips quickly went on the attack.

He punched Jimmy in the solar plexus hard and with precision, and as he went for his second blow, he felt pain in his kidneys as Mike began to pound them.

Phillips spun around and began trading punches with Mike and all the skill and precision he had started with had vanished, it was an out and out brawl.

Several times Phillips tried to plead with Mike to stop but Mike was having none of it, and continued to barrage Phillips with everything he had.

Phillips made one last attempt and threw himself at Mike, wrapping his arms around him in a bear hug but Mike was like a wild man.

Phillips once again felt pain in his kidneys as Jimmy who had composed himself came to Mike's aid.

This time it was too much for Phillips and he fell, as Jimmy and Mike continued to beat him into submission.

Once they were satisfied, he was within their power, they pinned him to the floor.

"Mike, get the rope," said Jimmy.

Phillips tried to protest but Jimmy slapped him.

"One more noise out of you and I'll knock you the fuck out."

"You know I'm a police officer," said Phillips.

"I know you're a fucking paedophile, now shut it," replied Jimmy, with a punch in Phillip's back.

Mike came back and put tape over Phillips mouth, "I'd do as I was told if I was you inspector, you're in a world of trouble and you're going to have to work very hard to survive today," he said.

Whippet had covered about a mile through the woodland, stopping every time he heard a noise and taking every precaution possible not to be seen.

He switched his phone on to silent as he approached the house, his movements more resembled a meerkat than a whippet, as he slowly edged his way to the building.

As he drew closer, he couldn't see a vehicle, or any signs of life in the house as he edged nearer.

He looked through the kitchen window and slowly worked his way around the building, looking through every window but he couldn't see very much.

He'd made his way all the way back to the kitchen and tried the back door which was locked, he thought about breaking in but decided to check with Boxer first.

Feeling a bit exposed, he headed back to his car, it took him about twenty minutes to weave his way through the woods.

Once he was sat in his car, he reached in his pocket for his phone, suddenly his door window smashed and he felt a sharp pain to the side of his head.

He was dazed by the blow and dropped his phone; he didn't have time to recover before a second blow rendered him unconscious.

Chapter 12
Chess

Dave had just finished his breakfast in the isolation cell and was laid down thinking about how much more time would be added to his sentence.

His wife wouldn't be happy but she must understand that Dave had no choice, he truly believed that his friends would do the same for him.

His obligation as a godfather was as much a promise to George and Abigail as if they were his own children.

He knew the horrors that awaited them and would do anything to spare them the tears that they would surely shed.

Time passed slower in isolation and Dave had lost all track of it.

Your other senses also come into play, every sound you hear is a blessing as it gives you something to ponder.

Are they bringing a new prisoner in or taking one out, are they coming for me or just bringing a meal?

Of course, meals evoked the sense of smell, and one surmised from the aroma what the meal was before it arrived.

Isolation was definitely an odd experience on the senses.

It had been a few hours since breakfast and Dave had kept himself busy with push ups, sit ups and stretches.

Some men lay on their beds philosophising about what's wrong with the world and how they would go about fixing it.

Not Dave, he only cared about what affected him and what he could control.

He heard a couple of peoples footsteps heading in his direction and thought to himself, it was about lunch time but he couldn't smell anything, and it didn't take two to deliver a meal.

The footsteps stopped outside his cell and he heard the rustling of keys.

"I'm getting a visitor," he thought to himself.

The door opened and in walked a prison officer closely followed by the governor.

"Good morning Dave," said the governor.

"Morning," answered Dave.

"It seems you're in the clear."

Dave looked confused.

"It seems another prisoner kind of confessed to Charmin's murder."

Still trying to figure out if this was some kind of trick, Dave remained silent.

"I don't like it, it stinks to high heaven Dave, if I had my way, I'd bring you up on charges anyway, but even I get orders."

The governor pointed to the door and said, "Back to your wing."

Dave followed by the officer left the cell and headed down the corridor.

"Dave," shouted the governor.

"I will find out what's going on here."

"Be sure to let me know if you do," answered Dave.

As they arrived on the wing the Nelson brothers and young Bobby watched as the prison officer escorted and left Dave at his cell.

They casually walked over and entered the cell with young Bobby standing lookout.

"What's going on Dave?" asked Carl.

Dave put his finger to his lip to signal to the brothers to be quiet, then tugged at his ear to suggest that the room may be bugged.

"It's been crazy boys, first they pulled me in for Charmin's murder and now they've let me go, cos his bodyguard confessed to killing him."

"The bodyguard is dead," said Lee.

"Dead?"

"Yeah, apparently he died on the way to the hospital from his injuries."

"And he confessed before he died, ehh?"

"That seems to be the story going around, you know prison, you can't keep anything quiet for long."

"Well it's all over now and there's no more to be said is there."

"I guess not," said Carl.

The brothers were basically testing Dave to see if he had said anything that may have compromised them.

Dave while trying to reassure them was worried that it was an elaborate plan by the police to tape a confession.

The brothers left the cell confident that they weren't in any danger, and Dave got himself a quick wash, as it was almost time to go to lunch.

The dining hall was so quiet you could literally hear a pin drop, and all attention was on Dave.

He grabbed his meal and walked casually to the same table he'd eaten at before with the lone diner.

The noise level slowly rose as Dave tucked into his meal but you could still cut the atmosphere with a knife.

After a few minutes, the lone diner broke the silence and said, "You made quite the stir in your short time with us."

Dave looked up for a second and then carried on with his meal.

"It's been a busy week, a man called Mike is found hanging in his cell and the finger was pointed in Charmin's direction, then he escapes from the hospital and has yet to be found."

Dave carried on with his meal occasionally looking at his dining companion.

"Next thing we know, Charmin himself is found dead, apparently at the hand of his own bodyguard."

This man's a lot more talkative thought Dave.

"There are those who say that Charmin was killed by someone else, as revenge for what he did to Mike, what do you think about that?"

"What do I think?"

"Yes."

Dave thought for a second.

"I'll tell you what I think, I think this lasagne is bland."

The lone diner smiled.

"It must have taken a deep loyalty to risk life in prison, to take revenge on someone like that, I can respect that."

"Can you respect the right to eat a meal in peace and quiet," snapped Dave.

"Sure."

Dave didn't trust anyone and felt uncomfortable talking. You can't slip up if you keep your mouth shut, a policy that had served Dave well over the years.

The meal passed without another word spoken and Dave went directly to his cell after, to give the day's events some thought.

The lone diner also returned directly to his cell which was at the end of the block with two empty cells between him and his nearest neighbour.

He made a quick survey of the area before entering to make sure he had privacy.

Once inside his cell, he turned the waist band of his trousers inside out and pulled apart a Velcro opening, that revealed a secret pocket.

From it he extracted the smallest phone, it was only as wide and long as two fingers and looked more like a toy.

The lone diner pressed the call button to redial the last and only number in the phone.

"Hello," said Haigh.

"Sir, It's Dug"

"What can I do for you, Dug?"

"I tried to speak to Dave sir and as I expected he closed up tighter than a camels arse in a sand storm."

"I knew it wouldn't work."

"What do you want me to do?"

"I think we need to take a leap of faith and tell him what's at stake."

"You want me to tell him everything?"

"No, get him to your cell and put him on the phone, I'll talk to him."

"How do you propose I do that sir; he doesn't trust me and it's not like I can drag him here."

"Give him some details."

"Is that wise sir?"

"They seem to know plenty enough already and if we don't put a stop to them, they could unhinge the entire operation, or worse hurt an innocent."

"Ok sir."

Dug hung up and headed out for Dave's cell.

As he approached Dave's cell he saw another prisoner enter it, it was Charmin's other bodyguard.

Dug moved close to the door so he could hear what was being said, and lend assistance if required.

"What the fuck do you want?" asked Dave, as he jumped off his bed to his feet.

The prisoner was definitely emotional and had clearly been crying.

"I know what you did."

"You've lost me," replied Dave.

"What you did to Charmin and the only friend I ever had in this world."

170

"Not following you, you clearly have some issues to work through, and I can't help you."

"You killed them," he yelled, "and tortured them."

Dave readied himself for an attack.

"If you think me capable of such things, in the interest of self-preservation, I would think very careful about your next move."

The prisoner thought on Dave's words, then said, "It ain't over," as he backed out of the cell, he didn't even notice Dug as he left.

Once Dug was satisfied he'd gone, he entered Dave's cell.

"Fuck me," said Dave, "Is it open day, is there a sign on my door that says welcome one and all."

"I need to speak to you, Dave."

"I thought I made it clear that I don't want to talk."

"I'm not asking you to talk, just listen, that can't hurt, can it?"

Dave sat in his chair, "You have 30 seconds, then you're going out on your arse."

"You need to come to my cell."

"I don't think so."

"My boss wants to speak to you."

"Tell him to come here."

"On the phone, there's more to this business than you realise."

"What business?"

"Mike Feather and his kids."

Dave's concentration intensified.

"I know you're connected to them and Jimmy Dutton. I also know that you're trying to trace the whereabouts of Mike's kids."

"You better start making sense, pal," said Dave, raising to his feet.

"We're on the same side, Dave."

"That doesn't explain shit."

"My boss will explain everything if you just come and speak to him."

"Who's your boss?"

"The guy who covered up Charmin's death, and got you released and in the clear."

Dave thought for a second. "Why?"

"What do you mean?"

"What do you want from me. You must want something?"

171

"We need you to call Mike off."

"That's not going to happen, even if it was in my power, you expect a father to give up on his kids?"

"Not give up on them, just stop taking out all the people that can lead us to them."

"Like whom?"

"Like Regan and the Welshman."

"Who else?"

"Dave, I'm not here to supply you with information. I'm trying to save your friend's children."

"From what I can see, your just trying to build a case, and you don't seem to give a shit that there are two little angels in danger."

Dug took a breath and a few seconds to consider Dave's point.

"We do care Dave but we have to look at the bigger picture and shut down this gang for good."

"And I don't give a fuck about the bigger picture, all I care about is finding them babies before they suffer any more pain or discomfort at the hands of them bastards."

"And if Mike should go to prison or die, who's going to care for them babies then?"

"Don't you worry yourself about it, them babies will be well looked after and will grow up with the knowledge that their father never gave up on them, and loved them enough to risk it all."

Dug could see that he was getting nowhere with Dave, and if he was honest with himself, he had to agree with what Dave was saying.

"Will you speak to my boss?"

"I'll listen to what he has to say but don't expect me to change my mind."

Dave followed Dug to his cell. Once there, Dug took out his phone.

"Shit, that's small."

"You never know when you may need to hide it."

Both men looked at each other, when it dawned on Dave that he was suggesting hiding it in his backside.

"And you expect me to hold that up to my head?"

"Don't worry, I haven't had to hide it in there," said Dug, then thought to himself.

"Recently."

Dug called Haigh.

"Hi sir, it's Dug."

"Hi Dug, did you get him?"

"Yes sir, but it wasn't straight forward, he needed some convincing."

"Ok Dug, put him on."

"Ok sir, just one thing, don't waste your time with the higher purpose speech, his only concern is recovering the kids ASAP."

Dug passed the phone to Dave and went to the door to keep lookout.

"Like I told your man, I can't call Mike off."

"Can't or won't. They're two different things."

"Either, it seems to me that none of you have children."

"What makes you say that?"

"Because if you did, you wouldn't be asking Mike to back off, let alone me having to explain to you why it's a ridiculous request."

"We do understand your point of view but we have a job to do, and Mike is not only risking nearly a year of preparation and work, he's also risking the safety of his kids and friends."

"Mike's friends are all big boys and make their own choices, and as for his kids, are you honestly trying to tell me they're safe where they are?"

"At least, they're alive."

"But for how long, and what cruelty are they having to endure while you play fucking Sherlock Holmes."

Haigh had a quiet little laugh but Dave heard it and lost his cool.

"Do you find something funny cunt?" he said.

"Sorry Dave, it's not funny but your friend Jimmy used that exact line on one of my colleagues a few days ago."

"You sent men to see Jimmy?"

"Yes, and Mike was with him."

"I take it that your men were sent away with a flee in their ear."

"Jimmy wasn't the politest of hosts, no."

"Then it seems you've already had your answer, so what do you think I can do for you?"

"We couldn't explain things properly to Mike and Jimmy but they'll listen to you."

"And again, I'm failing to see why we should cooperate, your priority is to build a case and Mike wants his kids back like about a week ago."

"We have had trouble penetrating this organisation, they're so well connected that they have nothing to fear, so getting any of them to talk is impossible."

"Not impossible."

"We don't have the luxury of your tactics unfortunately, nice work by the way."

"Sorry, you've lost me."

"Ok Dave, you don't have to admit to anything but I'll tell you what I know."

"I'm listening."

"You got Charmin to talk and he told you about Regan and the Welshman, you passed that information onto Jimmy via your wife, how am I doing?"

"I'm listening."

"Regan has taken the threat seriously and has gone into hiding, but he hasn't checked in and we can't find him anywhere. I'm beginning to wonder if Jimmy and Mike have already caught up with him."

A smile came across Dave's face at the news of Regan's vanishing act, he knew that Jimmy and Mike must have him.

"We need to get a hold of Mike and Jimmy before they do anything to Regan."

"Sounds like this Regan has something to hide."

"He does."

"Maybe they can make him talk, like you said, you can't make him talk because he's too well protected."

"But Regan is in fear for his safety now, because he's got a couple of lunatics wanting to burn his balls off, I can use that as leverage to get him to talk."

"So can they."

Haigh was fighting a losing battle and realised he was going to have to offer something in return to gain Dave's trust.

"How about this Dave, we work together to recover Mike's kids."

"You may not be police but you sure as shit are as dumb as them."

"What do you mean?"

"You try the frontal assault and when that doesn't work, you try saddling up to get behind the lines, and just like them when the time is right, you'll fuck us up the arse."

"I'm making a genuine offer, Dave."

"To find out what Mike and Jimmy are up to and use them to get your evidence and then throw them to the wolves once you've got what you need."

"I just protected you with the Charmin problem."

"Only because you thought you could manipulate me into helping you."

"Be realistic man, of course I want something but so do you, are you really going to turn down our help to recover the kids?"

"I am being realistic; you've already shown me your motivation is not to save the kids but to build your case."

Haigh took a breath as things were getting heated.

"Ok Dave, what is your suggestion to resolve this situation, where we both get what we want."

"Rescuing the kids would be a good start but unless you can guarantee people won't be charged, there's no incentive for any witnesses to be freed."

"We can't keep turning a blind eye to murder."

"Don't look at it as murder, look at it as a public service. To be fair, I don't think there'd be many people shed a tear over the death of a paedophile, except maybe another one."

"I'm going to see what I can do Dave, but if an innocent gets hurt, then all bets are off."

"There's two fucking innocents being hurt right now, if you want my help, find them kids now."

Dave hung the phone up and handed it back to Dug on his way to his cell.

"Dave," said Dug, "I heard what you said and you're right to a certain degree, none of us have kids, it's not the kind of job that gives you much time for family life, but don't make the mistake of thinking we don't care."

"You stood by while they murdered Tara and stole his children."

"We didn't know it was going down until after it happened. Our information was that they wouldn't be replacing the children they had for at least another year, but one of them died so they had to move quickly before the body started to decay."

"That may be but I just don't trust you."

"Could you at least give us a chance to earn that trust?"

"We'll see."

Dave went back to his cell and thought hard about Dug and Haigh's proposal.

Mike was attempting to wake the motorist up with little success, while Jimmy called Boxer.

"Boxer."

"Yes Jimmy."

"We got both of them."

"Who?"

"Phillips and the Welshman."

"That's great, are they talking?"

"Not yet, we've got a little problem with the Welshman. He's unconscious and we can't wake him."

"How hard did you hit him?" Boxer said with a giggle.

"Not hard enough, how's Whippet getting on?"

"He's just checking a house out that's a possibility but I'm waiting for him to let me know."

"Good, even though we have the Welshman here, I'd be happier if you were with him. We don't know who else is involved."

"What do I do about Regan?"

"Bring him here, it would help to have another person here to keep these bastards from telling us lies."

"Should I knock him out or get him drunk?"

"Best not do anymore damage, just tell him you're going to dump him at the hospital and if he makes any noise, you'll dump him in a ditch."

"Let Whippet know your plan to join him, then get here ASAP, without breaking the speed limit."

"I'm on it Jimmy," said Boxer, then hung up.

Boxer grabbed his things together and put them in his car.

He then opened the door to where Regan lay on the floor.

"I've been told to drop you at a hospital. This is how it's going to work, you're going in the boot, and when we get near enough, I'm going to let you out. Then you can crawl the rest of the way."

Regan nodded his head vigorously in agreement.

"Be warned, if you make one sound, I'll dump you in a ditch you won't be able to crawl out of."

Once again Regan nodded, Boxer grabbed the rope binding his legs and dragged him to the main door of the caravan.

After checking the coast was clear, he opened the boot of the car, he collected Regan and put him in.

As they were setting off Boxer called Whippet but got no answer, he probably can't talk, thought Boxer and left a text telling him to call back.

Phillip's was desperately trying to get Mike's attention.

"You'll get your chance to talk soon enough," said Mike, and he went to talk to Jimmy in the kitchen.

"This lad ain't waking up, Jimmy."

"There must be a problem with him."

"And Phillips seems desperate to talk."

"We have a bit of time to kill until Regan gets here so let's see what bullshit he comes out with."

They went in the dining room and Jimmy took a menacing position behind Phillips and left Mike to do the talking.

"We're going to take off the tape, the first time you raise your voice to cry for help, it goes back on and you get a beating."

Phillips nodded that he understood.

"Now before we start, let's get something straight, we know your involved and that you and the Welshman here, have got my kids and the only thing I care about, is getting them back."

Mike told Jimmy to remove the tape.

After the sting passed, Phillips looked at the motorist and said, "I can't talk in front of him."

"He's out cold."

"That may be true, but I can't talk in front of him."

"If you don't want to talk, we'll just put the tape back on" said Mike, gesturing to Jimmy.

"No, wait, you need to hear what I have to say but I can't talk in front of this man, please Mike."

Jimmy put the tape back on Phillip's mouth.

"What do you think?" Mike asked Jimmy.

"I think it's some kind of trick."

Phillips was shaking his head.

"We can't split them up," said Jimmy.

"OK," replied Mike, "Is what you're saying, that you don't want this man to hear what you have to say to me."

Phillips nodded. Mike went to the couch and grabbed a cushion, then ripped it open.

He grabbed two handfuls of fluff and shoved them over the ears of the motorist and told Jimmy to wrap tape around to secure them.

"That should do, now feel free to talk," he said, ripping the tape back off Phillip's face.

Phillips spoke quietly, "You're wrong about more than you are right."

"Make sense and do it quick, I'm not known for my patience," said Jimmy.

"You must be Jimmy Dutton, now I think I can see the connection to Dave Jackson."

"How do you know my name and don't tell me you got it from Dave."

"No, you're right about that. Dave wouldn't even open his mouth to tell me to fuck off."

Jimmy smirked.

"You actually met a couple of my colleagues the other night, in Leeds."

"I knew them bastards were police."

"No, they're not and neither am I. I'm under cover military intelligence."

"Really?" said Jimmy.

"I'll tell you one more thing, that isn't the Welshman, well, not the one you're looking for."

"Sorry, you'll have to forgive my stupidity, I'll just untie you all now and we'll be on our merry way," said Jimmy.

"We came here looking for you and a Welshman and guess who we found?" added Mike.

"Where did you get this information, have you got Regan?"

"I'm sorry I thought it was supposed to be us asking the questions and the only question needing answering is, where are my kids."

"The Welshman has them."

"We already know that, where, is what we want to know."

"I don't know."

"Well, we've heard different."

"If Regan told you that he's lying to save his own skin because he knows what you did to Charmin."

Jimmy lent in and said, "It cost Regan two of his toes for that information, I trust his word over yours right now"

"You're making a mistake, I'm on your side here."

"Really, and what side is that?" asked Mike.

"To get your kids back safely, isn't that what you want?"

178

"Then tell us where they are and we'll go get them."

"The Welshman has them but we don't know where he lives or where he's holding them."

Jimmy pointed at the motorist.

"I told you, that's not the Welshman."

"Then who is he?"

"His name is Devon Crabtree. He's a disgraced ex-policeman. He's now a private investigator who works for the Judge."

"What Judge?"

Phillips realised they didn't know about the Judge.

"The Welshman, it's a nickname."

"I don't believe him, Mike," said Jimmy.

"You say you're on our side and then lie to us, you're not gaining any trust."

"Mike I can't open my investigation to you but I am trying to save your kids, you and your friends are running around kicking doors in and grabbing the wrong people."

"At least we're doing something."

"Yes, you're getting noticed."

"You didn't see us coming," interjected Jimmy.

"I've been protecting you."

"How have you been protecting us?"

"When Charmin tried to hang you, it was my colleague that saved you and raised the alarm. Then I sent Peters to pick you up and you assaulted him and ran off."

"How do we know that Peters wasn't there to finish the job that Charmin started."

"I heard the phone call Dave made to his wife and for as careful as he was trying to be, it was clear that he had got his information from Charmin and I covered it up."

"Protecting yourself no doubt."

"I also shielded Dave from another murder charge."

"What do you mean?"

"He was being held for Charmin and his bodyguard's murder, I engineered it so it looked like a fight between Charmin and his bodyguard, killed them both."

"And why would you do that?"

"I was hoping I could get Dave to talk some sense into you."

"And how did that work out for you?" asked Jimmy.

"My colleagues are trying to talk with him now. If you let me call them, they may be able to arrange for you to speak directly to Dave yourself."

"Sure, I mean, why not?" Jimmy said sarcastically.

"There's only one way this is going to end, either I get my kids back or I'm going to make life very painful for anyone involved, whether they took the kids or stood by and let it happen, or tried to stop me from saving them."

"Well said mate," said Jimmy.

"Your making mistakes that will not only see you in prison or dead but you're also risking your friends and children."

Jimmy put his hand on Mike's shoulder and answered Phillips.

"Speaking as one of Mike's friends, whatever price there is to pay, is a small one to protect those babies and rid the world of a few diseased animals."

"What is wrong with you people. We have laws in place to deal with these problems, what makes you think you have the right to be Judge, Jury and Executioner."

"What's wrong with you that you think I should sit on the side lines while my children are in danger?"

"A Judge is just a man like me, Jurors are made up from normal hardworking people and the executioner himself is just a man with a stomach for the job," added Jimmy.

"But they aren't connected directly with the case and look at it dispassionately."

"Do I look emotional to you? Mike is, but believe me, when the time comes for clipping off your fingers, I want you to understand, there's no emotion involved."

Mike calmed Jimmy down. "We don't want to hurt anyone but you're not helping us or yourself, tell us something that can help us, otherwise you're of no use to us."

Phillips thought for a second. "You need to understand the bigger picture, Mike."

"Right, I'm getting a knife," said Jimmy.

"Wait," said Mike, "Go on."

"Have you ever played chess? You have all the principle pieces and then you have the pawns."

"Your point?" said Jimmy impatiently.

"The Welshman, Regan and even Devon here, they're all pawns and will never give up the king as they don't even know who he is."

"Do you?"

"No, we've managed to uncover a small part of a large international paedophile ring but we're only scratching the surface."

"While your scratching your heads and arses, his wife was murdered and his kids are god knows where."

"I swear Mike, we didn't know they were making a move on your family."

"Even if you did, you probably wouldn't have stopped it."

"Jimmy has a point."

"I didn't let them kill you," replied Phillips, "Let's work together, Mike."

"No."

"Why?"

"For one, I don't trust you. And this may not be the Welshman but we think we know where he lives."

"And how? Did Devon tell you, is that why you beat him unconscious?"

"That happened when he tried to kill me."

"You should thank us," said Jimmy.

"Why's that?"

"A man creeps into your house carrying a gun and clearly you didn't invite him, my guess, as he's paying you an unscheduled visit, he was here to kill you."

"Me?"

"Yeah, Welshman cleaning house?"

"What's the matter inspector, you seem to have gone quiet," said Mike.

Phillips was deep in thought, "There is another explanation."

"What's that?" asked Mike.

"He could have been here for you."

"How would he know we were here, that doesn't make sense?"

"Who told you about me, Regan right, tell me exactly what Regan said?"

"If Regan lied to us, we'll soon find out."

"Don't you see, if they know you're after Regan, they could have told him to send you here as a trap, which means they're on to you."

"Which also means they could be on to you, why set a trap at your house and not tell you about it?"

Phillips new that Mike was right, "You said you knew where the Welshman lived, who told you?"

"No one told us, one of our mates tracked him."

"We've been monitoring road cameras for months and can't get a hit on him."

"That's the problem with you people, you rely too much on technology, try getting off your fat arses and looking," said Jimmy.

"Your man has been following him, do you realise how dangerous this man is."

"He caught sight of him once but apart from that, he's been following his tyre tracks."

"Call him off, if the Welshman realises he's tracking him, he'll kill him without hesitation."

"My boys can take care of themselves and he knows not to approach the Welshman."

"The Welshman is armed and paranoid, if he sees your mate more than once, it will be enough to raise his suspicions."

"Yeah well, when Regan gets here, there'll be two of them and they're armed also."

"Mike, please, you need to untie me and let me help you."

Mike pulled Jimmy to one side out of ear shot.

"What do you think, Jimmy?"

"Met police or military police, they're all the same pal, they'll tell you what you want to hear to get what they want."

"Normally, I'd agree with you, but all I can think about is George and Abigail."

"Let's wait until Regan gets here, cos if Phillips is telling the truth, that boy's going to lose a few more toes."

"Ok Jimmy, better tell Whippet to back off and wait for back up though."

Jimmy went to the kitchen to call Whippet and Mike went back to Phillips.

"I want to believe you Phillips, but there's a voice in my head telling me you care more about your procedures and rules than you do about my kids.

In a few days, my friends it seems, have been able to do more than you with all your resources have in months."

"Mike, I want to find your kids and stop anymore being taken."

"Trust me, when I find this Welshman, he'll never take any more kids."

"You can't just go around killing people."

"He's not a person, like Jimmy said, he's a diseased animal in need of culling to protect society."

"Society will still be in danger, like I said, the Welshman is just a pawn, if we don't stop the principles, they'll find new pawns to take his place."

"I understand the rules of chess Inspector and I appreciate you are looking at the bigger picture, but I don't have the luxury of sitting back and playing the long game, my kids need me now."

"Fair enough Mike but you need to choose your battles carefully."

"My battle was chosen for me and I'm going to fight it the only way I know how. The war, that's your problem."

Mike put the tape back over Phillips face with him protesting all the way.

"Be quiet, Regan will be here soon and we'll have the truth out of him this time."

Jimmy returned and pulled Mike to one side, "I can't reach Whippet yet but I've left a message for him"

"What you thinking?"

"He won't answer if he's still creeping around that house, but I'll keep trying."

"Jimmy, hurting these creeps is completely fine with me but I'm not so comfortable with hurting Phillips, if he is who he says he is"

"I don't like the man but a lot of what he says makes sense, don't look so surprised Mike, I'm not fucking stupid. If he can help us find the kids faster, then great."

"So, are you going to untie him?"

"Not yet, let him sweat for a bit for being a dick, besides I'm not sure he'll approve of what I'm going to do to Regan when the bastard gets here"

"Just don't kill him, I have an idea how we can use him as a bargaining chip with Phillips."

"Don't worry, he may wish himself dead but the pain will remind him he's very much alive."

It was another half an hour before Boxer showed up and he called as he was approaching the village to check it was safe to drop Regan off.

Jimmy told him to reverse in the garden up to Phillips car and he'd come out to help.

Regan started to panic and cry when he saw Jimmy and realised, they weren't at the hospital.

As he started to mumble and moan, Jimmy back slapped him.

"Shut it you lying bastard, did you think we wouldn't find out you'd set us up?"

Jimmy dragged Regan through the kitchen to the dining room and made him take a good look at Phillips and Devon, before taking him to the front room to a waiting dining chair.

After securing him to the chair, Jimmy went to talk to Boxer in private.

"Have you spoken to Whippet?"

"Not yet, I sent him a message before I set off but he hasn't returned my call yet."

"I'm getting worried about him; I've been trying for the last half an hour."

"He wouldn't do anything stupid and he did have a mile of woodland to walk through."

"Still, he shouldn't be out of contact for so long."

"Who are them two in there?"

"One is Phillips and the other is a Welshman called Devon."

Boxer's attention peaked.

"Not the Welshman we're looking for apparently"

"Who is he then?"

"He does dirty work for them; we think he was sent here to kill Mike and Phillips"

"Phillips?"

"Yeah, turns out Phillips is friends of them boys we met in Whippet's place the other night."

"So, they were police?"

"No, apparently he's undercover trying to infiltrate this gang."

"Then he should have some information on them, like addresses."

"He reckons he doesn't know the Welshman's address and they've been trying to track him with street cameras."

"Do you believe him?"

"I think so but he did let something slip that I need to ask Regan about."

"Do you want me to go find Whippet?"

"I do, but let's see what info we get from Regan first."

Chapter 13

Trust Issues

Regan sat in the chair sobbing; Jimmy came back in holding a gun in his hand.

He back handed Regan and nearly knocked him over.

"Stop crying you cowardly little cunt," said Jimmy, who then composed himself and lowered his volume.

"You make me sick, plenty of tears for yourself but I bet you've not shed a single drop for any of the people you and your friends have hurt."

He pressed the gun against Regan's forehead.

"I could kill you just for the self-pity, but my only concern is the return of Mike's kids, so were going to try this again but remember you don't have many toes left," he said pressing the barrel of the gun into Regan's wounded foot.

Regan moaned in pain.

"Now, I'm going to ask you a question and you know what happens, if I don't like your answer."

Jimmy ripped the tape off Regan's mouth.

"Who's the man at the side of Phillips?"

"His name is Devon Crabtree."

"Off to a good start, what's his part in all this?"

"He's a private investigator."

"I didn't ask for his job title, I asked how he's involved?"

"He was sent to watch my back after what you did to Charmin."

"Didn't do too good a job at that, did he? So, if he's supposed to be watching your back, why is he here?"

"He didn't get to me in time so he probably thought he might catch up with me here."

"Be careful Regan, you sound dangerously close to telling me a lie."

"No, it's the truth, I was told if you came for me, I was to send you here."

"And who told you that?"

Regan looked uncomfortable at the question.

"The Judge," said Jimmy, looking at Phillips.

"Yes, who told you about The Judge?"

"A smarter man than you who still has all his little piggies."

Jimmy pressed the gun against Regan's toes.

"Please no."

"I warned you not to lie to us."

"I'm not lying."

"Not now you're not, but you sent us into a trap."

"I'm sorry, I'm sorry."

"Ok I'm a fair man. Tell me about The Judge."

"What do you want to know?"

"Everything, and if it don't match up with what I already know, I promise you won't get a third chance."

"His name is Robin Spruit, he lives at Churcham Hall, Gloucester. He's been a judge for over 25 years and he's got lots of people in his pocket."

"Like whom?"

"High ranking people, police men, ministers, doctors and civil servants and then there's the criminal element like Charmin and the Welshman."

"What's the Welshman's real name?"

"I don't know, I promise you, I would tell you if I did."

"Jimmy," interrupted Boxer.

The two men went to talk in private in the kitchen.

"What's up?"

"That estate that the judge lives at, it's right where Whippet lost the track of the Welshman's Land Rover."

Jimmy went back to the front room.

"You're doing well Regan; your story seems to be checking out."

"One question," said Mike, who had been stood patiently listening. "This Judge, is it the same one who sent me down?"

"Yes," replied Regan.

"I guess there's just one more question and it's a Biggy, so don't get this one wrong. Where are Mike's kids?"

"I didn't lie about that; the Welshman looks after them unless they're with clients but your kids are still in conditioning."

Mike lunged at Regan. "What do you mean conditioning?"

"It's what we call it when they're taught to do as they are told, not to cry or fight it."

"And how do they do that?" asked Mike.

"Mike, you don't need to hear that," said Jimmy.

"I need to know what they're doing to my kids."

"Ok Mike. Answer him."

"They used to beat them but it damaged the merchandise."

"Merchandise?" said Mike.

"I mean kids, then we tried drugging them but the clients didn't like it as they were unresponsive, so now the Welshman uses modern torture methods like sleep deprivation, starvation and stress positions."

"You sick bastards," said Jimmy.

"It's more humane than beating them."

"You don't do it because it's humane, you do it so you don't damage your merchandise."

Jimmy punched Regan square on the nose which made a loud crack as it broke, and Regan flew back and landed at Phillip's feet.

Then Jimmy approached Phillips and ripped his tape off.

"I knew you were lying to us."

"I have my orders and I can't just tell you everything I know, what would you do in my place?"

"For one, I wouldn't have opened my mouth in the first place, loose lips sink ships, didn't they teach you that in the military?"

"If I don't talk to you how can I gain your trust?"

"You can't earn our trust; you've already shown your true colours."

"Listen, I heard what he said, he can give me everything I need, so I can put all my efforts into helping you find the kids."

"And what use are you, we cracked your case in a week."

"We can't do what you just did, we have rules and consequences."

"The consequences for your inaction are his wife's murder and his kids torture, did you not hear what they're doing to them while you're following your rules."

"I did, so stop wasting more time, untie me and let me help."

Jimmy looked at Mike who nodded his head.

"If we turn out regretting this, I promise, you will too."

"You won't regret this; you're doing the right thing."

Once freed from his bonds, Phillips examined both Regan who lay unconscious on the floor and Devon.

"I can see why my boss likes you."

"What do you mean?"

"You're a blunt instrument, he's old school and doesn't disapprove of your tactics."

"Sounds like a man I could get on with."

"I'm sure you will when you meet him."

"Meet him?"

"We need to get these men to him to be interrogated properly and they need medical attention."

"Fuck 'em," said Boxer.

"Dead men tell no tales, that's a saying I learned in the army," Phillips said looking at Jimmy.

"Ok," said Jimmy "Boxer, you go find Whippet and we'll sort this mess out, but keep in touch at all times."

"I'm not sure that's a good idea," said Phillips.

"What would you suggest, we leave him in danger?"

"No, come with me and I'll send a couple of my colleagues with him."

"Ok, but understand this Phillips, we're not your men and don't take orders from you or your boss."

"Understood, and my name is Greg."

"Ok Greg, what now?"

"We need to get these two to my team so we'll need to put one in each boot and you and Boxer is it? can follow me and Mike"

"I don't think so."

"What's wrong?"

"Mike stays with me; I'm not having you drive him straight to the station with us in tow."

"What do you suggest?"

"I'll put both bodies in the boot of the Range Rover and Boxer will take you in his car."

Greg could see that Jimmy wanted to keep as much control of the situation as possible.

"That's fine with me Jimmy, but I need to get something from my car."

"What?"

"A phone, so I can tell them to expect us. We can't just walk in there unannounced."

"Fair enough but you make the call now and you do it on loud speaker."

Greg chuckled, "Ok, but you're going to have to trust me at some point."

"When you've earned it."

Greg retrieved the phone while Boxer and Mike swapped the cars in the drive for the Range Rover to load Regan and Devon.

After the bodies were loaded, the four men stood in the kitchen while Greg made his call.

"Hello," said Haigh.

"Sir, I've got Regan, Feather and three others with me."

"Are you ok, Greg?"

"Yes sir, we've come to an understanding and we're on our way in to base."

"Excellent, how long?"

"ETA is about 45 minutes, there's two men in need of medical attention."

"Who?"

"Regan and Devon Crabtree."

"Mike's friends given them a bit of a rough time, eh?"

"You could say that sir, on the bright side, Regan is in a very talkative mood."

"Really, has he said anything of interest?"

"He mentioned high ranking officials, police, civil servants and ministers."

"That's great, who else is coming in with you?"

"Two of Mike's friends but there's a third that is MIA. We think he may be in trouble, he was tracking the Welshman and they're pretty sure they've found his lair."

"Really, how?"

"That's not important right now, can you pull Peters and Mac in to go with one of these lads to find him."

"Sure, that's not a problem, now get yourself in here, I'm looking forward to meeting these boys who've done more in a few days than we've done in as many months."

"They're listening in, sir."

"Ok Greg, I'll see you all soon."

"Hello," said Mike.

"Yes," answered Haigh.

"Greg said you were in contact with Dave Jackson."

"Yes, I had a very interesting conversation with him not so long ago."

"Could you arrange for me to speak to him when we get there?"

"Shouldn't be a problem."

"We'll see you soon, sir," and Greg hung up.

"Happy?" Greg asked Jimmy.

"For now."

Greg shook his head in frustration, "Come on, let's go."

Whippet was waking to a throbbing headache and was struggling to open his eyes with how bright the light was.

It took a few minutes for his eyes to adjust but the throbbing in his head wasn't going away anytime soon.

The room he was in looked like a prison cell with concrete walls, except the door was a thick wooden fire door, and beyond the chair he was tied to, the room was empty.

The light looked like a 1000-watt security light designed for carpark and warehouses, not 8x10 foot rooms.

Whippet began testing the ropes that bound him but they held firmly.

He started to rock the chair to see if it was sturdy, or there was any chance he could break it and loosen the ropes.

He seemed to be loosening the joints of the chair but he heard a door close and stopped to listen.

It had gone quiet, and he was just about to try the chair again when he heard a lock go, and within a few seconds he heard another door close much louder this time.

Someone was coming. He wouldn't have been able to shout for help anyway, due to the tape across his mouth but he decided to listen.

He heard two bolts being undone and the door to his cell opened.

He could see the form of a man standing in the doorway, but he was unable to make out his features due to the light in his cell, being positioned just above the door and directed at him.

The figure advanced and was wearing a balaclava, he ripped the tape from Whippet's mouth.

"Who are you?" said the figure in a Welsh accent, "Why are you tracking me?"

Whippet just stared at the figure.

"You don't want to talk; I can insert needles in your eyes if that would loosen your tongue."

"I don't know what you're talking about dickhead, let me go, I've done nothing wrong."

"You're a northerner, are you a friend of Mike Feather?"

Whippet cursed himself for opening his lips and fell silent.

"You think giving me the silent treatment will save you, it's because you're not afraid, but don't worry, we'll change all that on my next visit."

The figure replaced the gag then closed and bolted the door.

Whippet listened as the second door closed and locked, a few seconds more he faintly heard another door go.

He kept listening for a few minutes but couldn't hear any movement at all, he began trying to break the chair again, thinking on the words of the shadowy figure.

The Welshman locked the cellar door and on returning to his kitchen he checked his emails.

He had emailed the judge, wanting a meeting to discuss the return of the joyrider and the lack of communication from Regan.

There wasn't a response yet and the Welshman's blood was beginning to boil.

He made himself a hot toddy to settle his frustration and checked the email again.

His email had been answered and he had to leave immediately to safely make the journey.

He took the most direct route he could, considering the urgency of the meeting he didn't have time to be too elaborate but he still kept off grid.

The Judge was waiting for him when he got there.

"Make this quick, I have a lot of meetings today."

"That joyrider came back and it looks like he's been tracking me."

"Are you sure?"

"He had a map on him, following my route from here to my house."

"Does that mean you've spoken to the man?"

"I've got him tied up."

"What, where the merchandise is, are you crazy?"

"He was unconscious and he's in a different cell."

"Do you know who he is?"

"No, he didn't have any ID on him but he is a northerner."

"You think he's connected to Feather and this man from the prison?"

"I do, and when I get back, I'm going to find out."

"You need to move the merchandise first; he could have called in your location."

"He didn't have a phone, I checked."

"Everybody has a phone nowadays."

"I searched him and his car, no phone."

"Get back there and transport the merchandise to the secondary location."

"What then?" asked the Welshman.

"I've been meeting with people all day to see if there's an investigation going on behind my back but it seems I've been talking to the wrong people."

"Who should you be speaking to?"

"An old friend."

The two men went their separate ways and the Welshman headed back home.

He approached his house with great caution.

He backed his Land Rover up to the kitchen door, leaving enough room to open the tailgate.

After a good scan of the area he made a bee line for the cellar.

Whippet, who had been trying to break the chair with little success missed the first door, but heard the second.

He sat in anticipation of his door opening but the two bolts he heard were not from his door.

He heard some talking but it was too quiet to make out.

Another two bolts went and although they seemed closer, it still wasn't Whippets door and again, he could hear some words being spoken.

Finally, the bolts to Whippets door went and the door flung open.

"Take a good look," said the Welsh voice from earlier. "Who is he?"

There was a short silence and the voice repeated the question louder with anger and impatience.

"I don't know," said a sweet but shaky voice.

"Are you sure you've never seen this man before."

"I'm sure, I'm sorry."

"I'll be back soon and then you're going to tell me everything I want to know."

The door slammed shut and Whippet knew that had to be one or both of Mike's kids.

He listened as the footsteps disappeared behind the closing of the doors and when he could no longer hear them, it gave him a renewed energy to break free from his bonds.

Greg got in the car with Boxer and gave him directions to follow with Mike and Jimmy closely following behind.

"He's a piece of work that Jimmy," Greg said.

"He is, but in all fairness, you are on his bad side."

"He's got a good side?"

"Jimmy's a top lad, you shouldn't judge what you don't know."

"So, tell me, what makes Jimmy a top lad?"

"Jimmy looks after all of us."

"You mean his friends."

"More than that, he looks after the whole estate."

"What do you mean the whole estate?"

"Kids can play out on our estate without fear of paedos or drug dealers, the old don't get robbed and Jimmy always throws the best bonfire night party."

"Really?"

"Yeah, he spends thousands on fireworks and sparklers for all the kids."

"A true beacon of generosity."

"Don't take the piss, when my mum was getting evicted, Jimmy helped her with the deposit for a new house, cos her scum landlord wouldn't give her the deposit back."

"I meant no disrespect."

"Of course you did, do you think you're the first to suggest Jimmy only does it to get people on side, to cover his illegal activities."

"I wasn't implying anything."

"Jimmy may not be a saint but to a lot of people, he is a god send and I won't have anyone pull him down."

"Your loyalty is admirable but I'm just trying to get an understanding of the man, and why he's risking so much to help Mike."

"Mike and Jimmy go way back, and Jimmy is god parent to them kids, he loves them as if they were his own, considering he doesn't have any of his own."

"But my understanding is that they haven't seen each other for years."

"It's called friendship and it doesn't have a time limit. Jimmy was proud of Mike getting away from the estate and making something of himself."

"And Dave?"

"Dave is cut from the same cloth, and you couldn't find a closer pair than Jimmy and Dave, and Mike is held in high regard by both."

"Dave could be in prison for the rest of his life for what he's done, that's a little more than friendship."

"He did it for the kids, Jimmy says one of Dave's favourite sayings is that (Real men protect the weak, regardless of the risk). Have you, as a soldier, never put your life on the line for another?"

"Of course, in war zones and battles, one has to risk themselves for their fellow soldiers, as your life is also in their hands."

"Mike, Jimmy and Dave have been in many battles, maybe not on the scale of your wars, but still they've risked their lives for each other and saved each other's lives more than once."

Greg could understand the bonds that soldiers formed with each other during combat but it never occurred to him that civilians faced similar challenges.

"Jimmy and Dave both seem to have brains in their heads, couldn't they have broken away from the estate?"

"They almost did, they were in the property market together with Mike but then Dave went to prison and Mike went his own way, Jimmy stayed on the estate and bought the house next door to his parents."

"Maybe I've misjudged Jimmy and Dave."

"People like you always do."

"People like me? Who's judging now?"

"You're a Dudley Doo Right, you think all criminals are evil and policemen are all saints."

"They are there to uphold the law."

"Yeah, well tell me this, why is it you're investigating them and not us?"

Greg fell silent thinking he'd set himself up for that.

"It's just a few rotten apples. You can't paint them all with the same brush."

"I knew you were going to come out with that same old stupid argument, you know there's an old country song that says. 'The cops say the bad guys are to blame and the bad guys say that both sides are the same', they knew it back then, and it's no different today."

"Society needs law and order to function and keep the majority of people safe, but there will always be a small minority find ways around the law to hurt people."

"Well, it's Jimmy that keeps our neighbourhood safe, not your laws and certainly not your policemen, the only time you saw a policeman on our estate, is when he was making a booty call on one of the young single mums."

Greg could see that Boxer had built up his hatred over many years and he would never change, he was also beginning to understand why he'd had trouble gaining their trust.

"About half a mile up this road, you'll be pulling into an industrial estate on your right, and you need to go to building 17 at the very back of the estate."

Boxer followed Greg's directions and found himself at a large warehouse with some built in offices.

Greg directed Boxer to a large roller shutter door and beeped the horn when he got there.

Within a few seconds the roller shutter started to open, as soon as it was high enough, Boxer drove in, followed closely by Jimmy.

As he entered, he took a good look at the man who had opened the door.

"He looks familiar," said Boxer.

"That's Mac, I believe you met in Leeds a couple of nights ago."

Boxer chuckled.

"I'm not so sure how happy he's going to be to see me, I had a shot gun pointed at his head last time."

"He's not one to hold a grudge."

Once inside the warehouse, Mac closed the roller shutter door and the men all exited their vehicles.

Peters, Dawn and Nipper came out from the offices to meet the men that had evaded them, and caused them many headaches over the last few days.

"Glad you finally came to your senses," said Peters.

"The jury's still out on that one," replied Jimmy.

"Enough of that," said Greg, "You'll have time to catch up in a bit, where's Haigh?"

"He's not here, he needed to pop out and said he'd be back as soon as he could, but we should crack on in his absence," said Dawn.

"Right, Mac and Nipper, there's two bodies in the back of the Range Rover that need taking to the interrogation rooms, and they both need medical attention."

"I can't," said Nipper, "Haigh told me to contact Dug as soon as they got here, so Mike could speak to Dave Jackson."

"Ok, you get on with that but then you get the interrogation room ready, as we need get these statements ASAP."

Greg looked at Dawn and Peters, when Boxer spoke up.

"I'll give Mac a hand."

"Thanks Boxer. Jimmy, can you show me where you think the Welshman lives and where your man tracked him?"

Peters led them all to an office which was filled with maps, with meeting places and possible routes of the Welshman marked on them, and Jimmy started marking all the points Whippet had text him.

Boxer opened the tailgate and Mac grabbed Devon and threw him over his shoulder and said, "This way."

Boxer grabbed the rope binding Regan's feet and dragged him off of the tailgate.

Regan landed with a thud, and a groan came from him. Mac looked at him with a blank expression.

"Well, at least we know he's still alive," said Boxer.

Mac walked on and Boxer dragged Regan after him.

"Whippet's last check in was this point here, that were calling the cross road," said Jimmy.

"Why, there's no road nearby," said Dawn.

"Yes, it's in the middle of a field but Whippet said there were multiple tracks, going in several directions over a long period of time."

"And what makes us think these tracks are the Welshman?"

"Cos Whippet says so, and I trust his word over yours, princess."

"Alright, calm down," said Greg, before a fight broke out.

"We'll work on the hypothesis that Whippet is correct. He did follow the tracks all the way to The Judge's estate so give him some credit, Dawn."

"Ok Greg, but tell that imbecile, he'll see what kind of princess I am if he disrespects me again."

Jimmy smiled.

196

"I think we all need to show each other respect and a little patience. We have very different backgrounds and approaches but the goal is to retrieve Mike's kids, agreed?"

"Agreed, sorry luv."

"Agreed and I'm not your luv either."

Jimmy turned to Mike, "Feisty, I like her."

"Jimmy, continue," said Greg.

"Whippet hid his car and went on foot, to check this property on the other side of the wood, and we haven't heard from him since."

"Do you think he's tried to play the hero and take on the Welshman by himself?" asked Peters.

"He's not that stupid, he knows his limits."

"Ok, Peters when Mac has tended to their injuries, take Boxer with you and find Whippet, and check this house out," said Greg.

"And if we come across the Welshman?"

"Grab the bastard," said Mike.

"You don't want us to follow him?"

"No, they're right, pull him in but your priority is to find Whippet and the kids," said Greg.

"Do we have authorisation to break into the house?"

"You don't need it," said Jimmy.

"We do things by the book here," said Dawn.

"If you suspect a crime is in progress you have the legal right to enter, it's a moot point anyway, Boxer isn't held back by your rules and can break into the house."

"He's got a point, Dawn," said Peters.

Nipper entered the room, "Mike, Dave will be calling in a few minutes."

Jimmy gave Peters the key to the Range Rover.

"Give this to Boxer, you may need to go off road and this can go anywhere the Welshman can."

"Thanks," replied Peters.

"Oh, there's tie wraps and tape in a tool bag in the boot, in case you bump into the Welshman."

"Don't worry Jimmy, we've got our own equipment."

Jimmy and Mike followed Nipper and Peters and went to find Mac and Boxer, leaving Dawn and Greg in the office.

"I don't like it, Greg."

"You don't like it or them?"

"Either, they're not professionals."

"Haigh would argue that they get the job done, and they're a necessary evil, where is Haigh?"

"After calling Mac and Peters back, he reported in to the minister that we had a witness for interrogation, and he was called in for a meeting."

"To London? He'll be gone all day."

"No, Hayes is up this way, they're meeting at the Dubrovnik, it's only 20 minutes away."

"Ok, you can assist me with the interrogation after I've cleaned myself up a bit."

"You look like you could do with some medical attention yourself."

"I'm fine."

"Did they do this to you?" she said examining a mark around his neck.

"Give them a break Dawn, Mike's been through a lot in the last couple of weeks and his friends are doing their best to help him, because no one else is."

"Men like that Jimmy just wind me up."

"Because you don't understand them."

"I've had to put up with sexist bastards like him all my life, I know him well."

"You're wrong, his remarks weren't given as an insult because you are a woman, he was testing you."

"Testing my patience is all he did."

"From an early age, boys are mean to their friends and girls that they like, it's just how we show our affection for people and weigh people up."

"Silly games, girls are far more mature, they just tell you straight."

"Where's the fun in that?"

Just then Peters interrupted them.

"The prisoners are ready for you Greg, and me and the boys are leaving now."

"Be careful, Jason."

Nipper handed Mike a ringing phone.

"Hello," said Mike, putting it on speaker phone.

"Mike."

"Yes Dave, Jimmy is here too, you're on speaker phone."

"How's it going boys?"

"We're doing well mate, we're almost at the end of the journey."

"Good, give the family a big hug from me."

"We couldn't have done it without you, pal."

"Don't worry about that right now. How are your new work colleagues?"

"They seem to be holding their end up and working hard, mate," said Jimmy.

"You take good care of him Jimmy, and Mike…"

"Yes, Dave."

"I'm sorry for doubting you."

"Don't you dare, it's gone from my mind as it should be yours."

"Get on and keep busy, whatever it takes boys."

"Yes pal."

Dave hung up and passed the phone back to Dug.

As he was leaving the cell he paused, "Thank you."

"You're welcome," replied Dug, and Dave was gone.

Haigh reached the Dubrovnik and headed straight for the bar, where he saw Hayes with a drink in hand.

"Minister."

"Haigh, do you want a drink?"

"No sir. I need to get back."

"All business. Ok let's grab a table away from eavesdroppers."

The two men found a table with sufficient privacy and sat.

"What's going on Haigh?"

"What do you mean?"

"Your mission is to gather intelligence covertly, not to take prisoners."

"I thought my mission was to infiltrate a paedophile gang and get enough evidence to shut them down."

"No, it's not your place to make arrests. You bring the intel, and the official police will determine who is to be detained."

"This man can give us the entire cooperative."

"Have you interrogated him yet?"

"Not yet, he wasn't there before I left."

"Well don't. I'm going to send someone to pick him up."

"Sir?"

"You've compromised yourselves by grabbing him. You need to shut your operation down."

"We didn't grab him; Mike Feather and his friends did."

"And you've made an alliance with these criminals?"

"He's a father looking for his children."

"That's no justification for what they've done, now seeing as you like to play policeman, you can detain Mike and his friends and hand them over to the real police."

Haigh's blood was boiling over.

"Anything else, minister?"

"No, it may be tomorrow before I can get Regan picked up so I will hold you responsible if he is harmed or interrogated by anyone."

"Understood, minister."

Haigh left before he blew a fuse, and all the way back to base his anger worsened.

On returning to the base, Nipper let the colonel in and closed the shutter behind him.

"Where is everyone?" asked Haigh.

"Greg and Dawn are interrogating Regan, Mike and Jimmy are getting something to eat in the kitchen and Jason and Mac have gone with one of their friends, to find the other one at the Welshman's house."

"Tell Greg I need to see him now."

Haigh popped his head in the kitchen to introduce himself to Mike and Jimmy but really, he was checking they were occupied, as he needed some privacy for his chat with Greg.

He found Greg and Nipper waiting for him when he got to his office.

"Nipper, go keep the boys in the kitchen company and Greg come in here and close the door."

"What's wrong, sir?" asked Greg, when they were securely in the office.

"We've been ordered to shut down the operation."

"What?"

"That little weasel Hayes has told me to shut down."

"Why, we're so close."

"He said we've compromised ourselves and allied ourselves with criminals."

"What does he expect us to do, just let them run free, doesn't he realise we now have a witness thanks to them, who is spilling the beans on the entire cooperative."

"We are to cease all interrogation and detain Mike and his friends."

"That's madness, and it's not going to be an easy task either, these boys are a handful."

"That's the orders I've been given."

Greg sat down and both men sat in thoughtful silence for at least ten minutes, until Dawn finally broke the silence.

Dawn came rushing in.

"I need to show you something, sir."

"What is it Smith?"

"I just had Regan write a list of all the people he knows are in the cooperative, and we were going through them to figure out what their involvement was."

"Yes, so you've clearly found something."

"Look at the list, sir."

Haigh looked down the list when his eyes flared, "That fucking weasel."

"What is it, sir?" asked Greg.

"Look for yourself," said Haigh, passing the paper over, "Minister Gordon fucking Hayes."

"That doesn't make any sense," said Greg.

"Why would he have us investigate a paedophile gang that he's part of."

"It actually is starting to make a lot of sense."

"Sir."

"He told me that we were only supposed to be gathering information and reporting back without breaking our cover."

"You think he's trying to get some insurance against the rest of the gang."

"Yeah, and that's why he didn't want us interrogating Regan, because it would compromise him."

"So, he's used us to strengthen his position, cheeky bastard," said Dawn.

"Right Greg, we're against the clock now so here's what we'll do. You and Smith get as much out of Regan as you can, we may need a bargaining chip of our own."

"We'll do our best, sir."

"If you feel he's holding out, threaten to throw him back to Mike's boys."

"What about Mac and Peters?"

"They're trying to locate Mike's friend to "detain" him, aren't they?"

"Yes sir," said Greg taking the hint.

"Send Mike and Jimmy in."

Dawn and Greg left and were soon replaced by Mike and Jimmy.

"Mike, I want to start by telling you how sorry we all are, for what you and your family have had to endure over the last couple of weeks."

"Thank you," replied Mike.

"It has to be said that you boys have shown all the qualities of some of the best men I've ever worked with, your resourcefulness alone is impressive. But your commitment to each other is second to none."

"No offence but you sound like you're buttering us up for some bad news." said Jimmy.

"What I've said is genuine Jimmy, but you are right that there's some bad news."

"We'll be leaving now then."

"Calm yourself Jimmy, your passion is a great credit to you but patience could be a better one."

"Patience is not a word in Jimmy's vocabulary," said Mike, "What's the bad news?"

"The guy who gave us this assignment is, it seems, involved at some level and he just shut the operation down."

"What does any of that mean?"

Haigh explained everything to the boys up to the discussion he just had with Greg and Dawn.

"So, this has now put us in a very difficult position."

"You can try and detain us but I wouldn't recommend it," said Jimmy.

"I don't think that's his plan Jimmy, otherwise he wouldn't have prewarned us."

"Unless he's playing for time."

"Time is against us and I believed being honest with you was the best way to save time. I've no intention of trying to detain you and every intention of helping you retrieve the children."

"So, what's your plan?" asked Mike.

"We've got Peters and Mac out with your chap, we'll let them follow that line. Greg and Dawn are back working on the list with Regan to see if there's any other targets who may have the children."

"What list?" asked Jimmy.

"He's been extremely cooperative since you made him pliable, and he's furnished us with quite a detailed list of members of this organisation."

"Who's at the top of the list?"

"I know what you're thinking Jimmy and it may not be the smartest move."

"Is it this Minister or the Judge?"

"As it looks to me, it's the Judge, but you can't just walk into his office or home Jimmy. He has a panic button that will alert armed officers to his location, and they will shoot to kill without question."

"Then we need to make sure he doesn't press it."

"There will be a number of people at both locations that can raise the alarm, not to mention the security."

"My experience is. If you go for the man at the top, you win."

"These are not football gangs and drug dealers Jimmy; they play by a different set of rules."

"We're more than happy to do this without you."

"Mike," said Haigh.

"They're my kids."

Haigh thought for a second.

"Ok, but keep quiet about this, Greg will never go along with it but let's have a plan before you go kicking doors down."

Haigh called Nipper and asked him to bring one of the tablets in, that they used for tracking vehicles.

"We struggled to place a tracker on the Welshman but the rest were easy, let's have a look where The Judge is right now.

He's at the far side of Cheltenham heading southeast, that area seems familiar for some reason"

"That's where my in-laws live."

"Do they know each other?"

"I don't know but it is possible as my father-in-law is a solicitor. Surely, he's not involved."

"What's his name?"

"Malcolm Briggs."

Mike began to feel sick and held his breath as Haigh checked the list of names.

"No Malcolm or Briggs on this list but I can ask Greg to check with Regan."

"Do it, god help him if he is involved."

"Listen boys, try not to let your passion control you out there. That's how mistakes are made."

"You don't have to worry about us," said Jimmy.

"Right, well there's two things you need to take into account. First is that if The Judge gets to his phone and presses the panic button it will be game over very quick."

"Got it, and the second?"

"There are two police officers stationed at the end of the drive until you are apprehended, so you'll have to avoid them and the last thing you need to do, is make a ruckus for them to hear."

"We will need to borrow some equipment as ours is in the Range Rover."

"I can't give you any weapons."

"No, we just need some tie wraps, gaffa tape and some rope."

"Ah well, in that case you'll find everything you need on the back wall, on the shelves."

"Thank you," said Mike, as they stood up to leave.

"You have earned my trust today," said Jimmy, and the two men left to prepare themselves for their task.

Chapter 14

Friend or Foe

It was 17:25 and as Mike and Jimmy were leaving for the Briggs residence, Boxer, Mac and Peters were driving through a field less than half a mile from the cross road.

As they came over the brough of the hill, they could see the woods up ahead, and on the ground just before it, what looked like tracks going in several directions.

"That must be the cross road," said Boxer.

"Where did your friend say he was hiding his car?" asked Peters.

"He'll have hidden it to one side or the other of the main track, no more than 20 or 30 feet in, just so it wasn't visible but easy to access."

Once Boxer reached the woods, he followed the tree line to the left scanning the woodland as he drove.

"Is that it?" said Mac, pointing to something shiny in the bushes.

Boxer turned into the woods and as he got closer, Whippets car came into full view.

"That's it alright, well spotted Mac."

The three men jumped out and while Mac stood sentry, Boxer and Peters went to investigate the car.

It didn't take long for them to see the smashed window and Boxer rushed to open the door.

There was a small amount of blood but not enough for a fatal wound.

The men looked at each other and knew what had happened.

"It would be wise to look around to see if we can find any tracks to determine what direction they went," said Peters.

"Or to see if there's a body in the undergrowth," answered Boxer.

"I didn't mean that."

"It's ok, I'm not stupid, it crossed my mind too."

"You could try calling him."

Boxer took out his phone and called Whippet, as the call connected, he could hear a buzzing coming from the car.

He frantically searched the car and retrieved Whippet's phone that was secluded between the passenger seat and centre consul.

Thirteen missed calls it read and four messages, all from Boxer and Jimmy.

After a quick search of the area, they decided to move on to the house.

"Do you think we should park the car up and walk in?" asked Peters.

"Didn't do Whippet any good did it, besides if the bastard tries to make a run for it, we'll need it nearby."

"Fair enough, but let's approach slowly and try not to let him see us coming."

"Agreed," said Boxer, and made his way back up to the main track through the woods and headed straight for the house.

Peters and Mac Checked and readied their weapons, and it wasn't long before they got their first glimpses of the house through the trees and bushes.

"Take it slow Boxer, I can't see any vehicles but we may have to move quickly so don't be panicking and running us over."

"You don't need to worry about me, pal."

They got to the tree line and Peters suggested that he and Mac proceed on foot and Boxer stay with the car.

Boxer reluctantly agreed and watched as the pair swiftly and silently covered the short distance to the house.

Peters and Mac searched all around the exterior of the house looking through all the available windows, as Boxer kept watch in case any vehicles arrived.

Peters waved Boxer over once he was satisfied that the property was unoccupied.

"Seems like no one is home," said Peters.

"Well let's get in then."

"How do you propose we do that?"

"Kick the fucking door in."

"Subtle, we prefer people not to know we've been in their homes, so we'll look for something a little less obvious."

"Ok," said Boxer as Peters walked off around the building to find an alternative entry point.

Boxer looked at Mac then suddenly launched an attack on the back door, he definitely did some damage but the sturdy door held.

Without hesitation he launched a second attack and the door flung open just as Peters came running back to see what the racket was.

"It seems someone left the back door open," said Boxer.

Peters looked at Boxer in frustration and then at Mac who just shrugged his shoulders as if he didn't care.

"What if it's the wrong house?" asked Peters.

"We'll leave them a note," replied Boxer as he walked in.

"Mac, keep watch," said Peters following Boxer into the house.

Whippet, exhausted from trying to break the chair, was taking a break when he faintly heard a banging.

His mind raced with thoughts the Welshman had returned to make good his threat and thought it's now or never.

He renewed his efforts to break the chair, he had made some little progress with it but the ropes that bound him were also giving more stability to it.

He tried stretching himself and rocking the chair and was even able to do a strange little hop to destroy the chair.

He put all his energy into it, fearing what was to come when the Welshman opened his door again.

"Let's stick together and clear the rooms before we start searching through cupboards," said Peters.

"Ok," said Boxer pulling a gun out from his coat.

"I'm guessing from the other night you know how to use that but do me a favour, and make sure I'm not in front of you when it goes off."

"I may not be a professional but I'm no fucking amateur."

They made their way from the kitchen to the living room, and Boxer tried the door to the cellar which was locked.

"Upstairs first," said Peters leading the way.

They searched all the bedrooms and attic space, anywhere that was big enough to hold a body before descending back to the living room.

"I'll be one minute," said Boxer leaving the house.

Peters looked around the room that was pretty well lived in, you could smell the alcohol everywhere from the moment you entered.

There was a two and three-seater couches and a coffee table with several empty cups and old newspaper strewn all over the room.

In the corner of the room was a TV on a stand with some kind of Hifi underneath it.

Peter's eye was drawn to it, as one of the speaker display needles was flickering quite frantically but the other two were still.

He wondered at first if it had been left on but turned down but it seemed the power was switched off.

He went closer to have a better look and was just switching the sockets off at the wall when Boxer walked in holding a crow bar.

"You found something?" he asked.

"Not sure, it's just a bit odd."

"What is?"

"This volume needle is bouncing around, even though the machine is powered down."

"Can't you play it through the speakers?"

"There aren't any speakers."

"He's probably got it hooked up through the TV."

"I don't think so, there are only three wires other than the power lead which seem to go to a hole in the floor."

Boxer rushed to the cellar door, closely followed by Peters and prised it open.

The door gave way pretty easily as it was old and they descended to the cellar to find a new fire door.

After several failed attempts to open the door Boxer handed the crow bar to Peters.

"You use that while I push," he said, sitting on the floor putting his back against the wall and his feet against the door.

It took some doing but they finally started to hear the frame crack, which gave them extra determination to carry on.

The door finally burst open and Peters readied his gun as Boxer jumped to his feet and charged in, throwing all caution to the wind.

Beyond the door was a room about 8 by 16 foot, it had two doors to the opposite side and one at the far end.

Each door had two hefty bolts but the first two doors were unlocked.

Boxer raced across the room not waiting for Peters and flung open the first door.

There was nothing in the room except a sleeping bag on the floor and a bucket that looked like a makeshift toilet.

Peters had caught up and told Boxer to slow down but Boxer was on a mission and hurried toward the next door, which led to a room similar to the first.

The final room was locked but Boxer wasted no time in pulling the bolts back and flinging the door back.

Both men were dazzled for a second by the brightness of the light that welcomed them.

It didn't take long for their eyes to adjust and see a man on his back, tied to a chair.

"Whippet?"

"Boxer!"

"Come here mate, I've got you."

Boxer rushed to his friend and picked him up but the chair wouldn't stay up as one of the legs was broken.

"The kids were here," said Whippet, as Boxer tried to steady him and untie him.

Peters came in to help steady the chair and passed Boxer a knife to cut the ropes.

"What's he doing here?"

"He's helping us find you and the bairns," replied Boxer.

"They were here pal and the bastard took them away."

"Do you know where?"

"No, sorry pal, he ambushed me and I woke up in here, he then brought the kids and asked them who I was but they didn't know, so he took them away."

Whippet began to cry as he was telling his tale and Boxer tried to console him.

"You've done a cracking job, lad, don't you fret, we're going to find them kids," said Peters.

"How long ago did he leave?" Boxer asked..

"I'm not sure, it seems like about an hour but I couldn't swear to it."

"Ok pal, let's get you out of here and then we'll figure it out."

Boxer helped Whippet to the Range Rover and gave him a can of pop and a chocolate bar to give him a boost of energy.

After checking his head wound, he turned to Peters and Mac.

"We need to call Mike with an update."

"Let's have a second to run through it first," said Peters.

"He'll want to know."

"I'm not saying don't tell him but let's try give him something positive, instead of telling him the Welshman has done a runner with his kids."

"He hasn't," said Whippet.

"Hasn't what?" asked Boxer.

"Done a runner, he said he'd be back shortly to get me to talk."

"That means he could be here at any moment."

"Mac," said Peters jumping into action.

"Take the Range Rover and Whippet and get out of sight, me and Boxer will wait here and set our own ambush."

"Where do you want me, in the woods?" asked Mac.

"There's no telling what direction he will come from."

"There's one direction he probably won't come from," said Whippet.

"Where's that?" asked Boxer.

"The road, we could take position on the road at the bottom of the drive."

"Excellent thinking lad, Mac take Whippet with you down to the road and keep out of sight, keep off your phones unless you see him."

Mac and Whippet left to hide the Range Rover from sight, Peters and Boxer hid in the Welshman's house closing the door behind them.

"As soon as he opens that door, he's going to know something is up, we'll have to be quick and whatever you do, don't shoot him."

"Ok Peters, I'll follow your lead but I'm going to give Mike an update while we wait."

"While you're on, I'll talk to Greg if you don't mind and see if they've got anything from Regan that we can use."

"Sure."

Boxer called Jimmy, "Go ahead Boxer, you're on speaker with me and Mike."

"We've got Whippet."

"Is he ok, where was he?"

"The Welshman nabbed him and tied him up in his cellar."

"What about my kids?" asked Mike.

"They were here Mike but the Welshman has taken them somewhere."

Mike was in mixed emotions knowing his kids were alive but not knowing what the Welshman had done with them.

"So, you don't have the Welshman?" asked Jimmy.

"No, but Whippet said he was to return shortly to interrogate him, we've set a trap for him when he does."

"Good man Boxer, then do some interrogating of your own and don't let them wet weekends tell you no."

"Don't worry Jimmy, if I get my hands on this bastard, he'll talk. Peters wants to talk to Greg, if possible."

"We're not with Greg."

"Where are you?"

"There's been a few developments and we're off chasing another lead."

"What's the lead?"

"I'd rather not say at the moment, don't be sharing it with anyone, Boxer."

"I won't, and I'll let you know when we get hold of the Welshman."

Boxer hung up the phone.

"I thought you was going to pass me on to Greg."

"They're not with him."

"Did I hear you mention a lead?"

"Yeah but they didn't tell me what."

"I better call in then."

Peters called the office and Nipper answered.

"Hello."

"Put Greg on."

"He's in the middle of interrogating Regan but Colonel Haigh is back."

"That's fine, I'll speak to Haigh."

Nipper transferred the call.

"Peters, how's it going?"

"We managed to rescue Mike's friend but the Welshman moved the children before we got here."

"Do you have any leads on where he's taken them?"

"No sir, but Whippet is pretty sure he's coming back soon."

"Whippet?"

"Mike's friend sir, there are three rooms in the cellar that are very well insulated where I think he keeps the children, and we found Whippet tied up in one."

"So, are you waiting for him to return?"

"Yes sir, but I thought I would just check in to see if Regan had given you anything useful that could help us."

"He's given us plenty but I'm not sure if there's anything new about the Welshman, I'll get Greg to ask specifically."

"Thanks sir, I heard Mike and Jimmy are chasing a lead."

"You just concentrate on the Welshman."

"Yes sir," and the line went dead.

"What did he say?" asked Boxer.

"Nothing, same as you."

"Jimmy didn't tell me where they were going."

"Fair enough, we just need to hope this bastard isn't too long."

"Yeah, as you've probably already noticed, patience isn't one of my virtues either."

"It's not that I'm impatient, it's just that the longer he takes to get back, the bigger the search area is for the children."

"What do you mean?"

"Obviously he's taken them to another location and the longer he's away, the further he could have travelled and the bigger the search radius is."

"That's only half the problem, what if he's passed them over to someone else."

"At least that's not the worst-case scenario."

Boxer looked at Peters, "Let's not even think that."

But the problem was, everyone was thinking it, had the Welshman disposed of the kids seeing the walls closing in around him.

"You're right Boxer, let's just focus on what we can control."

"Like snaring the Welshman."

"Exactly."

Mike and Jimmy were ten minutes off their destination after they'd taken Boxers call.

They'd been checking the Judges location all the way there and he'd definitely gone to the home of Malcolm Briggs.

"We're not far off Mike, what's the plan?"

"There's a turning on the left in about 5 minutes, but we need to go past it as the only house down that road is theirs, and the police will be parked down there."

"So how do we get in?"

"There's lots of horse paths around here and there's one that leads to the rear of the property."

"Great, how many people will be in the house?"

"At least three, possible more if Rose and family are there."

"Ok, we need to assume they all think you're guilty and won't appreciate your presence."

"Rose is the only loose cannon in that family, Malcolm and Bev are pretty level headed."

"Let's hope she's not there then, but whomever is there, we need to rush The Judge and secure him first, then it may be necessary to secure the rest."

"Whatever it takes pal, I'm sure they'll understand and be forgiving after they find out what's going on."

"Are you still worried that Malcolm may be involved?"

"For his sake, he better not be."

The judge arrived at the Briggs residence at about 17:30, and after identifying himself to the police officers on guard he made his way to the house.

Bev was in the Kitchen with Rose drinking a glass of wine and preparing dinner when the doorbell rang.

They both peered through the door to see Malcolm cross the hall to answer it.

All were at the point, where they didn't want any more news or updates about Mike.

"Hi Robyn," said Malcolm, "Come in."

"I hope I'm not imposing."

"Not at all, it's nice to see a friendly face, makes a change from the police officers who pretend to smile but think their time would be better spent elsewhere."

"They are necessary."

"I know, but my wife is sick of them and I must admit, I will be happy to see the back of them."

"I just thought I'd check on how you're holding up, it's a great loss to the world. Tara was a wonderful person and will be sorely missed by everyone who knew her."

"Thanks Robyn, come through and see Bev, she's just making dinner and we would love it if you could join us."

"Are you sure?"

"Of course, BEV, look who's here."

Bev and Rose came out from the kitchen and Bev gave the Judge a big hug.

"Thanks for coming Robyn, we know how busy you are."

"Nonsense, if I can't visit my oldest friends in their time of need."

"You'll stay for dinner."

"Of course."

"Great, you boys grab a seat and I'll bring you a drink, dinner is going to be about twenty minutes."

"Thanks, just a tea for me."

Malcolm and the judge went to the dining room and took a seat.

"I thought it better that I not come being the judge presiding over the case, but I had to see you."

"I understand and it's greatly appreciated, I understand that they still haven't caught Mike yet."

"Not that I've heard, it doesn't make much sense though."

"Which part, none of it makes sense to me."

"I thought Mike was an only child and a bit of a loner with no friends."

"He is, well no recent friends that we know of, but he's clearly got a whole secret life that we didn't know about."

"No recent friends, you mean there's old friends."

"He used to hang around a rough set of people but he stopped seeing them when he moved down here with our Tara."

"Have you told the police about these friends?"

"Yes, we even gave them pictures but I don't know what they've done with them."

"Do you know which officer you gave them to?"

"Yes, it was the inspector in charge, Phillips, that's right Inspector Phillips."

"I'll chase it up and find out what he's playing at."

"I'm sure he's doing everything he can," said Malcolm, but the judge was less interested in Phillips progress as why he had withheld the information.

The two men talked until dinner was finally ready, Bev and Rose joined them and they all tucked in to the food and conversation.

Mike and Jimmy had arrived just around the same time everyone had finished their meals.

They left their car a couple of hundred feet from the house, they travelled with stealth along the hedges and walls to the back of the property.

They worked their way around the house looking through windows, being ever so careful not to be seen.

When they arrived at the dining room window, they could clearly see all the occupants sat around the table.

"There's the bastard," said Mike, his blood boiling at the sight.

"Calm yourself Mike, we can't make any mistakes now."

"Don't have to worry about me, Jimmy."

"Good, now, how do we get in."

"The kitchen door is the best option."

The men backtracked to the kitchen door and found it to be locked.

"Shit," said Jimmy, "They'll hear us break it for sure."

"No need," said Mike, pointing to a box on the wall with buttons on it.

"I have the code."

"Good job."

Mike took out the key and quietly unlocked the door.

The two men entered the kitchen and positioned themselves by the dining room door.

"Ready?" asked Jimmy.

"Ready?" replied Mike.

Jimmy burst through the door closely followed by Mike and dove across the table past Rose, who he missed by inches.

He landed full force on the judge, knocking him to the ground.

Malcolm jumped up like a spooked cat but soon recovered himself, and went to the aid of his friend in the form of a kick to Jimmy's side.

Mike grabbed Malcolm from behind and threw him backwards to the ground.

Jimmy was trying to regain his hold on the judge who was reaching out for his phone.

Mike moved on the judge and stomped on his arm which broke so loud that everyone heard it.

He then dropped his knees on The Judge's shoulders to pin him to the ground while Jimmy secured his arms behind his back.

Malcolm regrouped himself and launched another attack, but stopped dead in his tracks when Mike produced a gun, and pointed it squarely at him.

The women who had been screaming at them to stop, also fell silent at this latest shock of behaviour from Mike, that they would never have expected.

"Mike," said Malcolm, "What are you doing?"

"Shut the fuck up and you'll find out."

"Get out of my house you murderer!" said Bev.

"I haven't killed anyone."

"What about my sister?" said Rose, jumping across the table, only to find herself in the firm grip of Jimmy.

"Get off me you arsehole."

"Calm yourself down, sweetie," said Jimmy.

"Don't call me that."

"Malcolm go around the table to Bev," said Mike.

As Malcolm moved, Mike picked the roll of tape up and tore a strip off and placed it over Rose's mouth.

"I've wanted to do that for fifteen years."

Jimmy then sat her down and tie wrapped her to the chair.

"Your turn," said Jimmy, to Malcolm and Bev.

"Not a chance," said Malcolm.

"I'm not asking, take a chair or I'll make you."

"Please do as he asks," added Mike.

"Why should we?" asked Bev.

"If you want to see George and Abigail again, you need to do what I tell you right now, we don't have long to save them."

"What are you talking about?" asked Malcolm.

"I don't have time for lengthy explanations, sit down."

They both looked at each other and complied with Mike's demand.

After Jimmy bound and gagged everyone, he and Mike picked up The Judge and sat him at the head of the table.

"Now, to save time, your all going to have to listen in and try and fill in the blanks for yourselves, over to you Jimmy."

Jimmy lent in close to The Judge, "Before you think of telling me you know nothing, be aware it didn't do Charmin any good, nor did it do Regan any good"

The Judge's eyes were transfixed on Jimmy.

"We have people in the Welshman's house right now, and we know that he's taken the kids elsewhere, all we want from you is where, you get one chance."

Jimmy ripped off the tape.

"You're crazy, do you know who I am, I'm a judge."

He barely had time to finish before Jimmy replaced the gag.

"One chance," said Jimmy as he left for the kitchen.

As Jimmy searched the kitchen draws, he saw a corkscrew on the side next to a nearly empty bottle of wine.

While he was gone Mike approached Malcolm and whispered, "You better not be involved in this."

Bev looked at Mike with questioning eyes at what he'd just said, as Jimmy marched passed her with the corkscrew in hand.

Everyone's attention was firmly on Jimmy though, when he grabbed the judges knee and started to wind the corkscrew deep into the judges knee cap.

You could hear his screams through his gag and tears where streaming down his face.

Bev and Rose were also crying over the spectacle.

Once it would go no further Jimmy asked where the kids were and ripped of the judges gag.

"FUCK YOU!" came the reply.

"You'll talk soon enough, it's just a question of how much damage I do first."

Jimmy went back to the kitchen and returned shortly after with a meat tenderising hammer.

He knelt down and took off the judges shoes and socks, the judge was shaking his head but Jimmy let loose.

He battered both of the judges feet until they were unrecognisable.

Giving the judge a little time to come around, Malcolm was frantically trying to get Mike's attention, so Mike removed his gag.

"Mike stop this, I've known this man for years and he's not capable of what you're saying."

"But I'm capable of abusing my own children and killing my wife?"

"I had a hard time believing it Mike, but the evidence is strong against you."

"Well, when this bastard tells us where they are, you can ask them yourself."

Mike replaced his gag and Jimmy asked The Judge again and removed the tape.

"You're making a mistake."

Jimmy replaced the gag and went back to the kitchen with a slower pace this time.

You could say he was trying to build on the judges fear but he was actually trying to think of how to escalate the pain.

Jimmy was looking around the kitchen and considered getting salt to rub into the wounds, when the answer presented itself in the form of a gas blow gun.

He held the gas gun up and pressed the button to expose the flame.

"Remember your friend, Charmin?"

Jimmy put the gas gun down on the table and uncoupled the judges belt then pulled his pants down to his ankles, exposing his penis and testicles.

"You had your chance; we'll find the kids without you."

Jimmy grabbed the gas gun and pressed the button igniting it.

He directed the flame at the judges testicles and the judge started throwing himself wildly trying to escape the flames.

The smell of singed hair hit everyone and the smell of burning flesh was soon to follow.

Rose started convulsing and Mike pointed it out to Jimmy, he leapt up as he saw vomit coming from her nose.

Jimmy ripped the tape from her face and a projectile of vomit exited her body.

Mike got her a drink of water and when she'd cleared her throat, she asked Mike to stop this.

"I'll stop when George and Abigail are in my arms."

"They're dead, Mike."

"No, they're not, that bastard has them and he's not leaving until he tells me where they are."

Jimmy went back to The Judge who was swaying around in agony, his eyes bulging red and raw.

"Where are the kids?" demanded Jimmy several times, with a few slaps to get his attention.

"They're fucking gone." The judge finally blurted out.

"What do you mean gone?"

"You're never going to see them again."

"What do you mean?" shouted Jimmy giving him a back hand.

"The Welshman has disposed of them."

"Where?"

"We knew you were getting close and we got rid of them."

Mike flew at him, "Your lying."

"I'm not, they're gone so all this was for nothing."

Mike stood back and raised his gun.

"It won't bring them back Mike," said the Judge.

"If my angels are truly gone, there's nothing else for me to do but avenge them."

Mike started to squeeze the trigger.

"Stop," shouted the judge, thinking for a second.

"We can make a deal."

"You've killed your only bargaining chip."

"What if I give you the Welshman?"

"We'll have the Welshman as soon as he returns home."

"He won't be returning home; I can arrange a meeting with him."

"How?"

"We communicate via an email account; we leave each other messages in the drafts to meet up."

Mike put the gun down and put the tape back over his mouth, he then pulled Jimmy to one side.

"What do you think Jimmy?"

"I think he's saying whatever he can to buy more time."

"If he's telling the truth and the Welshman has gone to dump the kids, maybe he can send a message to stop him."

"Ok Jimmy but again, I think he's lying. If he knew we were on to him, why is he risking running around on his own, Whippet said the Welshman asked the kids if they recognised him and they said no, so I don't buy it."

"He did also say that the Welshman was coming back to interrogate him."

"Exactly, let me check in with Boxer first."

"I'll see if Malcolm has a laptop to hand."

Jimmy went into the kitchen to make his call and Mike went to remove Malcolm's gag.

"Mike," said Rose still trying to compose herself, "Is it true, did he kill Tara and take George and Abigail?"

"Yes."

"But the police said there were three bodies."

"There were three bodies, they switched my kids for two they had that had died."

The judge was listening and wondering how Mike knew so much.

"Why?"

"It's what they do, they're a paedophile gang who find a family with a boy and a girl around 9 or 10, and when they've used up all the life out of their victims, they swap them and kill the family so there's no one to identify the bodies."

"Mike," Malcolm interrupted, "I don't want you to think I'm doubting you, but he's said nothing that I've heard, that proves him guilty of anything"

"What about all that talk about the Welshman?"

"You mentioned the Welshman had the kids, in fairness he could have said all that just to stop you hurting him, that's why torture is not an effective way to get information."

"Well, it's worked on all his colleagues."

"Probably weaker men, but your evidence here wouldn't stand up in a court of law."

"It doesn't have to stand up in a court of law. The only way that man walks away from this is if I get my kids back in one piece, otherwise, I will kill him." Mike said, turning and looking him straight in the eye.

"Mike, can we leave the gags off, none of us are going to make any noise."

Mike looked at Bev and she nodded her head in agreement.

"Ok but you need to be quiet and not interfere. Now Malcolm, where is your laptop?"

Mike popped his head in the kitchen.

"Can you keep an eye on them while I go up to Malcolm's office?"

"Sure, I can't get hold of Boxer."

"Leave him a message, his phone may be on silent."

"I have."

Haigh called Greg into his office.

"I've just had Peters on the line. They've rescued Mike's friend Whippet, stupid name, but he said that the children were there but the Welshman took them away."

"That's good news, at least we know they're alive."

"Unless he took them to kill them."

"Surely, it would have been easier to kill them there."

"Many a poor soul has been walked to his own doom."

"Still, I think it's encouraging."

"I need you to grill Regan about any other locations they may hold the kids."

"I'm on it, where are Mike and Jimmy?"

"Gone for some air, I think."

"Sir?" said Greg.

"I'm not their keeper, they said they needed to pop out and I didn't stop them, now haven't you got a job to do?"

"Right sir."

Greg headed back to the interrogation room and stopped at Nipper on the way.

"Do you know where Mike and Jimmy are?"

"No, Haigh asked me for a tracker pad and they left shortly afterwards."

"Any idea who they're tracking?"

"Sorry."

Greg returned to the interrogation and Regan was just explaining how The Judge controlled the media.

"Forget that for now. I need to ask you about the children."

Regan was a beaten man and the fear of being back at the mercy of Jimmy terrified him.

"Are there anymore locations where they might keep them?"

"They stay with the Welshman until he's broken them, and then they go to a house where they have a nice room and toys."

"How kind of you." Greg said sarcastically.

"It's part of the control. We reward them for being good and send them back to the Welshman for attitude adjustment if they're not."

"Where is this house?"

"It's a cottage on the Judge's estate, in a remote corner that is separated off by a 10ft wall, and staff are forbidden to go anywhere near it."

"How is it accessed?"

"Through a door in the wall."

"There's no vehicular access."

"No, it stops delivery and sales men calling by mistake."

"He once caught a burglar there and killed him."

"Who guards the children?"

"An oriental woman, I don't know her name."

"And this woman, she knows what happens to the children, what grip does the Judge have on her?"

"As I understand it, she was a child prostitute in Thailand, sold into it by her own parents. The Judge bought her and brought her here in secret, it's all she's ever known."

"Any other security?"

"There are cameras hidden all over, he uses them for security and to get blackmail material, and there is a panic button that goes directly to the Judge and his men."

"Is there anywhere else you can think of he may take them?"

"There is a quarry that has a deep mine shaft that they have used to dispose of a few bodies, like the burglar, but the judge won't give them kids away that easily."

Greg went to Haigh's office to report his findings.

"Should we get Peters to check it out, sir?"

"No, he's waiting on the Welshman returning, you'll have to go and take Smith with you."

"Me? Wouldn't it be better if I continued with the interrogation, what about Mike and Jimmy."

"Me and Nipper can handle the interrogation, you get out to that house."

"Yes sir," said Greg, still loitering.

"Is there something else, Greg?"

"Who are Mike and Jimmy tracking?"

"What do you mean?"

"Nipper said you gave them a tracking pad."

"Nipper needs to learn to keep his mouth shut, it's none of your concern, you've been given an assignment, now get on with it."

Greg left the office, feeling a little angry about Haigh keeping him out of the loop.

"Dawn, we need to go."

"What about the interrogation?"

"Not our problem anymore."

Greg and Dawn grabbed their equipment.

"Better grab two of them telescopic ladders and a lock pick kit," said Greg.

"Are we going in slow?"

"Yes, we don't know who is on that panic button list, better if we don't trigger it."

"Fair enough."

They packed the equipment into Greg's car and left, it would be a good thirty minutes to their destination and they spent most of it in silent thought.

Jimmy entered the dining room and headed straight for Rose.

"Are you ok?"

"Don't speak to me."

"Don't be like that. Mike had no choice. You would have brought the police in and things would have got a lot messier."

"You could have tried talking to us."

"We had to get control of that prick, before he pressed his panic button."

"And how could you do that to another human being?"

"Do you realise what they've been doing to your niece and nephew, and it's my understanding that your sister was still alive when they set fire to her."

"Stop it," said Bev.

"I'm sorry," said Jimmy.

"You need to all understand that these bastards are ruthless and Mike has had to live with this knowledge for two weeks now."

"We've been mourning too," said Bev.

"I appreciate that but you all turned your back on him and believed the lies, how could he approach you and explain, you would never have believed him."

"How could we, all the evidence pointed to him?" said Malcolm.

"How long have you been a solicitor, and you've never known the police to falsify evidence?"

"Point taken."

"It only takes a few key people to control evidence and this man has an entire network."

"And Mike thought I was a part of it."

"A list is being written as we speak and so far, your name isn't on it."

"Nor will it be, I've known this man longer then you have been alive and it's all just a little hard to digest."

Mike returned with the laptop.

"What's going on?"

Everyone fell silent.

"Jimmy?"

"Nothing Mike, just banging my head against a wall, let's get on."

Mike opened the laptop and Jimmy removed the Judge's gag.

"What's the email address and password?"

"I don't know."

"What do you mean you don't know?"

"It's preloaded on a phone at my house, I don't know it by memory."

"And you expect us to take you to your house, how fucking stupid do you think we are?"

"It's the only way I can contact him."

"I knew it was a scam to save your neck."

"It's not, it's the only way you are going to get to him before he disappears."

"I'm not so sure about that," interrupted Jimmy.

"We have Regan, Devon and Phillips, surely one, if not all, have access to the Welshman."

Jimmy took out his phone and headed off to the kitchen.

"It seems you've outlived your usefulness," said Mike.

"Wait Mike," said Malcolm, as Mike raised his gun.

"You can't be sure; he may be of use still."

"You haven't seen what I have Malcolm. If there is one thing I'm sure of, it's that this animal needs putting down."

"Please don't do this, this is not the action of the man my Tara fell in love with."

Mike stopped and looked at Malcolm.

"You're wrong, Tara knew exactly who I am and she saw past it. Unlike all you, she appreciated my loyalty and my willingness to do anything for my family."

"That's not true, we welcomed you into our family open heartedly."

"Really, Tara told me about your concerns and the talk you had when we first got together."

"I wouldn't have been a responsible father if I didn't try to talk to her about making informed choices."

"What about the look on Bev's face when I asked your permission to marry her?"

"Mike, I admit that I thought you were just a faze that I was hoping she would grow out of but you proved me wrong, you're part of this family now," said Bev.

"Really, I wonder how good the evidence really had to be, before you believed me capable of what they accused me of."

Malcolm, Bev and Rose all looked embarrassed.

"Seems you have a stay of execution, but when it's confirmed my children are dead, so will you be."

Mike left to go to the kitchen where Jimmy was deep in conversation with someone.

Mike heard some talking coming from the dining room and moved closer to the door to eavesdrop.

"Robyn, do you know anything about what Mike is talking about?"

"No, he's deluded."

"Are you sure?"

"You know me Malcolm, does it sound like something I'm capable of?"

"No, and I don't want to believe it but Mike seems pretty convinced."

"He's out of his fucking mind, look what they've done to me."

"I'll speak to him but you heard it yourself he'll kill you if he doesn't get his kids back and I believe he will."

"I don't have his kids; I've never even seen his kids."

"Ok Robyn, I'll do what I can to talk some sense to him."

"That's a lie," said Bev.

"What?" asked Malcolm.

"He said he'd never even seen the children but he has."

"Where?"

"At the village fate, last year."

"That's right, you were there."

"I didn't remember, it was one time."

"You bought them an ice cream and talked to them for almost an hour," said Bev.

"I just don't remember."

Malcolm had seen enough liars in his life to see that the Judge was trying to cover his tracks.

"Robyn."

"I honestly forgot but that proves nothing, it's circumstantial."

Malcolm was now on guard, and his attention was working overtime, watching the Judge's every facial expression and gesture.

"Who are these men they have?" he asked.

"I don't know."

"Isn't Regan the name of his solicitor, and Phillips the inspector running the case?"

"I don't remember."

That was it, Malcolm was convinced that the Judge was lying, so he pushed on with his questioning.

"You don't remember the name of Mike's solicitor?"

"Sorry, I know that his solicitor is Andrew Regan. I can't remember the details of all my cases."

"You have an incredible memory."

The Judge realised Malcolm was becoming suspicious.

"Age catches up with all of us but so what, he's going after everyone connected with the case, that doesn't make what he's saying true."

"No, but the fact your defence mechanism has kicked in tells me you know more about this than you're telling."

"Malcolm?" asked Bev.

"In our early days as a mental exercise we would all tell each other stories to see if we could recognise when people were lying to us, I could always tell when Robyn was lying because he got defensive."

"I'm not lying, I've been tortured, how would you be?"

"I'm sorry, what were you lying?" said Jimmy bursting through the kitchen door closely followed by Mike.

"My mates are chasing the Welshman through the hills now and believe me they will catch him. There's nobody better behind the wheel of a car than my pal, Whippet"

The Judge looked stone-faced.

"And the cherry on the cake, we have a team moving in on the cottage on your estate, what's the matter, you seem to be getting pale?"

Jimmy was right, the blood had drained from the Judge's face.

"How could you?" said Malcolm, "You're my oldest friend."

The Judge fell silent and looked away.

Chapter 15
Reunited

Boxer and Peters didn't have to wait too long before they heard the diesel engine of the Welshman's Land Rover.

Peters carefully looked out of the kitchen window then slunk back beneath the worksurface.

"It's him, get ready?"

The Welshman crept through the woodland in his Land Rover with his usual caution.

He parked up and switched his engine off and had a good look around and only when he was satisfied it was safe, did he exit his vehicle.

Boxer readied himself for the pounce after hearing the car door close, Peters raised a hand to steady his eagerness.

The Welshman headed for the door and then paused when he saw the damage to it.

Suddenly Boxer's phone rang. Peters looked at him as he tried to muffle it with his hands but then they heard the car door go and they knew their cover had been blown.

Both men bolted out of the house as the Welshman had started his engine.

The Welshman put the Land Rover in gear and drove straight for the men.

Boxer pushed Peters out of the way and jumped in the other direction.

The Welshman went straight between them and crashed into the backdoor, he put the vehicle in reverse and pulled back about thirty feet.

As he started moving forward again, he started to turn to flee.

Boxer was back on his feet and managed to jump on the side of the vehicle, he got a foot on the side step and a hand on the mirror.

He launched an assault on the door window which smashed on his third attempt.

The Welshman who was not easily panicked was definitely feeling the pressure and veered the Land Rover into a bush, which tore Boxer off the vehicle.

As the Land Rover disappeared into the woods, Boxer was joined by Peters who was just putting his phone away.

"Fucking phone."

"Don't worry about it, he's not got away yet, Mac's on his way up."

"But he was right there."

"I know but it's happened and you need to shake it off, you can beat yourself up after we catch him."

The Range Rover pulled up and they jumped in.

"Why are you driving?" asked Peters seeing that Whippet was behind the wheel.

"In case Mac had to assist you," Whippet answered, as he sped through the woods.

"Are you ok to drive?"

"Don't worry about him," said Boxer, "There's no one you'd rather have behind that wheel."

"What happened?" asked Mac.

"He got spooked," replied Peters.

"It was my fault; I didn't put my phone on fucking silent."

"Stop it, we'll get him."

Just then they were exiting the woods and the Welshman was nowhere in sight.

Whippet turned sharply to the left and followed a track that hugged the tree line.

"What are you doing?" asked Peters.

"He's gone this way."

"How do you know?"

"The new tracks up there that went in this direction."

"He could have made them on the way in or earlier."

"The spray pattern shows they were made leaving and the depth of them shows he was doing some speed.

As we know this bastard is cautious and drives slow everywhere, we can guess that he's just made them now."

Peters looked impressed.

"I told you, he's good."

"As long as he doesn't turn us over," replied Peters.

"You're lucky it's an automatic," said Whippet.

As they reached the end of the tree line which curled at the end, they could see a wooden farmers gate that had been pulverised.

"Looks like you're on the money, Whippet" said Mac, who was enjoying the ride a little too much.

The field took them up hill and you could clearly see the direction the Welshman had taken.

Just over the ridge they could see another gate in pieces.

"THERE," shouted Mac, pointing at a Land Rover in the distance.

"Seen him," confirmed Whippet.

"Fuck, he's moving."

"Not fast enough."

Whippet already flat out, just refused to slow down for any obstacles, and if he couldn't fly over them, he weaved around them at break neck speed.

"Jees lad, you should be a rally driver," said Mac.

"He almost was, but some little arsehole with a silver spoon up his butt took his spot after daddy pulled some strings."

"Couldn't you have joined a different team?"

"He might have been able to, until he got drunk and stole a car then ended his joy ride by launching it into a river."

"Took a dim view, did they?"

"The race organiser did, it was his Aston Martin."

Mac laughed loudly, "Yes Whippet, I like it."

Boxer turned to Peters, "I thought he was the quiet type."

"Nope, he's an adrenalin junky and is only happy in action."

The Welshman came to the end of his field and rammed the metal gate that led to the road, but it didn't give way and just bent around the front of his vehicle.

He backed up and went for the fence to the side which was an easier target and he was out on the road in seconds.

Once Whippet saw which direction he'd chosen, he adjusted his course to follow.

"Don't get stuck in the field," said Peters.

"Do you want to drive?" replied Whippet.

"Actually, yes."

"Well tuff shit, now shut up and let me do my thing."

Whippet saw his opportunity; he charged the fence and launched up a small embankment on to the road.

Everyone except Whippet was tossed around like a salad because they weren't wearing their seat belts, a mistake that they quickly remedied.

"Micky is going to kill you if you've scratched his paint work," said Boxer.

All four men laughed.

"He's made a big mistake going on the road," said Whippet.

"Why's that?" asked Peters.

"His 4x4 has spring suspension and is not built for fast driving on roads, whereas this has air suspension and corners like a car."

"Great, well let's get him then."

They had made up some ground on their prey but like any wild creature, he wasn't going to give up easily.

He weaved through the country lanes like a mad man and almost lost it a few times.

Whippet saw his chance and told everyone hold on to something.

There was a bend in the road that the Welshman had no choice but to slow down for.

Whippet prepared himself to hit the back end of the Land Rover causing it to spin out of control.

But the Welshman didn't slow down and nor did he take the corner, he crashed straight through the hedges which had a thirty-foot steep hill behind it with rocky patches.

"Fuck," shouted Whippet as he broke fast and hard.

They stopped on the brow of the hill and watched as the Land Rover was tossed around like a toy.

It eventually flipped over but landed back on its wheels.

The four men sat there trying to catch their breath after the near-death experience they just had, when the Land Rover began to move again.

"How the fuck did he survive that," said Mac.

"Well time to see how good this hill descent feature is," said Whippet, pressing a button on the Range Rovers centre console.

"And to a chorus of no's and holy shits, Whippet went over the edge of the hill."

It was like a scene from a cartoon where everyone is screaming until they realise, they're falling really slowly or not that far off the ground.

The Range Rover handled the hill with grace, unlike its occupants.

A few feet from the bottom, Whippet switched off the hill descent and floored it in hot pursuit of the Welshman.

Whippets three passengers had never been so silent that he had to check his mirrors to see if they were still there and alive.

Boxers phone rang and everyone jumped and laughed.

"It's Jimmy, hello."

"Boxer, how's it going over there, any sign of the Welshman."

"Yes, but he did a runner and we are up his arse now."

"That's excellent news, don't you lose him."

"Don't worry Jimmy, Whippet will kill us before he lets that bastard get away."

"Is Whippet driving?"

"Yeah."

"I have no doubt you'll catch him, there's no one more fearless behind the wheel than him."

"Hold that thought Jimmy because the Welshman drove off a cliff five minutes ago."

"A cliff, what did Whippet do?"

"He followed him."

"That's my boy, call me as soon as you've got him."

"Is he back at base yet?" asked Peters.

"We could do with them sending some backup to block him in."

"I heard what he said and were tied up me and Mike, but I'll call Greg and see what I can sort out."

"Thanks Jimmy, I'll catch you later," and Jimmy hung up.

"We don't need back up; I'll catch this bastard," promised Whippet, once again closing the gap.

The roll down the hill had damaged the Welshman's vehicle and he knew it was only a matter of time before they overtook him and forced him to stop.

He desperately scavenged around his cab, looking for his gun that had been tossed around.

He saw it at the far side in the passenger footwell but it was just out of his reach, he looked in the mirror and saw the Range Rover closing in.

It would only take one shot to their driver and his escape would be assured.

He started to shake his vehicle in the hope of moving the gun nearer to him but it was too heavy on the rubber mats.

He needed more thrust and turned the wheel sharply to the left and the gun came skipping across.

He reached for the gun but Whippet taking advantage of his sharp left turn hit the back of his land Rover and flipped it.

It crashed down on the driver's side and almost flipped onto the roof because of the hill it was on.

Mac, Peters and Boxer all leapt into action and jumped out of the Range Rover, dashing to drag the Welshman from the wreckage.

Whippet reversed back to a safe distance, while they approached the vehicle with caution.

The sound of glass smashing caught everyone's attention, and the Welshman popped up through the passenger door window.

They all scattered for cover as he took a pot shot at Mac, he then aimed at Peters who found himself looking squarely down the barrel.

The Welshman pulled the trigger but the bullet went whizzing past Peter's head, due to the distraction of Whippet driving the Range Rover on a collision course.

The Welshman fired frantically at the Range Rover to no avail, as it crashed into the land Rover and sent it tumbling down the hill.

It deposited the Welshman's body on the ground but not before crushing many of the bones in his upper body.

The three men ran down the hill to recover his body and make sure he didn't have his gun.

Peters checked him over, "We need to put a stretcher together."

"Why?" ask Boxer.

"We don't want to do any more damage to him until we have the children. Agreed."

Boxer agreed reluctantly.

"Boxer, break me two sturdy branches off that tree, and Mac get me the tool bag from the car and ask Whippet to give us a hand."

Boxer started breaking branches and Mac went to the Range Rover.

"PETERS," shouted Mac.

Peters and Boxer both sprinted to the vehicle to see Whippet struggling to breathe.

"He's taken a bullet to the chest," said Mac dragging him out from the driver's seat.

"We need to get him to a hospital," said Boxer.

"He'll be dead before we get a mile down the road," said Peters.

"Boxer, trust us mate, we know what we're doing," added Mac, returning from the boot with the medical kit.

"Is there anything I can do?"

"No, actually yes, build the stretcher because we need to get out of here as soon as we've drained his chest."

Boxer looked at his friend hoping it wouldn't be the last time, and ran back to the Welshman.

Mac pulled up Whippets t-shirt to reveal the wound and Peters put his hand around his back to feel for the exit wound.

"Whippet, this is going to hurt but you should begin to breathe and feel better."

Peters pulled the wound apart and a release of air came flooding out, sure enough Whippet began to respond quickly.

Mac passed Peters two patches; both were self-adhesive but one had a tube protruding from it.

Peters took the first patch and stuck it firmly over the exit wound.

"When I put this next patch on, this tube in the centre will go inside your body to release the air pressure, if you feel it getting tight you just turn this valve and you should be able to breathe again."

Whippet nodded and Peters went to insert the tube when a loud thud came from the back of the Range Rover.

"The bastards in the boot" said Boxer stepping out from behind the vehicle. "Are we ready to go?"

"Nearly," said Peters, looking at him disapprovingly.

Peters inserted the tube and firmly sealed the plaster around it.

"Let's just try it first before we leave," he said turning the valve.

Air came whistling out, and when it slowed down, Mac and Boxer helped Whippet in to the back seat of the car.

"I'm alright to drive boys," said Whippet.

"You've done enough driving today my friend, and it was a pleasure watching you work," said Mac, who closed his door and jumped into the driving seat.

After securing the Welshman, Peters took up position in the front passenger seat leaving Boxer to care for his friend.

Mac put directions in the sat nav for the nearest hospital and set off once it had loaded up.

Peters called in to update Haigh on their situation and cancel the backup he'd requested.

"How's it going Peters?"

"We've got him, sir."

"Excellent work, are you going to bring him here or interrogate him in the field."

"I'm not sure we're going to be getting anything out of him, anytime soon sir."

"What have you done to him?"

"He started shooting at us, and Whippet rolled his vehicle down a hill."

"Is he dead?"

"No sir, but I think there's a fair few broken bones."

"What was that kid thinking?"

"We were under fire and the Welshman had me bang to rights, if he hadn't acted so quickly, I'd be dead."

"Ok Peters, what's your plan?"

"Well there's one more problem, sir."

"What now?"

"Whippet took a bullet to the chest."

Haigh's tone completely changed to heartfelt concern.

"Is he ok, what's his status?"

"The bullet has gone right through but his lung has collapsed."

"And," said Haigh, impatiently.

"We've treated him and we're on our way to the hospital."

"Which hospital?"

"Gloucester royal, we need you to phone ahead sir, with it being a gunshot wound, they'll call the police."

"Don't worry, I'll make all the arrangements; you just get him there safely."

"Will do sir, don't forget that the Welshman is going to need treatment too, and we don't even know his real name."

"Don't worry, he's a terrorist who shot Whippet and he's in your custody, so his name is classified."

"Got it sir. You can also call off the backup."

"What back up, didn't Jimmy tell you?"

"No sir, he hasn't told us anything."

"He called awhile back asking for Greg to back you up but Greg and Dawn have gone to the Judges estate."

"Why?"

"It turns out that after the Welshman conditions the children, they're kept in a cottage that's secluded on his estate."

"And the kids are there?"

"We believe so."

"Do they need backup?"

"You just take care of Whippet and don't let that Welshman out of your sight."

"Yes sir, please let us know as soon as you hear something."

"I will, and you tell that young man he's done an outstanding job."

"Yes sir."

"What did he say?" asked Boxer.

"He's going to phone the hospital to prepare for our arrival, and Greg and Dawn are on their way to a possible location of the children."

"That's great, does Mike know?"

"I think so, Haigh said he told Jimmy."

"Shit, I'd better call Jimmy and tell him what's happened."

Greg and Dawn had arrived at the gate at the back of the Judge's estate that the Welshman uses.

Greg got a pair of bolt cutters from the boot and cut the chain which secured it.

Once it was open, he got back in the car and opened up a satellite map on his pad and guided Dawn to the cottage.

For as tall as the wall was, it was very well secluded behind a thick layer of evergreen bushes and conifers.

Even though they were looking for it they only caught glimpses of it.

They came across a path and stopped the car.

"I'll have a look before we get the equipment, keep your eyes peeled," said Greg, jumping out of the car and disappearing down the track.

It wasn't long before he was back sporting a thumbs up.

Dawn jumped out of the car and joined Greg at the boot to get the equipment out.

"There is a door in the wall that would need explosives to open, but these ladders will do nicely."

"Are we going straight down the path or should we find another entry point?"

"I didn't see any cameras so we'll use the path, there's a lot of thorn bushes at the base of the wall, probably to deter people."

"Scared of getting pricked?"

"No, it would be a nightmare to traverse."

"Whatever you say Greg."

Greg shut the boot as Dawn ran down the path chuckling to herself.

By time Greg got there, Dawn had already begun to extend one of the ladders while Greg readied his weapons.

Once it was at the right height, she leant it against the wall and Greg climbed up to put the other ladder on the other side, while Dawn readied herself.

When the ladder was in position, Greg went over the wall, closely followed by Dawn.

Years of training and working together had given them a fluidity, like they could anticipate each-other's movements.

It was roughly fifty feet to the house through more overgrown shrubs and conifers.

Their efforts to hide the property from prying eyes, gave cover to Greg and Dawns advance.

They moved close to the cottage and crouched beside the wall either side of the front door.

It was a double fronted property and they both took a window a piece.

Greg was looking into a sitting room with nobody in sight.

Dawns room was a dining room with some plates on the table but still no people in sight.

Greg gestured Dawn to work her way around the property and he went in the other direction.

They both moved as swift and silent as cats on the hunt.

They reunited at the rear of the property without encountering a single soul.

"They must be upstairs," said Dawn.

Just then they heard a door open in the kitchen and they both tightened their cover against the wall.

Greg slowly raised up to look through the back door and saw a small oriental woman who had her back to them, looking in the fridge.

"It's the woman, you try the door handle and if it's locked, I'll kick it in."

Dawn raised her hand and grabbed the door handle as Greg crouched in front of the door ready to pounce.

Greg gave the nod and Dawn slowly pulled the handle down.

The door started to open but just as Greg started to relax himself for a soft entry, a bell sounded, like an electronic shop bell.

Greg pounce through the door and the oriental woman who'd been given some advance warning by the bell, had lunged to the work surface and grabbed a knife.

Greg rushed her while she was still panicked and slapped the knife out of her hand.

He wasn't taking any chances and punched her in her solar plexus and she went down.

Dawn covered the door as he secured the woman's hands behind her back with a tie wrap.

He put his hand over the woman's mouth and told her to be quiet and she wouldn't be harmed if she cooperated.

The woman nodded her head and Greg removed his hand.

"Are the children here?" he asked.

She nodded her head.

"Is anyone else here?"

The woman shook her head.

"Good, where are the children."

She pointed upstairs

"Dawn, be careful," said Greg, sending her upstairs.

Dawn made her way into the hallway and checked all the rooms on the ground floor, before proceeding to the first floor.

Creeping up the stairs keeping aware of all doorways and the loft hatch, she made it to the top and started checking rooms in order.

The first was a bathroom which was clear, she quickly moved to the next room that was a large very nicely decorated bedroom, which didn't look like it was being used.

The third had a lock on the door and Dawn surmised that this was the children's room, so she passed it to check the fourth room first.

It was the smallest of the three bedrooms and was clearly the bedroom of the oriental woman.

The children who had heard the ruckus had huddled together on one of the beds in their room.

They listened in fear, to every sound of doors opening and quiet footsteps on the wooden floors.

The closer the sounds got the more their little bodies shook.

George hugged Abigail and shushed her as they could see the shadow of feet outside their room.

They heard the lock go and the door was flung open and in stepped Dawn.

Dawn immediately shushed the children as she examined the room.

Once she was satisfied it was clear, she lowered her weapon and crouched near the bed.

"Are you George and Abigail," she asked, but the children were too afraid to talk.

"I'm Dawn, I'm a friend of your daddy, he sent me to come get you."

The children started filling up with emotion and Dawn offered her hand.

"I'm George," said the little boy, as he took her hand, "And this is Abigail."

"Is my daddy here?" asked Abigail.

"No angel, he's not, I'm going to take you straight to him but first I need to ask you something."

The children looked at her with full attention.

"Is there anyone else in the house apart from the lady"

"The angry man was here earlier but he wasn't here at dinner time" said George.

"That's great, we're going to make our way down stairs to where my friend has arrested the lady, so don't be alarmed, he's very nice and then we'll take you to your daddy"

"And mummy?" asked Abigail.

Dawn felt sick in her stomach but she thought it best to lie for now and let Mike break the news.

"Yes, mummy too."

She led them down stairs keeping vigilant and one hand firmly on her gun.

When they reached the kitchen, she felt better for being reunited with Greg who had secured his prisoner to a radiator.

"Hi guys, I'm Greg."

"Are you a friend of our mummy and daddy too>" asked George.

"I am, and your daddy has been looking for you everywhere."

"Can we go home now?"

"Of course you can pal, we need to climb up a ladder to get over a wall first, and then we'll take my car."

"No key?" asked Dawn.

"Apparently not, she's as much a prisoner as the kids."

"Right come on guys, let Greg go first and we'll follow him."

"Abigail is scared of heights," said George.

"Don't worry, Greg is big and strong and can carry her over."

Abigail clung to Dawn; she didn't look happy at the prospect of a strange man carrying her.

"Would you prefer me to help you Abigail?"

Abigail nodded her head.

Greg headed up the ladder and once he was over the top, he encouraged George to follow him, which he did without hesitation.

"I'm good at climbing," said George as he reached the top and Greg helped him over the wall.

"I can see that you're very good at climbing," answered Greg.

Dawn gave Abigail a piggyback and started to scale the ladder.

"Hold on tight angel," she said, as she crossed over the top of the wall.

With all feet safely on the ground they made their way to the car.

Greg opened the back door and both George and Abigail climbed in and put their seat belts on.

Dawn turned the car around and followed the same track they came in on to get out.

Once on the road Greg picked up his phone and called Haigh.

"We've got them sir."

"The children."

"Yes, they're in the car with us now and we're heading back to base, is Mike back yet?"

"No but I'll call him immediately."

"Ok sir, tell him they're both fine."

"I will Greg, outstanding work."

"Mike, do you think you could remove these bonds?" asked Bev.

"Ok Bev, but I must ask you all to remain where you are."

"That's fair enough."

Jimmy cut Malcolm, Bev and Roses bonds while Mike kept his eye firmly on the judge.

"Mike, what's going on, what happened to my sister?" asked Rose.

Mike started to explain everything from when he first smelt the smoke to the recent position, they all found themselves in.

Rose cried when she heard how they tried to hang him on his cell and was a little more understanding of why he had resorted to the methods he had.

When he had finished, the room that had listened intently stayed silent, until Rose turned her attention to the Judge.

"How could you, how could you do all that, then sit at our table like it was nothing?"

Jimmy put his hand on her shoulder to steady her.

"Because he's a fucking animal."

"Animal or not, you'll pay for what you've done," she said.

"Don't worry, he will answer for his crimes," said Malcolm.

"You're right but not in the way you think, he's so well connected, there's no way you could take him to court, he'll be punished by my hand," replied Mike.

"It's not for you to punish him Mike, that's just vengeance."

"And what's wrong with that?"

"The law is there to punish men like him."

"Well, it does a piss poor job; you rob a bank and you get life but if you kill a woman or rape a child you get five to ten."

"The system isn't perfect."

"You're wrong, the system is perfect for people like him that control it, you've been in the game long enough to know what I'm saying is true."

"I still believe in the law Mike and I implore you to turn him over."

"This man murdered my wife, your daughter, and has my children, your grandchildren held up somewhere being tortured and made compliant, to be raped."

"But Mike—"

"NO, as a husband and a father, I have the right to take vengeance upon this creature, your laws are only there to protect him, not to bring justice for Tara."

Jimmy's phone rang, which was perfect timing considering the tension in the room.

"What is it Boxer, did you get him?"

"We did, Jimmy."

"That's my boys."

"We've taken a casualty though."

"Who?"

"Whippet was shot in the chest?"

"Is he dead?"

"No, Peters did some first aid shit, and he's ok for now but we're heading for the hospital."

"Good, you make sure he gets to the front of the cue and be careful Boxer, the hospital will phone the police, it's standard for all gunshot victims."

"Don't worry, Haigh is getting us special treatment, like we're special forces or something and we won't have to speak to no police."

"Excellent, keep me informed and tell that boy he's got something special to look forward to."

"Actually, you owe him a new pair of trainers?"

"He didn't get them mucky, did he?"

"Walked through a river apparently."

Jimmy laughed, "Can you put him on?"

"I'll put the phone to his ear, go on Jimmy."

"Whippet, don't you worry sun shine, you can have your pick of trainers."

"Ok Jimmy, thanks" replied Whippet, struggling for breath.

"No, thank you my friend."

"We need to go now Jimmy; I'll call you when I know more."

"Wait Boxer, has the Welshman said anything?"

"Not yet pal, he's a little fucked up at the moment."

"Ok mate, speak to you soon."

"What's wrong Jimmy?" asked Mike.

"They got the bastard but Whippet has been shot."

"How bad?"

"Pretty bad, but Peters is looking after him and they on their way to the hospital."

"I'm sorry for getting them involved Jimmy."

"Don't be, I'm sure he'll be fine, and in the summer when he takes his shirt off, it will be something to take the focus off his pigeon chest."

"One of your friends has been shot, and you're making jokes, do you not realise how serious all this is," said Malcolm.

"I do, but what would you rather I did, fall to my knees and cry?"

"No, just try acting like you understand the gravity of your actions."

"Like he should think of the gravity of his actions. Well, you don't have to worry about Mike killing him because if anything happens to Whippet, I will."

"I think it's best if we have a little quiet time, so everyone can calm down." said Bev.

"Would anyone like a drink?" asked Rose.

"That's a smashing idea. Come on sweetie, I'll help you carry them in."

"I've told you a thousand times, don't call me that."

Jimmy and Rose went to the kitchen to make a round of teas, while Mike, Bev and Malcolm sat watching the Judge in silence.

"It's been a while, how you been keeping?" asked Jimmy.

"You want to do this now?" answered Rose.

"I'm just making conversation."

"Well don't, I understand what Mike's been through and what is at stake but I can't unsee what you did in there."

"Ok, just trying to ease the tension, you've always been pretty tense."

Rose looked at Jimmy with a little annoyance, "James, stop it."

There wasn't many people allowed to use Jimmy's Sunday name but Rose was one who could get away with it.

"Sorry sweetie, do you have any biscuits to go with that tea?"

"I think my mum made a lemon drizzle cake to keep herself occupied but no one had the stomach to eat it."

She pulled the cake from the fridge with the milk and passed it to Jimmy.

Jimmy got a knife and cut it into slices and devoured one straight away.

After tea was made, they took it through to the dining room where everyone was still sat in silence.

Rose passed everyone except the judge a cup of tea and Jimmy offered out the cake with no takers.

Everyone was on edge, waiting for the results of Greg's search of the cottage.

It was getting intolerable, having to sit looking at the man who had murdered his wife and stolen his children.

Everybody jumped to attention when Jimmy's phone rang.

"Hello."

"Good news Jimmy, we've got the kids."

"YES," shouted Jimmy, "They've got them, Mike!"

"Who's got them, where are they?" asked Mike.

Jimmy passed the phone to Mike.

"Greg and Dawn picked them up about ten minutes ago Mike, and they're on their way here."

"Thank you Haigh, thank you."

"No need for that Mike, can you get yourself here?"

"Sure, I'm on my way."

"Mike," interrupted Bev, "Can you bring them here; you can't take them home."

"You're right, Haigh can you bring them to me?"

"Not a problem Mike, Greg can pick the Judge up at the same time, he is still alive, isn't he?"

"Just about."

"Good, you sit tight and we'll have your kids there before you know it."

"Thank you again."

"My pleasure, Mike."

Mike put the phone down and flung himself at Jimmy with an explosion of all the emotion that he'd been bottling up.

"Thank you, Jimmy," he said, as tears of joy streamed down his face.

"None of that now. Your babies are coming home, mate."

Which made him even worse.

"You have the emotional range of a cold wet stone James," said Rose, as she pulled Mike towards her to comfort him.

Malcolm had stepped towards the Judge.

"Everything he's said is true, I've sat there and defended you and everything he said, is true."

The Judge looked away.

"Look at me, you son of a bitch."

Malcolm slapped the Judge so hard, he sent him flying.

Jimmy stepped in front of him, "Your grandchildren are on their way; we don't know what they've had to endure but the last thing they need is anger and violence."

Malcolm nodded his head and was defused, then went and hugged his wife.

Haigh called Greg, "Hi Greg, can you take the children to Mike's in-laws?"

"What's he doing there sir? There's a watch on that house."

"He knows, but the Judge went there and Mike went to question him, and see if his father-in-law was in on it?"

"And you signed off on this, do you realise what they'll do to him?"

"I didn't have to sign off on anything. Mike's a big boy and can make his own choices."

"I hope he's still alive."

"I have it on good authority he is, so when you drop the kids off, bring him back here."

"What about the police watching the house?"

"Still there, and unaware as far as I know, you'll have to pull rank and get shut of them."

"I knew you was up to something."

"I'll see you soon, Greg."

"Yes sir," said Greg clearly annoyed by the news.

Jimmy picked the Judge up off the floor.

"All the pain you've gone through," Jimmy said, as he unscrewed the corkscrew from the judges kneecap.

"And being millimetres from death, you said nothing, you could have stopped all this by telling us where they were."

The Judge was clearly in pain, he barely had the energy to react but he was trying to mumble something.

"It's too late, we're not interested in anything you have to say."

"Maybe it's important," said Malcolm.

"No, it's more likely he's trying to bargain with us. Tell us how much trouble we're in and how he'll spare us if we let him go."

"How can you be sure?"

"Because I know his character, like most of his kind he has a god complex, he thinks he can control everyone and is never in the wrong."

"There are going to be questions that need to be answered."

"We know, but I don't ever want to hear that man's bullshit ever again."

"We need to prepare for the children," said Mike, who had regained himself, "They can't see any of this."

"We'll take them in the sitting room. They'll probably be hungry, I'll make some sandwiches," said Bev.

"Shall I get their beds ready?" asked Rose.

"No, we'll have a camp out in the sitting room so we can keep an eye on them."

"Ok, I'll get the blankets down and you boys can clean the mess you've made up in here."

The three men all looked at each other as the women rushed off with a new found energy and purpose.

"Jimmy, do you have Greg's number there, I want to hear their voices and tell them I love them."

"Sure Mike, here you go, it's ringing."

"Greg, it's Mike."

"Hi Mike, Haigh told me that we're coming to you, we're about thirty minutes out."

"That's great, I was just wondering if I could speak to George and Abigail?"

"Sure, oh, sorry Mike they've both crashed, do you want me to wake them?"

"No, let them sleep, they always sleep in the car."

"Mike, I've something I need to tell you."

"What is it?"

"They're looking forward to seeing you and their mum."

"They don't know?"

"No, and I didn't want to tell them, I thought it was better coming from you."

"Your right, thank you Greg."

"Don't mention it."

"No, I mean it, thank you for all your help."

"It's genuinely my pleasure, we'll see you soon."

The next thirty minutes felt like an eternity but they all made good use of it cleaning up the mess.

Mike kept having a peek through the curtains but it was so dark he couldn't see anything.

Greg and Dawn turned down the track that led to the Briggs residence and as they approached the police car, it lit up like a disco.

Greg told Dawn to stop a good two car lengths before them and he got out to approach on foot.

"Turn them god damn lights off."

"Who are you to be giving orders?"

"Inspector Greg Phillips," he showed them his ID and the officer turned off the lights.

"Sorry sir, it's been a long week."

"It's fine, who's your C/O?"

"Inspector Davis, why?"

"Could you call him for me?"

"Yes sir," the officer wasn't too happy at the request as he thought he was in trouble for something.

"Is something wrong Inspector?"

"No, I just need to speak to him, nothing for you to worry about."

The officer made the call, "Hello, I've got Inspector Phillips here sir, he wants to speak with you," and he passed the phone to Greg.

"This is Inspector Phillips; I need you to pull your men off the Briggs' residence."

"Why? Mike Feather hasn't been apprehended yet."

"Nor is he likely to be if we keep wasting resources like this, besides that, I'm trying to get Mr and Mrs Briggs on side, and they're constantly complaining about police at the end of their drive harassing their visitors."

"They're just doing their job."

"Which I can appreciate but I'm lead on this case and I want them gone, now."

"I'll have to clear this with the chief."

"That's fine and while you're at it tell him I said it's necessary."

"They'll have to stay until I get confirmation."

"The hell they will, I need to go in there and get those people to open up to me, I need to show good will and that good will is that these officers are going to leave now."

"Put me back on to them."

"Here, he wants to speak to you," said Greg, handing them back the phone.

"Yes sir."

"Come back to the station for reassignment, it's on his head."

"Yes sir."

Inspector Green hung up and the officers left.

Greg got back in the car and they continued to the house.

The car had barely had time to stop when the front door of the house flung open and Mike rushed out to embrace his children.

They were still asleep when he opened the door, so he gently unbuckled Abigail and started to lift her out, when he heard the sweet sound that had melted so many men's hearts.

"Daddy," said George, who had just woken up.

"Hi son," Mike said in his softest voice, "Take your seatbelt off and come here mate."

"Let me help," said Malcolm.

Mike looked at him and hesitated for a second, he just wanted to hug both his kids and never let them go.

Malcolm looked hurt by this hesitation, thinking Mike still had doubts on whether he was involved with the Judge.

"Mike."

"Sorry Malcolm, I just want to hold them so badly, of course you can help."

"Come here, George."

"Grandad," said George jumping into his arms.

The two men carried the children into the house followed by Greg and Dawn.

Both Rose and Bev were in the doorway, ready to greet the children and their rescuers.

Abigail started to wake up with the fuss that was being made.

"Take them straight into the sitting room Mike, we're all ready for them," said Bev.

They all entered the sitting room, where the coffee table had been moved from the centre of the room and replaced with a picnic blanket, which is one of the treats the children always looked forward to.

The children weren't really hungry but were so happy to see everyone they made an effort to eat.

The joy felt by everyone was suddenly over shadowed by the inevitable question, "Where's mummy?" asked Abigail.

The whole room fell silent as Mike took Abigail on his knee.

"Mummy couldn't make it darling, but she loves you so much."

Bev and Rose started to cry but tried to hide it, even the other adults had to keep their emotions in check.

"Can we go home to see her"

"Not tonight, we're staying here with grandma and grandad tonight."

"Why?"

"Because we're celebrating you being back."

You could see that Abigail was not going to let it go.

"Abigail, do you want to pick a film for us to watch?" said Bev, trying to change the subject.

It worked; Abigail went with Bev to choose a film.

"Mike," said Greg, "Can I have a word so we can get out of your hair, and leave you to be with your kids?"

Mike reassured the kids that he would be back shortly and to start the film, then left the room with Greg and Dawn.

"Bye guys," said Dawn as she left.

"Bye Dawn," the children said in unison.

"I'm not leaving them," said Mike, once in the hallway.

"You don't need to Mike, we'll take the Judge and take things from here."

"And what about the things we've done?"

"That's not my place to say Mike. Just concentrate on your children and I'll let you know as soon as I hear something."

"Make sure they put it all on me. I dragged the rest of them into it."

"Don't worry about it Mike, just leave it with me, now where's the Judge?"

"In the dining room with Jimmy," said Mike, pointing to the dining room door.

"Greg?"

"Yes Mike."

"Thanks again, you have no idea how much this means to me."

"I actually think I do Mike, and I'm only sorry I couldn't have done more."

"What more could you have done?"

"Nothing I suppose, but I swear if I'd known they were going after your family, I would have done something, and maybe your wife."

"Greg, they're to blame for my wife and them alone."

Mike went back to his children in the sitting room.

Chapter 16

Cleaning House

Greg and Dawn went to the dining room while Mike went back to the living room.

"Jimmy," said Greg, as they entered the dining room.

"I heard what Mike said and I'm telling you now, that man's been through enough. If there's a price to be paid, I'll be paying it."

"We don't know what's going to happen yet Jimmy, it's a complicated case."

"I'm not stupid Greg, the police always want their pound of flesh and he needs to be there for them little angels."

"Trust me Jimmy, now he's reunited with them, I'm going to do everything in my power to keep it that way."

Jimmy put his hand out and Greg shook it.

"I believe you, Greg."

"Does this mean you trust me now?"

"Baby steps Greg, Baby steps."

Greg saw the Judge who was looking at him with pure venom.

"Fuck me Jimmy, what's been going on here?"

"He's just drunk."

"Drunk, he's a bit more than drunk."

"Well, he tripped over his own feet and broke his toes, he then landed on the corkscrew he was trying to open another bottle of wine with, and it went right through his knee cap."

"Anything else?"

"Oh yeah, he jumped back in pain and landed on the fire and burned his bollocks."

"The fire isn't lit?"

"We put it out in the interest of safety."

"You got an answer for everything?"

"Just the facts, Greg."

"Really?"

"I have four other witnesses."

Greg looked at Jimmy in disbelief, and his feeble attempt to explain the Judge's injuries.

"Dawn, watch the door while we get him out of here."

Jimmy and Greg carried the Judge out and put him in the boot of his Range Rover.

"Do you need me to drive this back for you Greg?" asked Jimmy.

"I've got it Jimmy but if you wouldn't mind coming back with me so I can debrief you."

"Ok, but I need to pop in and check on Whippet."

"You go with Dawn then, and I'll see you back at base later."

Greg jumped in the Range Rover and headed back to base.

"Give me a second to say goodbye, Dawn."

"Sure, I'll be in the car."

Jimmy went to the sitting room where everyone was sat quietly watching Frozen, Abigail's favourite film.

"Mike," said Jimmy, "I'm getting off."

"Can't you stay, kids haven't seen you for years."

"No, I need to check in on Whippet and Greg wants to debrief me, you just relax with your family and I'll see you tomorrow."

"Kids, your Uncle Jimmy needs to go but he's going to come back to see you tomorrow."

The children looked confused as they didn't recognise Jimmy and Mike could see it in their eyes.

"We haven't seen him for a while but he sends you a birthday and Christmas card every year, and you write him thank you letters for his presents."

"God father Jimmy?" asked George.

"That's the one, we'll see him tomorrow and he'll hopefully have two friends with him who helped us find you."

"Bye everyone, see you tomorrow, kids."

Everyone bid Jimmy farewell and Mike told him to let him know how Whippet was doing.

Jimmy joined Dawn in the car and they set off to the hospital.

"You know I was only pulling your leg earlier," said Jimmy.

"You very nearly got kicked between yours," replied Dawn.

Jimmy laughed, "So we're good then?"

"Yes Jimmy, we're good."

"Super."

"I met a friend of yours, Jimmy."

"Who's that?"

"Mrs Cannon."

"Mrs C, how did you meet her?"

"They thought a woman's approach was best to try and locate you."

"Let me guess, she told you nothing."

"I was trying to gain her confidence when some mouthy little chav stuck her nose in and scared her off."

"People are protective of each other on the estate, especially of Mrs C, she's like everyone's second grandma."

"I got that message when the woman and her friend chased my car down the street, ripping my rear wiper off."

Jimmy bellowed laughter loudly and beamed with pride.

"Did you get their names?"

"No why, are you going to get my wiper back?"

"No, they've earned themselves a Christmas present."

Dawn was not impressed and Jimmy just chuckled to himself.

The rest of their journey pretty much passed in silence.

On arriving at the hospital, Jimmy and Dawn found Boxer, Mac and Peters in the cafeteria.

They all greeted each other, Jimmy could see how eager they were to hear about Mike's reunion, so he gave them the highlights as he was eager to hear about Whippet.

"He's still in surgery, so we don't know much more than that," said Boxer.

"He should be fine Jimmy; I've seen my fair share of these kinds of wounds and it's rare that the patient doesn't pull through," said Peters.

"How did it happen?"

"The Welshman had me bang to rights," started Peters, but he was interrupted by Boxer.

"Hold on, he had us all bang to rights and would have shot us one by one if Whippet hadn't crashed into his Land Rover."

"He's right," said Mac, "It's on all of us."

"Where's the Welshman now?"

"He's in surgery too, the Land Rover rolled on him and broke most of his ribs and his spine," said Boxer.

"Couldn't have happened to a nicer bloke."

"At least he won't be doing a runner," said Boxer, trying to lighten the mood.

"Don't give up your day job, Boxer," said Peters.

"What fucking day job?" replied Jimmy.

The five of them sat discussing the events of the last few days.

Making light of their near misses and talking like friends of old.

Over an hour had gone by when they were approached by a surgeon.

"Just wanted to let you know your friend's surgery has gone well and we expect him to make a full recovery."

"Excellent work, doc," said Jimmy.

"What about the other one?" asked Peters.

"The one who shot him?"

"Yes."

"His injuries are far more extensive and he'll be in surgery for a few more hours."

"Can we see Whippet, Doc?" asked Jimmy.

"He won't be awake for a couple of hours but then, sure, you can see him."

The surgeon left them and the mood of the group was definitely on a high.

"If he's not going to be awake for a couple of hours, we may as well go back to base and get your debrief over with," said Dawn.

"Sounds like a plan," replied Jimmy.

"You may as well take Mac with you," said Peters, "I can handle the Welshman, and there's a growing collection of prisoners back at base."

"Come on then," said Dawn, and led the way to the car.

Greg got back to base at about 10pm and Nipper helped him unload the Judge.

Haigh was sat with Regan who was still spilling his guts, it seems once people start baring their soul there's no stopping them.

Regan saw them carrying the Judge in who was in too much pain to walk. He went silent with a look of embarrassment.

"Don't worry about him Regan, he's the one who's going away for the rest of his life, and for your cooperation, you'll be back with your wife before you know it," said Haigh.

"Nipper get me the med kit," said Greg.

"What's wrong with him?" asked Haigh.

"According to Jimmy, he's drunk and fell over."

Haigh bit his lip and went back to his office.

After administering some basic first aid to the Judge and giving him something for the pain, Greg joined Haigh in his office.

He sat in the chair and Haigh poured them both a whiskey.

"Here Greg, it will take the edge off."

Greg took the drink and sipped it; he wasn't one for drinking on the job normally, but he made an exception today.

"I still don't approve of their tactics but I have to hand it to them, what they did in such a short space of time is pretty good going."

"I would hire them right now."

"I bet you would, there are rules for a reason, it could have all gone wrong with disastrous results."

"What you fail to understand Greg, is that for Mike, it was the worst-case scenario already, and he had nothing else to lose."

"Fair enough."

"And the Judge seriously underestimated the lengths a father will go for his children."

"I'm pretty sure he's regretting it now."

"I doubt it, I'm sure he's sat in there trying to work a way out of all this, and he probably still looks at them like they're the bad guys."

"Bad and good, they're just a matter of opinion. I prefer rules, at least with rules it's clear."

"Not always the case Greg, if you look at the rule book closely enough, you'll find there's always one rule to countermand another."

"So, we're making it up as we go along?"

"Pretty much. Yes."

"Thanks sir, you always know what to say to improve my mood," said Greg, sarcastically.

"You're welcome Greg," replied Haigh, with a devilish smile on his face.

Haigh's smile disappeared as two men entered his office holding hand guns.

"Who the hell are you?" he said.

"Your presence is required in the interrogation area," said one of the men.

Greg and Haigh got up and headed out of the office where they were confronted by two more men who were also armed.

"We need to check you for arms."

Greg and Haigh complied and raised their arms for a body search.

The men were clearly military and Haigh had an idea who they were but he was waiting to see their commanding officer.

When they got to the interrogation area, Nipper was on his knees with his hands tied behind his back and there were four more armed men with him.

"Assume the position gentlemen," said one of the men who was clearly in charge.

"I'll do no such thing and it's Colonel to you."

"Your rank has no standing here."

"Are you not military?"

"We are, but firstly, I'm under the orders of a higher authority."

"That doesn't give you the right not to acknowledge my rank."

"No, but secondly, the moment you stopped following orders and went rogue, you forfeited any privileges that rank held."

"Rogue?"

"You were told to close your operation down and despite those orders, here you are, still operating, and beyond and contrary to your original orders you've taken prisoners."

"There were children being held captive," interrupted Greg.

"Ours is not to reason why."

"So are you here for the prisoners?" asked Haigh.

"Our orders are to shut you down and to detain all involved."

Haigh knew that was a lie, you don't send clean-up crews to take prisoners.

"Now, we seem to be a few members of your team light, where are they?"

Haigh fell silent.

"I know one of your team is in prison with one of the civilians but by my count, there are three unaccounted for."

"Civilians?" asked Greg.

"Yes Greg, seven team men, five civilians and an unknown number of prisoners, now, where are they?"

Everyone remained silent.

"No matter, you, check the logs and see where the others are?" he ordered one of his men.

"Right team B, get the prisoners in the Judge's Range Rover and once you've dropped them, go straight to the hospital and two of you locate the two people who the Colonel here authorised for treatment."

"Should we retrieve them, sir?"

"No, the other team members may be there, so just observe and report back. The other two need to go to the prison and pick them two up."

"What do you mean pick them up?" asked Haigh.

"If you're not going to answer my questions, you can hardly expect me to answer yours."

"What do you want us to do with the targets from the prison?" asked one of the soldiers.

"Bring them back here."

"Yes sir."

Four of the men collected the prisoners and put them in the back of the Judge's Range Rover, then two men got in the front and the other two jumped in one of the two Discovery's they'd arrived in.

"Sir."

"What is it?"

"It appears Greg and another operative went to the Judge's estate to look for some children in a cottage."

"And then what?"

"There's no other entry after that."

"That must be where they picked up the Judge, ok what about the others?"

"Two of them went with a civilian to someone they refer to as the Welshman's house and he and another man are the two admitted to hospital."

"Right, we'll assume them two are still at the hospital, pass it on to team B."

"Yes sir."

"Right Greg, you left here with another operative and returned with the Judge?"

Greg said nothing.

"Clearly you left her at this cottage, as soon as my colleagues return with your friends from the prison, I'll have them pick her up."

Greg knew he was looking for a response but didn't give anything away.

The commander told his other two men to start to collect all evidence and weaponry together, in readiness for their departure while he watched the three men.

When they were ten minutes out, Dawn told Mac to call ahead to give them a heads up for their arrival.

"They're not answering," said Mac.

"Try Greg's number."

"I have, he's not answering either."

"What about Haigh?"

"I'll try now," but there was no answer from Haigh either.

"Something's wrong."

"Are you sure?" asked Jimmy.

"For none of them to answer their phones, there's definitely something wrong."

"What do we do?"

"We need to approach with caution and be prepared to get out of there at a second's notice"

"You people work for the government; can't you call the army in or something?"

"It doesn't work like that Jimmy and we don't know who's there, this organisation has people in high powered jobs who will go to any lengths to protect themselves."

"As they approached the industrial estate coming up on the left, two vehicles were emerging from it"

"Turn right here," said Jimmy quickly.

"What?" asked Dawn.

"Do it now, indicate and turn right," he demanded.

Dawn followed his order and turned right opposite the industrial estate, she pulled up fifty feet down the road.

"What's going on Jimmy?" asked Mac.

"You see them two motors coming out of the industrial estate."

"Yes."

"The front one is the Judge's Range Rover."

"Are you sure?"

"Of course I'm sure, I know my cars."

They all watched out of the back window and saw the two vehicles pass by.

"The Minister said he was sending someone the pick up the witnesses," said Dawn.

"Would that explain why they didn't answer their phones?" asked Jimmy.

"No."

"So, what are you saying?"

"They could have been detained."

"Or worse." added Mac.

"What do you mean worse?"

"He's just being over dramatic," replied Dawn.

"These youngsters are so optimistic."

"What do you mean Mac?"

"If they've sent the cleaners in, they could kill them."

"But aren't you on the same team?"

"You would think that's the case but these men are trained to follow orders without question, and if they're told you've gone rogue, they won't listen to a word you have to say, they'll just follow their orders."

"Don't listen to him Jimmy, it's just stories they tell new recruits to scare them, but it is possible they've been detained."

Jimmy looked at Mac and could see it was no scare tactic.

"How many men are we looking at?"

"Two teams so probably eight but that's my best guess."

"So, if at least two have left we're looking at six."

"No, at least four have left."

"How do you know; it only takes two drivers?"

"They do everything in pairs, there will be two in each vehicle, that was your mistake with Whippet, he was on his own."

"Ok well if there's only four left, with Greg and the others, we out number them"

"These men are trained killers, Jimmy."

"What are you, a fairy princess?"

"They'll all be armed and even if the others are alive, they'll be handcuffed."

"Ok then we have to hit them hard and fast."

"All the doors are alarmed and have cameras with a roaming camera on the corner of the building, they'd know we were there before we got a foot in the building."

"I bet you're no fun at parties Mac, these are your friends in there."

"Listen, unless you can parachute on to the roof, you're not getting into that building without being noticed, even then, they'd probably hear you hit the roof."

"Ok I get your point, actually you've just given me an idea."

"What?"

"How about we draw them out?"

"Again, they'll smell a trap and come out shooting."

"Depends on the bait, they shouldn't recognise me so I could play the lost delivery driver."

"They'd just tell you to fuck off and it wouldn't get them out of the building."

Jimmy was racking his brain when he saw something on the street that gave him a wicked smile across his face.

"Right I've got it, if you two circle the next warehouse, you should be able to get right behind the bins near the roller shutter, and when I draw them out you can get in and take care of business."

"You expect us to storm the warehouse?" asked Dawn.

"If I'm understanding Mac right, these boys aren't going to leave the job half finished, so eventually they will find us all."

"He's right," said Mac.

"Ok but how are you going to get them out?"

"A little trick I saw a friend use once, or maybe twice."

They drove onto the industrial estate, making sure to keep out of view of the warehouse and parked up at a safe distance.

Mac and Dawn got their equipment from the boot of the car and Mac offered Jimmy a gun.

"Better not, in-case they search me."

"Fair enough, but they won't hesitate to shoot you if they feel threatened Jimmy."

"Understood."

Mac and Dawn headed off to get in position and text Jimmy when they were set.

Jimmy started to walk down the deserted street slowly and, in an erratic manner, carrying a couple of beer bottles he'd picked up from where they were parked.

As he got in view of the warehouse, he started singing at the top of his voice and taking pauses like he was trying to remember the words.

He stopped near a wall bordering the warehouse and started shouting profanities at the building.

"Fuck you, go to hell you bastards, I fucking hate you," he sang at the top of his lungs over and over but he didn't seem to get any reaction.

"Sir, you need to see this," said the soldier that was going through the daily logs.

The commander looked at the monitor.

"Does he resemble any of Haigh's team?"

"No sir, I checked."

"Just a drunk then. He'll probably piss against the wall and piss off."

"He's making quite a bit of racket, sir."

"He'll run out of steam soon."

Jimmy upped his game and launched one of his bottles at the roller shutter door.

It smashed and Jimmy raised his hands and cheered in victory.

"I'll get the boys to run him off," said the Commander.

He shouted the boys over who were packing the intel up.

"Go get rid of that piss head, but don't be pointing your guns at his head, we don't need him phoning the police."

"Yes sir."

"Be careful, drunks are unpredictable and you never know who else is lurking around."

"Yes sir," and the soldiers left for the roller shutter.

"You monitor them, I'm going to keep an eye on Haigh and the others."

The soldier focused the camera on Jimmy, Mac pointed it out to Dawn that it had moved in his direction.

"Be ready to move Dawn"

"I don't like this plan; Jimmy will get himself shot and we'll be fighting on two fronts."

Just then the roller shutter opened and two men emerged.

"Agreed, we better take these two down and secure them first."

The two soldiers cautiously headed towards Jimmy.

"Oi," Shouted one of them, "Fuck off before we call the police and get you arrested."

"Fuck you," said Jimmy, who was sat on the wall pretending to drink from the empty bottle.

"Come on son, move on."

"You stole my job, you bastard," Jimmy staggered to his feet, "I've got kids to feed."

"Mate, I've no idea what you're talking about, you need to go home and sleep it off."

Jimmy could see Mac and Dawn advancing on the men, he raised his arm and smashed the bottle on the ground to draw their gaze, then started ranting about how he was sacked with no notice.

The soldiers were losing their patience with him and were about to grab him to bag and gag him until they had finished and gone.

"Don't fucking move," said Mac and the two men froze.

"Hands behind your backs now," he added.

As they complied, Dawn cuffed one of them but as she moved in on the other, he turned on her and went for his gun.

Jimmy reacted with the speed of lightning and punched him hard in the back of the head.

The soldier stumbled and dropped his weapon that Dawn kicked away.

Jimmy pinned the soldier to the floor while Dawn cuffed him.

"If you want to survive this night, I'd behave myself if I was you, son," said Jimmy picking him up.

"They'll know we're here now," said Mac.

"Here," said Jimmy, passing his prisoner to Dawn as he removed both their bullet proof vests, "They're not going to shoot their own men, use them to get close."

"That might not be true, Jimmy."

"Well, if they misbehave, shoot the two with guns first, come on."

Jimmy walked off towards the roller shutter, closely followed by an uneasy Mac and Dawn using the soldiers as human shields.

As he walked through the opening, he was greeted by the barrels of two handguns.

"Don't move," said the Commander.

"I have to," replied Jimmy.

"I said, don't move."

"I heard what you said but like I said I have to move, so we can bring your friends in."

Mac and Dawn entered tucked behind the two soldiers.

Jimmy drew everybody's attention when he pressed the button to close the roller shutter.

"I said stop or I will kill you."

"I don't think so pal, they tell me you're a professional which means you must be a clever fella."

"What the fuck are you on about?"

"Well, a clever fella would see a lost cause, but being a professional, you need to turn that lost cause to your advantage, and you do that by baring your chest, shout the loudest and put your opposition on the back foot."

"Do you have a point?"

"Not really, so if you want to shoot do it, because the second you pull that trigger, you and your three pals here are all dead because my friends are professionals too."

The commander looked around and could see while Jimmy had been talking that Mac and Dawn had flanked him.

"As you can see, you're bang to rights so do the smart thing, drop your weapons and live to fight another day."

"I can't do that."

"Drop your weapon son and you have my word that none of you will be harmed," said Haigh.

"We're all on the same side but your being used to hide another man's secrets, not because we've gone rogue."

The Commander lowered his weapon and told his subordinate to do the same.

Jimmy collected their weapons and took out his knife to cut Haigh, Greg and Nipper free.

"I said you were a clever boy."

"And who are you?" asked the Commander.

"I'm the international man of mystery," laughed Jimmy.

Greg looked at him and shook his head, "You're a damn fool with more lives than a cat."

"It's been said before Greg, all balls and no brains."

They secured the Commander and his team with several bounds and left Mac and Dawn to keep their eyes on them, as these men were well-trained in escaping from captivity.

"Now does someone want to tell us what the fuck is going on?" asked Jimmy.

"Come to my office," said Haigh and they were joined by Greg.

After the door was closed Haigh told Jimmy everything about the minister and the cleaning crew.

"So, these boys who've taken the judge, Regan and Devon are going to the hospital next and then the prison."

"Yes, but he clearly said the pair at the hospital were only supposed to observe and report and the pair going to the prison were to bring Dug and Dave back here."

"How are they going to get them out of the prison."

"I don't know, you'd have to ask them but there's no guarantee he'll tell you."

"He'll fucking tell me," said Jimmy heading for the door.

"Jimmy," said Greg, "You can't treat these men like you did the others; it wouldn't work and I wouldn't let you."

Jimmy looked from Greg to Haigh and could clearly see they were in agreement on this issue.

"They're just soldiers following orders, believe it or not, these are the good guys."

"Ok boys, I can be tactful."

Haigh and Greg didn't look convinced as Jimmy left the room and they quickly followed him.

Jimmy knelt at the side of the Commander and turned him off his belly on to his side.

"Listen pal, no one here has any animosity for you and your team, but I hear you are sending two men to the hospital and two to the prison."

Jimmy removed the gag and continued.

"We know that you're getting Dave and Dug out of the prison and they're bringing them back here, I just have a couple of points I need to clear up with you."

"What are they?"

"Firstly, we don't want anyone else getting hurt so are your men going to hurt them before they bring them back?"

"No."

"That's good, now how are they getting them out of prison?"

The commander went silent.

"I understand you might not want to say but the only reason I ask is because if you try and break Dave out, he won't go willingly."

"No break out, they're being released above board with the correct paperwork from the justice minister's office."

Haigh's ears pricked up from that little nugget of information.

"When they get back, I'm going to untie you so you can get them to give up their weapons and hand themselves over peacefully."

"They'll call before returning and I'll have to answer it."

"That's fine, now the boys at the hospital, what's their role?"

"To observe and wait for backup."

"And they won't move on my friends before backup gets there?"

"No."

"Everything seems to be going in the right direction," Jimmy said, looking at Greg.

"What have you done with the prisoners?" asked Greg.

"I can't discuss that."

"That means you've disposed of them." said Haigh.

"What, you mean they've made them disappear?" asked Jimmy.

"No, you can't make someone as important as the Judge disappear" replied Haigh.

"The body would need to be recovered in a way that can explain his injuries."

"Fire," said Jimmy.

"You're a bit clever yourself lad, yes they'll probably burn them all in the Range Rover together."

"Should we stop it?" asked Greg.

"It's too late, it's already happened," said the Commander.

"Fuck 'em, couldn't have happened to a nicer bunch of arseholes," said Jimmy.

Jimmy put the gag back on the Commander. "Sorry you're uncomfortable, boys, but we just can't trust you."

Haigh, Greg and Jimmy all returned to the office.

"We're going to have to let these psychopaths loose at some point, so how do we stop them coming after us again?" asked Jimmy.

"We need to get the Minister to call them off," replied Haigh.

"And how do we get him to do that?"

"With the same information the Judge used to blackmail him with."

"What's that?"

But Haigh tapped his finger against his nose.

"I need to have a word with Nipper, back in a minute."

"Is it always like this Greg?" asked Jimmy after Haigh left.

"It can be pretty hectic but I've never had a case as crazy as this."

"Is that our fault?" Jimmy said with a smile on his face.

"You and your friends are certainly all a piece of work."

"They're special boys, they just didn't get the right breaks in life."

"Whippet clearly got his name for being fast in cars, which I'm led to believe is a terrifying experience but what about Boxer, was he a professional fighter?"

"He wishes," Jimmy laughed, "No, the first time we saw him fight, he took a Boxer's stance and tried throwing jabs."

Haigh came back in and he looked like he was preparing to leave.

"Where you going?" asked Greg.

"I'm going to put a stop to this."

"Do you need some backup?"

"I'll come with you if you want," said Jimmy.

"No thanks boys, you two are needed here and I can take care of this myself."

"Are you positive?" said Jimmy.

"Jimmy I'd love to take you out on a mission one day but I need you here when Dave gets here, so I have a team left to return to."

Jimmy felt a certain satisfaction from that statement, and he was desperate to see his friend as he hadn't seen him since he'd been sent down.

Nipper came in and handed Haigh a piece of paper, then left just as quickly.

"Excellent, I should only be about two hours unless I have to go to London but I'll let you know."

"Ok sir."

Haigh sped out of the office with the speed and energy of a young man.

Greg called Peters and filled him and Boxer in on the situation and Jimmy did the same with Mike.

Afterwards, they made everyone coffees and teas and waited for the arrival of Dug and Dave.

Chapter 17
Justice

Dug who was a light sleeper, heard the footsteps long before they reached his cell.

He was expecting to be pulled out at any time but he'd had no notification from Haigh.

The footsteps stopped at his door and the key unlocked it.

Dug sat up and was confronted by two prison officers.

"Get your stuff together," one of them said.

"Where am I going?"

"Being transferred out, I think."

Maybe the text hadn't arrived from Haigh, he thought.

He grabbed his things that were already packed to go and he left his cell following the officers, but they made a wrong turn.

"This isn't the way?"

"You're not the only one being transferred."

Dug went along but kept on his guard. They stopped at Dave's cell and opened the door.

"Get up and grab your stuff."

"What's going on?" asked Dave.

"You're being transferred."

"To where?"

"Don't know, I didn't get told, I've just been told to collect you both and bring you up to be processed out."

Dave didn't have much but he got his stuff together and left his cell where he noticed Dug.

The two men didn't speak but Dave assumed it was something to do with Mike and Haigh.

They were led to the office block where they had to sign some paperwork and were given their outside property back.

They changed into their own clothes and were out of ear shot of the officers long enough for Dave to ask a few questions of Dug.

"Is this your doing?"

"I've been expecting to be pulled out but I haven't received confirmation yet."

"How do we know it's legitimate?"

"My team mates should be here to collect us."

The officer came over and hurried them along and once they were dressed, they were led to a room where they could hear a raised voice.

The prison officer knocked on the door which got a sharp response from within.

"COME IN," the voice said.

As the door opened Dave and Dug could see an angry governor and two other men that neither of them had ever seen before.

"I knew something was going on," said the Governor.

"What do you mean?" asked Dave.

"All the cloak and dagger, these two turning up with an official order to release you into their custody."

"Governor, the paperwork is in order and we need to leave now," said one of the two men stood in the room.

"Well, I don't like it, there's no one I can contact at this hour."

"It doesn't matter, you have your orders and so do we, so hand them over and you can make all the calls you want tomorrow."

"I don't appreciate undercover operations going on in my prison without being told, I assume that's what you two are, undercover officers."

"Sorry governor, I can't say anything," said Dave, feeling a little thrilled by the whole drama.

The governor looked between the four men and knew that he had to comply with the order to release them.

"Get out of my prison and I promise, I'll be on to your superiors first thing in the morning."

Dave and Dug followed the two men out of the room and were escorted by the prison officers out to the carpark.

"Your friends I assume," Dave whispered to Dug.

"No," came the quick short response.

This put Dave on edge, and he could see that Dug wasn't comfortable either.

Once all four men were in the Land Rover, Dug and Dave sat in the back where Dug questioned the men.

"Who are you?" he asked.

"Haigh sent us to pick you up."

"Why you?"

"Everyone else is busy sorting this mess out."

"I've had no notification; I want to speak to Haigh now."

"Listen pal, I don't answer to you, we've been ordered to pick you up and take you back to base and that's what's happening."

Dave and Dug looked at each other. Dave clenched his fist but Dug shook his head.

"Ok," said Dug, "Straight back to base, no diversions."

The Land Rover set off for the base with Dug and Dave on high alert and ready for action.

They made good time getting back to base with the roads being quiet at that time of night.

The driver told the passenger to announce their arrival when they were about five minutes out.

"They're not answering," he replied after trying.

Both the driver and the passenger readied their weapons.

"Is there a problem?" asked Dug.

"Just a precaution," said the driver.

"Give us a weapon then, we can help."

"No need, you just sit back, we can handle any problems."

The Land Rover turned into the industrial estate and slowly made its way to the warehouse at the end.

Dave saw Dug covertly unbuckle his belt and slowly remove it from his trousers.

He took it as a sign that a fight was imminent but he was unclear whether it was their escort or a third party that was the target.

They pulled up to the door of the warehouse and the roller shutter started to open.

Dug took his arm out of his seat belt and put his thumb on the button ready to release it and Dave copied him.

All four men were looking in the warehouse but nobody was visible.

The driver edged the Land Rover forward and as it passed the threshold Greg, Mac and Dawn appeared at both sides of the vehicle, pointing their weapons.

"LET ME SEE YOUR HANDS," Greg shouted.

The driver put the Land Rover into reverse and looked in his rear mirror but Jimmy had pulled up right behind them.

The passenger raised his weapon and Dug unplugged his seat belt quickly followed by Dave.

Dug lunged forward and threw his waist belt around the drivers neck pulling him tight back into his seat.

Dave launched himself towards the passenger and grabbed his right hand which was holding the gun and pressed the barrel into the side of the drivers head.

"Go on," Dave said, "Pull that trigger and your mate gets a brain full of bullets."

"Give it up boys, there's no way out of this but to hand your guns over," said Dug.

After a couple of second thoughts, the passenger released his grip on his weapon and Dave took it from him.

The driver passed his weapon back which Dave also retrieved.

"Good move boys, turn the engine off and unlock the doors," ordered Dug.

The driver complied and Dug released the belt from around his neck.

Greg and Mac opened the doors and placed both men in handcuffs, then pulled them from the vehicle and laid them down in front of it.

Dug and Dave joined them as Greg and Mac searched the men for weapons.

"These are my friends" said Dug to Dave.

"And there's mine," replied Dave as Jimmy walked into the warehouse.

The two friends embraced each other with an affection that only the closest of friends could appreciate.

"It's good to see you, my friend," said Jimmy.

"Don't start getting soppy on me," said Dave, trying to hide his own joy.

"When you two lovers are quite finished, can you pull these motors in so we can close the roller shutter?" asked Greg.

Greg, Mac, Dug and Dawn escorted the new prisoners to join their comrades, while Dave and Jimmy brought the vehicles in and closed the roller shutter.

When Dave and Jimmy joined the others, Greg explained everything that had happened and told them how they were now waiting on Haigh to contact them.

Haigh arrived at the hotel where he'd met Minister Gordon Hayes earlier that day. Nipper had told him that Hayes had a room booked there.

He passed reception and entered the lift to go to the third floor.

Once there he made his way to room 324 and knocked solidly on the door, and after half a minute he knocked again.

A light came on and Haigh new he'd got the Minister's attention.

When he saw the door peep hole flicker, he knew Hayes was standing there trying to figure out what to do.

"Open up, Hayes," he demanded.

"What do you want?" came the reply.

"To talk in private, and not in the hallway."

Hayes was uneasy with this unannounced visit, especially as he'd sent the cleaners in to shut Haigh down.

"Hayes, either you can open this door, or I can, all I want is to sort this mess out."

The door opened and Hayes tried to be authoritative.

"What do you mean by this, Haigh?"

"Let's talk inside," replied Haigh as he brushed his way passed Hayes.

Hayes closed the door and followed Haigh in.

"What do you think you're doing barging in my room at this hour."

"Are we alone?"

"What do you mean?"

"I half expected you to have company, a young lady or maybe a young boy?"

"I'm not into that sort of thing, yes we are alone."

"Ok, I'm just trying to understand why you would be in league with such horrible bastards."

"I'm not in league with anyone, what are you talking about?"

"I'm talking about you and Robyn Spruit. So what did they have on you if you don't share their fondness for children?"

"I don't know what you're talking about Haigh, you're completely off base with your accusations."

"Am I, what about your son?"

"What about my son?"

"Five years ago, two girls and a boy, all laid rape charges against him at his university dorm rooms."

Hayes slunk on the chair.

"It seems he drugged them and raped them but no investigation took place and the victims all dropped their complaints," continued Haigh.

"You seem to know enough, what do you want?"

"A little justice, but first you need to make a phone call and call off the cleaning crew."

"Isn't it too late for that, my understanding is that the Judge has already been disposed of."

"And two others, and in fairness, they got what they deserved, but my team haven't done anything wrong, so you need to put an end to it right now."

"Of course."

Hayes picked up his phone and called a number and Haigh listened carefully to make sure he wasn't passing any secret messages over.

"You made a serious error in judgement sending that team after us," said Haigh, after Hayes hung up.

"You weren't supposed to take prisoners or talk to any of them. It was information gathering only."

"And now we know why, you were trying to gather dirt on your friends while keeping your own involvement a secret."

"You don't understand, I've always been a law-abiding person and believe in the system, but I couldn't see my son go to prison, it would have ruined him."

"Your son is rotten to the core and covering up what he did isn't helping him, it's enabling him to carry on without fear of consequence."

"I've put too much work into him to just give up on him."

"He's an adult now and he must accept the consequences of his actions, by protecting him you've compromised yourself and other people and children have suffered for it."

"What sort of father would I be if I didn't try to protect my son?"

"Your son isn't an innocent, and he isn't a child either, but Mike Feather's children are, and now Mike and his friends are looking at long jail time for what they did."

"I wasn't involved in the kidnapping of any kids; I was trying to get information on them to stop it."

"You were trying to get information on them to get your own neck out of the noose."

Hayes hung his head, "I'm sorry about what happened to Mike and his family, and if I could have stopped it, I would have, but it would have meant prison for my son and an end to my career."

"Now we get to it, it's all about your job, not your son, to hell with Mike's wife losing her life and his kids losing their innocence."

"I didn't mean it like that, I'm just saying I've worked hard to get where I am, and it would all be for nothing if my son's actions came to light."

"Not if you had done the right thing from the start and made him face justice."

"I can't change what has happened, I wasn't thinking clearly and now it's too late."

"It's never too late to make amends."

"What do you mean?"

"I'm under no obligation to pass anything on to your or my superiors, so as long as things are set right, nobody need know about your involvement."

"How can I set things right?"

"Firstly, Mike and his friends walk away free and clear with compensation."

"Ok."

"Secondly, anyone else left in the cooperative loses their positions with no chance of reinstatement."

"That may be difficult without explanation and what if they won't go quietly?"

"Better they go quietly than go to jail or end up like the Judge and Regan."

"What else?"

"The Welshman goes to prison for the rest of his life."

"Done, is that it?"

"No, there is one more thing, your son."

"What about my son?"

"There are some privately run prisons around the world that are very discreet."

"You can't be serious."

"Do I not look serious. Your son is a rapist and needs to be punished for his crimes, I will give you the details of a contact I have and your son will spend no less than two years for each victim."

"Six years."

"Yes, six years, I think that's more than fair considering the alternative."

"How will I explain his absence?"

"That's your problem but these terms are non-negotiable."

"Is that everything?"

"Yes, except for a warning."

"A warning?"

"Yes, a warning. The men you just tried to kill are all highly trained individuals, and don't take kindly to people trying to kill them."

"It was a mistake, I panicked," said Hayes, realising the gravity of what he had almost brought down on himself.

"It was a mistake but rest assured if that mistake repeats itself, you're going to have eight very pissed off professionals gunning for you."

"There'll be no more mistakes."

"Good, well we have a long night ahead of us to close this case down, and then you have some recommendation letters to write for my men."

Haigh called Greg to fill him in on the situation, then got to work with Hayes to figure out the logistics of bringing the case to an end.

Greg had just got off the phone with Haigh when the commanders phone began to ring.

Greg cut the Commander free and gave him the phone.

The Commander coded in and received a message ordering him to abort his mission and return to base.

"It seems we have been ordered to stand down," he said.

"You need to call your boys at the hospital," said Greg.

"And you need to release my men," replied the Commander as he made the call to his men at the hospital.

"Untie them," ordered Greg.

"Hang on a minute, weren't these men sent here to kill us, and now you want to cut them loose?" asked Dave.

"It was just a misunderstanding Dave and it's been sorted now."

"And you trust them?"

"Yes, what would you have me do?"

"Leave them tied up and send the cops here in a couple of days to release them."

Jimmy laughed, "Don't worry Dave, Greg knows what he's doing."

The Commander and his men didn't seem too amused, but Dug and Mac were trying to conceal their smirks as they released the soldiers.

"Commander, ask your men to wait in their vehicles and I'll bring their weapons over shortly."

The soldiers did as they were ordered and Greg got a bag for all their weapons.

"Are you really going to give them their weapons back?" asked Dave.

"They're actually on our side, Dave."

"Well, that's one way to go," he said, as Greg walked down to the soldiers.

"Here's your weapons minus your ammunition, just in-case someone changes their mind."

Greg opened the shutter and the soldiers were gone as quickly as they came.

"Took their bullets, not as dumb as you look, after all."

Greg brushed the comment off and gathered everyone together, to brief them on Haigh's plan.

"What about my original sentence?" asked Dave.

"As I understand it, your sentence has been commuted and your time served is all the punishment you are going to get."

"So, I can go home?"

"As far as I know, yes."

"That's fucking great," said Jimmy, "Do you want to call Julie and let her know Dave?"

"No, she'll be asleep and we need to check on your man Whippet first. Then we'll all go home together."

Greg and his team felt great satisfaction at the way things had turned out and shared in Dave and Jimmy's joy.

"If any of you boys, or girl, find yourselves up our way, feel free to pop in for a beer," said Jimmy.

"Your always welcome at our homes," added Dave.

"Any chance you could retrieve my back wiper?" asked Dawn, everybody laughed except Dave and Dug.

"Wiper?" asked Dave.

"She was trying to question Mrs C and two local lasses chased her off, and pulled her back wiper off," replied Jimmy.

Everyone was now laughing as the debate started as to who the wiper swiper was.

After about another twenty minutes, Greg's phone started to ring.

"It's Peters from the hospital," he said, "What's up, Jason?"

"Them two boys who were watching us are leaving, they went outside and they're now in a Land Rover and it's driving off."

"Yes pal, they've been recalled."

"Thanks for the heads up."

"Sorry pal, there is some good news you can pass on to Boxer and Whippet."

"No," interrupted Dave "Don't tell them, we'll go over and surprise them."

"What is it?" asked Peters.

"Doesn't matter, Jimmy is on his way back to the hospital and he'll tell them."

"Ok, I better get back upstairs and check on them."

Greg hung the phone up, Jimmy and Dave sprung to their feet to set off to the hospital.

"Shall we send Peters back, we can take care of Whippet now?" asked Jimmy.

"He needs to stay there for the Welshman," replied Greg.

"Ok, for Mike, I just want to thank you all again for all your help."

"No need Jimmy, it's genuinely our pleasure."

In the thirty-minute journey to the hospital, Jimmy filled Dave in on everything that had happened and Dave listened quietly.

His mind was racing to take it all in, with his mind often wondering to thoughts of his own wife and child.

He was also enjoying spending time with his best friend, who he hadn't seen since he went inside.

The police keep records of visitors and known associates, so Jimmy kept his distance knowing he would see his friend soon enough.

Neither of them thought it would be this soon, or under these circumstances.

"We need to pop and see Mike before we set off, I owe him an apology," said Dave, as they parked up at the hospital.

"Not a problem Dave, but I don't think Mike wants or will accept any apology from you, after what you risked for him."

"I didn't do that for him, I did that for the kids but I should have known my friend better, I've clearly spent too much time around prisoners."

"No more though pal, time to be with family and friends."

"Right," said Dave, as they shook hands.

They exited the car and entered the hospital, they headed for the post op ward where Whippet was being looked after.

They approached the nurses station on the ward.

"Darren Mathews," Jimmy said to the nurses, who had not paid them any attention for the few minutes they had been stood there.

"He's in room five, but he has two visitors with him already," replied a nurse, who looked put out by Jimmy's impatience.

"They're not visitors, they're bodyguards and we're back up," added Jimmy.

"Is he in danger?" asked the nurse more concerned for her own safety.

"Not now," answered Dave as they walked past her with smirks on their faces.

"Just like old times," said Jimmy, as they got out of earshot of the nurse.

As they got nearer to room five, they saw two police officers sat either side of the door to room 6 opposite room five.

They gave the officers a nod as they entered room five and then shut the door behind themselves.

Boxer gave Jimmy a nod as he entered and jumped out of his chair when he saw Dave walk in behind him.

He rushed over with hand extended to greet Dave.

Boxer had only been with the crew for several months before Dave got sent down, whereas Whippet had joined afterwards.

Dave respected that they were friends and trusted by Jimmy which was enough to warrant his friendship and trust.

What they had both risked for Mike, just solidified Dave's appreciation toward them.

Peters stood up to greet the two men.

"What's with them two out there?" asked Jimmy.

"They've been sent to watch the Welshman; they're taking charge of him now," answered Peters.

"Can't you send them for a coffee, I'd like to pay that bastard a visit?" said Dave.

"I'm sorry boys, it's out of my hands and I'm happy to be rid of him, to tell you the truth."

"So, what is going to happen to him now?" asked Jimmy.

"Haigh has made it clear he's to go to prison for the rest of his life."

"Or until some solicitor helps him walk free?"

"You don't have to worry about that, Jimmy."

"Why?"

"That man will never walk again thanks to young Whippet there."

"What do you mean?"

"I'm saying that not only will he be going to prison for shooting Whippet, but when Whippet sent his Land Rover rolling down the hill, he broke many bones in the Welshman's body including crushing three vertebrae. He'll never walk anywhere ever again."

"Good lad, Whippet"

"My sentiment exactly, I'd be dead if it wasn't for him."

"As I understand it that wasn't the only time your life was in danger."

"What do you mean?"

"Whippets driving."

All four men laughed.

"You're not wrong, that boy is crazy good behind the wheel of a car."

"It's been a constant debate which he's more, crazy or good," said Boxer.

"So Dave tell me, how did you get out of prison?"

Dave and Jimmy filled Boxer and Peters in on their nights twists and turns.

The time passed quickly and the sun was fully in view before Whippet woke up.

"How you feeling, Whippet?" asked Jimmy.

"Hungry," he replied.

"Good man, Boxer you fancy doing a sandwich run?"

"Sure, text me a list."

"I'll come with you Boxer; I'm going to get off," said Peters.

"You're more than welcome to stay and have some breakfast," said Jimmy.

"Thanks, but I only wanted to be here when he woke to say thank you, Whippet you saved my life and I'll never forget it, Thanks."

After shaking Whippet's hand, Peters started to call Greg for a lift and walked out of the hospital with Boxer.

"As for you Boxer, you've made a friend for life."

"Same here Peters, when all this shit has settled, I'm sure Jimmy will be organising some kind of gathering, you and your team will all be welcome and we can share some beers."

"I look forward to it."

Boxer left to get the sandwiches and Peters sat on a bench waiting for his lift.

It was nearly ten o'clock by time Peters got back to base and Haigh had got back just before him.

Haigh briefed everyone on the outcome of his meeting with Hayes.

Using the newspaper contact from the cooperative, they arranged for a number of press releases.

Firstly, that early reports from Maple Tree House were wrong, and only Tara died in the tragic fire as the children were with their grandparents.

Secondly, the Judge, Regan and Devon died in a tragic road traffic accident after the three men visited a local meeting place popular with gay men.

And Thirdly, that Thomas Evans, a well-known paedophile and rapist, was arrested and charged with robbery, kidnapping and attempted murder of a tourist.

"Is suggesting the Judge was gay a good move?" asked Greg.

"We're using their own tactic against them; the wife and children will be embarrassed and therefore less likely to want a public enquiry."

"Sounds good, what about Mike's escape?"

"We believe keeping quiet about Mike and his friends is the best way forward but officially, he was moved for his own safety and all his charges have been dropped."

"Have you told him?"

"No, I thought you might like that pleasure."

"I would, thank you."

"You can tell him that him and his friends will also be receiving some compensation for their trouble."

"They may be insulted by that."

"Maybe, but they're getting it regardless."

"What do we get?" asked Peters.

"You all get a letter of commendation."

"How fucking generous."

"What would you like Peters?"

"Something involving sand and a colourful drink would be nice."

Haigh laughed, "I'll send you to the builders yard with a can of Iron Bru."

"Sounds about right."

"Right, enough of this, let's finish packing up and get out of here."

After they finished, it was about one in the afternoon and Greg went to one of the offices to call Mike in private.

Chapter 18

Reparation

Boxer returned with the sandwiches and as they all finished them the nurse came in to check on Whippet.

"When can I go home?" Whippet asked.

"The doctor will be along shortly; you're best asking him," replied the nurse, before leaving the room.

It was another hour before the doctor arrived and he'd barely had chance to check Whippets chart before he was asked the same question.

"You do realise how serious your injuries were."

"Yeah, but you've stitched me up, and I feel fine."

"Whippet you need to let the doctor do his job," said Jimmy.

"I would prefer you stay for observation; you can't be left on your own."

"I can't stay in here, I'm already crawling up the walls and I won't be on my own, Boxer will keep an eye on me."

"I can keep an eye on him doc but only if you say it's ok."

"I'll just sit on the couch for two week playing Forza."

"It's not ideal but they are trying to get patients home quicker, can you promise to keep an eye on him 24 hours a day for at least a week."

"We'll take it in turns, doc," said Jimmy.

"I'll approve your discharge but you'll have to wait for your medicine, and at the first sign of trouble, you call 999 for an ambulance."

"Definitely will, doc."

The doctor left and it seemed to take ages for the medicine to arrive.

"There's antibiotics and pain killers, so just take the prescribed amount and you should be fine," said the nurse.

Boxer went to get the Range Rover as Jimmy and Dave followed Whippet down who was being pushed in a wheel chair by a porter.

As they exited the front door, Boxer was already waiting for them.

"What the fuck did you do to Mick's Range Rover?"

Whippet started to chuckle, "Don't make me laugh, it hurts," he said.

Dave and Jimmy couldn't help but smile and even Boxer was holding back as he opened the back door.

Jimmy picked Whippet up like a child in the seated position and placed him gently on the back seat, then he took the car key from Boxer.

"Let's try and get home in one piece," he said.

Boxer wouldn't have been able to wipe the smile of his face with a brilo pad as he got in the back to fasten Whippet's seatbelt.

"Right, just one stop before we set off home, we're going to pop and see Mike, he's been pestering me all morning to get an update."

Everyone sounded their approval and Jimmy set off and drove like he was driving a hearse.

"Come on Jimmy, don't worry about me, I'm fine."

"Do you want me to turn around and take you back to hospital."

Whippet fell silent and Jimmy continued to Mike's parent-in-laws.

Due to his caution it took just over an hour to get there and Mike rushed out to greet them.

When he saw Dave walk around the back of the Range Rover, he made a bee line for him and flung his arms around him.

"Come on Mike, you'll be making the rest jealous," Dave said.

"How are you out, is it a day pass or something?"

"Nope, I'm out for good."

Mike looked overjoyed to see everyone, "Where's Whippet?"

"In the back, but don't be hugging him, or you might kill him."

Mike opened Whippets door and shook his hand, "Thank you, I can never repay what you've done for me."

"Don't worry about it, it's been a crazy adventure but someone does owe me a pair of trainers," Whippet replied, looking at Jimmy.

"As long as you do as you're told and rest, you can have whatever pair of trainers you want," said Jimmy.

"Come inside, Bev has prepared some sandwiches."

Mike led the men into the kitchen where Malcolm and Bev where preparing food and drinks for their guests.

Rose was sat at the table with George and Abigail who were eating sandwiches cut into the shape of teddy bears.

"George, Abigail these are daddies best friends and they helped to bring you home."

The children gave a little wave and continued with their meals.

"Abigail, this is my friend Whippet, he's very poorly and has just come out of hospital to see you, so can he sit here next to you to rest."

Abigail looked at her aunty Rose who smiled showing her it was ok, then she nodded her head and Mike helped Whippet into the chair.

"Cool," said Whippet, then turned to Bev, "Can I have teddy bears too please?"

"Of course you can," she replied.

"Don't be expecting me to be making you teddy bear sandwiches when we get home," said Boxer.

"It's ok, I'm going to live off Mrs Cs buns."

The room relaxed as the banter continued but Mike got a call and went to the hallway to answer it.

"Hi Mike, it's Greg."

"Hi Greg, what's up?"

"Nothing is up, I'm just checking in with you and updating you with what's been going on, but I will need to see all of you to brief you all about how to proceed from here on."

"The boys have just arrived so everyone is here if you want to come, you can tell us all together then."

"Thanks, but we need to close up shop here and make sure the wheels we've set in motion are on track."

"What wheels are they?"

"You're going to hear a few things in the media over the next couple of weeks and I must impress on you how important it is for all of you not to talk to anyone about anything."

"You don't need to worry; my friends know how to keep quiet."

"It's not them I'm concerned about."

"I'll talk to the in-laws."

"Good, as for you and your friends, you're all completely in the clear and free to go about your business."

"What about the fire and the bodies at my home?"

"The official story is that early reports were exaggerated and only your wife died in what was a tragic accident, your kids were with relatives."

"And the other bodies?"

"Officially, there were no other bodies."

Greg gave Mike a run-down of the headlines he may see over the next few weeks, as Mike listened with keen attention.

"There is one more thing Mike and I don't want you to take this the wrong way"

"What is it?"

"Haigh has organised compensation for you all and you will be being contacted about it at some point."

"Thanks, but speaking for myself, I don't want it."

"I completely understand Mike but hear me out, I know that there's no compensating for the loss of your wife and children's mother, but it's coming to you regardless, and even if you don't want it you can put it in a savings account for the kids."

"Ok Greg, I'll think about it, there is one thing you may be able to do for me."

"What is it?"

"I told my kids about the fire and that their mother passed away this morning, and all they want to do is go home, I suppose to be in familiar settings and be close to their mum."

"That's understandable."

"Can you get the house released so we can return and start repairs?"

"I'll get straight on with it, tell me, how did the kids take the news?"

"They cried for a little bit and asked many awkward questions but they've settled down now, and I think they're just processing it in their own way."

"Kids are extremely resilient Mike and I'm sure there will be good days and bad."

"Well, I'll just take it one day at a time and deal with the problems as they arise."

"Ok Mike, I'll get off and see what I can do about your house."

"Thanks again, Greg."

"My pleasure Mike, and I'll see you soon."

Mike went back in the kitchen where conversation was in full flow, even the kids were talking to Whippet who was playing, round and round the garden with his teddy bear sandwich on Rose's hand.

He gathered all the other adults to one side of the room to explain what Greg had just informed him, and the need for absolute secrecy.

To which everyone agreed.

"Are you sure taking them back to Maple Tree is a good move Mike?" asked Bev.

"I'm not sure of anything, but they keep asking to go home and it's where they will feel closest to Tara."

"Let me know when you get the go-ahead Mike, and I'll bring my builders down and we'll have that place right in no time at all."

"Thanks Jimmy but you've already done enough."

"Nonsense, I intend on spending a bit more time with my godchildren so you'll be seeing a lot more of me from now on."

"That goes for me too Mike," added Dave.

Mike knew once they'd set their minds on something, nothing on earth could change it and it would be nice to have them around.

After about an hour Jimmy announced that they were going to get off.

Whippet and Boxer protested as they were only halfway through the jigsaw they were doing with the children.

"Sorry boys, but it will be past your bedtime by time we get home if we don't leave now."

Everyone said their goodbyes, Mike and Malcolm walked them all out to the car and waved them off.

"I hardly recognised Jimmy today, a completely different man from the violent thug he was last night."

"Violent yes, but thug, not at all. If a man comes from where Jimmy does, he's a thug but the same man born with a silver spoon up his arse is called an executive."

"I'm sorry Mike, I didn't mean any disrespect."

"I might have thought that considering what we've just been through, you would realise it doesn't matter where a man comes from, there's good and bad at all levels."

"Your right, I should have chosen my words more carefully."

"Beyond my own father, there's no one I look up to more than Jimmy and Dave and almost everything that makes me the man I am today, I have them to thank for it."

"They certainly are loyal, which in itself shows a true strength of character and good morals."

"Like Dave says, men without loyalty are beneath animals, as even dogs understand loyalty."

"Interesting way of looking at it."

As the two men entered the kitchen Bev approached them.

"Me, Rose and the kids have decided, we're going to have a barbecue and invite all the people who helped rescue the kids, so they can give them thank you cards."

"That's ok by me Bev, but I need to check when they're all available."

"Great, make sure you invite your parents down."

"Shit, with everything that's gone on I haven't been in touch with them, I better call them now," and with that Mike disappeared to call his parents.

It had been two weeks since Mike had invited everyone to the barbecue and he was both nervous and excited to see everyone.

He'd seen Jimmy and Dave who had been down to Maple Tree House helping with the refurbishment.

The invitation was for two in the afternoon and it was now half past one.

Everything was prepared and Mike was watching the drive from the front window when he saw several cars coming down the private road.

He informed Bev and Malcolm who were in the kitchen, putting finishing touches to the food that the first of their guests had arrived, then went out to greet them.

It was Jimmy and Dave with their partners in the first car, Whippet and Boxer were in the second car with Dave's son Ashley.

Mike greeted everyone taking time to give all a proper welcome.

"Where's the kids Mike, we've got a few gifts for them," said Jimmy.

"There was no need for that."

"Well tell everyone, cos they've all brought something."

"They're around the back with Rose, playing with their cousins, follow me."

Just then Mike noticed two Land Rovers coming down the road.

"Actually, you know the way, it looks like Haigh is here so I better wait here"

They all walked around the building and left Mike to greet Haigh and his team.

Greg was the first to exit the vehicles and Mike went straight in for the man hug.

"Thanks for coming, Greg."

"We can't stop too long Mike, where up early tomorrow."

"Not a problem, we just wanted to show our appreciation."

"Like we keep telling you, there's no need" interrupted Haigh.

"How are your children, Mike?"

"Good days and not so good days, but it's a work in progress."

"It is Mike, this is the eighth member of our team Mandeep, he was on a different assignment but he's heard so much about you all, he wanted to meet the men that gave his colleagues a run for their money."

"Your more than welcome, Mandeep."

"And the rest you know."

"Yes, and you're all very welcome, please follow me, we have a good selection of food and drink, and a few familiar faces."

As they emerged around the back of the house, everyone got up to greet them.

"George, Abigail, come and say hello to everyone," said Mike.

The children ran over and stood by their father a little bit shy, until Abigail saw Dawn and ran over to her with the biggest hug Dawn had seen in many years.

Mike whispered something to George and he ran off into the house, returning with a bag containing envelopes.

George took half of the envelopes; Mike held the rest for Abigail and handed her one at a time directing her to the people named on them.

"They both wanted to write and draw their own cards to each of you to thank you"

"Awe bless you sweetheart," said Haigh, as Abigail handed him his card, "I'll treasure this."

Even those that weren't crying had water in their eyes ready to go but being held back by testosterone.

After the cards were handed out, Jimmy called the kids over and handed them the gifts that they had brought.

"Can we open them now daddy, or do we have to save them for our birthdays?" asked George.

"No sunshine, you don't have to wait, get them opened now."

The children thanked Jimmy and unwrapped the gifts.

There was a selection of cars and dolls and a jigsaw puzzle from Whippet, who made the children promise not to do it without him.

"Now that's out of the way, let's get you guys fed."

"Wait a minute Mike," said Jimmy "We have one more gift."

Jimmy passed the gift to Dawn who unwrapped it to reveal a cardboard tube, she opened the tube and tipped it upside down and a wiper blade fell out.

There was silence for a second as it sank in, then the whole patio erupted with laughter.

Malcolm, Bev and Rose looked very confused but the laughter was so infectious they couldn't help but to join in.

"Sorry about that, Dawn," said Cath.

"Don't worry about it, I can put it on my memory wall."

The rest of the afternoon passed with many stories and laughter as new friends acted like friends of old.

Haigh pulled Mike to one side and talked about how things should pan out over the coming months, he then said they had already over stayed and must call it a night.

"Surely you're not going to drag them away, they're having a wonderful time," said Mike.

"We must Mike, we're starting a new assignment and need to be up early and clear headed."

"Thanks for coming and if you're ever in the area, don't hesitate to pop in for a cuppa."

"I'm just going to use your bathroom if that's ok, it'll give them a few more minutes."

"Yes, of course as soon as you go through the kitchen into the hall it's on your left, under the stairs."

Mike went back to the patio, where Peters and Boxer had a firm grip on everyone's attention, with the epic tale of how they survived Whippets driving.

All Mac and Whippet could do was laugh at how exaggerated the story got, the more times they told it.

"It's not like we did a hundred and fifty miles per hour down Ben Nevis," said Whippet.

"We may have well as," replied Boxer.

Mike looked around at the friendships that had been forged in the wake of his wife's death, and in his mind, he felt assured that Tara would approve.

Abigail was asleep on Dawns lap and George was sat in front of Whippet, listening to the conversation.

"Past these kiddies bed time," Mike said.

Everyone protested but Mike remained firm.

"I'll take them up Mike, you stay with your friends," said Rose.

"I'll help," added Bev, as Rose picked Abigail up from Dawn.

"I thought I might wake her," said Dawn as she watched Abigail disappear into the house.

"At that age, they'll pretty much sleep through anything."

"You have two wonderful angels there, Mike."

"Thank you Dawn and it's largely thanks to all of you."

Mike dropped his head as he began to choke up but he quickly composed himself and changed the subject.

"I see you got your new pair of trainers, Whippet."

And with that comment, the laughter returned.

Bev and Rose got all the children into their pyjamas and tucked them up in bed.

"Can you read us a story," asked George.

"Ok, but then you all need to go to sleep," said Rose.

"Can we have Wind in the Willows?" asked one of Rose's children.

"Let George choose one, as he did ask."

"The Wind in the Willows is ok," said George.

Rose took the book off the book shelf and sat on the end of one of the beds, she opened the book and started to read as the children rested their weary heads.

Haigh was just finishing up when he heard a phone ring.

It sounded like a house phone, probably the one in the hallway.

He was just drying his hands when he heard footsteps coming down the stairs above him.

Whomever it was, answered the phone.

"Hello," said the voice.

"What do you think you're doing calling me on this number?"

Haigh remained quiet and moved nearer the door.

"I told you I'm out."

Haigh could make out it was a woman's voice.

"I don't want to be associated with an organisation that condones its members hurting children, and on top of that, not only did they target my grandchildren, they killed my daughter."

Haigh was shocked at what he was hearing but continued to listen.

"I don't want to hear your excuses and I don't care about the consequences so save your threats, leave me and my family alone, I've paid and then some for my freedom," and the phone was slammed down.

Haigh unlocked the door and opened it, trying not to rush so not to spook who he could only guess was Bev.

They thought it possible that Malcolm may have had a connection to the cooperative, but no one even considered that it could have been Bev.

Haigh exited the bathroom but Bev had already gone. He made his way out through the kitchen to the patio.

"Right gang, it's time to move," he said.

Despite a little protest from Mike and friends, everyone headed to the front of the house to see Haigh and the team off.

"Mike," said Haigh, pulling him to one side, "Keep an eye on them kids of yours and at the first sign of any trouble, you have our numbers and Nipper is always monitoring them."

"Do you expect trouble?"

"I'm a soldier Mike. Hope for the best but prepare for the worst."

"Thanks Haigh," said Mike, shaking his hand.

They re-joined the group who had all said their farewells and were ready to go.

"Just one more thing," said Haigh, "Whippet, you need to rest yourself, I may have a job for you in July."

"What's that?" asked Whippet.

Haigh and his team all had smiles on their faces.

"I'll be in touch," he replied, and they all jumped into their Land Rovers and left the Briggs home.

"What was that about?" asked Greg, as they drove down the road.

"I thought we could use his driving skills for the company competitions."

"I got that, but I meant the conversation you had with Mike."

"Just giving him a little reassurance that we'll be there if he needs us."

"There's something else you're not telling me."

"You know me too well Greg, but it's a conversation for another time. We need to get our heads into this new mission and leave what has passed to sort itself."

Greg left it at that as the team disappeared into the country lane.

Mike and his friends returned to the patio, and sat around the open fire that was barely taking the edge off the cold night air, that was rapidly approaching.

Bev and Malcolm brought out a selection of throws to keep people warm.

"Mike tells me you've got hotel reservations."

"Yes Bev, we've booked in a pub called the Hunters Inn," replied Jimmy.

"Ah yes, me and Malcolm often stop in there for an evening meal."

"We booked in before coming here but didn't eat, as we didn't want to spoil our appetites."

"And a good job we didn't, that spread was amazing Bev, you're a lucky man Malcolm," added Dave.

"I am, and I'm thankful for it every day."

They all continued talking for a few more hours until Dave finally said, "I'd love to stay, but young Ashley has been asleep for half an hour, and I think we need to get him to bed."

"Absolutely pal," said Mike.

For the second time, everyone made their way to the front of the house and hugged and kissed their goodbyes.

"We'll see you Monday at yours, Mike," said Jimmy.

"We'll be there too," added Boxer.

"Ok boys, see you Monday, thank you all for coming and thanks for the gifts."

The cars pulled out of the drive.

"Let's get cleaned up," said Mike.

"We can manage, Mike," replied Bev.

"Thanks Bev but I think I'll help if it's all the same."

Malcolm, Bev, Rose and Mike got stuck into cleaning up and made quick work of it.

"I'm going to have a coffee if anyone would like one," asked Mike.

"I think me and Malcolm are just going to bed, we're not used to these late nights."

"Ok Bev."

"I'll sit up with you, Mike," said Rose.

Mike made them both a drink and they sat at the kitchen table.

"Thanks Rose, that can't have been easy for you."

"What do you mean?"

"With Jimmy."

"It's hard to get the images out of my head but I understand why he did what he did."

"That's not what I meant."

Rose looked at Mike.

"He told you?"

"No."

"I should have known he would tell all his friends."

"You've got it wrong; Jimmy hasn't said anything and he wouldn't."

"You men all talk about your conquests."

"Men do, but gentlemen don't."

"Then how did you know, cos I've never told anyone, not even Tara."

"You told me."

"I did not. When?"

"The other night when you called him James."

"What do you mean?"

"Nobody calls Jimmy James, not teachers, friends or family, in fact the only people who even get away with calling him James, are his parents and women he's made love to, which suggests more than once."

Rose fell silent realising she had betrayed her own secret.

"Your secret is safe with me Rose, but don't go calling him James in front of Cath, or all hell will break loose."

They both finished their coffees in silence and Rose bid Mike a goodnight, then left for bed.

Mike sat as he often did in the evenings of late.

Contemplating the events that had almost destroyed his family.

Begging his wife's forgiveness for not being able to save her and promising to never fail their children.

Chapter 19
Epilogue

A month after the arrest of Thomas Evans, known as the Welshman in the paedophile community, for the kidnap, robbery and attempted murder of a tourist, he is to appear in Gloucester Crown Court today.

He's spent the last month recovering in hospital from injuries that he sustained in a car crash that not only led to his arrest but also left him paralysed from the waist down.

That was the news story that was playing on the radio of David Jones' car.

He had been following the case closely ever since Thomas's name had first been aired.

The traffic was light and he'd set off early to get to Gloucester city centre.

He parked his car in a multi-story carpark and bought himself some breakfast in a café just across the road.

David was a quiet man who lived alone, he had no children as he'd never been able to cement a relationship with anyone.

He even struggled with work as he was a bit of a loner and didn't quite fit in there.

He watched the people come and go as he ate his breakfast, continually looking at the clock to keep track of the time.

When he had finished his breakfast, he ordered a coffee to go and made his way over to the court house.

Once there, he sat on a bench to wait, as the court wasn't even open.

It was nearly an hour before other people started to turn up.

There were all manner of people, men and women in suits, some who looked comfortable in them and others that didn't.

Then some that just didn't care enough to make the effort, turning up to court in jeans and tracksuits.

David looked at them and thought he'd just lock them up for being scruffy and having no respect.

He was wearing jeans and a long parker coat but he wasn't attending court.

The media started to arrive and set up their cameras.

There for Thomas Evans no doubt.

A smartly dressed young woman sat on David's bench, he gave her half a smile and looked away, as was his shy nature.

From what he could see, she looked like she was with the press, sent to cover the big storey.

It was at least another thirty minutes before an ambulance arrived escorted by two police cars.

As David suspected, the police were going to wheel Thomas into court in front of the nation's cameras, to make a big noise about how great they were at catching this animal.

It disgusted him to think of how people like Thomas are allowed to do so many terrible things, and when the police finally stumbled on to them, usually by mistake, they try to make it out like it was some intelligent coordinated police effort, then make a big song and dance of it.

Of course, until they screw up the evidence and the animal goes free, then they retreat behind their impenetrable walls of PR damage control.

More commonly known as bullshit and passing the buck.

The lady sat beside David started to gather her things together.

David took a deep breath and turned to face her.

"Excuse me, are you here to cover the Thomas Evans case?"

"Yes," she replied, as she stood up to move off, as the paramedics had taken him out of the ambulance and the police had started to wheel him slowly toward the court door.

"You will need this then," David said, handing her an envelope.

"What is it?"

"The story you've come for, the story of a life time."

The woman looked confused but she had to rush to ask her questions before they got into the court room.

She took the letter and asked David to wait until she returned.

David followed her over to the line of reporters and stood at the end of the line.

The police were too busy peacocking in front of the cameras to see David pull out a sawn-off shot gun from his coat.

It wasn't until the first load of shot blew a hole through Thomas Evans' chest that anyone saw the gun.

Everyone either ran for cover or dropped to the floor.

"That's for my brother, Tommy, you bastard," said David.

David then pointed the barrel under his chin and emptied the second load of shot into his head.

The police jumped into action and retrieved the gun and the paramedics came rushing in but there was nothing to be done.

Both men were dead and the news reporters turned their cameras on the scene and barraged the police with questions.

All except one very shaken well-dressed young lady, who returned to the bench she shared with David just moments earlier.

As she looked at the scene in disbelief, she put her hand into her pocket to retrieve some tissue and pulled out the letter that David had handed her.

She cleared her eyes with her sleeve and opened the envelope.

It was a handwritten letter that said:

My name is David Jones.

What I have done here today was to rid the world of a vicious beast. This dark creature kidnapped and raped me and my brother when we were children and then he killed my brother. Because of the police losing evidence, he was allowed to go free and hurt more people.

I couldn't bear the thought of him getting off again and hurting anymore children. I hope my family will understand that I've never been able to move on with my life but in death. I will finally have peace.

D Jones X